Grey Lore

JEAN KNIGHT PACE

JACOB KENNEDY

To Kip, who stands beside.

—JKP

To my sweet, beautiful daughter and my strong son. May your lives be filled with adventures and become legendary tales full of sweet and happy moments worthy to be told in books of lore.

—JK

Grey Lore

Jean Knight Pace and Jacob Kennedy

Book cover designed by Deranged Doctor Design

The final approval for this literary material is granted by the author.

Printed in the U.S.A, 2017

ISBN: 978-1-7332550-2-8

All characters appearing in this work are fictitious. Any resemblance to real persons, living or dead is purely coincidental.

www.jeanknightpace.com

PROLOGUE

It was not a bad part of town, but even if it had been, the tall, well-dressed Italian would not have cared.

Above him the moon was a golden fruit—round and perfect in the midnight sky. It made him feel safe. And hungry. He rounded the corner and there, at the dark edge behind the restaurant, stood a scrawny figure wearing a dingy pink sweatshirt, with the hood up.

The beggar was thin and pallid, skin smeared in grime and bent in shadow. He held a small tin can with a lone piece that jangled inside, while the other hand remained tucked in his pocket.

The Italian flicked his hand dismissively and tried to walk past.

The beggar cleared his throat and took a gun out of his pocket.

"You've got to be kidding me," the Italian said, almost laughing.

The pistol was old—antique with mother-of-pearl grips and a barrel engraved in a filigreed pattern; tarnished, but elaborate. It was unlikely that it could fire properly, but even if it could, the Italian was not concerned. Not tonight.

"It's coming," the hooded beggar whispered—the voice high and strained as he waved the old gun.

"Is that so?" the Italian said, stepping closer.

"My time," the beggar added, hand tightening around the handle of the gun. "Though yours is ending."

The brawny Italian narrowed his eyes. "I'm not worried about your grandma's gun."

The thin beggar stepped forward and the Italian sneered—his white teeth sinister and gleaming in the moonlight. The Italian reached out a thick hand to grab the hooded man, but the beggar took a surprisingly quick step to the side, and cocked the gun.

The Italian jumped forward. "*You* can't kill *me*," he said, tearing his suit at the shoulders as he jerked the hood from the ragged beggar's head. Their eyes locked for only a moment before the Italian gasped and glanced down at the tin can to see that the silver piece was gone. He was too late.

The bullet moved gracefully through the layers of the Italian's skin, the muscles of the chest, shattering a rib, and then piercing his heart, before exiting through his back. He gasped only once before crumpling to the ground.

In the morning when the garbage man found him, his wallet and cell phone were still in place, but his teeth were completely gone.

CHAPTER 1

"Once…"

Ella had been dreaming of the word for days.

Once upon a time.

Once there was a boy.

Once upon a midnight dreary.

Once.

It was a word with promise. A word that implied there would be a twice. Maybe a thrice. Stories that started with once often led to a forever, a forever after, a happily forever after.

The stories her mother had liked to tell had always started that way —once—a beginning. And now they were ended.

Forever.

Forever after.

But not happily.

THE MORTUARY WAS WHITE AS SUN-BLEACHED STONE.

Ella walked, with the aunt she'd just met, through the halls and into the chapel where a simple brass urn sat at the front like a museum piece.

Because of the accident, there would be no body. The doctor had explained that, over the last nine days, her mother's face had swelled under the bandages almost as much as her brain had swelled under her skull. Head injuries weren't pretty. But it still seemed impossible —the silent urn, the fact that Ella would not be able to see her mother again.

Nine days. Nine days Ella had waited for the woman who had been her mother to shake herself awake and open her eyes. Just like the movies. Ella replayed the scene as it should have been. Lashes flutter, eyes open. Lashes flutter, eyes open. Lashes flutter—

Ella stopped, batting back the tears. It wasn't a movie.

Her aunt stood behind her and put a cool hand on her back as mourners began to enter. A trickle at first—soft padding feet that formed into a steady, slow river of people. There would be no other family among them. Her aunt Vivian—or Vivi as she'd asked to be called—had told her that her mother's parents had died years ago, and there were no other siblings.

Ella looked at the urn behind her. All her mother's secrets burned back to dust.

Now her aunt stood beside her as people greeted them. The social worker who'd found her aunt. Several of the waitresses from the restaurant where her mom had worked. Even her mother's boss, who walked toward Ella and pressed a twenty-dollar bill and a smooth, oval stone into her palm. "Your mother gave me this stone when my husband was going through chemo. Said I could rub it whenever I got worried. Which happened a lot."

Ella's throat ached as she nodded at the woman.

Other people came through the line, saying nice things as well. Her mother had once given all her tips to a waitress whose son was in rehab. She'd stayed late to bus tables when another broke up with her boyfriend. She'd been so kind to customers that a few of the regulars even showed up to pay their respects. Several of them handed Ella money or cards or earthy-blue stones her mother had given to them in times of sadness or need. Labradorite, lapis, kyanite, chrysocolla, larimar.

Stones.

For her mother's last birthday, Ella had made her a necklace by setting a loose stone from her mother's jewelry box in a funky wire, and then hanging it on a sturdy silver chain. The stone had been her mother's favorite—shiny gray with an almost metallic quality. Beautiful and offbeat, just like her mother.

Ella looked at her aunt who smiled at each of the people who came through the line. Ella had spoken to her aunt only three times now: once the day the social worker had called with the news that they had located her; once two days ago discussing the details of Ella's upcoming life; and today. Vivi wore a tailored black dress with a simple gold bracelet and ring. Ella looked at her thin, smooth neck and tried to picture her mother's chunky necklace on it. She couldn't.

The line snaked forward, the chapel door opening and closing. Opening. The doctor who had treated her mother came through in a trim, gray suit, waiting neatly in line.

Ella looked at him and paused. Her mother had not worn the necklace often, but she'd been wearing it the day she died. Her mother's other personal items—her wallet, keys, and ugly brown shoes—had been given to Ella in a sterile white package, but the necklace hadn't been with them.

Maybe the necklace had come off in the crash. Or been lost in the shuffle. There certainly had been a lot of shuffle. Two ambulances at the intersection just down the road from their apartment. Her mother had been flown thirty minutes away to a trauma center with a prestigious neurosurgeon.

The man in the gray suit.

Ella's neighbor, Rosetta, limped toward her with a fat wad of tissue and pink-rimmed eyes. Ella felt her insides relax a little. She'd been staying with Rosie while her mother lay in a coma in the hospital.

Rosie gave her a huge hug. "Oh you sweet little thing," she said, looking her over. "And your sweet, sweet mama."

"Thanks for helping me out these last few days," Ella murmured.

"Ah, now," Rosie said. "Wouldn't of had it no other way. You know your mama brought me dinner every night when I had the flu last winter and couldn't hardly get up?"

Ella shook her head. It made her feel good to hear it. But strangely sad too—had she known her mother at all?

And then the doctor stood in front of her. He was pale with a bolt of gray hair that sat impeccably in place like an obedient pet. Ella fought a sudden urge to reach out and mess it up.

"Thank you for coming," she said, hoping he'd leave quickly.

He didn't. He stepped a little closer, and when he did Ella could smell just a hint of something sour on his breath.

"I'm so sorry," he said.

Ella stepped back, bumping her aunt who stood behind her.

After staring at her for several uncomfortable seconds, the doctor said, "You look uncannily like her. Fair skin, dark hair."

Ella did not want to talk about this. She pressed her lips together, remembering her mother's necklace.

"Dr. Murray," she asked quickly, "my mother was wearing a necklace before the accident. It wasn't with her things. Do you know…do you have any idea what might have happened to it?"

The doctor looked at her for another long moment. "I'm sorry, sweetheart," he said, looking into her face with his own dark hazel eyes. They were swampy and rimmed with a firm line of gray, and when he talked, Ella felt like she was drowning. "Such things are often lost in cases like these. Perhaps it got caught up with her clothes." He paused. "Which couldn't be returned, of course, on account of the…stains."

He nodded to her aunt like he'd just made a comment on the weather, and then finally walked away. It was the first time Ella had met someone so much like the sky before a storm—calm, quiet, and perfectly terrifying.

It wouldn't be the last.

CHAPTER 2

Sam had lived in fourteen states in the last three years. And he wasn't an army brat either. At least in the army you got some sort of two-year commitment. His life held no such promises. His dad sold vacuums. Badly, it seemed.

This time they'd be staying in the Montgomery Mansion Trailer Park. That was better than their van, which had been their last residence. Apparently, the bright blue mobile home they now occupied only cost a few hundred bucks a month. On account of the fact that this spot had been hit by two tornadoes in the last five years.

Despite Sam's impressive track record with moves, he'd never lived in tornado country, so that was something.

The mobile home had come "furnished." That meant when Sam sat on the old brown couch, a puff of dust rose up around him. His father smiled and went to the car to get out his demo vacuum. At least when the next tornado came through, the place would be clean.

While his father vacuumed, Sam went outside to walk around the trailer park. The breeze felt good, and he shook off the smells of the muggy trailer. His father had promised to buy a window AC unit after he made a few sales, but one week into August, the trailer was hot as

Satan's spit. It didn't help that his father kept all the windows closed, so not even a whiff of air could blow through.

"Think," his father had said, "of what would happen if someone came in and stole the vacuums."

Sam snorted, walking along a crumbling curb where a line of ants marched by carrying crumbs. He'd thought about it plenty, and it sounded awesome. Maybe then his father would settle down and get a normal job. Maybe then they could stay in one place for more than a few months at a time. Maybe then Sam could start and finish school in the same place. What would that be like?

Sam stepped over a faded yellow speed bump and passed two empty lots where his beer-gut neighbor claimed the trailers had been lifted off the ground by a tornado. The lots looked so plain and uninteresting—like empty parking spaces, instead of the site where someone's life had ripped off the ground and spilled out somewhere else.

Sam rounded the corner. The road ended and a twelve-foot gate loomed in front of him with not one, but four chain locks to keep it closed. Behind the gate were trees—oak, maple, and ash. It marked the edge of the nature preserve owned and "shared" by the heir of the founder of the city, Charles Napper.

Sam had only been here for a day and a half, but he'd already seen Napper's name smeared all over everything—park benches, hospitals, elementary schools. The nature preserve that was Napper's back yard ran for several hundred acres through the middle of town. Sam had heard people refer to it as The Property.

In fact, any time anyone gave directions, it came up. "Oh, that's just about four miles west of The Property." Or, "You're going to get to The Property and then make a sharp left." And here it was—the epicenter of the town, as well as the point that delineated the mostly rich parts of town from the poorer quarter on its south side.

Sam held one of the locks. Apparently this was what rich old Charles Napper thought of the trailer park that bumped up against his property. It's not like Sam had ever met the guy, but he had a hard time with someone who could plaster his name all over half the town without ever seeming to care about the children who went to Napper

Elementary or the finches who roosted in the Napper Bird Sanctuary, or the crazies who made their home at the hulking Napper Psychiatric Institution.

It was like having an uncle who sent you fifty bucks on your birthday, but never bothered to show up for the party. Not that Sam would know what that was like either.

Past the gate ran a little footpath. For a minute Sam considered climbing the fence and finding out where it led. But the gate was definitely too high and, although Charles Napper hadn't topped it with barbed wire, it was made of pointed cast iron rods that didn't look very friendly.

Sam rested a hand on the warm metal of the gate, and stared through. There, at the edge of the trail, sat a tiny orange tabby cleaning her paws. When she noticed Sam, she turned and pranced up the path. Her tail had been cut clean off and was now just a furry stump.

As Sam watched her walk away, he noticed a building through the trees—a shack or camper or something sitting there at the edge of The Property. Maybe it was a groundskeeper. A weird, hippy groundskeeper with nothing to do but move tree trunks out of the hiking paths and maybe practice camping songs on an old guitar.

Sam envied him. On Sam's side of the gate were three huge garbage cans. And they stank.

CHAPTER 3

The drive from Indianapolis to Napper was quiet. Ella got the feeling her aunt wasn't exactly thrilled that she was now the guardian of a sixteen-year-old girl. Ella didn't blame her. It seemed pretty normal to *not* want to leave your comfortable single life to raise a stranger of a teenager.

The composite of Ella's life sat in the trunk, packed tightly into two suitcases. One with Ella's clothes, some books, and her journals. The other held a few of her mother's belongings: her mother's favorite jeans, her wallet, keys, a photo album, and a dark wooden box her mother had used for jewelry and her prettiest rocks. Ella had always loved the box, which was carved on the top, rustic and ornate.

Ella hadn't told her aunt what the second suitcase contained. She worried Vivi would find it too sentimental or impractical, that what she had left of her mother would be whisked away—bagged up like all their other things and given to Goodwill to be hung on racks, ready for the start of someone else's new life.

Her aunt turned off the country road onto a neat city block lined with cobblestone sidewalks that wove among a series of delicate shops and chic cafés.

Ella had never lived in a small town. Her mother had liked the chaos of tall buildings and eccentric people, stray dogs and cheap delis, run down tennis courts where no one cared what you wore when you played. She'd liked to get lost in a crowd.

Because of this, Ella had no reference for what a small town might be. She'd expected Napper to be a place like in the movies—quaint, but dusty—a short main street with old men playing checkers near the barbershop.

In reality, Napper was an oversized country club—an escape for retired businessmen, wealthy entrepreneurs, and a few hippy environmentalists who came from families with plenty of money to indulge the habit. As they drove further out, huge houses nestled themselves into hilly lots, large lawns draped across the landscape like lush Victorian dresses.

Occasionally, as they drove, Ella noticed a gardener planting trees or grooming the lawn. And she'd seen the cornfields that framed the land outside the city. Ella had lived long enough to know what that meant. There was another part of town—smaller, dingier, and filled with the poor that supplied the babysitters and lawn services for the rich.

Vivi turned onto a gated road that led up a hill. Trotting up the side of the street was a large, scruffy dog. Vivi gave it a glance, and scowled.

Brick houses marched along on either side of the tidy street. The lots weren't huge and they weren't as posh as many they'd seen on their way through Napper, but they were nicer than anything Ella had imagined having in her life. She swallowed the lump that threatened to overtake her throat, and took several deep breaths.

THE DOCTOR HAD BEEN WAITING FOR OVER A WEEK FOR THE TEST TO come back. Positive. Just as his employer had expected.

Now, he held the small vial of blood between his fingers in the same way he did his favorite Merlot before taking a sip.

After a few minutes he set the vial down and sat to make a few notes. On his computer, he wrote, "Cause of death: accidental trauma to the head." But on a neat, white slip of paper, he scribbled,

PTr4, confirmed strain, pure
Pt dcd. 1 remain.

This he slipped into a dull white envelope, which he sealed neatly and dropped into the post before heading home for his evening Chardonnay.

When you barely had a place to live, there was never much room left in the budget for things like cars or mopeds or bikes. Each day Sam's dad took their old minivan out to sell vacuums, leaving Sam with nothing more than his own two feet. That was good enough.

In the weeks before school started, Sam had run Napper up and down. His body was light and long, and his legs carried him past parks and over bridges, to the high school he would soon attend and around the large border of The Property. He'd run all along the wealthy stretch of restaurants with outdoor dining where people could eat better food than Sam had ever tasted—their leashed dogs sitting obediently by their sides. The cafés had handwritten menus outside their doors, while shops packaged their goods in bags that women were just as proud to carry down the street as their designer purses.

And then he'd run down the natty strip of fast food restaurants on the south side of town. At that end were the tire shops and resale stores, broken-down gas stations, dollar stores, and an old second-hand shop with several couches that had been left to sit out in the rain.

Almost every day, his jog led him to the Napper Psychiatric Institution. Sam thought they should have called it The Mr. Hyde—hulking, gray, and twisting, it dwarfed the more conservative Napper Hospital by a good bit.

The good city of Napper, apparently, had sick people of mostly one variety—a fact so intriguing and disturbing that Sam found himself drawn to the building like the sun to its dark stone exterior. The lawns were perfectly green with pathways that led through manicured gardens and around a large duck pond, home to several flocks of white geese—preening in the sun like lab assistants transformed by an evil witch.

If you were crazy, Napper was definitely the place to be. You would probably have the most comfortable crazy person life of anyone in the United States.

Sam wasn't the only one drawn to the public paths. Dozens of runners trotted along the garden loops that made figure eights around the Institution. The runners wore black spandex and bright shoes, Oakley sunglasses and designer visors.

Sam wore jeans or sometimes his one pair of basketball shorts with a torn up t-shirt that said, "Virginia is for lovers." He might as well have been running naked. Whenever he passed the other runners—and he always passed the other runners—they would look at him, slowing their pace, as though worried that the Napper Psychiatric Institution had finally loosened its granite grip, allowing one lonely, lost soul to slip through and break free.

CHAPTER 4

Vivi's house was layers of black. The walls were gray with paintings of modern art framed in black. The countertops were marbled charcoal granite, which matched the shiny dark tiles that marched in obedient formations along the kitchen floor. The carpets in the main rooms were white and creamy, which only accented the black, making it stark and striking. In the center of the largest room sat a shiny black grand piano. It looked as though it was not meant to be played.

In many ways the house was just like Vivi herself. Ella's aunt was beautiful. She had nearly black hair with eyes that seemed to swim between brown and gray. Her skin was pale, but perfect, like someone came in and airbrushed her every morning. Ella could tell Vivi wore mascara, but otherwise it seemed that all her untouched features were natural. Her lips were dark and smooth as was her voice. She answered every question Ella asked, smiled when smiles were due, and behaved just as perfectly as she looked. But that was all. Otherwise she lacked color, interest, contrast. With Vivi, it was all form and no flair.

Ella took off her shoes, though her aunt hadn't asked her to, and followed Vivi from room to room. The main floor included a living room, kitchen, office, and some kind of parlor. Below them was an unfinished basement that smelled like fresh-cut wood. Upstairs were three bedrooms, each with its own bathroom.

Ella took a deep breath and padded after her aunt, down the hall, to the room that was to be her own. Ella had never once in her life had her own room. For years, she had even slept in her mother's double bed, though at about age twelve, her mother had bought her her own twin mattress, which they'd crammed into the small bedroom they still shared.

One bed, one bath, mice optional—that's what her mom had always joked when they went to find a new apartment.

Looking at Vivi's house, the joke didn't seem funny anymore.

Ella's room was just like the rest of the house—the bed draped in a black bedspread with white and gold accents along the edges. The dresser and end table were dark black with a metallic square-shaped lamp next to them. There was a full-length mirror in the corner of the room—the kind of mirror that stood up on its own and didn't need to be screwed onto a door or wall. Ella stared at her reflection.

Behind her, her aunt smiled into the mirror—thirty-two perfect teeth lined up in two impeccable rows. "Will it work?" Vivi asked.

What could Ella say? No, would you share your bed with me and put some mice in the walls.

"It's amazing," Ella replied, which was absolutely true.

There were three paintings in the room—one with stark, gray lines that ran up and down in abstract spears, one like a gray and white checkerboard, and one with a huge, red sun rising over a crooked tree silhouetted at the corner. It gave Ella the chills.

"Way cool," she said to her aunt, who only nodded—the same smile in the same way it always was.

Her aunt set down the suitcases. "Well, you must be tired," she said, turning to leave.

Ella nodded.

Alone in the room, Ella turned two circles and then she felt it—the surge of tears she'd been trying to contain for the last thirty minutes.

Her mother had never been very fashionable, but she had had an artistic heart. She'd splashed their apartment with bright paintings from garage sales and pictures set in funky frames. She'd packed their walls with old shelves that she filled with thrift store paperbacks and large, interesting rocks.

Looking at the crisp, blank edges of her new room, Ella wanted to throw herself down on the dark, silky pillowcase and have a good cry. But the pillowcase wasn't one that invited crying. Or daydreaming. Or anything else, except perhaps good sleep and well-rested skin. So Ella sat cross-legged next to her suitcase, took out her mother's old jewelry box, and quietly sobbed into her palms.

IN THE LAST SEVENTY-FIVE YEARS, THE OLD GENTLEMAN HAD RECEIVED that slip of paper in the mail only two times. The first chance had been lost—taken from him by two interferers. Since then many other interferers had come and gone—some intent on changing his plans; others who wished to steal them. The most recent of the interferers called himself the Rogue.

The old gentleman supposed that the Rogue might attempt to get the stone from the doctor. Because of this, he would send one of the council to make sure it arrived safely. The doctor could be trusted only so far as his wallet was fat. And the gentleman could not risk letting this chance fall through his fingers as it had so many years ago.

He slid the slip of paper from its envelope and tucked it into his lapel pocket before picking up the steaming cup of Earl Gray. Whether this Rogue was the same killer who two weeks ago had shot a member of his council remained to be seen. But he could do without a council.

What he could not do without was the stone.

Or the child.

SAM SAT IN HIS HOMEROOM AND LOOKED AROUND. THE GIRL TO HIS left was hot. She hadn't looked at him yet. The kid to his right didn't even know he was there and wouldn't until Mr. Oblivious had flunked his first few math tests. Then, suddenly, Sam would become very important to him. And the goth/punk chick behind him already hated his guts. He could tell by the dramatic sigh as soon as she sat down.

Not a single friend. Just like his last school. And the one before that.

Sam didn't see the brunette slip in and sit in the corner—didn't notice the gray polo or the expression that said, *Nobody notice me, please.*

He didn't have to because other people noticed her. Not Princess Hottie or Mr. Oblivious—not yet anyway, but Gothy got another good sigh on, tapping her pencil repeatedly against her desk.

Sam turned around to see what her deal was. When he turned, he could see that she was sneering, not at him, but at a girl in the corner who was wearing scuffed up shoes that she'd tucked under her seat. Gothy's boots were brand new—black and purposefully distressed, but clearly expensive.

Sam figured those boots had probably cost a couple hundred bucks—a month of rent in Montgomery Mansion Trailer Park.

He couldn't help himself. "Nice boots. You ride?"

She ignored him, but he kept on. "I mean, they're motorcycle boots, right? My dad used to ride."

She turned her face just slightly towards him, a deep blush rising up from her neck, though her jaw was clenched. "I just like boots," she said, then pulled out her books and looked down, clearly annoyed at being called out.

Of course she didn't ride a motorcycle. Of course she didn't ride anything except maybe her daddy's beamer on her way to school.

Sam looked away from her.

In the corner, the girl in gray stared at the bulletin board to her left, but Sam hadn't missed the quick smile. It was a smile that reminded him of someone.

CHAPTER 5

Dr. Murray stood outside the pawn shop and held the sleek, round stone in his smooth, white hands. It was not a precious metal—not gold, platinum, copper, or even silver —though there was something very silver-like about it. Murray wondered why his employer was willing to pay such a high price for it, but he didn't dare take the stone to a jeweler. His employer had too many connections to the jewelry world, and Murray didn't want him to know he was asking questions. Instead, Murray hoped that the man at the pawn shop would be able to tell him why the stone was valuable.

Unfortunately, the guy in the flannel and jeans across the counter was ignoring him—hunched over an old coin, looking through a magnifying glass that was held to his eye.

"Excuse me," the doctor said. "I was wondering if I could talk to the owner."

"You already are," the guy replied without looking up from his coin.

Murray cleared his throat. "My mom just died and when I was cleaning out her things, I found this." He put the stone on the counter. "I'm not sure if it's valuable or not. It looks kind of like silver."

The owner of the pawn shop finished examining his coin and then put it in a case and stepped toward Dr. Murray. He picked up the stone, weighted it in his hand, examined it under a jeweler's light, then touched it with a magnet. "Interesting piece," he began. "It seems to be some type of natural stone and it may have a few veins of silver and maybe some other metals running through it, but I'm not really sure what it is." He held it close to his face. "I've never seen anything like it. I could do an acid test on it, but that probably wouldn't tell me anything more."

"I see," Dr. Murray said. "So it's not a metal you recognize."

"Correct," the man said, setting the stone down on the counter. "I could give you a couple bucks for the busted up chain that's holding it —that *is* sterling silver, but I'm not really willing to take a risk on the actual stone. Pretty cool though. Nice memento of your mother."

"Hmmm? Oh, yes," the doctor said, taking the stone back. "So—to you this is only worth a few dollars?"

"To me it's worth nothing. I'm not sure I could sell it, and I couldn't scrap it with my other metals. I'll give you a couple bucks for the silver chain though. That I can scrap and sell."

"Well, no, that's okay," the doctor said. "Thank you for your time."

He walked out of the shop and got into his car. He didn't know why someone would be willing to pay half a million dollars for something worth less than the metal chain that held it, and he didn't care. He was driving to Napper today.

Ella noticed the signs a few days after her arrival. They were yellow with a vicious-looking wolf that had an X stamped over it. At the bottom was a plea to write your congressmen and "stop the wolves."

When Ella asked Vivi about the signs at dinner, her aunt just waved her hand. "Oh, it's just political stuff. Napper is supposed to be the newest site for introducing the Gevudan wolf. It's kind of controversial." Vivi set down two dry-looking chicken breasts and a bowl of mushy green beans.

Ella could remember her mother reading obsessively about the progress of the gray wolf reintroduction in the West. Her mother had told her that before that, the government had attempted to introduce red wolves into the Smoky Mountains, but it hadn't worked.

"I didn't even know wolves were indigenous to the Midwest," Ella said. "I mean, are they?"

"Well, yes and no," Vivi said, scooping some more soggy beans onto her plate. "That's part of the controversy actually. None have lived here in the last several centuries, but recently a large body of evidence was discovered that seems to indicate that a genus of wolf used to inhabit this region. Regional scientists are very excited about it. The Gevudan are a Eurasian wolf. In fact, for the re-introduction—if it happens—they'll be bringing them over from France."

Vivi seemed kind of excited about it, but it sounded crazy to Ella. "So, the wolves lived here hundreds, maybe thousands of years ago, but they're still going to re-introduce them?"

"Sure," Vivi said.

"But isn't that sort of what made the Smoky Mountain reintroduction so unsuccessful—the wolves died off for natural reasons, not because of hunting by humans?"

Vivi set her fork down and looked at Ella. "You know a lot about wolves for a teenager. I'm impressed."

"Mom was kinda into that stuff."

Vivi nodded.

"So, seriously, why do they think it will work?" Ella asked. She didn't know why it seemed so interesting, but wolves in Napper—it was probably the coolest thing she'd heard about the city yet.

Vivi paused over her meal before answering. "Even though the wolves have been gone for a long time, there is evidence that they were pushed off this land by an outside force—perhaps some ancient peoples. So it seems they were eliminated through hunting, just hunting that happened a really long time ago."

Ella shook her head and smiled. "Still sounds crazy. And the government is bringing them in from Europe?"

"Well," Vivi said, hesitating. "No, not the government. The wolves will be brought over by a private party, a wealthy naturalist who lives here."

"So it's not a government reintroduction plan?" Ella asked, pushing the gristle from her chicken to the side.

"No," Vivi said. "The wolves have been gone for too long for the government to invest in reintroduction. But certain individuals are very interested in the idea. And Charles Napper, whose family founded the town, is one of them. He's paying to have them brought over."

"Wow," Ella said. "Where will they be reintroduced?"

"Onto his land," Vivi said. "Mr. Napper's property is quite extensive."

"And the government supports this—like, he has permission?"

Vivi sighed. "The government of Indiana allows certain people to have exotic pets if they've acquired the necessary permits—"

Ella interrupted, even though she didn't mean to. "Pets?" she asked. "They'll be pets?"

Vivi looked like she was about to explain something complicated, but decided against it. "Yes," she said. "I suppose they would be considered pets. At least until we see how successful the reintroduction is."

"And the yellow signs?" Ella asked.

"Just as in the West, some of the locals are very…nervous. They're encouraging others to write to their politicians to try to stop the wolves from coming, but the fact is that, as exotic pets, the wolves will have to be contained. It will all be very safe, very controlled, and perfectly legal."

Ella nodded. It was crazy, but cool. "And the supporters—they think it will help the ecosystem—restore trees and beavers, like in Yellowstone."

"I think the idea is definitely to restore balance," Vivi said before picking up her plate and walking to the sink.

THE DRIVE TO NAPPER WASN'T LONG, BUT MURRAY HAD GOTTEN A late start. He'd stopped to eat and then shared a few drinks with a tall blond at the bar. By the time they were finishing up, it was after ten.

He helped the tipsy blond to her taxi as the full moon stared down at him like a search light—high and searing. Afterwards, he sat in his classic Mustang for several minutes, letting the fan blow on his face. The strange stone was heavy in his pocket. He wished it was worth something at the pawn shop; he wished it had value for a visible, calculable reason.

Money, prestige, position—those were things he could understand. Sentiment, history, and artifact—they held no meaning to him. And Napper, the old fox, Murray didn't fully trust him. Murray decided that he'd ask twice as much as Napper had offered. If the old man wanted it badly enough, he'd pay.

The small freeway down to Napper was empty this time of night, and while Murray didn't feel drunk from his stint at the sports bar, he did feel tired. He opened the windows a few inches to let in some air, and turned on the radio. The black road rolled out in front of him, empty and quiet when, to his right, he thought he saw a tall, lanky man loping along the freeway.

Murray shook his head, and turned the radio louder. Then, after a minute, he rolled the windows up and locked them. A moment later, a large animal ran across the road.

Murray slammed on his breaks, cursing; and then it was beside him —the glowing, nocturnal eyes.

The crash hit him in a burst and then the stars seemed to fall from the sky and into his head before everything went dark.

THE RADIO PLAYED FOR THREE MORE HOURS UNTIL THE GAS FINALLY ran out.

The good doctor, for his part, was solidly dead. When the cops found him later that night, the car smelled like booze—an easy explanation for the huge dent in his car, the driver's head solidly imprinted into his steering wheel, a spray of blood across the windshield, deep scratches across his head and neck. The poor drunk looked like he'd been torn apart by Hades' hound himself.

When they checked his person, they found his wallet with several credit cards, $200, a receipt from a sports bar with a phone number scribbled on the top, and a driver's license. Other than that his pockets were empty.

CHAPTER 6

Sam knew that girl from somewhere and it was driving him crazy. When you'd lived in seventeen states, it wasn't always easy to place a face. Or a name. Her name was Ella. He liked it, but he was pretty sure he'd never known an Ella before. So why did her eyes remind him of his childhood, of trees and burning wood?

Sam had spent the afternoon going through the only yearbook he had—7th grade. No one in it looked like that girl. Or at least no one looked like the part of her face that haunted his memory—the dark brown eyes, the ivory cheekbones, the full but frowning lips. She was pretty, but he didn't think of her that way. He thought of her instead as weirdly…familiar.

Sam's father came home just before dinner—a small sack of groceries in his hand. Once, just once, Sam would love to have him show up with a pizza box instead. Tonight, it was canned pork and beans served over rice and topped with melted American cheese. His father ate with a napkin on his lap and made commentary on the sweetness of the beans.

Finally, when his father had cleaned his plate and Sam had choked down enough beans to avoid stunting his growth, his father leaned back and said, "Sold my first vacuum today. We should celebrate. Mr. Freezy's still have those sixty-nine cent cones?"

Sam really, really hoped they did. "Probably, yeah, sure," he said.

His father stood up, pulled several neat twenties out of his wallet and took them to his room. Sam knew his dad kept the money somewhere, though he'd never been able to figure out where. Truth be told, he hadn't tried that hard to find his father's hiding spot. What was he going to do—sneak money for video games so they could both starve to death?

Two hundred dollars was rent. Still nothing to cover food. And who knew how long it would be before his father sold another vacuum? His father never signed up for food stamps or free lunches. He said he didn't like the government to have its nose in his business.

Sam thought it'd be nice to have *someone's* nose in their business. Sam's mother had died when he was young. Too young to miss her. Although the idea of someone who could cook and fill in the budget did have some appeal.

His father came back out with two one-dollar bills and a jacket in hand even though it'd been wicked hot all month. "Those restaurants are always freezing," he said when Sam stared at the coat. Well, their trailer sure wasn't. Sam only wished he could store up enough Mr. Freezy's coldness to keep him from waking up sweating in the night.

ALL THE FAST FOOD RESTAURANTS WERE ON THE SOUTH END OF TOWN, and the booths at Mr. Freezy's looked like they'd been there for about 700 years. Also, the ice creams weren't sixty-nine cents. They were back up to their dollar menu status. Sam's dad didn't have the change for the tax. "We'll just get one for you," he said.

"No," Sam said. "Give me a minute." Quickly, he went out to the parking lot and walked along the curb of the drive through and then along the periphery of the grass by the huge garbage bin. When you didn't get a regular allowance, you got good at finding loose change.

Sam could spot a coin from forty feet away and usually scrounged up enough for a burger at school every week.

In the Mr. Freezy's parking lot, near the garbage gate by the Dumpster, Sam found a neat little quarter and two pennies, heads up. Sam took it all. The quarter would pay their tax with change. And Sam wasn't one to pass up pennies.

Or luck.

SAM AND HIS DAD ENDED UP EATING THEIR ICE CREAM CONES IN THE car on the way back to the trailer. Some kid had barfed all over the floor just as they'd gotten their order, and neither of them wanted to eat dessert with the smell of vomit wafting through the air.

Unfortunately, as soon as his dad turned on the radio, a story about the latest tooth-pull murder came on. It had happened almost exactly a month after the first bizarre murder, and the newscasters couldn't get enough of it—wondering whether it was a copycat murder or the same guy.

"Why don't you change it, Dad?" Sam said. "It's kind of sick."

"It's more than sick," his father said, not touching the dial.

"Then why don't you turn it off?" Sam said.

His father ignored him for a minute—letting the story play. The latest victim had been shot in northern Montana. He had owned a huge ranch that he oversaw from a lavish house that sat on a golf course nearby. He was about as different from the Italian computer genius who'd gotten killed in L.A. as he could be. Minus the money. They both had had plenty of money—money that seemed to be of no interest whatsoever to the shooter. Because just like the first murder, Montana guy had been found with a fat wallet in his pocket, his heart shot through, and his teeth torn out.

Sam shuddered.

"Sorry, son," his father said, putting his hand to the radio dial as the reporter said something about a silver bullet being found during the autopsy. His father flipped stations. "It's just that I met your mother near that town. It's strange to hear about something like that happening in sleepy, little Montana."

Strange didn't even begin to describe it.

Sam's father flipped through fuzzy stations until the local news came through—another morbid story about some guy who'd gotten into a car wreck on that same night, just about thirty miles north of Napper. Drunk driver, all torn up when they found him.

"At least he didn't kill anyone else," Sam said, glad when his father finally flipped the radio off entirely.

His father nodded grimly, looking out the window at the flat, green landscape ahead of them.

CHAPTER 7

A dark, mottled wolf turned circles in its cage—occasionally banging its body against the side.

"Do you think it will eat the others by the time it arrives in the U.S.?" a heavyset Frenchman asked his friend as they lifted the aluminum crate to place it on the large, wheeled baggage cart at the Paris Charles de Gaulle airport.

"If they're lucky," the smaller man replied. "Then they'll know it's crazy to welcome such an animal into your woods."

The wolves had been well-fed, vaccinated, and sedated. They now rested in a row of cages. Still, many of their eyes blinked open and the large one lurched around, looking anxiously through the narrow slats at the others.

The other man chuckled, but just as he did, the pacing animal let out a howl, and the man dropped his end of the crate. The lock banged against the tiled airport floor and sprang open. The wolf staggered out, breathing heavily. And then it howled again.

"What do we do?" the heavyset one shouted, as the animal stumbled forward once more before gaining its footing.

The heavyset man took a careful step back, and when he did the fur on the animal's neck rose up—spikes of dark fur surrounding a black face that ran into the deep abyss of its eyes. There was no glaze over them now, no dilation of the pupils.

Slowly the animal's lips curled back—black gums to yellow teeth—long, thick, salivating. The animal lurched forward, snarling.

"Kick it in the nose," the slender man screamed as the heavyset one stumbled backwards. "It doesn't even know what it's doing."

"*Comme diable*," the heavyset one stammered, kicking out a foot and missing, as the animal growled deep in its throat—a noise both men could feel as well as hear.

The slender man grabbed a small trashcan, holding it in front of his chest and then pulling it back as though to hit the animal with the flimsy, plastic edge.

The wolf lifted its snout, baring its teeth again, just as a tall American in khaki trousers and a plain cotton shirt appeared. He carried a large veterinarian's bag.

"Trouble, gentlemen?" he asked.

"*Monsieur*, it has escaped," the slender man shouted. "It is out of control."

The veterinarian raised one eyebrow—every other feature on his face unmoving. "Out of control?" he said. "Hardly." He smiled, lips lifting from his teeth in the same way the wolf's had. "You've merely spooked the poor creature through your panic."

The animal collapsed as the American spoke. The veterinarian calmly knelt by the animal, shining a penlight into its eyes. He reached into his bag and pulled out a small syringe, which he plunged into the animal's hide.

"Thank you, *monsieur*," the slender man said as the vet inspected the cages. "It is good you will be travelling with them."

"Yes," he said, looking to the men. "It is. Should I draw up a report about this incident?" he asked, reaching for a pen.

"*Non, monsieur*, that will be quite unnecessary," the heavyset man replied.

"Of course," the vet responded. "I trust then that you won't mention to anyone else what happened."

"Of course."

After they had left the American with the crates at the loading area, the heavyset man grumbled, "Spooked the *poor* creature, did we? Conceited American."

The slender man shuddered. "I'm glad he came anyway." And then he laughed—a thin, shaky sound. "Like an American movie, *non*?"

The other shook his head. "A bad movie," he muttered. "Those wolves should all be more heavily sedated."

"*Should* we report it?" the heavyset one asked.

"That we dropped a crate containing a deadly animal in the center of the *Roissy* and almost got attacked? *Non*."

ELLA HAD DEVELOPED A RITUAL. EACH NIGHT BEFORE BED, SHE TOOK down her mother's jewelry box. The smell of the wood was comforting, as was the clink of the small, inexpensive things inside of it—a few bicentennial quarters, several stones—some picked up at lapidary shows, but most found in nooks and crannies around the city. They held, as far as Ella knew, no value at all, but were beautiful and interesting to the touch. Every night as part of her ritual she rubbed each stone—the smooth and the jagged, and thought of her mother.

In the box, there was almost no jewelry at all except for her mother's wedding ring. It was a thin band with an unusual square of gold at its center in place of a diamond. On the gold square was a large swooping 'C'—her mother, Christa's, initial. Ella ran her finger over the shallow engraving. She might have hated the ring that represented her mother's lost marriage, except that her mother hadn't. Her mother had worn the ring often, almost always when they were at home.

Ella slipped it onto each finger. It didn't quite fit, but she liked how it felt—so polished and cool.

The only other things in the jewelry box were scraps of paper. Some of them were her mother's—a line of a poem, a Celtic saying, a nursery rhyme from Ella's childhood.

Lately, Ella had started adding to the stack of papers—a small observation, a sentence about Vivi's un-played piano, a little sketch of the stray dog she'd seen in the neighborhood. It was her own poetic contribution to her mother's little scrap journal.

Ella hadn't written in her real journal since her mother's death. Almost every day since she'd been old enough to write, her journals had gotten an entry, but now the pages sat naked and abandoned.

Maybe when she'd recovered a bit from the…the everything, she could paste some of her scraps onto the blank pages. She hoped for this —that one day these bits of paper, these scraps could be placed together to form a meaningful whole; to make some sense out of her mother's death which made no sense at all; to find some beauty in a situation that felt a lot like Ella's current journal—blank, empty.

<h1 style="text-align:center">CHAPTER 8</h1>

"O*ncle*," the young girl said. "Why do you ask if there are wolves on the plane?"

"Because I can feel them," the man replied with an American accent.

"But how," she asked. "*Comment le savez-vous?*"

The American shrugged. "One day you may understand." He stood and hugged the girl's mother—his sister.

She looked with some concern into his face. "Until next summer, then," she said.

"Yes," he said. "Or maybe Christmas if Antoine can change his holiday."

"*Oui oui, oncle,*" the child said, throwing her arms around her uncle. "I so want to see American Christmas."

The man untangled the child from his legs and kissed her cheek as he gathered his bag and papers. "Maybe Christmas," he said. "But for now I must get back to my job and my class."

He took a deep breath. He could smell them—the wolves the ticket agent had said couldn't possibly be on the plane. There were nine.

The passengers still had not begun boarding and the man was feeling antsy. As was his niece.

"*Oncle*," the girl said. "Tell me a story."

"A story," he asked. "But which one?"

"Well," the girl said with a small, mischievous look in her eye. "Since you like wolves so much, you must tell *Le Petit Chaperon Rouge*."

"I do not like wolves. At least most," he said.

"All the better then, for the telling of the tale," his sister injected, staring out at the plane as though trying to see through it and biting her nail.

The man sighed. The would-be passengers were milling about and someone who looked like the pilot was arguing with a tall man in khaki pants. It did not appear the passengers would be boarding any time soon.

"Very well," he said, looking at his niece.

"*Once upon a time there was an impetuous and persistent young girl.*" He tapped his niece on her nose. "*She was like a bright spot in a land dense with woods and darkened by wolves. Every night, each cottage that sat near the woodland path locked its doors and shuttered its windows, leaving candles like talisman to frighten away the bloodthirsty beasts.*"

"David," the girl's mother said in a warning voice. "Don't make it too scary."

"*Non maman, c'est bien.*"

Her mother sighed and her uncle continued. "*Only the bravest families lived among the trees, gathering roots and plants by day, spinning and weaving by night. The girl's grandmother was the bravest of all—living alone at the path's far end—gathering berries and baking pies to give to weary travelers and to trade with the roaming merchants.*

"*The old woman seemed to the child as sturdy as one of the 200-year trees and the girl expected her to live just as long. Which is why it was a shock when one day a rumor floated through the wood, dusted onto the lips of a tall tradesmen: The old woman had fallen ill and lay in her bed, wasting away into twigs and loose skin.*

"That very day the girl packed a basket with maple nut rolls and a fat round of butter, and set off in search of her dear grand-mere."

The story stopped as the airport intercom crackled a moment and then went silent again. The man's niece poked a finger into his thigh. "The cape, *oncle*, you have forgotten it."

"I have not," he said. *"Naturally the child could not trudge through the cold wood with nothing but a frock and boots, so she tied her favorite red cloak about her neck, tucking her dark hair into its hood, then set off to cheer her grandmother back to health.*

"It was fortunate she had brought so many buns, for by noon-time the girl's stomach rumbled and she sat to eat.

"Just as she did, a most handsome creature came up beside her. He was, unfortunately, clearly a wolf, though he looked nothing at all like the monsters she'd heard described in her mother's frightening tales. His fur was light gold with a bronzed sheen that reflected the sun in a magnificent way and when he came up beside her he bowed politely and spoke. 'I pray thee, tiny maid, could you spare but one roll, for my limbs grow weary from hunger.'

"The child was quite surprised and not foolish enough to deny a hungry wolf his request for a bit of bread. Quickly, she tossed him a sweet roll.

"As the creature devoured it, the child scurried along on her way, though she had not gone much further when the wolf appeared before her again, this time standing on hind legs and bearing a posy of flowers, which he presented to her with his thanks.

"He really was a tremendously fine-looking animal with stone gray eyes that stared into her own. 'Perhaps,' the girl said, taking a careful step back, 'I will give these lovely blooms to grandmother. She lives at the furthest end of this path, and does not fare well, you see.'

"'I do,' replied the wolf, delicately licking his upper lip. 'There are many bright flowers off this path. If you've a few moments to spare, perhaps you would find many more to your liking.'

"The girl hesitated. She had been warned never to leave the path, no matter the cause, yet she would not need to stray far, for she could smell the perfumed blossoms from where she stood. Besides, the

gentle wolf had already run on, which meant she would be quite alone.

"It was nearly dusk when the flower-laden child arrived at her grandmother's house. The door was unlatched, although the child tapped on it thrice before entering. Her grandmother must have been very weak because she did not so much as murmur bonjour. *The girl pushed open the door. In the dimming light she could see the still form of her grandmother in the bed.*

"'Grandmother,' she said softly, searching the cupboards for a match to light the candle.

"Grandmother cleared her throat and it seemed she must have been very ill indeed because the sound of her voice rumbled low like tumbling rocks.

"'Let me butter you some bread,' the child said, giving up on her search for matches.

"'Non,' whispered grand-mere. "Come closer. I wish only to see your sweet, soft face."

"'Goodness, grandmother,' the girl exclaimed, stepping closer, 'what a very hoarse voice you have. Shall I not make you a pot of tea?'

"'No, child; come closer.'

"'And grand-mere, your soft white hair looks course and ashen in this darkened cottage.'

"'Well, of course my dear; closer now.'

"'And your ears, so black. Your teeth so..."

"Now boarding flight 375 to John F. Kennedy International Airport."

The young girl jumped at the cackling of the intercom, as did several of the passengers nearby who had been soothed into listening to the story.

"*Oncle*," the girl said, stamping her foot. "You must finish it. *Vous devez.*"

"I'm afraid I can't, *cherie;* it will have to wait for another visit."

"But how does it end?" she begged.

"You know how it ends, Emmaline," her mother chided, handing the man his bag before kissing his cheek.

"No, I don't," the girl said, almost in tears. "The stories never end in the usual way with *oncle*."

"True, *cherie*," her uncle said. "Not all wolves are bad. And not all men are good. And most are unfortunately stuck somewhere in between."

"Oh, *oncle*," the girl said. "It is always a riddle, *une enigma*."

The man bent down and gave her a hug. "At Christmas," he promised.

"You will finish it then?" she asked, sniffling.

"I will try," he said, dashing out to the plane, trailing after the other passengers.

HIS NIECE, HE THOUGHT, WAS RIGHT TO WONDER. IN THE DARKEST versions of the story, young Red Riding Hood got eaten and that was that. The Grimm brothers had introduced a huntsman to rescue both girl and grandmother. And in many versions—both very old and very new, the child and the old woman had devised a way together to escape from the crafty wolf—stitching up stomach or mouth, filling him with stones, drowning the beast. But in this story—his story—he wasn't quite sure how it would end.

In the coach seats, the smell of the wolves onboard was undeniable, at least to his senses.

"*Mademoiselle*," he asked as the flight attendant walked past, "there wouldn't be any animals on this flight, would there? My allergies are giving me quite a time."

"Animals, *monsieur*? Of course not. *Non*."

"Of course." Not that she would know anything about them. Not that any normal person would.

It was inevitable, he supposed. The wolves, their masters. They had gotten grandmother years ago, and mother only recently. It remained now to see what would happen to Red.

CHAPTER 9

Napper, Indiana, was pretty much tragically boring. Mornings at Vivi's house were stone silent. Afternoons Vivi was at work. And evenings got twenty uncomfortable minutes of forced banter over dinner before they settled into their own quiet corners of the house. It was a stifling silence—the kind that made you feel like you not only had to shut the bathroom door without a click, but also that you shouldn't be thinking any loud thoughts either.

Maybe that's why Ella felt compelled to reject her aunt's offer to drive her to school. Sure it meant that she had to trudge along the shoulder of the road most of the time, like the stray dog that sometimes hung out at the edges of their neighborhood. But it was just over a mile, and she kind of enjoyed it.

Walking to school was still quiet, but Ella's thoughts could scream all they wanted. She turned over the funeral in her mind. She kicked at puddles. She listened to the bugs and birds. And she walked past the entrance to The Property—the huge estate with the copper plaque reading, "Napper, Indiana, established 1803."

Most of Napper was flat as Vivi's pancakes, but this section rose up to a tall hill and was covered with trees and flowers. Ella could see paths that led around the property and once, early in the morning, an owl had swooped down in front of her and picked up a mouse from the ditch. It'd been kind of cool. And scary. Which is how the grounds made Ella feel in general.

Strangely, it was a feeling she loved.

Today instead of an owl, Ella saw an old grocery cart in front of the gates and a man screaming inside the preserve. The man was balding with thin, pale lips, torn pants, and a dirty flannel shirt that was unbuttoned nearly to his waist. He had stained hands and an old backpack that maybe used to be purple, but now just looked brown.

He shouted, "This used to be my land. My domain. I can come here whenever I want. I know these woods better than anyone—even you, *Mr. Napper.*"

The name smeared through the air like a curse.

Ella looked through the fence to see a tall, trim man in a black suit walking toward the homeless guy.

Charles Napper walked with a cane, but had a full head of gray-streaked hair and a perfectly trimmed beard. He stopped in front of the shaggy man and took out his phone. "I'm sorry, sir, but the grounds are closed today. If you don't leave, I'll be forced to call the authorities to have you removed."

"Removed," the man shouted almost hysterically. "Removed!"

Mr. Napper started to dial. It seemed as though this had happened before. The homeless man stomped down the hill, still screaming. "I used to be a king. A KING!"

Ella didn't want to be at the gate when he came through. She ran the last six blocks to her school and stopped in front of the doors. She'd seen Charles Napper arguing with some homeless guy. Awesome. And the homeless guy had been terrifying, but hilarious. Ella caught herself thinking that she couldn't wait to get home and tell her mom.

The tears sprang to her eyes before she could stop them

SARAH PRICE HAD PLENTY. PLENTY OF FOOD, PLENTY OF CLOTHES, plenty of money. She was smart too; and not even ugly. It was all intensely boring—school, clothes, her parents, their jobs. She wanted to go to Africa and fight disease. Or Paris and fall in love. She'd even settle for a summer job. But her parents wouldn't have that. They'd be sending her to acting camp again this summer.

Sarah Price regretted that when she had turned twelve, she'd told her parents that it was her heart's desire to be an actor when she grew up. Maybe some accountant-dentist couples would have balked at the idea, but her parents lovingly and aggressively—with all the type-A-fervor of their souls—threw their support behind their only child's dreams. Thank goodness she hadn't told them she'd wanted to be a lion tamer.

The thing was, she did want to be an actor. It's just that it seemed kind of hard to pretend to be all these other people when all you'd known was white upper class suburban life. She'd been doing the goth thing for nearly a year now—listening to Bauhaus, wearing black, dying her hair. Lately, she'd added some steampunk jewelry to the mix —a cuff with cogs, a leather corset over a black silk blouse. And it did stress her parents out.

Half the time, her mother was convinced that she was a pathologically lying drug addict. With all the helicoptering her mother tried to do, it was a wonder she wasn't. But the truth was that her parents' stress and all her mom's worrying didn't really change her life or anything in it. She was still the same—smart, rich, and bored.

Today she'd driven to school early. That new girl, Ella, had come running to the school, then stopped, sat on the steps, and started to cry.

You weren't supposed to envy someone for being a nut job, but Sarah Price kind of did. She smiled, thinking of how her mom would feel to see her running along some ditch by the road and then sobbing on the school steps. Her poor mother would probably have to double up on the restorative yoga to rebalance after the horror of it all.

Sarah walked right past Ella on the way into school. And then she paused. Did she want everything in her life to always be the same predictable blah or not? Why not talk to the crazy girl?

"Hey," she said, turning around. "There's a box of tissues in the theater room on the south end."

She hadn't meant for it to sound snarky, but maybe it did. Sarah didn't dare turn back to see which way Ella had taken it. After all, the girl in black wasn't supposed to care.

CHAPTER 10

The truck driver arrived right on time, ready to crate and transport the animals. Normally, he transported zoo animals from the airport, and several times he'd been hired to pick up exotic fish. But wolves were new. That didn't bother him too much. The rich guy who had hired him for this job had offered to pay as much as the driver normally made in nine months. Transporting a pack of wolves all over the eastern United States wouldn't be fun, but he wasn't about to turn down a job with that kind of pay.

Before they left, the wolves were fed, re-crated, and re-sedated. For the month-long journey, they would drive through document checks and red tape until sometime in October, when they would find their way to a sleepy little town in southern Indiana.

When the wolves were ready, the driver buckled himself in and looked over at the veterinarian who sat in the passenger's seat next to him, frowning at a strange pack of seemingly stray dogs that trotted toward the van.

"That's unusual," the driver said.

"Hmmm," the man responded.

"The dogs," the driver said. "I've never had a bunch of dogs so interested in my van before."

"I can't stand dogs," the veterinarian said.

"Really?" the driver asked. "That surprises me with your work and all."

"Wolves are different than dogs."

The driver didn't argue, although the main difference he could see was that no one was going to put out kibble for a pack of wolves or invite them up onto the couch at night. Except apparently Mr. Vet Guy.

They were nearly out of town when one of the dogs started barking loudly and another ran up along the van, nipping at the wheel. A third bit hard into a wheel on the other side.

"What the…" the driver said.

The veterinarian cursed and then suddenly reached over and grabbed the steering wheel, jerking the van to the side so that it hit one of the dogs. Two sets of wheels thumped over its body.

"Holy mother," the driver said, gaining control of the van and slowly moving over to the shoulder.

"Keep driving," the vet shouted.

"Sir, I gotta pull over. We just ran over that dog."

"That dog is dangerous," the vet said. "Keep driving."

"That *dog* is dangerous?" the driver replied, his voice rising. "I'm sorry. I'm going to have to stop."

"You have been paid to do a job. Now do it."

"My job isn't to run over animals like a lunatic," the driver said, then looked over at the vet. The man's eyes were sharp-edged, his face set like it had been cut from a mountain. His hand was clenched on a large, black bag beside him.

The driver had driven poisonous snakes, bears, mountain lions, and even a young tiger. He had never once felt afraid. But now, looking at the man beside him, he felt the hair at the back of his neck rise. He remembered a story that had shown up on his newsfeed only a few weeks ago about a man who'd shot his friend in a fit of rage. And this guy wasn't even a friend.

The driver did not pull over to check on the dog. He had a wife and twin sons. He'd report the crazy vet after he got home. "Look, I'm just trying to do my job," the driver began as gently as he could.

"Then do it," the vet said, staring straight ahead.

CHAPTER 11

M r. Witten was short and stout—and that was putting it politely. He was bald on top with a ring of gray hair that circled the rest of his head. He was wearing a button-down shirt as though dressed to impress the new group of juniors, but he'd missed a button, and as a result, his shirt hung crookedly. Gothy couldn't resist a snort.

Sam could. Mr. Witten reminded him uncannily of his father. And, unfortunately, Sam had to admit that he would never ever buy a vacuum from this man. Perhaps his father should have gone into creative writing. That was a field that, apparently, required no aware-ness of your personal appearance. The only proof that Mr. Witten had actually looked in a mirror that morning was a silver bracelet set with a large copper square that gave him a sort of Bohemian look. It had probably worked for him during his college years, but seemed a little silly when he was facing a room full of teenagers.

Their new teacher was directing them to a place in their syllabus with assignments for the semester. Mr. Witten had missed the entire first week and a half of school, which seemed like a big offense, except rumor had it that he was a big wig folklorist and had been doing some reading at a prestigious university overseas. The two girls in front of

44

Sam said the school had been fighting to get Witten here for years. And when a school with as many rich kids as this one fights for a teacher it wants, they usually get him. Though, apparently, a week late.

The girl named Ella was in the class too. He still couldn't place her face, but there was something about it he found comforting.

Gothy sat in front of Ella. Looking at her didn't make Sam feel comforted. Looking at her made him feel something else. The truth was he was finding it increasingly difficult not to look at her, and that bothered him. She wasn't exactly sweet as sugar candy. And the dark hair and nails and punk jewelry weren't his thing. But he'd noticed that her hair was starting to grow out. It wasn't black at all—more of a copper red. Sometimes he wondered what else she was hiding under the charcoal veneer.

She turned toward him and for a second their eyes met. Gothy's eyes were a deep, clear green. They caught Sam off guard. He wasn't sure what he expected—black demon eyes or something. All he knew was that mean girls didn't deserve eyes like that. He dropped his gaze, staring at his syllabus.

Mr. Witten droned on. "You'll be studying several fairy tales, folk-lore, and tall tales—each from different countries, some well-known and others not." Witten paused, looking around at the class. "You'll also study several modern retellings of common fairy tales, and will be expected to participate in class discussions as well as write a one-page paper on each story. Then at the end of the semester, each of you will get to create a retelling of a story of your choice."

Sam thought that Witten sounded like he actually believed that this would be fun for some of the kids. His teacher concluded, "Your story retelling will be ten pages long and will count for a quarter of your grade."

Sam frowned. When he'd signed up, he'd thought Folklore and Writing sounded easier than plain old grammar-based English.

He set his pencil down and looked over at Gothy just in time to see her close a notebook—her name written in sweet, swirly letters across the top of the page. Sarah. The 'S' draped itself across the corner like a dress. Sam must have heard her name in class—he was pretty sure his teachers didn't call her Gothy, but there was something about that sweeping 'S' that made the name stick. Sarah—one of the most old-fashioned, feminine names around. Sam couldn't help but enjoy that.

She shoved her notebook into her bag, and shot him a weird look. Sam wished he could shoot her a look of his own. He had a feeling she'd like him better if he could. But all he could do was shrug as he walked out of the building to the module where he had his shop class.

Normally, it was a relief to head out of the main building to the sparse room where tools lined the tables, where he felt like his brain and body could connect in a way they couldn't when he only had pencil and paper. But today he couldn't help but notice that Gothy-Sarah walked the same direction he did—veering off into the stage area for her theater class just before he got to the exit door. When he got into shop class, he found that the thought of Gothy-Sarah across the way distracted him. He failed to let the metal of his soldering iron cool and burned his finger. Twice. That was weird.

THE DOG WAS THE SAME ONE SHE'D NOTICED WANDERING AROUND HER neighborhood—a dark-eyed mutt with eyebrows that seemed to lift when she looked at him, like he was ready for a chat. He'd been following Ella ever since the four-way stop across from the school. She'd never had an animal follow her home, and she was enjoying the cliché.

He looked pretty clean for a stray—his fur anyway. Two of his toenails were cracked and broken. Which didn't stop Ella from sitting down next to him in front of the gates of Napper's preserve. The dog put a paw in her lap, like it belonged there, and Ella felt she'd finally made one friend. It had taken long enough.

Both of them stared at the gate that blocked off the opening to The Property. Up a long cobblestone road Ella could see the huge Napper residence—mansion and museum wound together in an intricate series of turrets, columns, and large twinkling windows. Behind it, a tall hill rose up, arching on its left into a dangerous overhang. On the right side of the mansion, an expanse of woods stretched into a few rolling hills that were almost entirely lost in trees.

Ella wished her mother could see it. She could have named every tree, and the rock formations to boot. On the plaque that hung on the gates, Ella read that in the 1800s, treasure seekers had often come to these hills searching for silver nuggets, although over the years such stones had become increasingly rare.

The dog, Ella noticed, was looking to the right through the trees in an intense way. Ella wondered if he'd seen an animal moving. She stared hard, but nothing cool like a deer or wild turkey came into view. After a minute, her eyes started to water from staring and a stiff breeze caught the tree branches.

Beyond the trees, Ella swore she saw a column of smoke at the edge of The Property. She blinked and looked again, but she couldn't see anything. She shook her head and smiled at the dog. "What do you think?" she asked him. "Are my eyes playing tricks on me, or is there something back there?"

The breeze blew again and the dog barked like he was answering her.

"Go on," Ella said, laughing. "Tell me all your secrets."

The dog looked at her with big, plaintive eyes.

Ella smiled and stroked his ear. "And now I'm begging animals to give me the low down. I must really want something exciting to happen in this crappy little town."

She turned from the gate and hurried home. The dog, she noticed, stayed behind watching The Property like he was guarding it. He was just as crazy as she was. She'd call him Loco.

EVERY TIME DAVID WITTEN SAW THE HOMELESS MAN WITH HIS CART full of cans, hovering around the iron gates of The Property, he handed him a twenty. It was more than kindness or community concern or a hand out. It was a familial responsibility. You didn't choose your distant relatives. And Witten surely wouldn't have chosen this guy, but that didn't mean he wouldn't help him out when he could.

The old man's name was Cres. When Witten had first come to town, he'd offered him dinner and—against his better judgment—a place to stay. But Cres was having none of it. He wanted to live only one place and would not go anywhere else. And so he loitered around the The Property, sneaking in, then getting kicked out, then waiting to get in again.

CHAPTER 12

It was a small stone that would fit into the palm of a child's hand. Simple, gray, with metallic streaks and glints of blue and green. The stone had had a difficult journey here. Or, rather, those who carried it had had a difficult time of it. The bearer and the thief were both now dead. Gruesome business—automobile accidents.

The police had done a remarkable and clueless job of handling the incidents, as the police did a remarkable and clueless job of handling so many things that were within this realm. He appreciated that.

The good doctor's drinking problem and penchant for women hadn't hurt either.

Now the stone that most adults would have overlooked sat in a locked glass case next to the other valuables in his study. For the last two weeks it had remained there—safe and unusable—a reminder of the behemoth undertaking ahead of him.

Dangerous as this stone was, the task of bending a human will would be even harder. But she was young. And she had spent many, many years tragically poor. If her dear mother were still around, he would thank her for that.

A human without money was clay in his hands.

~

Loco always met Ella just before The Property as she walked home from school. He stayed close to her heels as though he was protecting her from something very fierce behind the gate. It was the sweetest thing Ella had ever seen.

Ella's mom had loved dogs, treating strays like they were long lost friends. Looking at Loco, it was easy to see why—the big-eyed loyalty, the willingness to protect you even when there was no danger, the companionship.

It was proving a little difficult to find any of that at school. So far the closest thing she had to a human friend was that weird kid Sam who always stared at her like he was trying to remember something.

He wasn't exactly creepy. He had nice eyes and dirty brown hair exactly the color her mother's had been, plus the same sort of smile. He just never said anything. And you couldn't be friends with a mute. Unless, she thought smiling, that friend was a dog. In which case you didn't have to talk because dogs wore every emotion on their faces.

When they got to Vivi's house, Ella went in to get Loco a couple of meatballs from the freezer. Then the two of them settled down on the grass. Ella did her homework and Loco rolled over for a nice belly rub. Ella was pretty sure her aunt wouldn't approve of scratching a strange dog's belly. She was pretty sure her aunt wouldn't approve of scratching a strange dog period.

Not that her mom had gone around scratching strays. But every time they passed a stray her mother would feed it, even if it meant going into a store or restaurant to buy something. It used to bother Ella —the way her mother had treated the animals like they were people, maybe even better than people.

In Napper there were precious few people in need on the streets— only the one crazy grocery cart man that she'd seen—so Ella didn't have to feel guilty doling the meatballs out to a dog instead of a man.

She watched Loco eat and then, as had happened so many times since her mother's death, a long-ago memory stabbed into her—vivid and fresh. It always made her sad—the rush of the recollection, the ache at her mother's absence, but Ella didn't push it away. In the memories she often found her mother again—renewed, young, alive.

Ella had been little—maybe five or six. It had been night and they were walking home from her day care. The moon had hung so full and bright it'd almost outshone the streetlights, which was saying a lot in the city. They'd stood near several tall, blackened buildings waiting for the last bus of the night.

There, on the corner, had been a scraggly, dirty mutt. The ends of the fur by his belly had been tangled and clumped almost like dread-locks and her mother had looked at the pitiful animal and sighed. "Let me guess," she'd said. "You're down on your luck and need a bite to eat."

The dog had cocked his head to the side as though he didn't appreciate her mother's sarcasm.

"Well, sorry pal, I've got nothing and it's late; everything's closed."

The dog had nodded to the fluorescent lights that dripped down a crumbling building—'BAR,' only the 'A' had been burned out so it read, 'B R.'

"I'm not taking Ella in there. I couldn't if I wanted to," she'd said, motioning to the bored bouncer in the doorway.

In Ella's imagination, the dog had actually answered back. "Come on; just tell them you want a few peanuts. I love peanuts."

Ella had loved peanuts too. She smiled at the way her imagination had given that line to the dog.

Her mother had stood for several minutes—forehead wrinkled practically to the hairline. The animal had looked at her—so hungry, hungrier than most.

"I'll watch the girl," the dog's imaginary voice said in Ella's memory.

And her mother had paused, considering. No—Ella wrinkled her nose trying to straighten out the memory. No, her mother had actually left her at the dog's side and walked several paces toward the door. Then she'd shaken her head and come running back. "I must be out of my mind. This is going too far."

Even so, they'd walked out of their way—it had seemed to Ella hours, but had probably been only twenty minutes to go to the nearest taco place. They'd bought two chicken burritos—one for the dog and one for Ella. Her mother had gone without.

After that her mother had avoided the strays most of the time, though she'd regularly bring leftovers from work that she'd place outside the trash cans where she knew the dogs liked to forage. And her bedtime stories had become peppered with tales of the talking dogs —a noble race equal to the humans, packs of animals who played and worked and sang. Ella had often gone to bed wishing just once to hear a dog sing.

Sitting on Vivi's perfectly soft, perfectly green, perfectly cut grass, that life of walking home past strays and garbage cans seemed far away. Maybe that was part of what had drawn Ella to Loco. Maybe feeding him had given her a piece of her mother back. Lounging on the lawn, Ella could see how her mother might have talked so much to the dogs. Every time Ella looked into Loco's face and said something, Loco looked like he absolutely wanted to answer back.

He sat at her heels and nudged her hand with his head as soon as she stopped scratching.

Ella laughed. The dog's ears were soft and she bent down to look at him. She'd been trying to figure out what type of dog Loco was. He was some type of mix with light gray fur underneath and a large black patch on his back that made it look like he was wearing a super hero's cape. "You're part shepherd," she said. "And maybe a little husky too."

Loco seemed to nod.

Ella laughed again. "Maybe I'll become a crazy animal person," she said, rubbing the dog's ears. "I'll take you in, and we can be weirdo orphans together."

Loco seemed to like the idea. He lay down on the sidewalk and stretched out for a good back scratching.

CHAPTER 13

Twenty years ago, the Psychiatric Ranch Retreat had promised full recovery from the hallucinations for next to nothing. It was a deal no parent who was worried for the sanity and well-being of their children could refuse. The arrangement was set up so that the teenage sisters would stay on site.

Later, when their parents died in a late-night car accident, it was determined that the girls would stay on permanently—taking classes, going to therapy, working through their rehabilitation.

Caring for the girls was not easy. They were used to their ways. They resisted the things The Ranch taught. Most infuriatingly, they insisted ever more strongly that they hadn't been hallucinating at all— that every full moon they could hear dogs talk.

In time, however, his treatment for the pTr4 genome had been more and more successful. Without exposure to dogs, the girls had begun slowly—so slowly—to forget their memories of their life before. His medications had helped dull the symptoms as well, though he was always distraught that they did not completely cover them.

The Ranch would need to keep the girls many, many years for the treatment to have the desired effect. He would need them, he estimated, until they were in their late thirties.

For a while, it seemed like it might work. The girls were allowed free run of The Ranch. They rode horses, hunted for chicken eggs, and hiked along the trails. The older girl loved puzzles; the younger, books. In the fall, they made cider and picked apples. In the winter, they learned to sew and cook, and spent extra time on their lessons and recovery meditations.

Several years passed. The Ranch prospered; the girls grew. He thought that it would be his life's greatest—and final—work.

But it wasn't. He was rarely caught off guard, but the day—two decades ago—when he'd learned the girls had run off with two of his hired men, he was shocked. Even more so when he learned they'd left with his people's most valuable artifacts. When the girls' stolen car wound up at the bottom of a gully, he'd felt that his life's work had been crushed with them.

After many years, Napper had built the Institution in hopes of one day finding others like them. And he had found many with similar symptoms and similar blood. But, until recently, he'd been unaware of any whose symptoms and gifts were *exactly* the same.

You should never name them. Ella knew this. I mean, it was Stray Animal 101.

Loco was gone. For two weeks they'd spent their afternoons together, but now Ella hadn't seen Loco for five days. And it hurt. It hurt like her mother's funeral all over again.

Ella knew that was stupid. She knew it was really stupid. It was a *stray* dog. It strayed. But that afternoon she didn't go inside. She sat on the back step, poking a stick into Vivi's immaculate lawn, digging up little clumps of sod. She might care when Vivi got home, but she didn't right now—and right now was all she could see.

Why hadn't her mother told her more about her father? Or any of her grandparents? Or her aunt? Or anyone at all? Ella didn't even know where her mother had grown up. All she knew was that her mother had left her. Just like that dog.

Ella tossed the stick she'd been holding, then held her head in her hands.

When Vivi found her, her aunt looked at the sod, but didn't comment. Quietly, she said, "Someone will be coming to meet with you later this week, someone the doctor's office recommended. His name is Jack Sanderson and he's a grief counselor."

Fabulous, Ella thought. A counselor. For the freak. A freak counselor.

To her aunt, she said, "Okay." And then, because it seemed like she should, "Thank you."

CHAPTER 14

Sam watched the rain sheet down the window like a rich lady's drapes—folding over itself until it seemed to be piling onto the window, not just splashing and breaking apart. He had spent the last twelve moves in the southwest and could remember nothing like this.

Watching the water was liked being hypnotized. He forgot to be afraid until the first thunder struck—the sound of a gun—quick and uncompromising. It shook the floor of the trailer. Sam reviewed what he'd read. The safest place if there was a tornado was a place with no windows or doors—a closet or the hall of their trailer. But Sam thought of the empty lots where the other tornado-struck trailers had been, and knew that the only safe place in a trailer was no place at all.

The thunder rumbled, vibrating his bones, and the panic burst into him. Sam ran. He ran from the closed walls of the home that could be lifted and dropped at the whim of a crazy funnel of air. He ran against the purple-bruised sky, down the road, to the locked gates.

Later, he would try to remember how he'd gotten through. What had happened to the four padlocks? Had they not been there at all or simply left open? But that part of his escape gaped from his memory— a spot as black as the sky.

All he knew was that he'd run through the open gate, up the path, and behind the little shack he'd seen when he first got to Napper.

A small line of smoke puffed out of the chimney, which seemed impossible with the waterfall of rain. He might have pounded on the door, except that it opened on its own, just like in a horror movie, with no one standing behind it. Sam walked toward it anyway. After all, the little house was dry; and anchored to the ground.

There, at a small table, sat a very old woman sipping a cup of tea and eating a cookie. An orange tabby sat on her feet like a fluffy pair of socks. It was then that Sam wondered if something had fallen on his head and he was unconscious and dreaming. Or maybe the trailer had crushed him and he was dead.

Either way, the woman spoke. "Come in, child, and have some tea. What were you doing out there anyway?" She had a big, bright smile with white square teeth that seemed too big for her lips—dentures he guessed.

"I'm sorry," Sam stammered. "I didn't mean to disturb you. I—" He had no idea how to finish the sentence. *I panicked and ran through a storm like a mental patient and then walked into a stranger's house.*

"Sit child," she said.

The woman or trippy dream character or post-death apparition poured him some chamomile tea. Sam sniffed, then took a sip. It was hot—crazy hot. It burned all the way down.

He waited to wake up. He didn't.

"Watch your mouth," she said. "It's hot."

Yeah. Two minutes earlier that would have been nice to know. Sam was about to get up and leave when another jolt of thunder and lightning struck with barely a millisecond between the two.

"Stay child," she said. "You're safe here."

Sam didn't know what else to do. Unless his drink had been poisoned, he was pretty sure he could take on a hundred year old woman if he had to. She pulled her feet away from the cat and used an old wooden walking stick to get up and stir the fire.

The stick she used was a coffee-colored wood, smooth from use, and engraved with a tangle of leaves and birds, butterflies and flowers.

When she pulled it from the fire, there was no charring to the tip; and the fire settled and crackled like there were no bigger sounds in the world.

"So," Sam said, "are you the..." He didn't know what to say. The woman was obviously too old to be a groundskeeper, but she must have had some job in order to live on Napper's land. "Are you a gardener here or something?"

The old woman chuckled. "Well, child, in a way I once used to be, but my extremely long life has finally gotten in the way of all that."

Sam smiled and asked, "But Mr. Napper lets you stay here? On his property?"

She smiled. "Napper might think he owns everything in the world, but he doesn't quite." She hobbled back to the table and helped herself to a second cookie. "This house has been here for a long time. It's a historical structure. Old Napper can't knock down an old house with an old woman in it—it'd be bad for his image."

Sam decided that if this woman was a crazy killer, then at least she was an entertaining one. It was better than his trailer taking him to Oz at any rate.

She got up and hobbled to what looked like a very old stove to retrieve the next batch of cookies. "You may call me Zinnie," she said, even though Sam hadn't tried to call her anything. "Now, what is your name?"

"Sam," he said, clearing a spot for the cookies she was carrying.

The cookies were thin little things, like puddles on the pan. If Sam had pulled them out of the oven, he would have thrown them all in the garbage. But the old woman didn't. She handed Sam a dish towel, which he put on the table so Zinnie could set down the hot, flat cookies.

"Help me out, dear," she said. Expertly, Zinnie took a cookie and, using the handle of a wooden spoon, she rolled the flat cookie around the handle so that it formed into a small cone while it was warm. She looked at Sam, waiting. "Give it a try," she said, handing him the spoon. "It's not that hard once you get used to it. And after we're done, we'll fill them with cream."

Sam spent the next thirty minutes rolling delicate cookies into even more delicate tubes and then piping them full of whipped cream. By the time they were done, he was surprised to look out the window and see blue sky surfacing.

Zinnie smiled. "Go on, now, the rain has cleared. Every Friday I make cookies. Come whenever you want."

Sam stood slowly, unsure of what to say.

"Go on," she said. "I bet if you leave now you'll catch the rainbow."

Sam left, and as soon as he walked through the gates, there was a rainbow—doubled up—one stream of colors sitting fat above another. Tornado country—it had its perks.

CAREFULLY, THE SILVERSMITH PACKAGED ONE SILVER BULLET—BUBBLE wrapped, then triple boxed just as the buyer had requested. Usually he got bulk orders for his bullets. They were one of his most popular novelty items for party favors, Halloween decorations, and occasionally a redneck wedding. But for the last couple months, he'd gotten an order for just one—the tedious instructions typed below it with an offer to pay five extra dollars for his trouble.

And, sure, why not? Since he'd started his side business of selling silver trinkets, he'd learned not to be too surprised at anything. This order would be shipped to a local P.O. Box even though he was getting payment from a European bank.

It was strange, but not any stranger than ladies who ordered the bullets for their divorce-is-final parties or the men who wanted them as gifts for their best men. The silversmith just rolled with it. Growing corn and raising chickens didn't bring in a ton of money. It was the dogs and the little side businesses that kept him afloat, not to mention sane.

Watching Vivi carefully carry in her umbrella and hang her coat was like watching a movie with Mr. Rogers as the lead. Ella sighed. It sounded terrible, but Ella just couldn't picture her aunt as her mother's sister.

Her mother hadn't been wild or anything. Her mother hadn't even had a boyfriend. But there'd been something alive in her mother's eyes —verdant, feisty, mysterious.

Vivi was a stone—a gorgeous stone, polished and faceted, but a stone. Vivi had bought Ella school clothes and new boots. Vivi had stocked up on marshmallow cereal as soon as Ella mentioned them. Vivi had taken Ella to her fancy country club and signed her up as a member. She had made dinner every night, and each day she gave Ella four times as much money as she needed for lunch, and told her to keep any change for spending money. In fact, Vivi had done everything it seemed she could possibly do for a niece she had never met. And yet, there was no warmth, no light. Vivi was a closed door, a locked safe.

Ella stood in the kitchen staring at her impeccably groomed aunt and all the sudden she couldn't stand to look at her anymore. She turned to go to her room without even saying hello.

From the kitchen, Vivi called, "I think I'll order a pizza tonight. You up for it?"

Ella stopped in the perfect white hall. She was a jerk. It's not like her aunt wasn't trying.

"Yeah, sure," Ella said. "That'd be great."

Maybe she just needed to give her aunt more time. Maybe Vivi was just shy. Ella had noticed at her other schools that if a girl was gorgeous and quiet, everyone assumed she was snobby. But often, she guessed, they were just shy. I mean, being stunning didn't make you automatically outgoing.

Maybe it was the same sort of thing with Vivi. Certainly this whole adjustment was throwing her off too, especially since it seemed she'd been used to living alone. Her aunt had given up life as she'd known it. The least Ella could do was try to be pleasant at dinner.

When the pizza arrived, Ella was almost convinced that Vivi would just break out a chicken breast and some carrot sticks for herself until her aunt actually picked up a slice of supreme pizza and said, "Dig in."

Ella took her own slice and looked at her aunt. "So, Vivi," Ella began. "Tell me more about yourself."

Vivi turned to her as though Ella had just asked her to explain the principles of quantum physics.

Ella waited.

Vivi paused and then asked politely, almost chirpily, "What would you like to know?"

Ella realized she had no idea what she'd like to know—something, anything. She didn't even really know what her aunt's job was. "Well, um, what exactly do you do at your job?"

"I work for the Napper Nature Conservatory."

"I know," Ella said. "But what do you *do*?"

"I write grants actually. It's kind of dull."

Ella nodded. It sounded dull. "What kind of grants?"

"Oh, stuff for the city. Parks. Preserves. Animals. Whoever needs money."

Ella nodded again. It was absolutely too dull for words. She finished her pizza and was about to go back to her room when she stopped. "Aunt Vivi," she asked.

"Hmmm."

"Do you have a favorite color?"

Judging from the décor, it was black or white, but for some reason Ella wanted to hear her aunt say it.

"Oh, I don't know," Vivi said. "I guess if I could, I'd paint the sun red and the sky purple."

It was an odd answer, but definitely the most interesting thing Vivi had ever said.

Ella went into her room and wrote it down. She didn't know why. It's just that somehow it made her aunt seem like more than an empty space.

Ella took the little slip of paper and opened her mother's jewelry box. She set the paper on top of the others—her aunt's words blinking at her like a strange lizard in a nest of birds. She got out her mother's old wedding ring. Since the accident Ella had worn it every night. She couldn't explain why; it just felt right. Her mother hadn't wanted to let her father go. Now Ella didn't want to let her mother go. The ring was too big for her, and she usually put it on her middle finger or thumb, but tonight she slid it over her ring finger—the same finger her mother had worn it on.

"Ella!" Vivi called from the living room.

Ella jumped and the ring flew off her finger into the box, making a strange little plink where it should have made a plunk. That's weird, Ella thought. The ring had made a sound like there was another section under the jewelry box, though Ella was almost positive the box had just one compartment.

"Ella!" Vivi called. "Mr. Sanderson is here."

Ella would have to investigate later. The freak counselor had arrived. She took a deep breath, shut the jewelry box, and went downstairs.

CHAPTER 15

Jack the freak counselor showed up in jeans and a grass-green button down shirt with the sleeves rolled halfway up. He was hot. And probably only twenty-six. Which made being the freak all the more embarrassing.

As soon as Ella came in, he stood and held out his hand. Ella wished she could ignore it and just stand there staring, but that would probably only earn her more points in crazy. She held out her hand and when he took it, she noticed that his palm was just a little callused while the skin on the back of his hand was soft and tan. He pressed her hand lightly and then gestured to the couch like a gentleman.

Ella sat down and Vivi brought out two glasses of water, lemon wedges, and grapes before retreating into the kitchen.

"So, Ella," Jack began, dropping a lemon wedge into his glass. "How long have you been in Napper now?"

"About a month," Ella said trying to squeeze lemon in the delicate way Vivi always did.

"And how are you liking it so far?" Jack asked.

Ella wasn't sure what to say. Telling Jack she hated everything about it seemed both impolite and like something a freaky, depressed teenager would say. "It's nice," she lied.

"Whatever," Jack said. "It's completely lame. I'm just glad there's the wolf controversy so there's something in the paper now besides the 4-H winners."

Ella smiled. Not the polite, careful smile she'd been mastering at home and school, but a genuine, toothy smile. She'd forgotten how it felt. "Yeah, it can be a little slow."

"On its worst days it's absolutely comatose. How are things with Vivi?"

"Oh, they're good," Ella said quickly. "She's been so nice."

"That's great. Vivi's a little shellacked, but inside she's punchier than she seems."

"You know her?" Ella asked, dropping her lemon wedge on the floor.

"Sort of. Our moms go way back. Actually—" Jack smiled almost shyly. "Vivi used to babysit for me."

Ella realized Jack didn't look at Vivi like other men did. He looked at her like they were relatives. Ella was totally cool with that.

"You've been through some crazy tough stuff," Jack said, leaning in to look at Ella's face.

She looked down.

"It's tough to transition to a different town even without having to transition to a completely new life," he said.

"Yeah," Ella mumbled.

Jack leaned back and let her think. After a few minutes he asked, "So what do you think has been the hardest part for you? Besides losing your mom of course."

Ella hadn't really thought about it. Losing her mom had been such a shadow over everything else that Ella if you took that out, she didn't really know exactly what the hardest part of the transition had been. "I don't know. Vivi's done her best to make it easy. It's just so…"

Jack leaned in. Ella could smell the musky aftershave on his face.

"You know there was this stray dog," Ella began. "And…" And what? He left and she was sad? Maybe she really did need counseling. "I guess I just really miss having someone to talk to," she said.

"Hmmm," Jack said, "so maybe a phone would help."

The suggestion caught Ella off-guard. She'd never had a phone, much less any friends to call. But she wasn't about to say that. "I couldn't ask Vivi for a phone," she said. "They're too expensive."

Jack smiled, crinkles by his eyes and a deep dimple in his right cheek.

~

THE NEXT MONDAY WHEN ELLA GOT HOME FROM SCHOOL, A NEW phone was sitting in a box on the table.

Ella was too shocked to do anything, but stare.

"If the phone doesn't work for you," Vivi began, "we can look for something else; I just thought it'd be easiest to add you to my plan."

"Oh no, it's good. It's…it's awesome," Ella said. It must have cost more than her mother had spent on her entire wardrobe in all the years Ella had been alive. Holding the expensive phone felt like a small piece of treason. But there wasn't really a graceful way to reject such a nice gift either. Especially when Ella was pretty sure Jack-the-gorgeous-freak-counselor had suggested it.

Ella spent the evening reading the owner's manual and adding a few apps. She tucked it away well after 11:00 and brushed her teeth quickly before falling into bed.

It was the first night in a long time that she didn't pull down her mother's jewelry box to sift through stones and slips of paper. Ella felt a little treasonous in that, but tonight she was too tired to care. She fell asleep in moments, the phone just a few feet away.

CHAPTER 16

Sam had a headache like he'd never had before. His father often got migraines when the moon was full—he said it was common with the extra gravitational pull.

"Everyone's bodies get off when the moon is full. Most people just don't notice it," he'd told Sam once after a particularly bad migraine. "Did you know that statistically women have more babies during the full moon? It's a fact."

Sam wasn't sure about that, but tonight his father was in his room moaning with the whole jar of Aleve. Which was too bad because Sam could have used a couple.

Sam went to the bedroom door and almost knocked, but then he heard the bathroom door open and slam shut. Sometimes his dad got headaches so bad he puked all night long. Sam wasn't going to go pounding on the door, whining for a couple of pills.

Instead he sat very still and pressed his fingers against his temples. Through the window he could see the bright moon propped up on the horizon like a fat, shiny coin. And then an animal jumped in front of it —a dark silhouette with the outline of a cat.

Sam blinked. The cat sat on his window sill like a paper cutout, staring at him with amber irises and fat black pupils. Sam recognized her from the old woman's cottage, but something looked a little different.

"Well, hello," Sam said, charmed by the animal in spite of his splitting head.

She mewed a reply, which seemed hilariously polite. Sam let go of his throbbing temples and went to the fridge. Pickings were pretty slim, but they had a half-eaten can of tuna, the mushy pink flesh still sitting in the can. Sam got that out, scooped out a spoonful for himself, and then opened the front door and set it on the concrete step.

The cat looked at him, but did not move.

Quietly, he shut the door, turned out the lights, and went to bed.

In the morning, the tuna can was licked shiny clean. Sam smiled. His headache was gone and he felt pretty good. His father was puttering around in an old robe—pale-lipped, but otherwise okay.

"Next time leave me a couple Aleve, will you?" Sam said, smiling.

His father buttered a slice of toast and said, "Be grateful you don't need them."

"Hmph," Sam said. "Well last night I kinda did."

A look passed over his father's face—green-gray clouds of worry.

It made Sam feel bad for complaining and he quickly added, "Not like you or anything. Just a little headache."

"But you've never had one before," his father sputtered, setting down his toast.

"Well, sure I've had a headache before," Sam said. "And it was no big deal." Sam was starting to feel annoyed that he couldn't complain about a little headache without his dad freaking out when his dad didn't freak out about anything, including the fact that they had maybe twenty bucks to get them through the rest of the month.

"But not at the full moon. You've never had a headache during the full moon," his father muttered.

"What does that matter?" Sam said, annoyed.

"How old are you now?" his father asked. "Fifteen? Sixteen?"

"Dad, that's something you should know," Sam said, still irritated and grabbing his backpack.

"Sixteen," his father said, staring off into a corner for several blank seconds before getting up, wandering away, and dropping his uneaten toast in the trash can.

Sam stared at the place his father had been, then looked at the edge of the toast peeking up from last night's onion skins. His father was a weird guy—Sam knew that. But he also knew that in all of his sixteen years his dad had never thrown out a perfectly good piece of bread.

It worried him all the way to school.

TWO DOGS WERE DEAD AT THE EDGE OF HIS FIELD—RIGHT BY THE SIGN that read, "Free range eggs $4/dozen." The chickens, it seemed, were untouched in their coops. Strange. The farmer held two large plastic bags near the bodies of the dogs—they were torn up pretty badly— chests and stomachs ripped open and several organs eaten out. He didn't want to look at them, but his curiosity pushed through his revulsion. And his sadness. He'd been working with them for months. And they'd been good animals—well-trained, sweet-hearted. They never would have touched the chickens. That's why he left them out here at night when coons and foxes liked to prowl around and carry off sleepy hens.

Jones knelt beside them, wrapping the bodies in bags, trying to figure it out. Nothing chose a dog over a fat, dumb chicken. Nothing normal anyway. There were no bears in these parts. And, as far as he knew, those cusses of wolves hadn't gotten here yet.

His glassed neighbor said he'd seen two hairy men crawl onto his property last night on all fours. Which was just what you said when you ran a drug factory from your white trash trailer and were spooked by stories of wolves coming to your town. The farmer wasn't thrilled about the wolf news either, but he knew that people got stoned or scared or both; and soon enough there were crazy rumors running around like chickens without their heads—no brain, no direction, plenty of speed.

He'd bury the mutts before the school bus got here. He shook his head—it would have been awful if any kids had seen the torn up dogs; he was glad he'd found them first. Later that week, he'd head down to the Humane Society to see if they had any good dogs for cheap.

THE SILVER SHOOTING—THAT'S WHAT REPORTERS WERE CALLING IT ON account of the silver bullets used, probably from some type of antique gun. It was all over the national news. And this time—the third silver shooting in the last three months—it was all over the local news as well. It had happened in Indy—the hospital where her mother had died.

Ella couldn't get away from it. But she had to. Pictures of the hospital, images of the trauma rooms. Empty. White. It was just like Vivi's house.

Ella had to be where there weren't clean white walls. She ran to the bus stop and then from stop to stop until a bus finally came. She got on.

It had been the lab administrator at the hospital who'd been shot. The lab administrator who handled the blood work—found in a pool of her own blood, vials of other people's blood knocked to the floor around her. Blood, blood, blood on white, white, white.

And no teeth of course. All gone. An empty gaping mouth of blood. Her mother's hospital. All over the news.

When Ella had found out, she had suddenly, perversely, needed to know if her mother had had her teeth. She'd called Dr. Murray's office, but he was gone—not out, but gone. Dead. Killed in a car accident almost exactly one month ago.

Ella put her head against the bus seat in front of her. Above her, the radio played.

The lab administrator had been born and raised in Napper. The locals were shocked, mourning. The victim had been a couple years ahead of Vivi in school. The town was reeling, services planned in a large stone mortuary at the edge of town. Vivi had texted to say she was going and wouldn't be home until late.

Ella tried to feel their pain—the collective sorrow for this small town daughter. But all she could feel was her own pain. White walls, red blood, death.

About an hour out of town, her hysteria stilled. The woman who'd been killed wasn't her mother. It wasn't anyone remotely like her mother. Just the same hospital. A terrible murder. But her mother hadn't been murdered. Her mother had been in an accident. Those were different things. Same result, but different events. Ella took long, deep breaths. The radio played dull music.

When Ella finally got back into town, she got off at the hardware store, bought brushes, a roller, and a drop cloth. There was one thing still that she couldn't face.

Vivi might ground her for the rest of her life, but Ella didn't care. By the time her aunt got home, the flawless, white walls in Ella's bedroom would be replaced by a color as blue as the sky.

CHAPTER 17

Ella felt, with a perverse sort of pride, that Vivi must have called Jack as soon as she'd come home to find one room of her perfectly black and white house had been painted blue. But Ella couldn't be sure. Vivi had looked at the room with not much more than a blink while Ella had stammered about how she'd just wanted a color change. Vivi had nodded. And that was that.

Now Jack sat in front of Ella for their second session. If that was her punishment, it could have been way worse.

"So," he was saying, as he nursed the soda water Vivi had brought out. "Do you go to the local high school or has Vivi hooked you up with one of the private schools?"

"Oh, no," Ella muttered, not touching the gross fizzy water. "I go to the normal high school."

"Normal," Jack said smiling. "If normal means all white, rich kids."

Ella giggled. "Yeah, well, Indy was a little different. But they're not *all* rich, white kids."

"Eh, mostly," Jack said, still smiling. "My little brother goes there, so I should know."

"Oh," Ella said a little surprised.

"Not that he's particularly little," Jack added. "He's probably four inches taller than me and broad as a horse."

Inside Ella kind of gagged. Definitely not her type.

"What's his name?" Ella asked, to be polite.

"Brant," Jack said. "Brant Sanderson."

Ella hadn't expected to know the name, but she did. Everyone did. And Jack was right—he was huge, probably 6'4" and all muscle everywhere. He played football and usually spoke at the pep rallies.

"Oh, yeah," she said out loud. "He plays football, right?"

"Yup. Wide receiver."

"Oh," Ella said.

"You don't know what that is, do you?" Jack said.

"Not really, no," Ella said with a weak smile.

"It's okay," Jack said. "Neither did I till he started to play."

Ella's smile widened.

"He's the guy that catches the ball, then runs as far as he can until he gets tackled. I go watch him every Friday since my mom's usually out of town for her job. You should come sometime."

Ella stopped herself just before saying, *With you?* Of course not with her twenty-six-year-old grief counselor. Oh my gosh, she was a freak.

"Yeah," she said slowly. "Maybe."

"Or not," he said, still smiling. "But it really is pretty fun. There's a lot of energy at the games. Even if you don't like football." He winked.

Ella felt the blush burn at her neckline. Maybe she would go to a game. The question was, with whom? Because you didn't have to know the rules of football to know you didn't just show up in a packed stadium all by yourself and take a seat.

SAM HAD BEEN IN A LOT OF SCHOOLS, BUT HE'D NEVER SEEN A KID get hit so hard that a tooth flew out. He saw it now, even from a distance, as he was walking past the football field where the football team ran along in sloppy formation banging into the practice sleds like an army of zombies. Although right now, the kid who looked most like a zombie was the one by the bleachers, dripping blood onto the grass—black eye, red mouth. Sam was pretty sure it was a scraggly kid from his science class, Howard Simms. The other kid—tall, fast, strong—was one of the football players. He laughed as he hit the kid again.

Sam hopped the fence and started running toward them. Across the field, the football coach was turned away, not moving a muscle—visor over his face. The rest of the team was running through their drills, oblivious to what was happening past the bleachers.

Sam felt his feet pounding into the hard summer soil, gaining ground as the bigger kid pummeled the other one in the back, then neck, forcing him down to the ground before kicking his ribs, then stomach. The kid screamed, rolling over to cover what was left of his face, as the bigger kid gave him one last kick in the neck before trotting off to the football field like he'd just been out for a drink of water.

Sam came up on Howard Simms as he rose to his knees. Howard's whole body was shaking, trembling in a way that Sam worried looked a lot like a seizure. His bloody, bruised face was stoic, eyes blank.

"Here, wait just a minute," Sam said, groping through his bag until he came up with a scraggly pack of old tissues. He held them out for the kid, trying to flag down the football coach.

"You got a phone? I'll call somebody," Sam said, opening the tissue packet that the kid was just holding in his hand.

"Screw you," Howard Simms said and then threw up.

Sam jumped back. "I'll go grab a teacher. You'll be okay." But the kid flipped him off, stood up, and staggered away toward the field. Sam ran back to the school and banged on the locked door. A janitor finally opened up and asked what he wanted.

"Some kid just got beat up outside," Sam stammered. "He was bleeding all over the place."

The janitor nodded to Sam. "I'll call someone. We'll get it taken care of." He looked at Sam. "And calm down, kid. You look like you're going to faint."

Sam kind of felt that way too. He sat down on the cool hallway floor and leaned his head against a locker while the janitor went into an office and mumbled into his walkie-talkie.

"Alright son," the janitor said when he came back. "I got stuff to do and you look a lot better, so head out."

"Did they send somebody out there?" Sam asked.

"Don't you worry about it," the janitor said, dipping his mop into a bucket. "Ain't nothin' for a kid to stick his nose into."

But Sam did worry. When he felt like he had his legs back, he ran back to the field. Strangely, it looked like everything had been all cleaned up, including the puke. And the kid was nowhere to be seen. Sam promised himself that he'd find Howard the next day at school, and try to talk to him.

But the next day at school, Howard Simms was gone. Not absent, but gone. His locker sat empty and the desk he'd had at the back of Sam's physics class was given to a new kid.

Maybe he'd wound up in the hospital. Or his parents had sent him to a private school. Maybe he'd died of a brain hemorrhage for all Sam knew.

And that was the craziest thing.

In this little, upper class high school, gossip floated when a girl got a new pair of earrings and exploded when somebody found a cigarette in the boy's locker room. Nobody mentioned the fight. The kid who'd thrown the punches—some senior named Brent or Grant or something went to his classes smiling like nothing had ever happened. And even though Sam nudged a couple of his classmates with questioning comments about the scrawny kid, no one ever said anything at all about him. It was like he hadn't been here. It was like he'd never existed.

ELLA PULLED OUT HER MOTHER'S OLD JEWELRY BOX. ON A BLANK SLIP of paper, she jotted the word "Jack" and dropped it into the box. She sat next to the window and looked at herself in the little jewelry box mirror—she could sometimes see her mother in her features and definitely in the pale skin that would never tan. But the mouth and brown eyes—they belonged to somebody else. She would give almost anything to know who.

She pulled out her mother's wedding ring again. Her mother had never said a bad word about her father. Not one. Of course she hadn't said any kind words either. Her father's name was Patrick—that's all she knew. Not even a middle initial. So where was he? Why had he left? Who could she ask? Vivi couldn't produce so much as a wedding invitation.

Ella rubbed the ring between her thumb and forefinger, and then she remembered the strange sound it had made when it had dropped into the box a few days ago. She leaned over. There was definitely not another drawer or opening. She let the ring fall into the box. And there it was again—the plink that should have been a plunk. Ella emptied the jewelry box of the quarters, papers, and rocks, and tapped on the bottom. Still sounded hollow.

"Weird," she said, and then she did something she never would have done if she'd taken a moment to think about it. She peeled away the cheap velvet from the inside of the box to see if anything was underneath.

The wood beneath had a tiny inscription with the initials P.P. and a small silhouetted tree. Ella ran her hand over it. The inscription was etched into the wood and beautiful. Still, Ella couldn't see that there was any compartment underneath—it just looked like a wooden box. But somehow she felt positive her mother had glued that velvet on to hide something. Which made Ella more confused than ever.

Something was in the bottom of the box. But Ella didn't want to tear her mother's only keepsake apart to find it.

Absently, Ella picked at a line of glue left from the velvet and when she did, the wooden piece that looked like the inside bottom of the box lifted just a bit.

"Oh my gosh," Ella said. She picked at the glue again, and again it lifted. This time, she picked at a corner of the glue so she could hold it between her fingernails and use it as a teeny tiny glue handle.

She lifted and up came the bottom of the box. She caught the edge —an edge that was so well fitted to the box that it had looked as though it connected to the wood on the sides—and held it there, shivering with excitement.

She removed the square of wood and there underneath she found… paper. Several sheets. They weren't treasure maps either. Just plain, white paper with plain, black words.

Ella was still pretty sure it was a treasure because there on top of the pile was a slip of paper folded four times with her name written neatly in her mother's handwriting.

"Ella."

She read her name over and over before unfolding the note. It wasn't a letter as Ella expected it to be, just a simple story, the kind her mother used to tell her before bed.

Once upon a time in a world filled with howlings and madness, a child sought a stone that had fallen through the cracks of her life, now lost in a wood of rock and ashes. Each day the child wandered through the petrified trees—the trunks cool against her fingers, their leaves brittle as they fell to the earth. Each day the child grew colder, her skin losing color, her eyes growing in pallor.

"A ghost," the child thought. "If I don't find my stone again, I will become a ghost."

And so it was that as the waif-like girl wandered the woods, she heard a small voice through the trees.

"You cannot hear me," it said, "but you must follow me if you wish to live."

"But of course I can hear you," the girl said.

"Then you must not," sang the voice in a rumbling baritone. "Now come."

The girl stepped toward the voice, and when she did, the howlings began—deep, feral, threatening.

"Quickly," the voice said, and a dog ran forward, leading her away as the howling ones trailed behind.

Outside it had started to rain. Ella looked out the window at the damp sky. She leaned her cheek against the windowsill as the rain began to hit the glass, trickling in bent lines down the panes. It was a comforting sound—the sky mourning with her, releasing its tears.

Ella realized she had never seen one of her mother's stories written down. She held the paper against her skin. It was soft and creased all over from having been pressed into her mother's own hand.

Ella put it in her lap and picked up another paper from the stack, but just as she did, she heard Vivi open the front door. Ella stopped. She didn't want to uncover her mother with her aunt nearby. Ella re-folded the note, re-covered the jewelry box, and replaced the box in her closet before Vivi's voice came echoing up the stairs.

"Ella...Ella are you home?"

Ella looked into the full-length mirror and realized she'd been crying. Which made sense. Her mother had died two months ago. As she hurried to the bathroom to wash her face, Ella realized that she hadn't seen her aunt cry. Not once. "Must have been some feud," she mumbled. It made her mad. Could her aunt not find enough forgiveness in her heart to grieve just a little?

When Ella went downstairs, her aunt was making tiny little pieces of meat that Ella realized were some kind of animal innards.

"Hearts," Vivi said without looking up. She plunked one down on Ella's plate. "I got them for a steal today at the farmer's market."

Ella must have looked as grossed out as she felt because her aunt quickly added, "They're really nutritious." And then, "I made gravy."

Vivi's gravy was definitely not good enough for Ella to choke down her repulsion. She ate the potatoes and even the soggy asparagus, but for the first time since she'd come to Vivi's house, she didn't graciously finish what was on her plate.

Vivi didn't say anything. Of course. But Ella thought she noticed the shadow of a scowl as Ella rose from the table, put the meat in a Tupperware, and left the kitchen.

CHAPTER 18

Sam had found her—Ella. Well, sort of. At least he'd found the reason she looked so familiar to him.

All he'd had to do was chase a mouse into the hall closet. There, behind his father's coat, two ratty boxes with vacuum parts, and an old pair of boots, he'd found—not the stupid mouse—but a dusty, green suitcase he didn't even know they had. An old, yellowed tag hung from the handle with his father's name—Robert Calhoun—scribbled across it in fading ink.

Maybe Sam wouldn't have bothered to look inside, except for the dust. His father may not have been able to match his socks to his shirt or cook a decent meal, but he was meticulously neat. Besides, they moved every few months. Most of their stuff never had the chance to get dusty. Yet, there it was—lines of dirt stuck in the creases and latches of the suitcase.

Sam lifted the suitcase out of the closet. He could think of only one reason his father would keep a thing but never touch it.

The suitcase contained mementos of his mother.

A dried bouquet of flowers, two framed pictures from their wedding, and at least one letter written in a swooping cursive. Sam didn't dare read the letter and he didn't care about the flowers, but he could have looked at the pictures for hours. Maybe he did.

His stomach had started to growl by the time he began to put everything back. It was then that he saw, at the bottom of the suitcase, an unframed picture, old and yellowed. His mother's mother. She was young in the shot—dark hair, fair cheeks, brown eyes.

It was like Ella had stepped into a dress from 1970. "Wow," Sam said.

In the picture his grandmother stood in the woods—a bright bonfire burning beside her, a big smile on her face, and a large dog at her side.

He stared at it until he heard his dad's key in the door. Sam thought about shoving all the stuff back in the closet, but he felt soldered to the floor, unable to move.

His dad came into the room, took in the mess, and the suitcase. He didn't respond how Sam thought he would. He just stepped toward the suitcase and peered over Sam's shoulder. "Well, I'll be," he said. "I'd forgotten about all this stuff."

Sam didn't find that perfectly believable, but he didn't argue.

His father sat beside him and looked at the wedding pictures just like Sam had—his face lost for several long minutes. "Guess I shouldn't have stashed this stuff away."

"Sorry I got into it," Sam said. "There was a mouse."

"You get it?"

"Nope." Sam was quiet for several minutes.

"You okay, son?"

Sam shrugged. "This is gonna sound crazy, but there's this girl in my class who looks just like this picture of Grandma. I kept thinking the girl looked familiar, but couldn't place her face. Now I can." He pushed the picture toward his father. "I must have seen it sometime when I was younger. And remembered."

His father was silent for several minutes, staring at the photograph. Finally, he cleared his throat and laughed. "Well, you should ask that girl where her people hail from."

Just then the orange cat hopped onto the ledge outside the window and stared in.

Sam jumped. His dad stood up. "Shoo now. Go on."

The cat didn't shoo. It just narrowed its amber eyes and flicked its tail nub.

THE NEXT DAY THE CAT WAS BACK. BUT IT WASN'T ON THE windowsill. It had crept through the window Sam had opened, even though his father told him not to, and then it had plunked itself down into the old suitcase with the picture of Sam's grandmother.

"Shoo," Sam said, just like his dad had.

The cat licked a paw.

"I mean it. Out." Sam reached in to pick up the animal. He lifted her out of the suitcase and then lifted the picture to blow off the fur. On the back of the picture were the words, "With love, to my two beautiful daughters." It was a perfectly normal inscription. Except that as far as Sam knew, his mother had been an only child.

ELLA TURNED OFF HER LIGHT SO VIVI WOULD THINK SHE'D GONE TO sleep. She used the dim glow from her cell phone to see into her mother's jewelry box. Once again she lifted up the fake bottom, and once again she held her mother's note. Ella ran her finger along the cursive letters of her name—written on a secret paper, found in a secret compartment, a glance at a secret part of her mother's life.

She held the note for several minutes before setting it aside and looking at the stack of papers. On the top of the first sheet, her mother had scribbled, "If you've found all of this, I'm guessing that things aren't great. Since I can't tell you much or kiss you good-night, let me finish the tales I always told before bed."

Ella sat in the near darkness, holding the stack of papers. These words, these stories—they were her mother—her voice, her handwriting. And yet, hidden like this, they were her mother as a secret agent—

as something more than a waitress at a diner who came home after midnight with a pocket full of ones.

Ella sighed, flipping through the stack. She'd listened to her mother's stories until she was twelve when, suddenly, she felt way too old for bedtime stories. They hadn't been just stories either—poems, riddles, rhymes. They were all here. Her mother's tales had involved monsters and monarchy—evil werewolves, beautiful queens, and sometimes beautiful werewolves and evil queens. Ella had always fallen asleep with teeth and swords, betrayal and impossible loyalty swirling through her dreams.

Now Ella wished she'd never asked her mother to stop. She blinked away the tears that threatened to splatter her mother's beautiful words. And then, she began to read.

Once, in a world before our world, when a garnet sun sat in an amethyst sky, a werewolf king ruled, offering neither love nor mercy to any who opposed him.

Ella settled into the corner of her closet, flipping through the pages of her mother's manuscript. This was a familiar story, and one her mother had loved.

While the wolves wore the fur of beast, their masters could also don the skin of man. Called the Veranderen, or the Changers, they were a nearly immortal, magical race of man-like creatures who could shift at will, day or night, full moon or no moon, into hulking, intelligent, wolven beasts. No one dared speak the ancient and degrading name "werewolf." In the land of the great red sun, one ruler reigned supreme...

The words were a blur of tears, memories, and sadness. The words were her mother right there, but not; her mother was gone. Ella would never see or hear or hug her again. Even so, she could hear her mother's voice as she read—the voice that knew the story up and down. "Oh my gosh," Ella whispered. "She was writing a book."

CHAPTER 19

The farmer, Mitchell Jones, wanted that dog. It looked strong and had clearly been trained. Not only that, but when it looked at you, you got the feeling it was saying something. Jones liked that.

"I'm sorry, sir," the acned boy at the Humane Society desk mumbled, looking down at his half-eaten roast beef sandwich. "The papers say I can't give this one up. He's fit to be put down come morning. Fancy lady in some shiny black car dropped him off last week and said he'd done took a bite outta her little toddler."

"That so?" Jones asked. "'Cause it doesn't look like he's gonna take a bite out a nothing, much less a baby. "

"I'm sorry, sir. I just can't set you up with him. We got other dogs."

"Yup," the farmer said. "I see 'em, but I don't much like 'em. That one's a good dog. I'd say he's even worth more than the fifty dollars the pound asks for these mutts."

As he said it, the dog let out a whimper like he was pleading his case.

The boy looked at the dog and Jones could tell that even though the kid was skinny and pimpled and talked like he'd just been dumped off the pumpkin cart, he wasn't really dumb. Sometimes kids were like animals—if you could see past the dirt and scruff you got a much better look. It was clear that the boy knew the animal wouldn't do any harm either. In fact, as the farmer watched the boy look at the animal, he got a hunch. "You know, son, I'm not much of a gambling man, but I got a little bet for you."

The boy looked up.

"You stick that half a sandwich in that cage. I'm going to tell that mutt not to touch it. If he so much as licks it, you win and I pick another dog. If he leaves it alone, I walk off with that animal today."

"But what'll I tell Miss Mandy?" the boy asked, looking down at his sandwich. "I mean, if you take the dog."

"You tell her to come talk to Mitchell Jones," the man said. "She knows a good animal when she sees one just like you do. She knows that dog didn't do nothing."

"Sure didn't," the boy grumbled, handing the man his sandwich.

Jones put the half-eaten roast beef sub in the cage. The dog looked at it, hungry.

"Stay," Jones said loudly. The dog lifted its head, then laid back down on the floor of its kennel.

Jones looked at the boy, and the boy grinned. "I knowed he didn't do nothing to no kid," the teenager said.

"Nope," Jones said. "Sometimes fancy ladies'll say whatever they can to get a mutt away from their pretty grass."

The boy nodded.

"You know where my farm is?" Jones asked, fishing five ten dollar bills out of his wallet.

"You train dogs and sell trinkets and run the corn maze every year, sir."

"That's right," Jones said. "You got a girlfriend?"

"No, sir."

"Well, get you one, and come on out to the corn maze for free."

SAM HAD BEEN THINKING ABOUT THE INSCRIPTION ON THE BACK OF HIS grandmother's picture for the last two days. He wanted to ask his father about it, but didn't know how. Bringing up potential family skeletons was always awkward.

As soon as his dad walked through the door, Sam took a deep breath and cornered him, waving the picture in his dad's face like a lunatic.

His father looked at him and said, "Sold two vacuums today," then walked past Sam into the bedroom to put the money away.

His dad's announcement was enough of a shock that for a minute Sam forgot about the picture. He forgot about the fact that his mother might have a sister, which meant he might have an aunt, which meant he might have a cousin. He forgot about everything.

"Two?" Sam asked, letting the picture hang at his side.

"Two," his dad practically sang from the next room. "*Dos. Twee. Deux.*"

"That's awesome, Dad," Sam said.

It was kind of a record. Sam couldn't remember his dad ever selling two vacuums in a day. "Where'd you go?"

"West side of town," his dad said. "Nice folks."

"I guess," Sam mumbled, looking down. He saw the picture in his hand, read the inscription again and then said, "Hey, Dad?"

"Yeah," his dad said. "Let me get my coat. We'll go get one of those five-dollar pizzas."

Sam shook his head. It had to be a dream. Getting a pizza with his dad was possibly even weirder than finding a mysterious inscription on a picture or running through a pouring thunderstorm into an old lady's house and eating her food. So, yes, pretty weird.

"Dad," he said again, looking at the picture.

His father strode out of the room, jangling his keys like a teenager. "Come on, son, I'm starving."

Sam was too. He set the picture back into the box, inscription-side down and followed his father out the door.

CHAPTER 20

The Silver Shooter settled down on the couch, watching the news special about the shootings. All around the country other people were doing the same thing—curious to know the gory details of the murders, to surmise about what the killer's motivation might have been, to gawk over the senselessness of the crimes. To wonder whether it would happen again.

The Silver Shooter smiled, sipping a macchiato.

The teeth, the reporter was explaining, were not just broken or bashed from the mouth, but carefully extracted. A forensic scientist had come on and was describing the procedure and displaying replicas of what the teeth would have looked like once pulled. After that, they brought out an old gun that was similar to what they believed the killer was using, as well as silver replicas of the bullets that had been found in the bodies—oblong silver discs that had travelled through healthy, beating hearts.

The reporter concluded, "At risk of making light of these horrible murders, these crimes could be compared to graffiti: They serve no practical purpose, require quite a bit of effort, and make no clear statement. Yet the cost is so much higher than graffiti. These deaths aren't something that can be washed up or painted away."

Indeed, the shooter thought. That was pretty much the point. To make an impression that would only be understood by those who were involved, to leave a blood trail that could not easily be cleaned up.

VIVI'S COMPUTER HAD BEEN LEFT OPEN. IT WAS ONE OF THOSE THINGS that wasn't weird until you realized it was. Ella really didn't mean to look at it, but she was drawn to the bright screen like a person might be drawn to an unusual piece of art, reading the words before she even realized what she was doing.

A photo of a much younger, surprisingly handsome Charles Napper was in the upper left corner with a brief bio underneath. Ella guessed that her aunt was writing a grant for the wealthy philanthropist. Which should have been boring enough to make her stop reading. Except that near the bottom of Napper's bio was a little blurb on the Central Indiana Hospital—a hospital famous, apparently, for the pioneering and funding of various types of genetic testing. And the place where Ella's mother had spent the last few days of her life.

Ever since the latest silver shooting, Ella had been sucked in by almost any headline having to do with the shootings, or the hospital.

Years ago, Napper had been a chemist there.

"Crazy," Ella muttered to herself and sat down. She didn't know what chemists did in hospitals. And she didn't know what you could do in chemistry to make the kind of money Napper had made.

It only took a tiny click to find out.

Napper had worked in genetic testing, developing a blood test from a strand of ancient DNA—extracted from a piece of primordial human ear that had been found and preserved. The whole thing was kind of gross, yet fascinating.

The test had been developed to detect whether you had a certain genetic disorder—pTr4, Napper called it.

He went on to develop special test tubes that could be used for the testing. After their experimental stage at Central Indiana Hospital, the tubes had been given to every hospital throughout the U.S. This meant that any time a patient went in for any kind of blood work, they'd find out if they had the disease.

The disease itself seemed like a strange combination of physical oddity and mental disorder—people whose skin didn't react to certain elements like other people's did, people who would begin to hallucinate and see animals speaking to them. The disorder was often associated with premature death.

If it wasn't for that last part, Ella might have laughed. The disease seemed so random, almost ridiculous. Who on earth would have such a disease? And supposing you did, who on earth would think to study and develop testing for this disease? And why were so many hospitals willing to conduct that testing? It seemed like the perfect example of bad bureaucratic spending.

Ella reached out to scroll down just as the door shut behind her.

"Ella Peterson."

She swung around to see her aunt standing there with her arms crossed in front of her chest. Her aunt had never before spoken to her so sharply. Ella stood up and fought the urge to hide her hands as if she'd been caught stealing. She must have looked sorry because Vivi's face softened.

"Listen, Ella," Vivi said. "I'd really appreciate it if you didn't read anything from my computer. Most of the reports I write for the Conservatory are confidential. Honestly, you should know not to snoop around on someone else's laptop."

Ella did know. It had been really rude. "I'm so sorry," Ella stammered. "I just saw it there and didn't really think."

Her aunt didn't argue.

Ella squirmed, searching for something to say that would release a bit of the tension between them. "So I never would have guessed that Mr. Napper started out in chemistry."

"He's definitely an interesting man," her aunt said, clicking the page closed.

"Or that he'd been so good looking."

Her aunt actually laughed. "Well, I'll tell him you said so."

Ella smiled. "Do you know him?" she asked, curious.

Again her aunt laughed, though this time the sound wobbled a bit like it'd lost some air.

"No, not really," she said. "The whole town kind of knows him, of course. And, in working for the Nature Conservatory, I naturally do work for him sometimes. But mostly he keeps to himself. So I'd never really have the opportunity to tell him you found his thirty-something-self good looking."

"Thank goodness," Ella said, expecting another laugh, but her aunt had turned to gather up a file that sat near the computer, neatly tucking all of the pages out of view.

"I'm really sorry," Ella said again.

"It's not a big deal," her aunt said, but she didn't meet Ella's eyes when she said it. And that made Ella feel even worse. Why couldn't she and her aunt just find a spot where they could be *not* awkward.

CHAPTER 21

Sam came home from school Friday afternoon determined to talk to his dad about the picture. He slipped down the hall. The suitcase wasn't out like it had been. Sam figured his dad had put it away. He dug back behind the coat, boxes, and boots, and pulled it out.

When he opened it, the contents were a wreck. Some postcards had come out of their rubber band and were all over the place, and a few colored stones were mixed up with everything else. Sam was worried that when he found the picture, it would be scraped or bent. Turns out he didn't need to worry. Because he couldn't find the picture at all.

He went through the items in the suitcase three more times. Sam stacked and unstacked the postcards like they were face cards he was shuffling and replaying. He moved all the rocks into a corner. He checked each pocket of the suitcase and felt around for any he might have missed. The picture was gone.

He turned a circle in the room as if that would help him see the picture—like he'd look up and find it tacked to the wall.

When Sam turned back to his original position, he still didn't see the picture, but he did see the orange cat running out the front door. Where she had come from or been, he had no idea, but he followed her.

The cat ran down the road and squeezed through the wrought iron bars of the gate, then sat there looking at Sam, as though inviting him to join her. Sam might have been a skinny kid, but he definitely wasn't going to be able to fit through the gates that way. He went to the locked gate and shook it. The chains rattled and the four padlocks banged against the iron.

"Did you steal it," he asked, looking at the cat. "I mean, you couldn't have, but where did it go? I know I put it right there."

The cat looked him squarely in the eyes and it was then that Sam noticed a long pink tail hanging out of the cat's mouth.

"You got the mouse," Sam said, a little grossed out, but also impressed.

"Now dear," a voice said, and Sam jumped. "You mustn't talk to the cats like they can understand you, or people will begin to say you're crazy."

The old woman stood on the other side of the gate, walking cane in hand.

Sam didn't know what to say.

"You haven't come back for cookies, dear," the woman said.

Sam should have thought of some polite, yet reasonable excuse, but all he could come up with was, "It's locked."

"Of course, dear, that's why you must come in through the back door." And with that she turned and walked back up the path to her house.

As Sam watched her, he realized she wasn't crazy or creepy. She was just senile, a lonely old lady with dementia.

Both of Sam's grandmothers were dead. His mother's mother, Grandma Jagerson, the one in the picture—she had died before he was born in a car accident. But his dad's mom—Granny Calhoun—had been alive until a couple years ago.

When he was nine or ten, she'd been diagnosed with something— probably Alzheimer's. And it had been horrible. She'd wandered around telling crazy stories about wolves in her bed to anyone who'd listen. Finally, she had to be put into a home.

Once there, she'd grown violent—cursing and threatening the

nurses so that she had to be restrained—her legs and arms strapped to the nursing home bed. Even then she would writhe around, fighting the bands. Until one day she broke one of her restraints and stabbed her nurse in the wrist with a fork.

After that his granny was always medicated, never herself again. She'd died just a few weeks later. Sam's dad said that was probably the best thing that could have happened to her, but Sam knew his father still felt guilty about everything.

Sam did too. He shook the memory away and watched as Zinnie disappeared behind the trees up the path. He heard the old woman open her front door and watched the cat as it pranced along the path to join her.

Sam walked back to his trailer.

His dad was out front, and furious. "What on earth are you doing?" he shouted. "You shouldn't be by that gate."

Sam didn't know what to say; he didn't have the energy for arguing. He was feeling worried about the old woman, guilty about his granny, and still confused about his Grandma Jagerson's picture. "Dad," he blurted, choosing the last thought and clinging to it. "Dad, I lost her picture. Grandma Jagerson's. And it had something written on it. It said, 'To my two beautiful daughters.' But Mom didn't have a sister. Right?"

Sam felt like a little kid when he looked at his dad, waiting for the universe to be explained.

His dad rubbed his forehead as though trying to push a headache away and said, "Son, you must have misread it or something."

"No," Sam said. "That's what it said; I read it a billion times."

His dad turned to go inside. "You know, your mom had a really good friend in high school. She always used to say she was like a sister. Your grandma used to say that too—called them her two little girls. That's probably what it was. Where's the picture? I'll have a look."

"No, Dad. She wrote an inscription to her 'two beautiful *daughters.*'" Sam followed his father inside.

"Are you sure it didn't say girls?" his dad asked.

Sam was almost sure. He wished he could find the picture. "Dad, I can't find the picture. It was right there in the suitcase."

"That's strange," his dad said. "You must have just set it down somewhere else."

Sam could picture it as he'd placed it in the suitcase before they went out for pizza the night before.

"Don't worry, son," his dad said, patting his shoulder. "I'm sure it'll turn up."

Sam wasn't sure at all. He felt like he was just as nutty as the old woman.

CHAPTER 22

The wolves were here. Nine of them. There were a few picketers by City Hall and several more by the Napper Nature Preserve. But most of the town had lined up outside the gates—protest-sign-free—to see the animals taken from the truck and escorted into The Property by a grumpy guy in khaki's and the mighty Charles Napper himself.

There was a local band playing a pitchy version of "Hungry Like the Wolf" and several food vendors selling tamales and burgers. Ella didn't even know the city of Napper had street vendors.

As soon as the song ended, some guy stood up at a podium and began a long explanation of the process the wolves had gone through to get to Napper. Ella couldn't help but listen.

She was surprised to hear that the wolves had landed in the states nearly a month and a half earlier. They'd started off in New York City and followed a slow route, being subjected to a number of document checks in a number of towns. They'd been blessed by a shaman in Tennessee before continuing into the Midwest. In Indy, they'd undergone a final series of vaccinations and medical checks and then, finally, they had been allowed to make the last leg of their journey.

The driver who had brought the wolves was puffing a little desperately on an e-cig and talking frantically into his cell phone. Apparently, transporting Gevudan wolves for a month and a half was stressful.

Ella wandered through the crowd. Several kids from her high school were here ignoring her as usual, although Jack's brother Brant did catch a glance of her and tip his head up in hello. She had to admit that when he wasn't spouting out football terms at a pep rally, he was actually sort of intriguing—good looking, so tall it kind of made you quiver, and with the exact same eyes that Jack had.

She nodded back quickly and hurried along until, near a hamburger stand, she saw that kid Sam. For once he wasn't staring at her. He was digging in his pocket like he was mining gold.

"Just a minute," she heard him say to the vendor, "I know I've got some more here." The vendor looked bored and annoyed and suddenly Ella felt really bad.

"Here," she said, plunking down a couple dollars. "And I want a cheeseburger too."

"It's okay," Sam said, recovering a small stack of pennies from his pocket. "I can pay for mine."

"No, seriously," Ella said. "It's no biggie. It's like ten cents."

Sam didn't argue, though he looked like he wanted to. "Well, thanks," he grumbled, looking into her face like she was haunted.

Ella had to repress the urge to shout, "Boo." Instead she said, "So where should we eat these. They're huge."

Sam looked pretty pleased about that part and nodded to a bench nearby where two old people were leaving. They raced to it and plunked down. Ella laughed. And then it was awkward.

Sam was back to his staring, but this time it wasn't at her. Near the band stood the goth-punk girl, Sarah, though the black dye in her hair was fading and today she was just wearing dark jeans and a red shirt with a simple leather cuff on one wrist—not too crazy. She was also smiling and talking politely to an older woman who seemed to be complaining about a pain in her tooth. It was such a different picture than the crusty, cynical Sarah they saw at school that Ella found herself staring too. A woman who had to be Sarah's mother came over and Sarah stepped away.

Ella wasn't sure if Sarah had seen them looking at her, but slowly she started walking in their direction.

Ella looked down. Sam kept staring. Sarah Price walked past.

"You know her?" Ella asked when the girl was gone.

"Nah," Sam mumbled, shoving bites of his hamburger into his mouth like he hadn't eaten all week.

"Me neither," Ella said. "She is hard to miss though." They both smiled and then the awkwardness was gone. "So where'd you move from?"

"New Mexico," Sam said.

"Seriously," Ella asked. "Why'd you come *here*?"

"For the bugs," Sam said in a deadpan so perfect that it took Ella a minute to process the joke.

"And so my dad could sell vacuums to rich people," Sam added.

"Well, you came to the right place," Ella said as two designer-clad teenagers walked past with lattes.

"You need one?" Sam said.

"A rich person," Ella said. "Nope. I've already got one."

"Well then, how about a vacuum?"

As far as Ella knew Vivi had never vacuumed her perfectly white carpet. "I don't think so," Ella said. "My aunt doesn't need make-up or cleaning devices to maintain perfection."

"Sounds frugal," Sam said.

"I doubt it."

"And where are you from," Sam asked.

"Indy," Ella said. And then for reasons she didn't think through she added, "My mom died."

"I know," Sam said.

For some reason it kind of stung to hear that people knew, but it felt good too—having it on the table.

"It's a small town," Sam said, seeing her face. "People talk. A tragic tale is their favorite kind. Why do you think we're all here to stare at these wolves?"

"Because they're cool," she said.

"And dangerous," he added.

"And mysterious," she finished.

"Definitely mysterious," Sam agreed.

As he said it a man in khaki's led the obviously-drugged animals from their cages in the truck to the cages at the preserve.

Ella had never seen a wolf in real life. Their coats were a little scragglier than she had expected and varying shades—some rusty and brown, others dark gray or silvery. And one seemed to combine all the colors. Their eyes, like their fur, were a gamut of color from amber to steel to chocolate. Yet, there was nothing unkept or imprecise about their eyes. Even with the drug their eyes looked sharp and clear. Oddly, the eyes struck her as their least dog-like quality—less liquid, more stone.

HE'D COME TO NAPPER, INDIANA, BECAUSE IT WAS A SMALL NOTHING town with a bunch of wealthy people. He'd gone to DeWitt, Maine, and Parkhead, New Mexico, for the same reason. He'd done his time, sold a few vacuums, and left before social services or some local church charities noticed them and came knocking at the door. It was far from a perfect life, but they'd always had food to eat and some sort of shelter.

But this town was different. He couldn't see it at first, but he could feel it, smell it. There had always been some of his kind in the places they lived, but very few. Here there were many. Here they owned businesses, built parks, sold houses, owned land. Here they ruled.

He should have known, should have recognized the name of the Alpha. But he had thought it just a coincidence and then he'd gone and plunked them down practically at the Alpha's back door.

He'd lain low, trying not to see or be seen. But he could not help but notice the girl—the girl who had now befriended his son. She looked just like her grandmother—a face even Sam had unwittingly recognized.

And now the wolves were here. He and Sam had to leave. Soon.

But for once Sam wasn't ready. Sam had made a friend. Sam was acing math. Sam had his eye on that black-haired girl.

He'd torn his son from towns before, but usually Sam had been drifting just as much as he was. Now something had focused in his son, something had settled, something that reminded him of their life before —its sweetness and stability.

Robert Calhoun stopped sleeping at night, his sheets a tangle of tumbled thought and unmade decisions. He started sleeping in the day, parked in his car under a tree. He didn't sell anything, had to tap the golden goose. Which didn't make him sleep any better. He saw the woman, walking stick in hand, cat at her heels. It gave him a breath of relief to know she was there, but only a gasp. She had aged, weakened. For now she was a barrier, but soon even she would crumble.

And then, as a final blow, he had started to crave meat. Craved it like he hadn't in years. But he couldn't eat it, not even a little. If he did, they would smell him; they would know he was here. Alive.

ELLA AND SAM HAD SPENT THE WEEKEND DISCUSSING FAVORITE FOODS, favorite classes, different cities, and how it felt to move a lot. Sam had been all over. Ella had only been in a few big cities, but they'd changed apartments almost as much as Sam had changed towns.

So now she had a friend. And he wasn't a dog. That was progress.

Sunday night, after she'd gotten ready for bed, Ella shut her door, and got down her mother's jewelry box. On a small slip of paper she wrote, *Sam. Reminds me of home.*

She dropped the scrap of paper into the growing pile among her mother's stones, and then peeled off the wooden bottom of the box and began to sift through the hidden stories. It was a ritual that never lost its appeal, or its sadness.

She chose a story near the middle, one that had a pencil sketch of a small gray ring drawn to the side.

Once, in a land turned around and back again, a human queen rose up with skin like flower petals and words like silk.

She began to mine the mighty Grey, renaming it Silver for the sleek lines and satin tones of the word. She did not mine it for its power, nor for its usefulness, but because of its beauty. It was brought down in cartfuls, and as the mines grew deeper, the queen's vanity did as well. Some of the metal was fashioned into tools, even weapons, but most was used for the queen's favorite purpose—adornment. Soon all wealthy humans adopted the trend.

The wolf-shifters shrank to the far reaches of the kingdom, their needs, rights, and interests no longer acknowledged by the fashionable queen.

It was not long before the witch's wood again became a refuge—a place of leaf and branch where those who wished could find rest and restoration. Perhaps the shifters would have hidden ever on the outskirts and in the wood were it not for a small discovery in the southern hills. From deep in the bowels of these insignificant foothills, a small man discovered a new metal—a variety of gold with the blush of a rose.

This man presented the queen with a delicate ring formed from the rose-colored gold. The substance did not tarnish or deteriorate in the air as silver did; and its scarcity made the queen grow hungry.

Within months, a series of mines was excavated and erected. The silver jewelry was cast off by the human socialites, and the shifters could return in relative safety to their homes and lands in the head city.

But many did not.

Instead, they harbored a silent fury at the way in which the most basic concerns of their kind had been ignored and discarded on the altar of the queen's couture.

It was not long after the discovery of the southern rose gold that the monthly killings began. Soon, none could venture outside the city on the night of the fullest moon unless he wanted to vanish into a pile of clean, white bone.

Ella shuddered. The stories her mother had been telling her for her whole life were connected to each other, sparse pieces to a dense whole. Her mother had been writing something that was part fairy tale, part wolf lore, part origin story—one of those everything-you-didn't-know-about-the-myth-you-already-knew stories. Mr. Witten would love it.

CHAPTER 23

Sam stood in front of the iron fence with the four padlocks, wondering how he could go in and check on Zinnie. His dad had started watching the news in the evenings and it was disconcerting—every national channel covering the Silver Shootings, while all the local channels were talking about the wolves. Sam wasn't even sure Zinnie knew about the wild wolves that now wandered The Property with her.

Just as he was imagining them un-drugged, the orange tabby pranced into his view, her striped tail high in the sky. Zinnie followed, leaning on her staff and looking perfectly unafraid of wolves or any other troubles that might befall her in the wood. "Hello Sammy," she said without looking at him.

"I was just thinking about you," he said, staring through the bars.

"Well, of course," she said.

Sam stared at the old woman for just a beat before saying, "There are wolves in the wood, Zinnie; you should be careful."

"Oh, those old pups can't hurt me. As long as my house stands, nothing in this wood can. Besides," she said, with a grin much too wide for such an old woman. "I can control the weather. And wolves don't like rain."

Sam opened his mouth to say something and then stopped. He knew that arguing with a person who had dementia would be useless.

For a minute, he wondered if he should tell his father about Zinnie. She was putting herself at considerable risk, wandering around with wolves loose on The Property. Thinking of his father made him think of the picture of his grandmother. He stared at the cat. She seemed to stare back—a dare.

"Zinnie," he said, pausing. "Did that cat bring a picture to your house? She was sleeping on it and then it was gone." He knew he sounded like a total loon.

Zinnie laughed. "One thing I'm sure of is that the picture is not here, but there."

"There?" It was like talking to the Mad Hatter in *Alice in Wonderland*.

"At your house, dear boy."

"No, it's not in the house; I've looked everywhere."

"That's unlikely," the old woman said. "You've looked where you think it might be. That's obviously not where it is."

"Obviously," Sam muttered.

"Try looking in a spot it oughtn't be," she said. "That's usually how lost things get found."

The orange tabby scampered in front of Sam.

"Ah, little Gabby has an idea. She often goes where she oughtn't and sees more than most humans."

"I noticed," Sam mumbled.

"She should be able to help," the woman replied cheerfully.

Gabby pranced through the gate like she actually had some idea what the old woman had said. Which was ridiculous.

DAVID WITTEN WAS PRINTING OFF HOMEWORK ASSIGNMENTS FOR THE retelling of Beauty and the Beast, and thinking about wolves. The day Napper's wolves had arrived, Witten had stood near the edge of the crowd in a carefully chosen spot so he could see the place on The

Property where the temporary cages were situated. The old beggar had been in a similar location, digging through his cart of cans and muttering, then sniffing, then muttering some more. When he'd finally looked up, Witten had held out several dollar bills, but the old man had ignored them, staring, fixated, on the wolves. He sniffed. They sniffed.

Witten had stepped away from the homeless man and watched the veterinarian carefully release the animals from their shackles and bed them down. One of the creatures had caught his eye, and for a long moment, he had held its gaze.

David Witten thought about that now. What better creature to inspire the writing of folklore than the centuries old Eurasian wolf. It had inspired the fairytales of France, Norway, and Germany. Native American stories were brim-full of wolf-lore, and Puritan America—with its perfect fear of the unnatural—had nursed a vengeful terror for the men they suspected could shift to beast.

This particular bit of lore carried the strength to fuel hundreds of years of stories and fears, pressing its way into mainstream America through both the terrifying and the absurd. It was this particular bit of mythology that America couldn't seem to get enough of. Man to beast or beast to man. Either way, it was a theme rich for discussion.

Witten finished printing out his lesson plans and then picked up his phone. "Hello, *cherie*," he said. "Yes, the classes are going well. It's nice to have interaction with humans instead of just old books." After that there was a long pause while his sister spoke. When she was done, he hesitated before responding, and finally in a quiet voice he said, "Yes, *cherie*, they have arrived. Nine of them."

When he hung up the phone, he was not so sure his niece would still be coming for Christmas.

CHAPTER 24

Ella and Sam stood by The Property. They'd spent the whole hour of Witten's folklore class discussing wolf lore and had stopped at The Property as they walked home. Ella pressed her face into the bars of the front gate, like a convict planning her escape. "I wish we could go in there," she said.

"Why?" Sam said.

"I wish we could see them."

"Who?" Sam asked.

"The wolves," Ella said, laughing. "I'd been hoping they would do some community access thing, where we could come in and observe them getting used to their new home."

"Yeah," Sam said, "I don't think community access is really Napper's thing."

"Mmm," Ella said, staring deeply into the woods.

Sam thought about the padlocked gate. He thought about Zinnie and her "back door." Sure, she had dementia, but maybe that was her confused way of telling him there was another opening, a safe way into The Property.

"You wanna try to get in?" Sam asked.

Ella pulled back from the gate and looked at Sam suspiciously. "How?" Ella asked. "You going to climb over that?"

"Not if I can help it." He smiled.

Ella cocked an eyebrow at him, waiting.

"Come on," he said, and started to run.

She followed, jumping over the ditch and running along the shoulder of the road. He was impressed with how well Ella could keep up. She ran like a gazelle—all limbs and air, like she didn't care if anyone else was watching.

"There's this old shack I found one day when I got onto The Property," he said, panting as he ran. "It's pretty cool, and…well, you'll just have to see."

They came around to the trailer park, then to the south gate. All four padlocks were tightly secured. "It's up there," Sam said, pointing through the trees.

"How'd you get in there?" Ella asked.

"Once," Sam started, not wanting to explain too much. "One day it was open."

"Weird," Ella said.

"It was." Sam wished he could remember how it had been open. He'd been so scared that he'd run just like a rabbit—seeing only the straight ahead, the moment, the escape. "Anyway, supposedly there's some other entrance near that shack that you can go through, although I've never seen it."

He inched through his neighbors' back yards—the ones that were closest to The Property.

"Back door," Sam mumbled to himself. What did she mean? He looked for another gate and when he didn't find one, he inspected the fence, hoping for a missing pole or something. Most of the leaves were turning and some had dropped, but the forest was still dense enough that he couldn't see the shack through the trees. When he thought he was in the right area, he walked back and forth along the fence, touching it.

He expected to turn and see Ella looking at him like he was crazy, but she seemed just as intrigued as he was. She followed several paces after him, touching each wrought iron bar.

"This metal fence must have cost a fortune to put up," she said.

"Probably. Even the metal as scrap is worth $100/ton."

"That's strange," Ella said.

"I know."

"No," she said. "There's a little path. And a cat staring at us."

And there was.

Gabby sat in the woods, looking thin and mischievous. Right at their feet was the path. The strange thing was that the path, well-worn and cat-sized, went right under the bars as though the center bar hadn't been there—as though the cat had just swung the bottom two feet of iron open like a bendable doggy door.

Sam touched each bar at chest level. They seemed solid, but the path the cat had made definitely plowed straight through one. Sam knocked on that pole. Thick iron and not moving. Then he kneeled down in the muddy path and looked through the fence at the cat.

"Gabby," Sam cooed softly. "Here Gabby."

She ignored him and cleaned a paw—taking special care to get between the toes.

"Gabby," he said, and tapped on the bottom of the bar to get her attention. The sound did not tap back at him like cast iron should. It didn't make any noise at all.

Ella dropped down beside him. "You're kidding," she whispered, touching the bar. She pushed on the bottom half of the vertical bar and it bent. "It's candy," she said.

That was impossible. Sam had taken every shop class ever available. He'd tinkered and fixed things in the trailer and had always been his dad's go-to guy when their old beater van broke down. There was no way anyone could make candy look like cast iron.

He licked his finger and placed it against the bar. It was sticky. Ella did the same and then stuck her finger in her mouth.

"Candy," she said. "Licorice—super gross." She looked at him. "So what now? We eat our way in?"

"No," Sam said, pressing on the bar.

It was impossible, yet there it was—a bar with the bottom three feet made of candy, candy that was so expertly connected to the iron top that no one would ever know it was different unless they noticed an animal push through.

For the second time on the way to the woman's house, Sam thought he might be dreaming. He and Ella bent the gummy candy post out of their way and crawled through. Sam had never been on drugs, but he was pretty sure this was how it would feel.

They stood, dusted off, and walked to the house. No smoke spiraled out of the chimney even though it was chilly. Sam tapped on the door. No one answered.

Outside the cat mewed loudly. Sam knocked again and then noticed that one of the windows was broken when it hadn't been before. He knocked louder as Ella walked around the short periphery of the house.

"Sam," she said, as his knocking got even louder. "I'm not sure anyone lives here."

The comment annoyed him. He pinched his lips shut, and—remembering his granny wandering helpless and lost around her own house—he gently pushed open the door.

They both stepped in and Ella said, "See," while Sam stood there like a stone.

Several windows were broken, age-old soot stained the wall above the fireplace, and leaves that had blown through the holes were scattered on the floor. The house was completely empty. No furniture, no fire, no cookies, no life. Sam turned several times in the center of the floor as though dancing a slow song with himself.

"Cool," Ella said, wandering into the abandoned kitchen.

The cat had followed them in and was rubbing her neck on the corners of walls, marking them with her scent.

"No," Sam said, but couldn't say more.

Ella came back out and looked at him. "You okay?"

"No," he repeated, looking away.

"It's a cool, old shack," Ella said. "How'd you find it? What's wrong?"

"It's empty." Sam walked to the corner of the room. The fireplace was filled with cobwebs. The floor was coated with dust and dirt. It wasn't possible.

"Yeah," Ella said, "and has been for a while."

"No," Sam said for the third time. "Last time I was here it wasn't empty. An old woman lived here. There was a fire and furniture and she had made cookies and tea. We talked."

"That's not possible," Ella said, drawing a deep line through the dust on the window ledge with her finger.

"I know," Sam said.

THEY SAT IN SAM'S TRAILER AND ATE SALTINE CRACKERS. WELL, ELLA ate. Sam just sat and stared at the wall.

"Maybe," Ella said, "maybe you just imagined it. Maybe in your panic during the storm you, like, had some kind of hallucination or something."

"Maybe," Sam muttered. That didn't much explain the other little chats with his imaginary friend. Zinnie had told him to look for a back door.

And there was the cat Gabby, the orange tabby. Suddenly Sam bolted up. "Ella," he said. "That cat—did it have a tail?"

"Nope," she said. "Cut clean off. I kind of liked the little guy."

"Girl," Sam said.

It hadn't had a tail the first time he'd seen it either. He remembered it now, but most of the other times, he was pretty sure she'd had a tail. He could picture the tail hanging down off the window sill, and then later curled around her body as she'd lain in the suitcase. The suitcase. With the missing picture. Had he somehow imagined the inscription too? Sam leaned his head into his arms on the table. "Oh man," he said. "Oh man oh man oh man."

"Hey," Ella said softly. "It's okay. I'm sure there's an explanation."

Yeah, Sam thought, *There had to be, right?* But even as he thought it, he saw his Granny Calhoun rocking back and forth in her nursing home bed, moaning about things she swore were there that weren't.

Ella finished her crackers and sat back in the old chair that Sam's dad had found by their neighbor's trash.

"Now *this* is a home," she said, looking at the pictures and old furniture and stained rug.

"Ella," Sam said, ignoring his junky house. "The post—it was candy, right?"

"Crazily enough, yes," she said, tipping back in the chair. "I wonder who put it there? Probably someone who likes to go hide out or make out or sleep in that shack."

"But it was licorice?" Sam said. "Thick, black licorice."

"Yes," she said.

"And you'll tell me that tomorrow if I ask?"

"Yesss," she said slowly.

"Okay," Sam said, pressing the sides of his head like his dad did when a migraine was coming on. "Because tomorrow I'm going to ask you."

BUT TOMORROW HE DIDN'T.

By the next morning, his head was burning so badly that he threw up twice before the sun even came up. His dad sat by his bed, urging him to take tiny sips of ginger ale. The soda was a precious luxury, but all Sam wanted was to lie still and never move again. He slept in and out of the next several days, nightmares about the Silver Shooter and Zinnie's empty house conjoining and clashing through his consciousness, until at last they faded, misty and distant.

Just when he thought he would live and die on a diet of flat ginger ale, his fever broke. Thursday morning he woke up starving, sent his father out the door, and polished off the rest of the ginger ale and a cold piece of toast his father had left for him. But that wasn't going to cut it.

He closed his eyes, thinking about food for the first time in days. What he really wanted was a hamburger—juicy, thick, tender. It was a strange craving, but thinking about it made Sam smile. He took a quick shower, grabbed a stack of change and put on his tennis shoes. He wouldn't be running today, but being out of the dank trailer sounded really nice. Some Mexican guy sold tamales and hamburgers from a food cart just south of the trailer park. He'd go there.

The cool air felt good on Sam's face and neck. And it made the warm burger even better. The juices dripped onto his fingers as he walked, and he stopped when he got to a foot path that meandered outside the east edge of The Property.

Sam licked his fingers, savoring every greasy drop. His dad was a vegetarian and he was always telling Sam not to eat meat. Beans were cheap and, supposedly, there was a family history of heart disease.

Sam didn't care. He was sixteen and he was hungry. Especially since they'd moved here. A small glob of cheese and two lettuce bits were stuck to the wrapper. Sam used his finger to peel them off and pop them in his mouth. He might have licked off the wrapper itself if some homeless guy hadn't wandered into his view. The man pushed a cart full of clothes and Coke cans. It looked like he hadn't had enough to eat for a long time—he was scrawny and scraggly and his chest was covered in patches of greasy hair. If Sam had had any burger left, he would have offered it to the guy.

Sam had known more than one homeless person in his life. Which meant he knew to be nice, but wary. Sometimes they were strung out, sometimes they were not all there. This guy was one or the other or both. He looked at Sam with bloodshot eyes that were covered by lids so wrinkled they sagged down, almost covering the rusty irises.

Sam tipped his head at the guy and the homeless man took a step closer, staring into Sam's face. Technically, Sam had been homeless himself—because living in your van in New Mexico doesn't count if you tell a social worker. But, to be fair, he'd never really *felt* homeless. He had his dad, some kind of roof over his head, and—well—his sanity. Lots of homeless guys didn't.

Sam took a step back.

"You smell," the old man said, the 's' lisping since he was missing all his front teeth.

Sam had to resist the urge to laugh out loud. Instead, he just smiled and said, "Do I?"

"That's right," the homeless guy said. "I can smell you. They can't yet. You're too young and they're not close enough. But they will. Just wait."

"Okay," Sam said, scooting backwards, preparing to walk around the man. "Well, you have a good day."

"You have to listen to him," the homeless man said. "Your old man. Otherwise, they'll smell you."

"Okay," Sam said, walking cautiously around the shopping cart. "I'll do that. I'll listen to the old man."

The homeless man snorted as though offended and walked off, picking up two cans from the gutter just a few feet away.

Poor guy, Sam thought. He wandered around the periphery of The Property, wanting to move his limbs and avoid another run-in with the homeless guy. But he overestimated his energy or underestimated the distance. By the time he came around to the area near the mental institution, all he wanted to do was sit down and rest. But he didn't.

So far in his new city, the people most willing to talk to him were a crazy cat lady who may or may not exist, and a homeless man with no teeth who told him he smelled.

No teeth.

Sam thought about the latest news story of the Silver Shooter. He always took the teeth. Nothing else. Sam shook off the chill. There was no way *that* homeless guy was wandering from city to city killing rich people. Still, as Sam walked past the mental institution, his legs moved faster and faster until he broke into a run. He might have been tired and weak, but at this time of day, the institution cast a long shadow.

CHARLES NAPPER DID NOT TOUCH THE STONE. INDEED, HE COULD NOT. That was part of what was so pesty about it.

He wore thick leather gloves whenever he handled it and even then, he usually felt ill afterwards. His nephew had collapsed after handing the stone over and had taken a full three days to recover.

In this way, it would have been nice to have the good doctor still available. But he'd become a bit bulky to carry around—rather like an overstuffed suitcase when you're travelling—convenient until the weight becomes too much. At that point, it's freeing to unload some of the baggage, especially if you have the things you most need.

And Napper did.

Well, at least one of them. The other he'd moved within his range. The veterinarian Tomas thought they should test her as well—just to be sure. What if she'd been adopted? Or was a stepchild from the father? It seemed unlikely considering the fact that her face was the picture of her mother's.

But it didn't seem worth the risk. When you could only change a thing every hundred years, there was no point in betting on the wrong horse.

Of course, he didn't want to damage the child so much she couldn't be used. The incident with her mother had been necessary to obtain the stone, but unfortunate. It would have been nice to have two heirs still available. Now he had only one, and he needed her whole for the solstice.

But as Tomas had pointed out, all he needed was a small sample of blood. And that, he reasoned, could be procured at the next changing. He wouldn't do it himself—he'd gotten too old for such business. But he knew those who would help, and gladly.

CHAPTER 25

The corn maze stretched out over two hundred acres, bumping up against a little creek and occasionally turning its way around a dark stand of trees.

Supposedly, the corn maze had made the major news channels twice for losing someone inside for over twenty-four hours. The average time to make it through was four hours. And it wasn't just a maze. It was a haunted maze. And a treasure hunt. So, while getting lost for long enough that you might miss your next meal, you could also get chased by zombies, vampires, bats and—naturally—children of the corn.

It was easy to get Sam on board.

Because somewhere along the haunted labyrinth was a small token —a literal silver bullet. If you found this, it could be cashed in for a hundred dollars. The girl who sat next to Ella in folklore told her that years would go by with no one finding it. Which made sense. With the maze and the darkness and the zombies and all.

Still, there was nothing Sam loved more than a treasure hunt. Except maybe a treasure hunt that was also a puzzle.

It hadn't taken Ella long to realize that Sam was good at puzzles. He'd been bumped into both calculus and physics—two classes basically dedicated to puzzles. It hadn't exactly helped him socially, but Ella figured he could rock a corn maze.

And find a token. He was oddly good at that sort of thing too—picking up quarters and dimes that seemed to sprout from the ground in front of him. He was like a human witching rod—metal calling to him instead of water. Of course, really he just had the habit to look.

The truth was that Sam was a strange guy in general—fast and slow, dull and bright, happy and not. Maybe that's what Ella found so easy to like in him. He pulsed with realness in a school that mostly pulsed with rich kids who had their teeth whitened on a regular basis. Ella was pretty sure her partner in biology had come back with a new nose after missing school for a week.

That was the type of place where Ella would never really fit in. Sam didn't either. And it was nice to be able to not fit in together.

Ella plunked her crisp five dollar bill onto the folding table set up outside the maze and watched Sam sort his money into his palm—two ones, six quarters, eight dimes, and a heap of pennies. Seeing him sort it out gave Ella a pang—it was just like seeing the money her mom used to have from tips laid out on the table. In fact, going somewhere with Sam was a lot like going somewhere with her mom—quirky, fun, and cheap.

Ella felt her throat tighten up.

Fortunately at that moment ghoulish howling crackled through the loudspeaker and they entered the gate to the maze. It was crawling with kids from school—girlfriends and boyfriends, a group of football play-ers, three girls from biology class, and there, near a corner, was Sarah Price.

At first Ella thought she was one of the actors who volunteered to jump out and scare people—a vampire or steampunk ghost or some-thing, but then Ella noticed she was staring at Sam. The two of them locked eyes for just a moment, and something about it made Ella feel excluded. Then Sarah noticed Ella and walked over.

"Hey," Sarah said. "Did you guys come together?"

"Yes," Ella said.

"No," Sam said.

Ella was ready to laugh, but Sam looked like he was hoping the chainsaw massacre guy would find them and take him down.

"Well, we *came* together," Ella said. "With Sam's dad. As friends. Not…you know," Ella said, nodding to a couple ducking into the maze —the girl clinging tightly to her date's waist.

"Got it," Sarah said, staring at nothing in the opposite direction from where Sam was also staring at nothing.

Ella didn't have a degree in psychology, but she wasn't an idiot. "Um, want to join us? Or are you waiting for someone?"

"Actually," Sarah said, "that'd be cool." She held up her phone. "Just got a text and my friend isn't coming."

Sam nodded casually, but Ella thought he looked like he wouldn't mind living another day after all.

THE CORN MAZE OPENED IN THREE DIRECTIONS AND SPREAD OUT IN front of them like a tall, golden lake. Through and around it ran dozens of dogs. On their way into the farm, Ella had noticed a sign reading, "Jones' Dog Rescue and Training." And after they'd paid, they'd been given a whistle they could use if they got lost in the maze. Supposedly, a dog would follow the whistle, come and find them, then lead them out. It was pretty impressive.

"Yeah," Sarah said. "The whistle thing is newish. He started doing it a couple years ago when someone was stuck in here for thirty-six hours or something. They threatened to shut him down, but he's been doing this since then and no one's gotten lost like that again."

"That's kind of amazing," Ella said.

Sarah shrugged. "Jones has been training dogs for forever. If you've got a bad dog or a dog that needs a home or anything at all like that, you can bring it here. In fact, the Humane Society always brings Jones the dogs that are going to be euthanized soon. He'll take them, train them, and then either give them away or take them back to the Humane Society where they can find homes. Everyone wants a dog; they just want good ones."

"So this is like doggy rehab," Sam said.

"Pretty much," Sarah replied. "He's good at it too. Supposedly some reality TV show called him wanting to do some kind of dog whisperer thing."

"You're kidding," Sam said.

"Supposedly." Sarah paused. "But Jones wouldn't do it. He said he couldn't train dogs with a camera crew in his face."

"So how do you know all this?" Sam asked. "Or are you just messing with us?" He led them around two sharp turns and looked at the full moon, rubbing his forehead.

"That would have been funny," Sarah said, "but I'm not messing with you. My mom's gotten two dogs from Jones. They're perfect animals. Seriously. Mom sends Jones a Christmas card every year. She says he must have the best karma in the universe."

"So any dog at all can come here if it gets picked up and taken to the Humane Society?" Ella asked, looking more closely at the dogs than she had before.

"Yup," Sarah said. "Except the dangerous ones. If they've bitten or attacked any people or livestock, they get put down."

They walked past a couple tucked into a corner kissing, and Ella noticed that among the maze-goers there was a lot of touching. Their group, however, remained platonically stoic.

The girls followed Sam who looked skyward half the time and ground-ward the other half.

He wants that bullet, Ella thought. And she wanted him to get it. He'd come and dropped his last five bucks on this. He deserved to get it.

Ella started to look at the ground too. It was as she bent to examine a suspiciously shiny bit of dirt that a one-eyed doll jumped out at them. The doll's face was gray with stitches up the side, her right arm a bloodied stump. Ella screamed like a child. Sam just swatted the doll away, leading them left. And Sarah—Sarah laughed. Ella was still sort of screaming when the doll monster was out of sight.

"Calm down, Ella," Sarah said. "I think that was Annabelle Pete. She's in my drama class. Pretty good, huh?"

Ella was still trying to get her heart to not burst out of her chest. She felt dizzy and a little sick from the adrenaline. Sarah looked like she was about to laugh again, like she thought Ella was messing around or exaggerating, but then she looked into her face. "You're paler than me," Sarah said.

Ella smiled weakly.

"They're just actors," Sarah said.

"I know," Ella said. "But…the blood."

"It's only make-up, Ella."

"I know," Ella said quietly. "It's just—"

Ella didn't say that it reminded her of her mother's accident. She hadn't seen the worst of it, but she'd seen them carrying her mother away and even then she could see the blood. And there'd been blood on the street and bloody bandages at the hospital. Ella paled even more remembering it.

"Come on," Sam said. "We can go back."

"Sure," Sarah said. "No biggie; we can leave."

"No," Ella said. "You two stay."

"Whatever," Sam said. "We're not going to leave you to wander back on your own."

"Seriously, you guys stay," Ella said, and then she turned as if to leave. The sun had set since they'd entered the maze, changing the landscape. The pathway back looked convoluted. And haunted.

"Okay, never mind," Ella mumbled. Why had she wanted to do this? And a week before Halloween.

"Come on, Ella," Sam said. "I'll take you back."

"No," Ella said. "It's okay. I'll stay. I can do this."

"Sure you can," Sarah said, smiling. She reached over and took Ella's hand. Ella was so startled, she almost pulled back. Sarah's hand was surprisingly warm. Ella didn't know why it wouldn't be—it's just that Sarah was so…so *goth*.

But her hand wasn't. Her hand was warm and soft and kind. Ella realized that no one had touched her—really touched her—with intention and kindness since Rosie at the funeral. Ella squeezed Sarah's hand and then reached forward and took Sam's. He turned back, startled, and then smiled.

Ella should have given him a chance to get to Sarah. She promised herself she'd nudge them together later that night. But for now she wanted to feel herself at the center of a human chain—hand to hand, skin to skin, warm blood connecting her to her friends.

And then something stumped behind them. Ella screamed again and they ran—to the bend at the right, following Sam, and laughing.

IT WAS NEARLY NINE O'CLOCK, AND ELLA COULD TELL THEY WERE WAY ahead of most of the maze-goers. The clouds traveled in wisps over the full moon, which made the night feel dark and cold. Ella shivered.

"I think we're almost there," Sam said.

Only occasionally did they bump up against a dead end. When they did, Sam would rub his head and say, "Sorry, my head hurts a little. I must be off my game."

"Are you kidding?" Sarah asked. "I've never gone through it this fast. Never. And I've been doing it since I was ten."

Sam just shrugged. "It's a pattern," he said.

Ella smiled. They were near the edge of the maze. Through the rows of stalks, she could see a large field stretching out to a cluster of trees. Just then, the moon broke through the clouds and a group of dogs started howling.

"Creepy," Sarah said, stopping suddenly.

"What?" Sam asked, looking up and casually stepping closer to her.

"Never mind," Sarah said. "It's just the howling spooked me. I thought I saw a wolf out there in the field, but it's probably just a dog."

"Or an actor," Ella added.

"No," Sarah said. "The actors always stay in the maze. They're not supposed to wander through Jones' other fields."

Ella nodded just as a huge thing jumped in front of them. For the first time that night, Sarah screamed. Sam staggered back and stumbled. Ella did neither. She stood stone-still, her voice dead in her throat.

The creature was hairy—that's what she registered as it reached out and grabbed her arm, pulling her through a thick stand of corn, which scratched her face and arms.

Her voice found itself and she screamed, "Let go of me."

He pulled her deeper into the maze.

She kicked the actor-monster and would have bit him, except that he was too quick. He shoved her onto a new path, dark and empty. Ella realized that earlier with her friends when she thought she'd been afraid, she hadn't been, not really. Now her fear shot through her skin and sank into her bones, heavy and poisonous. She didn't know what was wrong with this actor, but he was dangerous.

He reared up on his hind legs—long yellow teeth bared, hairy chest and shoulders, pointed ears, black, black fur. He was a werewolf.

His costume made him seem huge, and he smelled. Ella wondered if he was on something. "Leave me alone," she screamed again—realizing that Sarah had their group's dog whistle.

The werewolf grabbed her arm and dragged her through another corn wall, further away from where she thought her friends were. The moon hung high and bright, but instead of making her feel better, it made her feel trapped, like a spotlight was being shined onto her face. The werewolf actor moved on two legs, but still like an animal, never tripping or stumbling in the dark.

Ella dug her heels into the ground, and her screams became cries. "Stop it. Somebody. Help."

In the distance she heard something start to run, then it growled near her—low, quiet, and oddly familiar.

The werewolf heard it too, scooped up a rock, and threw it at the growl. It plunked against its target, but instead of a yelp as Ella had expected from the dog, she heard a sort of groan.

She kicked the werewolf hard in the back of its leg, and for a minute it released her. She scrambled up and started to run away, but the monster had her again—this time holding her ankle and dragging her over the ground.

Ella started to cry. "Somebody," she screamed. "Help me!" But they were far from the crowds now and everything seemed too quiet.

She picked up a rock and threw it at the monster. He laughed when it hit him, and kept dragging her.

She heard the running sound again, soft through the fields. And then a voice, even softer. "Ella," it said.

Ella drew in a sharp breath. The voice wasn't Sam's. Or Sarah's. Who else would know her name?

"Ella," it repeated. "Listen and don't speak."

The werewolf turned to the sound—its ears twitching.

Ella breathed deeply, and the person whispering to her breathed with her breaths.

The werewolf removed something from around its neck and Ella heard the whisper again. "Even a werewolf has a weakness. Look down."

Ella did and there by her arm was the silver bullet—half buried in the dirt. She held it tightly in her fist as the monster turned toward the noise. It threw another rock—a huge one this time. The rock soared through the air as though it was a tiny pebble, and an animal in the fields darted off before it could get hit.

"Loco?" Ella whispered to herself, clutching the bullet tightly. The animal that had run off looked just like him—light paws, dark back, rust-colored ears. But who had been talking?

The werewolf turned to her, grabbed her wrist, and lifted—not a rock—but what was clearly a scalpel. Ella screamed as he jerked up her coat sleeve and sliced her arm, swabbing the blood just as quickly.

When he did, she swung at him with her left arm—the fist that held the bullet. She had never hit anyone before, but her fist landed squarely on his cheek. She could tell it was a weak hit. Even so, the werewolf pulled back, dropping to all fours like an injured animal.

She swung again—hitting his thick, hairy neck, and as she did, Ella heard running—fast, two-legged, human running. Sam jumped through the trampled corn hedge and barreled into the werewolf like he was a 200-pound wrestler who took down monsters every day, not a scrawny junior who'd never played a sport in his life.

When he hit the werewolf there was a loud crack and a howl. The werewolf stood and ran on his two legs. Which made Ella feel strangely comforted. She had almost forgotten he was an actor and had begun to believe he was an actual monster.

Sam followed him a few paces before turning back to Ella. Sam looked surprisingly tall and strong in the moonlight—like he'd gotten a crazy high from the chase.

"Oh Ella," he said, kneeling down. "Are you okay? That was crazy. Crazy."

Ella didn't say anything. She rocked back and forth, holding her cut arm and crying.

Sam put his arm around her, muttering, "Crazy," over and over.

THEY NOW HAD A HUNDRED DOLLARS OF PRIZE MONEY FROM THE silver bullet, a large strip of gauze on Ella's arm, and a story from Mr. Jones about how he hadn't hired anyone to be a werewolf.

They sat at Burger Barn with the three largest burgers Ella had ever seen. Neither she nor Sarah could eat even half. Which didn't matter because in a feat almost more impressive than rushing a strung-out werewolf at fifty miles per hour, Sam had finished off their burgers too.

"Anybody up for a shake?" he asked.

Ella groaned.

"You're the monster," Sarah said, nudging him.

"I'm buying one," Sam said, "but then I'm done."

"You might have to eat it on the way home," Sarah said. "I texted my parents with a very watered down version of the night, but it's still super late. My mom's going to think I snuck off to some rave or something. Not that watching Sam eat isn't kind of the same thing."

Ella's arm throbbed, but she smiled at the two of them. She'd kept her promise to herself after all. There, under the plastic table, Sarah and Sam were touching hands.

~

SARAH DROVE THEM HOME. SAM SAT UP FRONT WITH HER WHILE ELLA dozed in the back seat.

"Seriously," Sarah said, putting her free hand on the armrest between the seats. "How'd you do it?"

Sam moved his own hand closer to hers, touching her fingers with his fingers.

"Must have been the adrenaline," Sam said. But it wasn't true. It was like something had overtaken him, changing his body—giving him speed and force. He'd never felt like that before—so powerful, so alive. Also, his headache was gone. And he was still starving.

"That's some adrenaline," Sarah said, staring straight ahead at the road as she scooted her hand under Sam's.

Ella had been a good friend to Sam—the best he'd ever had. She'd been a good enough friend that he'd torn through a corn maze chasing a guy who was twice his size to help her out. Still, at this moment, Sam really hoped that Sarah would drop Ella off first and then go for a long drive after.

Sam didn't expect his father to be awake when he got home. But he was. Before Sam came in, he could see the green-blue glow of the old TV through the window. Sam took a breath. He didn't really have a curfew, so he couldn't really break one. But he was pretty sure that when a parent stays up to wait for you, it's kind of bad news.

And it kind of was, but not in the way Sam had expected. When he unlocked the door, his father didn't budge, his face only inches from the TV screen.

"Go to bed, son," his father said.

He didn't sound happy, but Sam realized it wasn't because he'd just walked in late. In fact, Sam was pretty sure his dad had no idea what time it was, or anything else. He was fixated on the screen, watching the news break—a reporter discussing a new shooting while a banner of more news snaked across the bottom of the screen.

People got shot all the time, but Sam had to admit that these silver bullet shootings were disconcerting. This time it was the Parisian CEO of an airline company. When you looked at the picture of him, it was clear that he was dripping money. But, as usual, it wasn't money the killer was after. And, as usual, the shooter—

whoever he was—was psychotically uninterested in shifting the blame to anyone else.

Silver bullet shot from an antique gun.

No teeth.

Sam's dad was sitting so close to the TV that every image that popped up reflected several times—on both lenses of his glasses and on his shiny, balding head. Sam's dad reached up to wipe the sweat off his face and popped an Aleve into his mouth, no water, just a quick swallow.

"Nice stuff, huh?" Sam said

"I told you to go to bed," his father replied.

Sam didn't listen.

They were now showing a picture of the type of gun they thought the killer might have used. It was strangely delicate—white-handled, intricately engraved, pretty. And then a psychologist came on to discuss the potential motivations for such a crime.

Sam was pretty sure his dad didn't blink. Once his father opened his mouth like he was going to speak, but then closed it again—not so much as a snuff of air escaping.

When Sam looked at his father again, he was touching his teeth, one by one, as if counting.

It was nearly dawn, but there was too much to think about. His dad was obsessed with a serial killer, he hadn't kissed Sarah, and Ella had been chased by some crazy drug-head.

Sam watched the full moon as it tilted down toward the horizon. His dad was right about one thing. When the moon was full, the world went insane.

Sam had felt so good right after he'd helped Ella—all that adrenaline, or whatever it was. Now, it was gone. His head hurt like it had never hurt before and the moon seemed like a laser, sharp and searing. He lay down, pressing a pillow over his eyes.

Outside, he heard the low rumble of thunder—a storm headed in their direction. Inside, he heard a small, close sound—breathing, and then a tiny meow.

He moved the pillow just a bit and opened his eyes. The orange tabby sat at the end of his bed—a fat queen, her tail curled round her body. He closed his eyes again. He didn't care how she'd gotten there or if the door had been left open. Someone could come try to steal something if they wanted. What were they going to take? The pork and beans?

Again, the cat meowed—this time getting up, stretching her back, and then carefully padding up the bed toward Sam's chest. She cuddled up against him like a baby, breathing and purring. It was surprisingly soothing, and Sam felt his own breath come in calmer, slower waves. When he slowed his breathing, the pulsing and light-headedness got better too.

And then he heard the thunder again—still distant, but moving closer.

"You hear that?" he asked the cat.

"No, hun. No one hears that but you."

Sam bolted upright—migraine and all.

The cat stood, looking at him with sleepy eyes that seemed to say she wasn't happy at being shaken from her resting spot.

"No one spoke," he mumbled to himself, lying back down. "I just drifted into a dream."

The thunder rumbled again. He sat up, got off the bed, pulled the old blinds up. It was dark, but clear. Sam had always loved a fat, full moon, but tonight looking at it hurt his eyes.

He stepped back, feeling dizzy, and when he did, it felt like he was stepping into a tornado—long and fierce. But it didn't feel bad. In fact, it gave him a strange release. He felt stronger, bigger, calmer. His hands, when he held the ledge of the window seemed to have doubled in size.

"Weird," he said and when he did, his voice was low, grumbly.

He couldn't tell where the bed was, but he wanted to sit down—at least part of him did. The other half wanted to break through the window and *eat*.

He moved back to where he thought the bed was and bumped it. Around his ankles, he became aware of something—soft, vibrating. The cat wove between his legs, purring, pressing. Again, his breathing slowed. He felt as though he shrank—the blood beating against his skull. He sank onto the bed and fell back.

"It will pass," he heard the voice purring beside him. "Just breathe and it will pass."

It was so soothing, he didn't even care now that he was imagining the cat speaking. As long as she could calm him down, as long as she could shrink the blood vessels in his head. He breathed.

And in his breathing he remembered something, something so long forgotten he wondered if it was a memory or just his imagination.

"Lovely Luna Lunatic," his mother's voice said in his head. "Longed a lolly to take a lick. Instead she found a licorice stick. Lonely Luna Lunatic."

She'd told him silly poems at night. He'd been so young when she died—maybe three. But the migraine had tapped into his mind, squeezing out the memory. He could see her blond hair, dark eyes. She was beautiful.

And then another memory jolted forward—his Granny Calhoun— alone in bed. She was in a room with monitors and drips. But she did not have Alzheimer's. His father's mother had gone insane.

"Lovely Luna Lunatic," a voice in his head murmured again—this time whispering, fading. It felt almost like an accusation, a prophecy. He burst out of bed and toward the window. He broke through the glass, tearing out the shards with hands that seemed too thick to bleed.

The cat yowled behind him and he leapt through the window, toward the moon. As he did, the storm clouds rolled in—pressing out the stars, inking over the moon. The thunder clapped and Sam fell onto the cold dirt by his trailer as the freezing rain pelted his face and back.

It felt good. His head and hands cooled, the migraine faded into the puddles at his feet, and he took a long, sure breath before standing.

The window, he could see, was completely banged out. He walked around to the front door, which was locked. So he climbed back through the window and dropped to his floor, cutting his foot on a piece of glass. Exhaustion washed over him. He staggered into bed, and slept.

IN THE MORNING, HIS ROOM WAS FREEZING, HIS THROAT HURT, AND HIS body ached. Also, his window was still broken. Awesome. Because of all the parts he wished he'd dreamed, that was number one. Sam paused. Had he dreamed? Or had he hallucinated? Had the migraine messed with his mind somehow? He shook his head, trying to toss the worry away.

Strangely, he'd managed to break the window without a scratch to anything but his toe. Sam broke down an empty cardboard box and taped it over the bedroom window. Then he swept up the glass and went into the living room. His dad was already gone.

Sam sat on the couch and closed his eyes. It seemed his dreams and his imagination were trying to stitch something together—something that wouldn't make any sense unless he could see it as a whole. Which he couldn't.

Sam opened his eyes. He needed to find the picture with the inscription. He needed to put some parts together, recover some pieces of himself it seemed he'd lost.

CHAPTER 27

Ella scrolled through her phone, reading news stories about the silver shooting the week before. She was glad that this shooting had been farther away. Much farther. A fancy hotel in New York City where some rich CEO from Paris was staying. Definitely no connections to Indianapolis or Napper. But at the same time, that made it extra troubling. The shootings stretched from Los Angeles to New York. No connections between the victims except wealth, and even their wealth seemed oddly discordant—earned in entirely different ways. Ella swiped the screen closed and plugged her phone into the charger.

She still hadn't told Vivi about the corn maze. She hadn't told anyone. Her aunt had been out of town the weekend it had happened, and by the time she got back, Ella felt like the story was stuck in her skin.

The attack had been scary and bizarre, but probably just some druggy prank. Yet, she definitely would have told her mother. Ella sighed. Jack would be here in about five minutes, and she wondered if she should tell him. It seemed like someone should know.

As soon as Jack came and Vivi left, Ella blurted out the whole story

—the chase, the cut on her arm, Sam barging through the corn. It felt surprisingly good to talk about it.

"Ella. Oh, wow," Jack said, reaching out and touching her arm. "Are you okay? Let me see."

He lifted her arm, gently rolling up her sleeve so he could see the cut. For several seconds he examined the thick, raised line that tracked an inch and a half up her forearm.

"Oh wow," he kept whispering, touching the pink line in a soft way that made Ella feel like the entire night had been worth it. "Did you call the cops?"

Ella hadn't. The farmer had offered to, but looking out at the intricately mowed corn maze and the dogs he'd taken in, Ella hadn't had the heart to call the police. What if they shut the maze down? What if it hurt his business? It wasn't his fault there were strung-out sickos in this world.

"Ella," Jack said firmly. "You need to write up a police report. It's dangerous to think of people like that roaming around and taking advantage of certain situations."

He must have seen the set in Ella's face because he said more softly, "Look, I know you don't want to hurt the farm, but the maze really is the perfect draw for drunks and perverts."

Ella had to admit that this seemed true. "Okay," Ella said slowly. "I'll think about it. But listen." She paused. "You can't tell Vivi. Or anyone. I told you this in confidence and there's no present danger," she said using a phrase she remembered from TV. "So you can't tell her. Please."

Jack nodded. "I can't make you call the cops. But you really should let the police know. I wouldn't want anything to happen to anyone. Least of all you."

ELLA LAY IN HER BED THAT NIGHT THINKING ABOUT WHAT SHE MIGHT include in a police report if she did fill one out. And then she remembered something she'd forgotten. The voice. That strange voice telling her to look down to where she'd found the bullet. Who had it been? And why hadn't he come and helped her?

Granted, a guy in a werewolf suit had been brandishing a scalpel, but still—who sits back and lets a teenage girl get threatened like that, and then just vanishes. He hadn't even called 911. And how had he known about the bullet and where it was?

Maybe he'd been in on the prank somehow, and then regretted how far it was going. Maybe. She remembered being relieved to hear that voice, that there had been something almost familiar in it.

As she drifted to sleep, Ella pictured Loco speaking those words, and in that place between sleep and waking, it seemed possible—even probable—that a dog under the full moon would call out to her.

WHEN ELLA WOKE IN THE MORNING, SHE'D DECIDED *NOT* TO WRITE UP a police report. Her dreams of the dogs had been too sweet. She didn't dare cut off some of the income to the farm that was their home.

She'd decided something else too. Next week she would find out if there was a bus that ran all the way out to the farm. She had to know if Loco was there.

NAPPER WALKED THE NEAT TRAILS OF HIS PROPERTY. NORMALLY, THE foliage along the trails was in perfect condition, but with the wolf population increasing, he could see the wear of having so many animals in such close proximity. Certain areas looked trampled, as though the wolves had been pacing them at night. And the wildlife that consisted of their prey was decreasing at an alarming rate. He'd had to order more hare and goats to be brought onto his land.

In addition to more food, the wolves needed more space. He hoped that soon he would be able to give it to them. Napper hiked deeper into the dense woods of his land, and as he did, he spotted the group of Gevudan in the distance, chasing a young deer. Wolves were beautiful creatures—smart, organized, efficient. They were connected in packs that worked together to kill, that reproduced with order, creating offspring from only the strongest of their kind.

In a wolf pack, each animal had jobs that they performed without complaint. Though occasionally, one would break away, fight for dominance. Or leave the pack, finding his own way and fending for himself until—if he proved strong enough—others would follow him, forming a new pack with the new wolf as their alpha.

Napper respected that. Yet he also understood that these lone wolves could be a threat to the existing pack, sometimes encroaching on their territory, sometimes drawing wolves away from the pack, threatening their solidarity.

The Rogue had long been a lone wolf—one of their kind, defiant, anonymous. Yet, thus far, unable to draw his own following.

Each time Napper thought he knew who the Rogue was, that person wound up dead—hearts shot through, teeth torn out. As though the true Rogue knew his thoughts and was saying, "Nice guess, but try again," before dancing out of view. It was a game well played, but Napper was tiring of it.

He didn't know if the one the humans called the Silver Shooter was the same as the Rogue or hired by the Rogue. Whatever the case, he knew that the Rogue was trying to lure him into the game, hoping he would attempt to stop the shootings.

But Napper disliked the rules of others. He played his own game. And it had only one winner.

CHAPTER 28

For Halloween, Witten had let them watch the movie "The Wolf Man." The '40s were weird, that's all Sam had to say about it.

Near the end of class, Mr. Witten asked, "So, what'd you think?"

Most of the class groaned and Witten laughed. "Hokey or not," he said, "this stuff is also part of the enormous body of wolf lore that our country enjoys. And there are certain elements that are almost always the same. Silver, for example. Werewolves don't like it. They can be killed with silver bullets. Or, as you saw in this film, even silver staffs and silver stakes can be used against werewolves. Wolf-shifters and silver just don't go together. Usually."

"What do you mean 'usually,'" one of the girls asked.

"I mean," Witten said, "that in some very, very old lore, there are tales of certain werewolves who couldn't be harmed by silver. Werewolves who were strengthened or even healed by it. But that part of the mythology has been eradicated in pop culture."

Sam had stopped listening and was staring at Sarah, watching her scribble drawings into her notebook. He hadn't talked to her much since last week at the corn maze—a nod hello or maybe a question about homework. After that Sam never quite knew what to say.

As the weekend neared, Sam found himself even more frozen. How did you go about inviting a girl to spend time with you? Sam had no idea.

～

AT THE END OF THE DAY, SAM HURRIED TO HIS LOCKER, GRABBED HIS books, and then circled back through the hall.

Sarah stood by her locker, slowly stacking up books.

"Hey," Sam said, walking past.

"Hey," she said, turning to him.

He cleared his throat. She just looked at him, bright-eyed, waiting. But his mind was blank. "Well," he said, "I'll see you Monday I guess."

She looked back into her locker. "Yeah, I guess."

Sam walked home slower than he'd ever walked home before. It was Halloween night and a few little kids were already out in costumes, walking with their parents, holding pillow cases and plastic pumpkins, winding their way through the trailer park.

Sam unlocked his front door, dropped his backpack on his bed, and walked back outside. He just wanted to be alone in a world that was bigger than he was dumb. But he wasn't sure that was possible.

A tiny princess wandered past him, the train of her dress dragging the ground. "Trick or treat," she sang at the woman who opened the door.

Sam remembered how Sarah had looked the weekend before when he'd left her car—her eyes leaning in though her body had stayed still. He wanted to forget that he hadn't kissed her. He'd wanted to kiss her more than anything. But he was sixteen and he didn't know how. Where did your arms go? How did your lips go? He suspected that Sarah knew all these things and that made it worse.

Truth be told, Sam hadn't been kissed by anyone for years—no grandmother or mother or portly aunts. Nobody. His dad gave him his best; for physical affection that meant an awkward pat sometimes.

And that is what Sam had ended up opting for with Sarah. He'd patted her hand and watched her eyes pull away from him. He wanted to forget that too. And now, after this afternoon, he was pretty sure she never wanted to talk to him again.

He walked to the end of his street, right up to the gate by The Property and kicked it. He heard a click and it swung open. Just like that.

Sam pinched his arm. It hurt.

He stepped through the gate and walked up the path. It felt good to be swallowed into the preserve, the leaves of the trees changing and falling; it opened his mind.

Next time, if he got a next time, he would ask her if she wanted to hang out. And next time, if he got a next time, he would kiss her, no matter how badly. At least if she ignored him after that, he'd know he'd given it a shot.

When he looked up, he found that he'd walked straight up to Zinnie's house. The door was open, the fire lit.

"Hello, Sammy," the old voice said.

Sam had trouble finding his own voice. He pinched his arm again. Harder. It still hurt.

"You were gone," was all he could say.

"It happens sometimes," she said. "More and more lately. With these awful wolves about."

Sam had forgotten all about the wolves. He'd just walked through a wolf-infested wood and not given them the tiniest thought.

"Have a gingerbread," Zinnie said. "They're fresh."

They were the most elaborate gingerbread men Sam had ever seen —candy buttons, peppermint clothes, licorice eyes. And they were delicious. At least Zinnie's Alzheimer's hadn't spread to her baked goods yet.

The empty house kind of made sense now. Zinnie's family or someone must come and find her here and take her away—things and all. And then she'd come back.

"So where do you go," Sam asked, trying to be casual and taking another bite of the intricate cookie. "When you're gone?"

Gabby was curled up by the fire, her tail wrapped around her body like a blanket.

"Where they want me to be."

It was as good an answer as any.

"They've even taken my staff," she said clucking her tongue against her big teeth.

Sam looked to the stove where she often rested it. Sure enough, her walking stick was gone. He felt bad for the old woman, though he had to admit that a senile woman with a big stick didn't seem like the greatest idea ever.

"Now Sammy dear," she said, "I need you to remember something."

"Okay," Sam said, his mouth half full of cookie.

"1891471121681."

Sam stopped mid chew. "Um, what's that?" he asked.

"My number," she said. "For the hospital. If I ever need you to check me out."

Sam smiled. "You expect me to remember it?"

"I do more than expect it," she said.

And he would remember it. The numbers had already lined themselves into a neat pattern in his brain.

Sam felt an unexpected warmth toward the old woman. "Okay," he said, "I'll remember." He stood to leave.

"Use the back door," she said. "The wolves won't find you that way."

Sam nodded. "Zinnie," he said. "Would you care if I ever brought a friend?"

"Of course not," the woman said. "Though a family member would be even better."

Sam smiled. A friend would have to do; his dad would never fit through the "back door" even if he wanted to.

As soon as Sam had squirmed his way past the licorice post, he started to run. He had to tell Ella—he wasn't crazy.

It was two miles to Ella's neighborhood. The houses rose up like clean, straight teeth and Sam paused. He knew where she lived because Sarah had dropped her off, but he'd never gone to her house before. He hoped it wouldn't embarrass her. He stopped on the porch and took a few breaths, then rang the bell.

Ella answered. "Sam!" she said. "How'd you find my house?"

"I just…I remembered," he said.

"So how'd it go with Sarah," Ella asked, stepping outside.

"Um, okay." He paused. "Hey, listen, that old shack—the lady's there. I think she's got dementia or something and comes when she sneaks away from her family."

Ella raised an eyebrow. "So she's crazy, not you."

"Something like that," Sam said.

"Hey, I'm freezing. Come on in," Ella said.

Sam stepped into the warm house. He'd never seen so much white and black. It pressed against him like the walls of an institution. Sam shook it off. Ella's aunt must have the best vacuum ever, that was for sure.

"Hey Ella," Sam said. "Come with me to see it. I want you to meet her."

"And tell you you're not crazy."

"A little, yeah," he said.

"Okay," Ella said smiling. "I'll call Sarah for a ride." Ella took her phone out of her pocket.

"No," Sam said, too quickly. "Maybe we could. Well, could we…"

Ella looked at his face. "Okay, we'll run."

It took them less than twenty minutes to get to the licorice post and crawl through. Sam hurried forward, pushed open the door, and stopped.

Ella came up behind him, bright-faced, and then she stopped too.

The house was empty—completely, one hundred percent empty. No Zinnie, no furniture, no cookies, no fire.

"Sam," Ella said, reaching out and putting her hand on his shoulder.

He shook it off, ran to another room, and then another. All empty. Zinnie couldn't have left that quickly. It'd only been forty minutes since he had left her house. He swallowed the lump in his throat and took a deep breath. "I don't know what to say," he said, walking back into the main room.

Ella looked at him with big, wet eyes. "It's not a joke?" she said.

He shook his head, imagining his granny muttering about the non-existent things she saw before she died. "I think something's wrong with me." He turned to the door and Ella followed, then stopped.

"Sam," she said, as he touched the knob. "I smell gingerbread."

Sam hadn't told her what he'd eaten.

"Seriously, Ella," Sam said. "It's not a joke."

"No," she said. "Smell."

She pointed to a little spot on the floor. A pile of crumbs was there, and from it went a little trail of crumbs into the kitchen and up to a tall, human-sized pantry.

They both stopped in front of it. A person would have fit in it perfectly.

"Open it," Ella said softly.

Sam just shook his head. A fear had started to boil under Sam's skin—not just a fear of being crazy—but a fear of what he might have done during a crazy spell.

He pictured his granny straining under her restraints, swearing at the nurses, threatening people. And then, later, docile as a lamb, unaware of the bout of violence that had overtaken her just minutes before. Sam bit into his cheek. Was he really crazy? And if he was, had he done something to the old woman? Had he hurt her somehow? It was like the worst horror movie ever.

"You guys," a voice shouted from behind them.

Ella screamed. Sam jumped.

Sarah stood by the door looking red-faced—mad or worried or cold —it was impossible to know.

"You're crazy," she said. "There are wolves on this property. And you crawled through a *fake* fence. I saw you. I followed you. And you two are here. Alone." She looked at Sam accusingly.

"And who does this?" She gestured at the house. "Who comes to a place like this unless they want to smoke pot or make out?" Another accusing look. "But you two are just staring at that cupboard like a couple of nut-jobs."

"We think there might be a body in it," Ella whispered, so white she almost looked gray.

Sarah stood with her hands on her hips and glared at them. Her face was hard as ice, but Sam could tell the eyes had softened.

"And who," Sarah said loudly, "would have put it there?"

"Hopefully not me," Sam muttered under his breath.

"Whatever," Sarah said, and with three long steps, she went to the cupboard and jerked it open.

Ella screamed and Sam thought he might throw up. But there was nothing.

Well, almost nothing.

At the bottom of the cupboard was a small, white appointment card. In neat print it said, "Napper Psychiatric Institution—Havensborough Unit. November 7th—9 am."

Sarah picked it up. "Nice dead body," she said, though it was clear that all the bite was gone.

"I came to see if you were home and wanted to go for a drive," she said, looking at Sam. "Glad you were busy ghost-hunting with your girlfriend in an abandoned shack."

"It's not what you think," Ella said. "It's crazy."

"It's not," Sam said, "but I think I am." He took a deep breath. "I thought an old woman lived in this shack. I thought I visited her with a fire and a cat and cookies."

"But whenever *I* come, it's empty," Ella said. "Abandoned."

The rest of the story came out like that—monotone confession from Sam, worried whispers when Ella jumped in.

Sarah sighed and plunked cross-legged down onto the floor. "You guys are so weird," she said. "I try to be weird and I can't even manage it. I've got rich parents and good grades and my own car. But you guys just…" she motioned around the house. "What'd you say her name was?" she asked Sam.

"Zinnie," he said, staring at the wall.

"Too bad it doesn't have a name on the card," Ella said.

"Doesn't need one," Sam said. "It's just a coincidence.

Ella was chewing on her nail. "The post *is* licorice," she said.

Sam shrugged.

"You're kidding," Sarah said. "I thought it was rubber or something."

"Taste it," Ella said, a touch of challenge in her voice. "And, Sarah, what does it smell like in here?"

Sarah breathed deeply. "Spices," she said. "Sweet spices."

"Gingerbread," Ella said. "And the trail to the pantry is made of cookie crumbs."

"Maybe I did it," Sam said. "With, like, my eighth personality or something. Maybe I made the cookies and the path."

"Right," Sarah said. "Because your other self baked a bunch of gingerbread in your house. Sam, do you even own any ginger?"

It was the first ray of light Sam had felt. He was pretty sure that they did not, at all, own any ginger. But maybe he'd stolen it. At this point, that seemed as likely as anything. Sam shrugged.

Sarah rolled her eyes. "Only one way to find out," she said. "Next Friday morning I'll meet you at the mental hospital at nine. If we see your old woman, we know at least that she exists."

"What about school?" Ella said.

"What about it?" Sarah asked like she skipped it every day, though Sam knew for a fact that she was there every morning, and early.

Sam sighed. Whether Zinnie was at the mental unit or not, he was still schizo. She couldn't have emptied out this house in the forty minutes he'd been gone. He was just glad he hadn't killed her.

WHEN HE GOT HOME, THE ORANGE TABBY WAS SITTING ON THE STEP outside the door—stump of a tail.

"I hope you're the evil twin," Sam said to her. "Otherwise they're probably going to leave me at the mental hospital too."

The cat looked at him like she planned to say something back. Sam just turned and unlocked his door. When he went in, his trailer smelled old and slightly moldy. Not a hint of gingerbread anywhere. Sam would take the good news where he found it.

CHAPTER 29

Jones scouted the periphery of his land with a loaded gun. Two more dogs were dead—guts ripped out. And lately the rest of the dogs had taken to barking at night.

For a little while after the wolves had arrived in Napper it had looked like everything would die down, like the wolves really would become the eccentric pets of an eccentric billionaire.

Then the sightings had started—a wolf in a field, a calf dragged off during the night. And the howlings—lone calls as though from a stray dog. But soon the lonesome howls had been joined by other voices.

They were not dogs. Jones knew that. These howls were more ancient, more ghostly, more *organized*.

Wolves were gathering. It was the craziest thing—as though they were being drawn by the Gevudan, as though some father wolf was calling them home.

Jones might have thought he was just being paranoid, but his neighbors had seen wolves too, shot at them, missed. And then, when researching wolves on the internet, Jones had found a tiny article from a tiny hunting journal in Montana. There had been a movement—slight and seemingly insignificant. But the wolves were moving—as a group mostly, but occasionally one would break from the pack and leave, heading east.

Jones had not printed the article. He wished he had because the next week when he looked it up, it was gone. The page came up with a message that said, *We're sorry; this content is currently unavailable for viewing*. When he searched the magazine, it looked like it had gone under—publication ended.

Bad timing and bad luck. But Jones wasn't going to lose more dogs. He wasn't rescuing and training them so they could be torn apart by wild animals.

Jones thought about the girl who'd been attacked on his property a week ago. At first he thought the attacker had been his pill-head neighbor—dressed like a werewolf and scaring teenagers half to death.

Now he wasn't sure.

When Jones had gone to confront his neighbor, Jimmy-Duke, later that night, Jimmy-Duke had been passed out on the floor. That was probably nothing out of the ordinary, but his face was gray as ash and his breath wasn't coming as regularly as it should have. Jones had called 911 and they'd somehow managed to get his heart and lungs moving properly again.

Jimmy-Duke came to sputtering about a werewolf in the cornfields —taking blood from a child. He'd seen it all through his binoculars, he'd said. And he had it on film. He swore up and down he was calling a reporter. Ever since then, he'd been in the mental unit under surveillance.

Which wouldn't have meant anything, except that Jimmy-Duke wound up in the ER on a fairly regular basis—overdosed, talking nonsense and threatening to tell the news about whatever crazy story his unstable mind had cooked up. The hospital had released him all the same. Every time—back to his house with his pain meds and his drug factory. And no one cared. Until now.

Jones heard the soft tread of one of his dogs as it came up beside him. It was the caped one he'd gotten from the Humane Society. The dog walked step for step with him and it made the farmer smile. "We'll get it, won't we, boy?" he said, patting the young dog's head.

When the animal looked at him with the dark round eyes, Jones could have sworn the dog was saying, "I hope so, sir, I do."

Which was an observation the farmer planned to keep to himself so he didn't wind up in the psychiatric hospital with Jimmy-Duke.

～

Once, before the great red sun fell from the sky replaced by its small white brother, the race of dogs ran in free-ranging packs —singing songs and spinning tales like colored yarn through a child's hat.

The dogs gave their voices to free their friends—the humans who had sheltered, fed, and fought for them in their times of need. But they missed their song, and their story.

One night, many moons into the era of the high white sun, the dogs took their petition to the Holder of Woods, the Worker of Magic.

The young witch could not bring their voices back—they'd sacrificed them willfully as they'd known they must, but she promised them that if, at the next full moon, they brought the humans who were dearest to their hearts to her cottage, she might be able to give them something. And so they did. And so she did.

To those humans, young and old, who showed up to support their voiceless friends, she gave a gift—touching their lips with a beam from the moon, promising that when they both were kind and good to one another, each month at the fullest moon, dog and man could hear and understand each other again. And so it was.

The gift filtered on through generations, this fleeting bestowal of speech passed to those who loved each other.

Now there are but few remaining who can hear the voices of the dogs at full moon. But they walk among us—keeping their secrets so as not to arouse suspicion or distrust. For we, my child, must not put the dogs at risk.

ELLA RUMBLED ALONG IN THE CITY BUS ON TUESDAY AFTERNOON thinking of Loco. She'd spent the night before reading story after story that her mother had written. She'd begun typing the hand-written tales into her computer late at night. Which explained all the weird dreams she'd started to have. Every night since the corn maze, she'd dreamed about Loco; and every time, he spoke to her.

In the magical world her mother had created, all the dogs talked. And sang too. Ella found herself wishing that Loco would sing to her in her dreams. She had an urge to hear the melody, the *hondsong*, as her mother called it in the stories—earthy, variegated, beautiful. But in her dreams, Loco never sang. He mostly gave archaic, chilling warnings like, "They come." Then Ella would wake in a sweat.

Between her mother's stories, Napper's wolves, and her folklore class, it was little wonder that dog and wolf stories were wrapping around her mind, like a song set on repeat.

The bus stopped on a dusty road that led through two walls of dried cornstalks. "Last bus comes at 6:00, hun," the bus driver reminded her. "Don't miss it."

Ella didn't intend to.

WHEN JONES ANSWERED THE DOOR, A TEENAGE GIRL WAS STANDING IN front of him. She looked familiar, although he couldn't place her face immediately. The truth was he could remember a dog's face better than a person's.

And then she spoke. "Um, hello, Mr. Jones. My name is Ella Peterson and I was here a little over a week ago at your corn maze."

Good mercy. She was the girl who'd been attacked. "Oh yes," was all he could think to say. "I remember."

Ella nodded.

If she'd come with her parents, he'd fully expect a lawsuit. Truth be told, he'd been waiting for some kind of legal letter to come all week. But none had. And now she stood here alone and looking not angry.

Jones stepped outside and did something his lawyer brother-in-law had told him not to do. He apologized.

"I'm so so sorry," he said, "about the corn maze. I know I didn't hire any werewolves that night. I," he began and didn't know how to finish. "I don't like them." The truth was that the idea of a man shifting into something else had scared him since childhood. He liked to look at a person and know what he was about. Maybe that's what he liked so much with the dogs.

"I know," Ella said. "It wasn't your fault. I mean, I didn't really figure he was hired." She paused to look at Jones. "I guess someone took advantage of a situation to scare some people. I don't think..." She paused again. "I don't think he was right in the head."

Jones agreed.

"But that's not actually why I'm here." Ella took a deep breath. "When I was here, I thought I saw a dog—he was rusty colored with a dark back that I think looks like a cape. Is...is he here?"

Jones smiled. "Well, I believe he is. Good dog, that one."

"Could I see him?" Ella asked.

Jones closed the door behind him and walked to the field. It was the least he could do for the girl. He whistled shrilly three times and the dog came running.

Loco stopped when he saw Ella, and she looked at him like she might cry.

"This dog yours?" Jones asked, seeing her reaction.

"No sir," she said, kneeling down to rub Loco's belly. "He was in my neighborhood." She looked like she wanted to say more, but stopped.

The farmer nodded. "Your parents ever see him?" he asked.

"I live with my aunt on the northeast side," Ella answered, avoiding the question.

The farmer got his answer anyway. Rich girl befriends poor dog— like star-crossed lovers, that story. He'd seen it before.

"What do you call him?" Ella asked politely. She sat on the ground with the dog's head in her lap, like she had no intention of leaving.

"I call him Buddy," Jones said. "Truth is, I call all my dogs Buddy till I find them a home or they make it clear that this is their home." The farmer squatted low and looked at the girl. "What'd you call him?"

"He wasn't really mine to name," Ella answered, looking down.

"That's not what I asked," Jones replied.

"I called him Loco," the girl said, looking up and meeting the farmer's eyes.

"Loco," the farmer said, rubbing the dog and then holding his snout in a big hand.

"But he's still not mine to name," Ella said.

"He's yours as much as he is mine," Jones said. "And the name's a good fit."

Other dogs had come to the front yard. Ella smiled to see them and several bumped against her legs, beating her with their tails. She scratched one behind the ears—the fur soft and clean.

Jones looked down the dusty driveway. "How'd you get all the way out here?" he asked.

"Bus," she said, rubbing another one of the dogs—scratching all down its neck, like a doggy masseuse.

"It's a good mile walk from the stop," Jones said.

"I wanted to know if it was him." Ella shrugged.

Jones nodded and was quiet for several long minutes, save for a small, nervous click that he made with his mouth. The dogs pressed against the girl, vying for her attention. In the middle of them, she looked like some kind of queen. The farmer pressed his lips together.

Ella looked at him. "Is there any way," she began, "that I could come out several afternoons a week? To volunteer on the farm?"

Jones glanced down at the dogs. Generally he didn't like help and he didn't need it, but the dog Loco was staring at him like a little kid asking for candy, and the other dogs were still sniffing and licking on her like she was family. The farmer sighed. "You get yourself out here and I'm sure I can find something for you to do," he said.

He walked with Ella down his driveway, the dogs following the girl like a royal entourage. It was strange, honestly. They didn't treat all his visitors this way. They didn't even treat Miss Mandy this way.

For whatever reasons, the dogs seemed to really like the girl—to attach to her in a way he'd only ever seen them attach to him.

When they got to the end of his long driveway, Ella turned to wave and then she caught sight of the beat up trailer Jimmy-Duke used to live in. It hadn't been a beauty before, but now three of the windows were broken and the bottom step was split in half. "That trailer looks pretty rough," the girl said. "Does anybody live there?"

"Used to be my no good neighbor," Jones said. "Now it's nobody. Hospital admitted him for mental help."

"Well, I guess that's good for you," Ella said, wrinkling her nose at the stinky, ruined house.

The farmer nodded half-heartedly. Jimmy-Duke wasn't coming back, and while it was a relief, something about it nagged at the farmer, refusing to speak.

CHAPTER 30

The Havensborough Unit of the Napper Psychiatric Institution was closed on Fridays. The sign clearly said so. It looked to Sam like it was closed most of the rest of the time too, with only a few visiting hours posted. It appeared to be some type of assisted living facility, probably for the mentally ill.

"But the card," Ella said, walking back and forth by the side entrance where they were standing.

"Is probably ten years old," Sam said.

"No," Sarah said. "It doesn't look old at all."

Sam shrugged.

The Havensborough Unit had a narrow gray door and limited hours, nothing like the gaping mouth of the main entrance at the front of the building. It was a place with a quieter purpose. Sam couldn't decide if that made it for the more crazy or the less crazy. You weren't visiting your strung out son or bipolar aunt; you weren't rushing someone in after a suicide attempt. You were there because you had a recognized and regular need. You were there with intention. Several office windows lined the side—all covered with blinds, all locked up tight.

Sarah banged on the number pad to the door, like that would let her in.

Suddenly Sam drew in a sharp breath.

Number pad.

The numbers Zinnie had told him flashed through his head. He tried to ignore them. How would Zinnie know the code anyway? And, wait, Zinnie probably wasn't real.

Still, his fingers felt twitchy. What was the harm in trying? He was already crazy.

He moved Sarah's hand off the key pad. Her fingers were so soft and small. He shook his head, and typed the number. A red light flashed atop the number pad. Denied. He typed it again. Same thing. The girls, he could tell, had no idea what he was doing, but still Ella put her hand on his shoulder and said, "Third time's a charm."

But Sam took her hand off. No, he thought, crazy is crazy. He didn't need to make himself look crazier.

"What number was that?" Sarah asked as they walked back to her car.

Sam shrugged.

"Come on, tell me," she said.

"It's a number my imaginary friend gave me," he said.

Ella looked at her watch. "Looks like we'll make it in time for Folklore."

Sam stopped at the car door. "Look guys, I think I'm gonna walk home."

"No," Sarah said. "Come on." She nudged him into the car and Sam let himself be nudged.

IN WITTEN'S CLASS THEY DISCUSSED HANSEL AND GRETEL—TWO children, crumbs, candy, gingerbread, kill an old woman. Halfway through Sam jumped up and ran to the bathroom. He banged into the stall, locked the door, and leaned his cheek against the cool metal, his head pounding, his stomach sick. He was hovering near the toilet when Mr. Witten came in and spoke.

"Guess you better head to the nurse, Sam," he said kindly.

"Yes, sir," Sam mumbled.

"You know," Mr. Witten said as he walked with Sam to the nurse's office. "All fairy tales have retellings—twists and turns and whole new stories. It's part of what makes them so timeless. And interesting."

Sam wasn't listening. If his teacher wasn't there, Sam would have run out of the school and all the way home. A little pig. Scared.

ELLA SAT AT THE PEP RALLY BY HERSELF IN THE BLEACHERS. OF course, she wasn't really by herself. She was surrounded by people, sardined between two screaming girls who were in biology with her. Though she was almost sure that neither one knew her name. Ella wished she could have found Sarah in the mob. And she wished Sam hadn't gone home early. Ella was a little worried about him.

Everyone around her started to clap as the marching band began to play. Ella touched her hands together, scanning the crowd for Sarah.

All at once, the clapping stopped and the crowd erupted into cheers and whistles. One of the cheerleaders jumped off the shoulders of two others, doing a twist in the air. The entire student body burst into an enthusiastic shout. Ella caught herself clapping too—for real this time.

The cheerleaders ran through the crowd, throwing candy. Ella reached up to grab a piece when she felt a sharp pang on her left cheek. Someone had thrown a hard candy at her.

One of the girls from biology was trying to hide a giggle. "Sorry," she said, and then the girl next to her giggled too.

Ella turned away, threading her way out of the gym as quickly as possible.

As Ella walked back to her locker, Jack's brother, Brandt, ran through the hall, shouting, "Go Royals!" and throwing more candy.

Ella scooted out of the way, but Brandt caught her eye.

"Hey, Ella," he said, tossing a lollipop in her direction.

Ella was surprised he knew her name, and even more surprised that she caught the lollipop.

Brandt smiled, slowing to a walk, and came up to her. "Nice catch. You coming to the game?"

"Um," Ella said, almost dropping the lollipop. "I don't know. I hadn't thought about it."

"You should come," he said. "Maybe I could meet up with you after or something."

"I…" she said.

"Give me your number," he said before she could finish. "I'll text you and then you'll have my number."

"Um," Ella said again. "Okay." She messed up her own phone number twice before finally getting it right.

Brandt smiled. "Okay then, maybe I'll see you tonight."

The crowd moved him down the hall before she could answer. Which was just as well since she felt like a football was stuck in her throat. There was no way she was going to that game. Who would she sit with? What would she do with herself? Did she want to see Brandt afterwards? I mean, sure he was good-looking, but… Ella almost bumped into her locker.

She dumped books into her bag and then noticed the lollipop she was still holding. She placed it on the top shelf of her locker, unwilling to eat it just yet.

His father put his coat away and walked to the fridge. "You hungry?" he asked, looking at its Spartan contents.

"No," Sam said. And his dad turned around.

"Something wrong?"

"I think I'm sick," Sam said quietly.

His dad sat down beside him and laid a hand against his forehead.

"No," Sam said, "not like that." He paused. "I think…I think something's wrong with my head. I think I might need to go to the hospital."

"You hit it on something?" his dad asked, slowly, as though he knew that's not what Sam meant.

"No," Sam said, looking his dad straight in the eyes. "I've been seeing things—things I thought were real, but," he paused again, "then they're not."

His dad stood up. "Maybe it's your vision, son. Maybe you're catching a glance of something that looks like something else."

Sam laughed—a hard sound. "Only if what I 'glance' talks, smells, and makes cookies."

His dad said nothing, but held the back of an empty chair. After a long silence he said, "I'm sure you don't need a hospital, son. Tell me what you see."

Sam closed his eyes and pressed his fingers to his temples. He could still see her, smell the cookies, feel the fire. "I see an old woman. I thought she lived in this shack. Then I took Ella. And the woman wasn't there. Nothing was there. It didn't even look the same—it was all dusty and old."

"You took Ella there?" his father asked.

"Yeah," Sam said miserably. When he opened his eyes, he noticed that his father's knuckles had gone white from clutching the chair. "Dad, I need help. I don't want to end up like Granny. Please."

"That's ridiculous," his father said, pushing the chair away.

"Look. I know it's expensive, but I'm scared. I'm worried," Sam said, picturing the human-sized pantry in the shack. "I'm worried I'm going to hurt someone."

His dad tried to hide it—the look that passed over his face—but Sam had seen it. His dad was worried Sam might hurt someone too.

"I'm not taking you to any hospital," his father said.

"Please," Sam said, his throat tight.

"No," his father said. "Your mind is fine."

"Dad, I know it's hard. But I feel like if I get checked, they might be able to help me. I'm young…"

"They will not help you," his father shouted. "Or anyone like you. Never forget that." His father pushed past the chair with such force that it thundered against the table and broke.

"Dad," Sam said so softly he knew his father wouldn't hear. "Dad."

CHAPTER 31

David Witten surveyed his collection of candied porcelain houses. You got unusual gifts when you were a folklorist. These houses were some of his favorites. Like all fairytales, Hansel and Gretel had dozens of retellings, some even taking the witch's side.

But there were none in which both the old woman and the children paired up to fight the evil forces that had thrown them together in the first place. Though surely, when a woman winds up living alone in the middle of the forest, and children are left to wander the woods until they stumble into her, one can assume there are many other malevolent forces at play.

Somewhere in there was an opportunity for an interesting retelling.

Witten sighed. Retellings. He wasn't sure how healthy it was to have your life's work focused on changing old stories. But, healthy or not, it was what he had chosen.

He selected a small, bright house, sprinkles and sugar glaze sparkling on the roof, peppermint sticks standing as pillars, gumdrops lining the path to a cinnamon-spiced door. He packaged the ceramic house carefully in a box with tissue paper. Then he took out a dainty pink card and began to write.

My dear Emmaline—

He paused, his pen in the air like a wand, wound up with a spell.

I am still hoping to see you for American Christmas, though your mother is concerned that the timing may not be quite right. In the meantime I've written a version of one of your favorite tales, and one I've been thinking about these last few weeks. I hope you enjoy it.

Once... He glanced out the window at the dark clouds that were gathering in the distance. *...in the dark of the wood lived a very old woman in a very old house. Both had stood in the forest for much longer than such things should; and both had grown old and crooked from time. The woman, as you can guess, was possibly the loneliest creature in the entire world, having only her gardens and the animals for company.*

To soothe this ache, she spent hours each day baking cake and boiling confections of every kind—things that reminded her of times long past. She baked so much and so often that soon the little house was overflowing with sweet treats. The woman began to pile pound cakes against walls like bricks, filling in the cracks of her old, aching house with frosting, spinning hot sugar through the floorboards, and plastering the walls in crisp chocolate.

As the years went on, the house became more and more solid while the woman continued to stoop and crumble.

And then one day a flock of birds flew over her house, cackling and pecking at the shortbread shingles of her roof. "You're lucky, old crone," a fat bird chittered, "that we're not hungrier. For we've just devoured an entire path of sweet, white breadcrumbs, and don't have room for your roof today."

The old woman shooed the crows away just as two small children came into the clearing, the youngest one crying as the older pulled on her hand, begging her to keep moving. They stopped when they saw the house, and the old woman tucked herself behind the poppy seed door, watching.

Now, in many a tale you've heard, that old woman tricked those poor children into her house, and tried to eat them.

But the truth is that there are many things about children that are sweet beyond what lips can taste and sustaining beyond what bellies can feel.

For many moons the children stayed with the old woman, drinking her tea and patching her old bones in a way only bright, young creatures can.

But both witch and children possessed things that powerful people sought. And, in time, the birds brought news of a stepmother's hunger and an old mayor's greed.

Digging into her speculoos cellar, the woman brought out several bright rubies and a pair of diamonds. "Take these, my sweets," she said. "And tell them you've pushed the old hag into the fire. In this way, we might both remain safe."

The woman sent the now-rich children back into the dark wood.

The jewels, she knew, would buy the children some freedom. And the story would buy her some time. But there were those in this world who would not be quick to be satiated. And so she watched through her butterscotch windows. And waited.

WHEN ELLA GOT TO THE GAME, IT WAS COLD AND THE AIR FELT THICK and damp. Kids wandered past her, holding hands, wearing letter jackets, gossiping, and laughing.

She didn't belong here. It was just too obvious. She'd invited Sarah to come, but Sarah hated football. It was one of the first things they'd talked about, one of the surprisingly many things they'd had in common.

Now Ella paused near the entrance, wondering if she should leave, but the smell of winter hung in the air, shot through with laughter and cheering. People were carrying mugs of hot chocolate and baskets of fries, which smelled amazing. Jack had been right—there was a lot of energy here. And in a strange way, it *did* feel nice to be a tiny part of it, wandering through crowds, catching bits of conversation, pulling her sleeves down over her cold hands.

Ella had purposefully come late, and now the second half was starting. All around her people were stomping and cheering, while in the bleachers the marching band played a loud, honking version of the fight song.

Ella took a deep breath. She figured she could hang out in line at the concession stand. That would kill a few minutes before she actually had to make her way to the bleachers and find a spot.

Ella felt the first drop of rain as someone from the student council handed her a hot dog. It hit her on the nose, then another on the hand, her jacket, her hair—picking up speed as the ground around her darkened in the increasing rain. Then, through the trees that surrounded the stadium, she heard the rush of wind as the heart of the storm crashed down on them, a wall of water pounding into the crowd. All around her people scattered, pulling up hoods and running for cover as the fat rain drops beat against the aluminum bleachers and the thin roofs of the concession booths.

Ella pulled her collar tight around her neck, stepping under a row of bleachers. Above them a crooked spear of light bent down from the clouds, and when the first clap of thunder hit, several girls screamed and everything rattled. Some people put umbrellas up. Ella hunched into her jacket, wishing she'd brought a coat with a hood.

More lightning jumped from the sky, a twisted branch of electricity. Through the pounding of the rain and the chatter of the crowd, Ella heard the unified squeal of whistles as the players were hurried off the field. Streams of purple and blue uniforms fled to opposite sides of the stadium.

Ella craned her neck, trying to catch a glance of Brandt, but with their uniforms and the rain, all the players looked the same. Around her, people were gathering their soggy belongings and leaving.

Several more cracks of thunder followed quick bursts of light, and the screen of the scoreboard lit up with a cartoonish frowny face. It looked like the game was cancelled. Everyone was packing up now, even the diehards.

Ella pulled her coat collar tighter around her neck and threw her soggy hot dog into the trash. She had walked here. It was going to be a wet trek home. She stuck her hands in her pockets and started toward the exit when she heard someone call her name.

She turned around, thinking it was Brandt, but there in front of her was Jack—dripping in a thin jacket, his wet cheeks flushed like he was having the time of his life.

"You're not walking home, are you?" he asked.

Ella shrugged, embarrassed.

"Here," he said, coming up to her. "I'll give you a ride. It's not safe to walk in a storm like this."

Ella shrugged again, but followed. Jack was even more gorgeous sopping wet than he was dry. Ella shivered in the car as Jack turned on the heat. He handed her a River High Royals blanket. "For that," he said, "you can thank my brother. He gets me something football themed every year for Christmas."

Ella wrapped the blanket around herself and snuck a peek at Jack's profile. He was smiling.

Ella wondered if Brandt would text her later that night like he'd said he would. She wondered if that was what she wanted. She took a deep breath. The blanket smelled like Jack—his cologne, his shampoo, and something muskier underneath. It was all kind of confusing.

Controlling the winds had always been an easy task for the old woman. A few tilts and taps with her staff and she could bring a storm in or push one out.

Now that her staff was gone, it was so much harder. She had to connect herself to the earth, sway with the winds as she drew or deflected them. She had to dig for moisture, or reach for dryness. And she was so very, very old.

She caught a horrible cold the first time she'd done it without her staff, a cold no amount of tea had been able to soothe. This time she would catch more than that.

The Alpha was not pleased with her interference. He had thought that taking the staff would stop her. Now that he knew it wouldn't, there was only one full-proof way for him to control her.

It wasn't that she feared death. She had yearned for it in a way that only a person of her age and experience could ever understand. But her death could not come until her life was done. And that was a trickier matter.

CHAPTER 32

Brandt never texted her. She'd picked up her phone a couple times that weekend, and stared at it, wondering if she should text him first, but she hadn't.

Now she was glad. That week at school, Brandt stalked through the halls ignoring her, and everyone else—angry, it seemed, that his precious win had been taken from him by the storm.

Ella still had the lollipop in her locker. She took it out and was going to toss it in the trash can when she walked past Lila and Nicole from her homeroom.

"Do you really think he'd date her?" Nicole was whispering to Lila who was fixing her lip gloss in the tiny mirror that hung in her locker.

"I don't know," Lila said. "He's, like, so much hotter than she is, but he seemed kind of interested last Friday. He got her number."

They could have been talking about any of the hundreds of students at the school, but for some reason Ella slowed down, gripping the lollipop tighter.

"He's got my number too," Nicole said, laughing. "Doesn't mean anything."

Lila puckered her lips together, evening out the gloss. "Seriously," she said. "I mean, she's really not good enough for him. I don't even know how he noticed her? But whatever. Maybe he just feels sorry for her because her mom died and stuff."

Ella stopped. She was a few lockers past them. Quietly, she wound through several halls and back to her locker. She put the lollipop on the upper shelf. Her mom would have told her the comment wasn't worth crying about, and she didn't. But now she found herself hoping Brandt would call after all.

SAM WALKED TO SCHOOL. HE PAUSED IN FRONT OF THE ENTRANCE, AND then he kept walking. At the edge of the fence, the janitor stopped him. "Headed the wrong way, ain't you?"

Sam looked at him. It was the same janitor who had called for help when Howard Simms got beat up. For all the good that had done. "I, um, forgot my homework," Sam said. "I have to go back and get it."

"You're probably better off just heading to class and asking if you can call your mom to bring it."

Sam had no doubt that he would be better off if that was the way his life worked. "She's, um, not home."

The janitor grunted, looking towards the school. "Still probably better off in class."

Sam nodded, about to turn back to the school, and then hesitated. "Hey, um, sir, you know that kid that got beat up a little while ago over by the football fields?"

The janitor grunted again, but didn't say anything.

"Do you know what happened to him? He hasn't been back."

"He a friend of yours?" the janitor asked, moving his mouth like he was chewing cud.

Sam shrugged, looking past the school in the direction of the fields. "No, I didn't really know him at all. Just seems weird that he hasn't come back to school."

The janitor shrugged. "You know, kid. You'll learn that a lot of weird things happen in life. Usually, it's best not to ask too many questions about them."

Sam bit the inside of his lip, tasting blood on his tongue. "But you do remember that kid, right? You know what I'm talking about?" Sam looked into the janitor's face. The man's eyes were blue, a little inky at the centers and lighter at the edges. "Do you know what happened to him?"

The janitor just moved his mouth, tucking what Sam guessed was a wad of chewing tobacco into his cheek. "I don't know nothing," the janitor said, almost spitting out the last word. "Now get yourself back to school before the final bell rings."

The janitor stalked off, spitting into the grass as he walked.

Sam stepped outside the gate of the school property, stood there for a second, and then stepped back in. The final bell rang. Sam ran, then sprinted, taking the front steps three at a time. The janitor was right— so far nothing good had come from asking a question, nothing at all.

CHAPTER 33

Maybe Jones didn't name the dogs, but Ella did—every one. She didn't call them their names when Jones was around, but when she was alone with the dogs she called them with all the sweetness of a mother. Which was how she felt. Like a mother to dogs. Why was she such a freak?

What Sarah had said in Zinnie's empty house bothered her—she and Sam *were* different and it *was* like they couldn't be normal. Everything Ella did or cared about seemed different than what all the other kids did or cared about. Clearly, scooping dog poop on a random Wednesday was her idea of glamour. And she wondered why she only had two friends—one of them probably insane, and the other rebelling against her parents by hanging out with lonely kids on the fringe, hoping to become as nutso as they were.

It wasn't working. Sarah was as normal as ever. She'd be picking Ella up to go get hamburgers at six o'clock.

Before then Ella was supposed to shovel and dump any poop that was in the yard, then bathe the dogs. In summer they might not have cared, but on this late autumn day, Ella could tell the dogs were all dreading it.

The sky was still blue and clear, but as the sun started to set, a smile of a moon made its way to the horizon.

It occurred to Ella, as she tied up the bag of poop and unwound the long hose, that she was going to end up smelling like wet dog just as much as the dogs were.

Ella got the bucket of soap ready and looked at the dogs. "Okay, who's first?" she said, shaking her head.

None of the dogs moved, but she caught the eye of one she called Sheila. "Come on girl," she said. "Don't you want to smell nice?" Ella swore Sheila gave her the equivalent of a doggy eye roll—shaking her head and then stepping forward an inch, like an unwilling, but resigned volunteer.

Ella washed Sheila, then the others. At least two of them were filthy again by the time she'd finished the group.

"Seriously guys," she said, looking at the now-dusty little pug and the muddy husky.

Ella dumped out the buckets and put them in the barn. Dusk was settling into darkness and the wind bent through the dry corn, murmuring and rustling. Ella couldn't see anything clearly and she felt a little of the old fear come back to her. She hadn't been at the farm at night since the corn maze.

In the distance, she thought she heard a howl. Ella looked up and over her shoulder. The memory of the werewolf and the scalpel were too close. She jumped up and ran toward the lighted windows of the farmer's house.

She pounded on Jones' door and he opened it quickly. "Are you okay?" he asked, clearly alarmed at her face.

"I just," she said. "I was hearing things and I—"

The farmer ushered her in. "I don't see anything," he said, looking out the front door. "But Loco and I will look around after your friend comes to get you."

Ella stood awkwardly in the entryway.

"Come on in," Jones said, gesturing toward the living room.

Ella walked through the dark wooden door frame into a spacious warm room while Jones went into the kitchen. The couches were old blues and greens—outdated, but clean and comfortable. The walls and floors were made of wood in various colors and grains. But the most striking thing was that Jones' house was filled with metal. There were small silver objects everywhere—belt buckles, bracelets, cufflinks, coins, spurs, and even crafts made from used bullet shells.

It was super tacky and Ella loved it all. She walked from end table to end table. Her mother would have swooned over each item, though a lot of it was surprisingly masculine for a bunch of silver stuff. Ella picked up two cufflinks and put them down again.

From the next table she picked up a picture frame made from used bullet shells. Jones came in with two hot chocolates and saw her holding the frame.

"Cool, isn't it?" he said. "I take old metal and recycle it into different pieces—mostly silver, but also bronze and copper—like those bullet shell frames."

Ella nodded, distracted. "Where is this?" she asked, squinting at the fuzzy picture.

"Oh, that. That's in northern Montana—from my hunting days. I don't hunt much now—just some rabbit or duck here or there. But when I was younger, I went after much larger game."

Ella held the photo closer to her face. "I'm sorry," she said, "but is that Mr. Witten?"

"Yup. We've known each other a long time."

"He's a hunter?" she asked.

"Pretty good one," Jones said, setting down the mugs. "Though he doesn't go out much these days either."

"You made that bracelet he wears," she said.

"Right again," Jones said, sitting down to sip his chocolate.

Ella looked around. "Do you make anything for women?" she asked. "Anything more delicate?"

The farmer leaned back and looked at a distant point across the room. "It's not my best stuff," he said. "I don't really have what you'd call a delicate hand."

She nodded.

"Oh come on," he said, setting his mug down. "I'll show you what I've got."

From inside a small box, he pulled an ugly linked chain, several pendants, and a long hair pin that was sharp at one end like a slightly clumsy lightning bolt.

Ella almost laughed. She'd thought Jones was just being humble, but he really didn't have a delicate hand. Nothing reminded her even remotely of her mother's taste in jewelry. However, some of these things might be the perfect fit for a goth-punk girl. Ella held up the chunky chain and a pendant that held a jagged slab of obsidian.

"How much?" Ella asked.

The farmer hesitated. "Oh, you've come almost every day this week; you can have that for free."

"No, it's okay." Ella said. "The metal itself must be worth quite a bit—it's heavy."

"Bathing those dogs is worth more," he said stubbornly.

"At least let me pay for your costs," Ella insisted.

"Fine," he said. "You can have it at cost—ten dollars."

Ella pulled a twenty from her purse. "This is all I have."

Jones raised an eyebrow. He put the chain and pendant in a small white bag, then slipped in the two cufflinks that she had first picked up.

Ella opened her mouth to argue, but Jones held up a hand. "Thank you," he said, "for all your help on the farm this week."

CHAPTER 34

Robert Calhoun paced his small bedroom, balling and relaxing his fists. He wanted to leave, his whole body itched to throw everything into the van, pick Sam up from school, and head out of town. But the body, he knew, was better preserved when it listened to the mind. And for now they had to stay.

For now they had to look like they were just normal folks with nothing to hide. The trailer park, their poverty—it gave them an advantage. Napper didn't expect ex-members of The Pack to live like paupers, didn't look for its retirees among the dregs of his own city.

To run would draw attention to themselves. To run would wave a red flag in Napper's face.

But to stay was dangerous too.

Robert Calhoun had more to lose than Howard Simms, the boy who'd been beaten half to death, then institutionalized—all because his parents had tried to run. Unlike the boy's family, Robert had not only left the Pack, but he'd left it to marry and then preserve one of the sisters—one of Napper's most prized treasures. He'd hidden her so long and so well that Napper would never be able to get his hands on her. Calhoun had paid a high price for their hiding. He'd lost his wife.

He was terrified about losing his son. And so they would stay in plain sight.

For now.

~

Sam had wandered through the last week in a haze, barely talking to Sarah or Ella. Seeing them just reminded him he was crazy. The fact that they were still nice to him only made it more embarrassing.

Sarah had asked him if he wanted to go to a movie that weekend, but he'd said he had to do a project for physics. It was a lie. What he had to do was find the picture, the picture of his grandmother with the inscription.

If he could just do that, if he could just read it and see that it said, "To my two beautiful daughters," then maybe he wouldn't feel so off-kilter. Maybe he could regain a piece of his old, sane self.

Sam stood in his living room for a minute, and then he started slowly—walking to each room, looking at each picture, then in the closets, behind furniture. With each less likely location, he felt his panic grow.

He started tearing open drawers, throwing out the clothes. He and his dad didn't have much; a picture shouldn't be hard to find. He looked between the mattresses, took food out of cupboards. He banged against the floor and then the walls.

When the house had been torn into bits, Sam still had nothing. He grabbed the knob of his father's bedroom door and slammed it shut.

Then he found it.

The door—it was bottom heavy. Sam slammed it again just to be sure.

Yes, it was a cheap, hollow door, but the bottom seemed heavier. He knelt down and put his hand under it, then lay on his belly, feeling around. And there it was—a tiny latch that locked a tiny door.

When Sam opened it, several dollar bills slipped out. His father's money-hiding spot. Sam stuck his fingers in and more bills came out—

fives and tens, then a twenty. He wiggled his hand in, flat-palmed, pulling gently on the corners of the money. More twenties fell out and then a hundred.

A hundred dollar bill just lying on the floor of his trailer. It must have been bundled with more of its kind because the more he tugged, the more money came out, until he was sitting in thousands of dollars of cash.

Sam started to cry. Clearly he wasn't the only one with a mental illness.

The picture was almost the last thing to come out—crumpled from being shoved into its tomb in the door. Sam turned the old photograph over and read, "To my two beautiful daughters."

His dad was a liar.

The word seared through Sam's skull in a way that made his head burn like nothing else ever had. He had loved his father. He had trusted him. Completely. He'd eaten canned beans and worn clothes with holes and hunted for coins on the sidewalk all on account of that trust. Now he stood, picture in hand, and the money fell off of him like dust.

And then he realized—maybe he was wrong. Maybe he was hallucinating it. He bent over and picked up a hundred dollar bill. He folded it into a tiny square and put it in his pocket. He wanted to see if it would be there in the morning.

When he looked up, his dad was standing at the front door.

Sam held his father's gaze for a long moment. "Is this real?" Sam asked.

His father stepped into the house, shutting the door and locking it behind him.

"Am I standing in a pile of money?" Sam asked.

It seemed as though his father refused to breathe, locking the two front windows, and closing the blinds in perfect silence before turning to Sam. His father was crying.

Sam still didn't know if he was standing in money or if it was a pile of dirty socks he'd stacked around himself—lunatic style. Or maybe it was nothing at all.

His father opened his mouth to speak and then choked on his sobs —red face, eyes and nose streaming.

Sam wasn't sure if he wanted to be crazy or not. Lying, thieving father in the sane corner; shockingly vivid hallucination in the crazy one. Sam felt as though he stood in the middle of the ring and waited.

"If only she hadn't died," his father kept repeating.

"Dad," Sam said again. "Please. Is this money? Just tell me."

His father took a deep, shivering breath and spoke. "You're not crazy."

Sam bent to pick up several bills. "I see," he said, his voice ice.

"No," his father said, wiping his nose and then shaking his body as though shaking the tears off. "You don't see."

"Then tell me," Sam said, tossing the money up in the air so that it fluttered to the ground like a game show. "Tell me what I don't see. Tell me why we've starved and moved and lived in a van. Tell me why I've never had any friends or known anyone outside of you. Tell me!"

"Because the things you don't see can hurt you," his father shouted back. "But if you don't see them, they can't get to you as quickly. Or as easily." His father stopped. "Sit down, son. And not in the money."

Sam remained standing, defiant, in the thousands of dollars his father had hidden from him. "So…" Sam began sarcastically. "No, wait, let me guess. You love to camp, so you thought it'd be fun to spend the last twelve years living out of cars and trailers and eating refried beans."

Sam's father pressed his fists into his temples and took a deep breath. "Son, all money comes from somewhere."

"Right," Sam said, laughing meanly. "Like how this money came from a hollow door where you were hiding it."

His father took his fists off his temples and stared a straight line into Sam's eyes. It hurt for Sam to hold the stare. He glanced down and his father spoke. "And some money comes from places it shouldn't— from crime and murder and coercion. In some circles, they call that dirty money. That's the kind of money my family left to me. Money that never should have been gotten the way it was. When I met your mother, I saw a reason for change. Ever since then, I've been trying to make it on my own."

"But you kept it," Sam said accusingly. "This 'dirty' money."

"I kept it so if I ever couldn't make it on my own—and trust me, it's not easy when you're moving every few months selling something no one wants to buy—I could feed you. And I did. Not well. Not on roasts and Italian cheeses, but I fed you. And clothed you. It hasn't been easy, son. Especially without your mother." His father paused. "I know it might sound crazy, but I've done all this so that you could have a normal life."

That did sound crazy. Sam laughed—a choked sort of sound. "So how did your family get the money?"

"The truth is that I don't want you to know. They did a lot of things they shouldn't have. Developed things they shouldn't have. My father's side anyway. He was involved with several dealings with a group called The Pack, which controls a *lot* of money. Your mother was familiar with this group too, but for a whole different set of reasons."

That was not nearly enough explanation about how they were standing in thousands of dollars, but Sam would ask more later.

"And the picture?" he said.

"I didn't want you to know about your aunt."

"Why?" Sam asked.

"Because your mother's sister is dead too."

"Did she marry into a bunch of mobsters as well?"

"I would not exactly call my family mobsters. And no. Your mother and her sister grew up in a compound—mostly secluded from the outside world."

"A compound controlled by The Pack?"

"A compound controlled by the people who control The Pack, and other groups like it."

"So…a master mob."

His father did not contradict him. "The Ring of the Alpha," he said.

"What?" Sam asked.

"That's what The Pack called them—'The Ring of the Alpha.'"

"And was it like one of those weird religious compounds?"

"Sort of. Minus the religion. But, yes, isolation and a different sort of indoctrination. When your mother and her sister were young women, they broke out with some help from some of the servants within the compound. Your aunt actually ran off and eloped with one of those servants. And shortly after that, your mother and I met." He took a deep breath. "For several years, the sisters were thought dead. Our life was pretty good. And then your aunt's husband was found alive. He didn't stay that way for long.

"After that, things got tough. After that we started to move. We became rovers; vagrants. It's been a hard life and one I never anticipated, but I haven't looked back. Through it I got both your mother and you. I've lost one and couldn't bear to lose the other."

"So how did she die—my mother?" Sam asked. "Really."

"Uterine cancer, like I've always told you."

Sam raised an eyebrow.

His father sighed. "But the reason it advanced as quickly as it did was that your mother hid it. I didn't know until she collapsed one day —just standing there by the sink in the kitchen. I rushed her to the hospital, though she'd always refused to go to the doctor or any medical facility after her years on the compound. But it was too late. She never regained consciousness. The cancer had spread everywhere. I'd just let her die under my nose."

Sam looked at his father who was crying again. It was all super crazy—so crazy that it seemed it would be difficult for his dad to be making it up.

"If what you say is true," Sam said, "then why would we still have to run? Why would they care about you? Or me? You didn't help her break out of that compound like my...my *uncle* did. And it's not like I know anything about their compound; it's not like I could report them to the police or anything."

His father made a face. "The Ring of the Alpha does not fear the police. But it also does not enjoy losing face. I took more than money. I claimed your mother—one of their greatest prizes. And then I hid her from them."

Sam shook his head, confused.

His father sighed. "Your mother and her sister had a gift, a gift that this group needed." He paused. "Luckily the gift has not been passed to you. Your mother's marriage to me took that away from you. This has made us less of a priority to them. That's a good thing. Even so, I know more than I should. And you might know more than you think you do. Though I hope not."

Sam could only stare at his father. He had no idea what he was talking about.

"Listen," his father said. "Whatever happens to you in the next few weeks or months or years, know this—anyone from The Ring of the Alpha claiming to want to help you doesn't. No matter how much it might start to seem that you're like them, you're not. They know it. And they don't like it. Your kind—a child created by two people like your mother and me—this world has no place for you. The world will fear you. And The Ring of the Alpha will do worse than that. It will hunt you—try to control you. Don't let them. Please."

His father's last plea was so earnest that Sam couldn't do anything but nod. Still, he was worried his dad was crazy. What was he even talking about? Of course Sam wasn't going to go off with some gang or mob or whatever The Ring of the Alpha was.

He thought of his father's mother with her strapped arms and writhing body and then the words came to him—psychosis, paranoia. "Dad," he said. "I think we need help."

And with that his father roared—deep, throaty, heavy, almost inhuman. "No," his father shouted, the raspy deep word, pressing through Sam's skin. "Now sit down."

Sam sat.

"There are a few things you should know. I'm not..." he began. "I'm not normal. That's true. There are times...times when I could change into something I don't wish to be. As you get older, there's a part of you that might feel this too. And there are a few things you must do to avoid becoming like them—like I was before I met your mother."

Bi-polar, Sam added to the list of his father's possible mental illnesses.

"And if you ever…" his father went on and then stopped. "If your body ever starts to feel out of control, then just don't…"

Sam bit his lip, remembering the night he broke the window.

"Well, if you ever lose control, just don't—well, never mind, it won't happen. It can't."

"If I ever what?" Sam asked.

"Listen. Sometimes you'll have headaches or dizziness. And hunger. The hunger is the worst part. It feels like it will eat you. But it won't. Trust me, it won't. Just fight it."

Sam didn't want to talk about hunger, about control. "The picture, Dad. Tell me about it. Tell me about my aunt."

His father sighed, a long, deep breath that seemed to empty him. "After her…after your aunt's husband died—your aunt cut herself off from the family. She'd stolen some sort of artifact from the compound and she seemed to believe that it was putting the ones she loved at risk. So instead of getting rid of what she stole, she distanced herself from the family. She always sent your mom postcards though—every few months—always from a different location. And she had a little girl. You should know that." His father looked away. *You should know that.*

Sam did know that. In a way, he'd always known it. "So you think it's her," Sam asked, forgetting to be angry. "You think it's Ella? She's my cousin."

"I don't think anything," his dad said, still staring into his corner.

"It is," Sam said, catching his father's eye. "It is her and you *do* know it. And you know that there *was* something about her mother."

"There was something about the whole family," his father said. "They wind up dead. If she is Christa's daughter, then she's the only Peterson left. Stay away from her."

Sam looked at his dad. "But she's my cousin."

"All the more reason."

When David Witten showed up at Mitchell Jones' house, Jones barely cracked open the door. "What?" he said gruffly.

"She's been here," Witten said.

"That's no concern of yours," Jones retorted.

"It wasn't a question," Witten replied. "The child is in danger—carries danger around her like the flu."

"Yes," Jones said slowly. "Yes, I had noticed that."

"Take this," Witten said, shoving a small item into the farmer's hand.

"What is it?" Jones asked, fingering the silver chain.

"I found it on one of the carriers—the doctor. The stone that belonged to it was already gone."

"And what am I to do with it?" Jones asked.

"Make it into something," Witten replied. "Something the child can use to protect herself."

The farmer pressed his lips together. "I hate getting mixed up in all of this."

"The day you picked up your first stray dog, you got mixed up in it," Witten said.

"The day I picked up an injured young man in the woods of Montana I got mixed up in it worse."

"I know," Witten replied.

"I should have taken you back to the commune."

Witten smiled—a long, slow change to his face. "But you didn't," he said, then held out his hand to shake.

Jones took it, and for a moment the two men were friends again.

CHAPTER 35

Ella sifted through the old stones in her mother's jewelry box. A chipped moonstone a vendor had given them for free at a lapidary show. A long, straight shard of kyanite, blue like the sky. A smooth chunk of sea-wave green chrysocolla. And labradorite, one of her mother's favorite stones—gray with oil spots of color puddled throughout. Ella fingered the stone. She had almost used it for her mother's necklace. But she hadn't.

She set it down, thinking about the stone that had been gray shot through with streaks of silver—the stone she'd used on the necklace that was now lost.

Ella was pretty sure it was the inspiration piece for the stone in the stories her mother had written. Maybe that's why her mother had treasured it so much. Ella flopped onto the floor near the jewelry box and pulled out a page from her mother's stack.

There were few who could carry it. The stone of source.
None of the Changers, except the rare but mighty Silverlords. And

few of the humans. The alchemy of the stone was odd, perhaps enchanted. Created during an ancient time when the metals of the humans were wound through with the magics of their world, only a few strong and pure of heart could bear the stone.

Through the ages, this human bloodline began to fade. They were hunted by Changers, shifters hungry for the power to change the suns; and they were hunted by the humans desperate to thwart any change. Hunted. Through the dark ages and crusades and witch trials. Until only a thin strand remained.

One could find this small line of descendants because they could still hear the voices of the dogs at every full moon—a gift they learned to hide so well that eventually their children's children's children did not think to look for such a gift, and worried if they happened upon it.

And perhaps that blessed-cursed bloodline could have remained hidden were it not for the shifters and madmen of this world—those who concocted potions and brews—elixirs intended to uncover the gifted humans whom they sought. Year after year, century after century, they experimented. Eventually, the human hunters died off— science replacing mythology.

But shifters had longer memories and hidden ways. Over the years, one rose to power, stumbling upon a serum that would change color with the blood of the Bearers. And so he began to work in blood —white coat, clean hands—his methods for hunting advanced, refined, evolved—alchemy giving way to chemistry.

ELLA LOOKED DOWN AT HER POLO SHIRT. SHE'D BEEN PICKING AT IT AS she read, and now she'd managed to unravel half the hem. She dragged herself off the floor and stumped downstairs to see if she could find a pair of scissors.

She couldn't. But there in Vivi's kitchen drawer was a tiny spool of red floss. It was soft and smooth, almost garish in Vivi's black and white house.

Ella had never seen her aunt do any kind of crafting or sewing. As near as Ella could tell, there was no other thread or even any ribbon anywhere. Vivi's house was as clean and as sparse as a monastery—void of extras or sentiment of any kind.

Finding the spool of floss was like finding a piece of colored glass in plain, brown sand. Ella took it out and might have just kept it in her pocket as some kind of good luck charm if she hadn't thought of her mother's ring.

Ella ran back upstairs and dug the ring out of the jewelry box, then unraveled a bit of the floss, looping it over the band of the ring until it fit her finger snugly, until she was sure she wouldn't lose it.

Wearing the ring felt comforting—like a piece of her mother could be with her all the time. Everything about it—from the decorative 'C' to the blocky, funky square—reminded her of her mother. Somehow Ella knew that hundreds of secrets were contained in that tiny ring, secrets Ella would probably never know, but she wanted to have close to her anyway.

WHEN JACK CAME A FEW MINUTES LATER FOR THEIR SESSION, HE noticed the ring immediately. "Where'd you get that pretty thing?" he asked, touching her hand and holding it up so he could examine the ring more closely.

Jack turned her hand over, and then raised an eyebrow when he saw that it was wrapped with floss. "It's not yours," he said. "Do kids still give each other their rings when they're dating?"

The word 'kids' stung, and Ella stumbled over her explanation. "Oh, well, no, I mean, maybe, but it's not from anyone else. I mean, it kind of is, but not at school. It's, well, it was, it's my mother's." She blushed as she spoke—hot streaks of red shooting from her neck to her forehead.

Jack laughed and squeezed her hand before letting it go. "Oh good. I thought you'd gone and gotten yourself a boyfriend."

"Oh, no," Ella said quickly, "I...no, I didn't." The blush felt like a fever now.

Jack laughed again. "Well, good. If you had a boyfriend, you might get too busy for me."

He was obviously kidding, but Ella felt like she wanted to stick her head in a bucket of ice. Fortunately Vivi chose that moment to come out with two glasses of water in hand. Ella took quick gulps, which almost made her miss the meaningful glance Jack shot Vivi as he nodded at Ella's finger.

"Oh, Ella," Vivi said, setting the pitcher of water down. "That's pretty. And unusual. Where'd you get it?"

Ella was relieved that Vivi wasn't also surmising that Ella had found herself a significant other.

"It was my mom's," she said between sips of water.

Vivi took Ella's hand and looked slowly at the ring—turning it so she could see it from each angle.

"It's gorgeous," she said. "The 'C' is for Christa I suppose."

"I guess," Ella said. She was actually kind of surprised at the attention her aunt gave it. And a little pleased. There were times, many times, that Vivi had seemed almost uninterested in anything about her mother. Ella was glad to see that her aunt seemed to appreciate the small artifact from a part of Christa's life that she had missed.

"May I?" Vivi asked, touching the ring as though to slip it off.

Ella took it off and handed it to her aunt, who peered closely at the small square of metal, touching the engraved "C" as though some dark secret would be released. She didn't look like she wanted to give it back.

Finally, gingerly, Ella held out her palm, smiling at her aunt. Her aunt smiled back and returned the ring, her fingers cold.

SAM JOGGED TO THE ENTRANCE OF THE HAVENSBOROUGH UNIT—THE door with the code that he couldn't crack. It was different from the main entrance with its urgency and bustle. At Havensborough, very few people went in. Employees occasionally—men and women in quiet suits or white lab coats. Nurses with plain, green scrubs.

Sometimes other people went in too—never in handcuffs or straight-jackets, never fighting police officers or laid out on stretchers. But they went in. A slow walk, an empty gaze—every step seemingly willing, yet somehow forced. Parents and children with tear-streaked faces, adults leading their elderly relatives with a sad, stoic grip.

The more Sam came to stare at the building, the more he realized that even the walkers and joggers avoided this entrance, preferring instead the hurry and rush of the front doors or the distant, winding paths of the grounds.

Even the door seemed to discourage entering or leaving—a slender gray line against the pale limestone face of the building. One thing, though—you could be young or old, ugly or beautiful, poor or rich. The Havensborough Unit did not discriminate. At this door—you could slip in, but it seemed to Sam that precious few slipped back out again.

This was the door Sam had to face. Somehow he was sure it held Zinnie and it was the door he worried would someday hold him.

He fingered the $100 bill in his pocket. He wasn't, at least, crazy, though part of him still wished he was. He hadn't hallucinated the money that had fallen from the inside of his father's bedroom door, or the lie his dad had told him about the picture of his grandmother. He hadn't hallucinated Ella's resemblance to his maternal grandmother or the headaches he'd started to have.

Because of that, he was pretty sure that the number that danced through his head and the old woman who had given it to him were also real. But he needed to know.

He believed now that the number was a code. If he could crack the code and get in, the code was real. If the code was real, the code giver was real, too. If the code and code giver were real, then he could get inside this door.

He wasn't quite sure why he would want to, why he would enter the one place that had scared him since they'd gotten to this town, but he did.

He needed to know why he'd found a woman who seemed to be able to disappear and reappear and make posts out of candy for children to crawl through.

Was she trying to trick him into the stove, or save him from it?

CHAPTER 36

The senator walked in wearing a trim navy suit—fitted and double stitched. The hemline rested tastefully below her knees, hiding all but the tip of a dark scar peeking out.

"To what," Napper said politely, "do I owe the honor?"

"To my nervousness," she said bluntly, sitting down and waving away the cup of tea Napper pushed toward her.

"Over what, my dear?"

"You may call me Senator McKinney."

"I made you, child, and I may call you what I will." He blew gently across the top of his tea, no anger in his voice, or eyes either, though she felt the pulse of it heat up the room.

"I'm just worried," the senator said, her tone softer. "One of the pieces has been discovered. When we thought it completely destroyed; when you gave us your assurance that this was so." She straightened her skirt as she spoke, tugging it over the ugly scar.

"Yes," he said slowly. "It is somewhat miraculous that it survived the crash all those years ago."

"And the other piece—the Ursa Major," she asked. "Have you made any kind of search for it?"

"None whatsoever," he said smoothly. "If it is in existence at all, there is no need of recovery. Even with the discovery of the smaller Ursa Minor. Once the minor and major are broken apart, one would have to find both pieces—a near impossibility. And then one would have to realize they must be fitted back together again. And then, of course, a genius would be needed to know how the device must be used."

"There are geniuses," she said matter-of-factly. "You of all people should know that."

He smiled. "As well I do. And a terrible burden it is, my child. But to find the pieces, which even our best could not, then to reassemble them into one, and to make use of the object. It is a statistical impossibility."

"There are more than statistics at play," the senator said.

"The old woman has been committed."

"And for how long this time?"

"For as long as necessary."

"Unless you plan to kill her in there, it cannot be long enough for me." The Senator looked to her knee where she knew the long scar bulged up above her otherwise flawless skin.

"We have no plans to kill her, but the dear cannot cheat death forever, can she?"

Senator McKinney knotted her delicate brows together.

"Her medicine has been more heavily dosed; her time is close," he said.

"Not close enough," the senator replied, touching the scar on her knee. "And if the minor and major are reunited…"

"Then what?" he interrupted. "It is too late. The wolves gather, our people convene, the girl is here."

"Then they will know, and knowing, they will resist."

"The powerful ones of their kind have been able to do nothing. Look at your own human-filled councils. And as for the child, she is young. She can hardly resist her own hormones, much less a force such as ours."

The senator pinched her lips together. "And the Rogue? The Rogue will surely make a grab for the girl if given the chance. "

"The Rogue is annoying as ever, but easily enough contained. Our goals, at least, are the same."

"Hardly," the senator said.

"Mostly." Napper drained his cup of tea. "We need the girl, the solstice, and the stone."

"The Rogue is a potential threat to the council, your plan, every-thing. And we don't even know yet who he is."

"No," Napper replied. "The Rogue has left surprisingly few clues concerning identity. However the Rogue would not stop the sun change even if it was possible to do so."

"But the Rogue is not on our side."

"Obviously," the old man said, to the clear annoyance of his protégé. "But he is not on their side either. The Rogue, I'm afraid, is on The Rogue's side—a lone wolf." Napper paused, the sides of his mouth turning up almost imperceptibly. "If you will."

The senator sighed. "We are not the only ones with power."

"Perhaps not." Quietly, he looked at the now empty tea cup in front of him. Pulling back a long finger, he suddenly tapped the cup with such focused force that it crumbled to pieces on its plate. "But we are the only ones with clear focus. With intention. And it is only that focus that can shatter this lesser existence that has been thrust upon us"—he pressed a finger into the ceramic bits and then blew the tiny particles toward the senator's dark suit—"to dust."

CHAPTER 37

Ella went into her bedroom, dropped her bag, and walked past the full-length mirror before she saw it—the long red dress laid out on her bed. It was an impossibly deep color, floor length with slender sleeves, shimmering and heavy against the tissue paper and white blankets beneath it. It was a stark point of color in the bland room, matched only by the red sun in the painting on the wall. Something about that made Ella shiver. It was beautiful.

She reached out to touch the dress. It was made of smooth, satiny fabric and had a fitted bodice with a skirt that moved like water. It was weird that Vivi had left it there. She must have brought it up here for some reason, laid it down, and gotten distracted. Which seemed very un-Vivi.

"So what do you think?" Vivi asked from behind her.

Ella jumped. Her aunt wasn't usually home from work yet, and she had come up to the bedroom door as quietly as an animal.

"It's gorgeous," Ella said. "What will you be wearing it for?"

"I won't," her aunt said, laughing. "It's for you."

Ella just stared at her.

"The Festival of the Red Candle," Vivi said, answering the question Ella hadn't asked.

"Your fundraiser?"

"Yes," Vivi said. "A poem is read and a ceremonial stone is placed after the candles are lit every year. They wanted someone from the high school to do it; they were thinking of holding a contest. But I had a better idea. Beautiful niece. Clear voice. It seemed a lot easier. Mr. Napper liked the idea too. The thought of tryouts with dramatic high-school-aged teenagers made him nervous. He didn't want the entire female body of the Thespian club to eat each other." Vivi smiled, but Ella was still too shell-shocked to return it.

"So I volunteered you. Will you do it?" Vivi asked.

Ella was flattered, but a little worried too. She thought about Sarah. Sarah might have eaten someone to be able to do a reading at The Property. But probably not—she was all teeth and no bite. Instead she would have spent the night bawling into her pillow if she had auditioned and not gotten the part. So it *was* probably better just to pick someone. Ella just wasn't sure if it was better to pick her.

"Well," Vivi said, "go try it on."

Ella could barely touch the dress much less put it on her body. It had probably cost more than her mother's last month of rent. Plus, waltzing out of the bathroom to display it to her aunt instead of her mother made her feel like crying. "Well, okay, maybe," Ella said. "I…"

Vivi picked up the dress, lifting it from the tissue paper. She let the heavy fabric fall through her hands and over her fingers. It looked like sand the way it moved, like blood-red sand through an hourglass—smooth, glittering, suffocating.

"I don't know," Ella said suddenly. "Do you think I'm the right person for it?"

"Oh, of course," Vivi said, looking up from the dress. "And it'll be a really good opportunity for you to meet lots of influential people. Mr. Napper, of course. And the mayor, the head of the school board, lots of other people too."

Vivi must have seen the way all those names seemed to discourage Ella more than encourage her because she said, "But don't worry, not all the faces will be unfamiliar. Mr. Sanderson will be there."

"Jack?" Ella said, trying to sound nonchalant and looking at the dress. "How come?"

"Oh—I guess I never told you. His mom is well connected with Mr. Napper."

"Oh," Ella said, touching the dress.

"Here," Vivi said, putting the gown into Ella's arms. "You don't have to decide now. Just think about it."

Ella held the heavy red dress and nodded.

"I didn't mean to thrust this on you," Vivi said. "I just thought it might be a good opportunity. And a lot of fun. But you don't have to do it if you don't want to." She nodded at Ella and left.

Ella held the dress a moment more, then turned to the mirror. She let the full skirt fall down and held the dress in front of her. She had never owned something so expensive or beautiful before. She had never been *that girl.*

She slipped out of her clothes and put the dress on. It fit like a magical glove—tight and loose in all the right places, bendable, but gorgeous. At the bottom were tiny stitches of shimmering gold that formed a sort of sun and moon pattern along the hem.

Downstairs she heard Jack's voice. She looked once more at her reflection in the mirror. Maybe she would go. Maybe.

She slid out of the dress and back into her normal clothes, which seemed scratchy and stiff in comparison. Across the room, she looked at her mother's jewelry box—so plain and square and small. Then she laid the dress on the bed and went down for her session with Jack.

Vivi set fruit and cheese on the table.

"So," Jack began. "Vivi tells me you might be at the Festival."

"Maybe," Ella said, slightly annoyed that Vivi had said anything at all. "It'd be a really great opportunity."

"Absolutely," Jack said. "It also comes with a decent little scholarship."

Ella looked in Vivi's direction, but her aunt had already left the room.

"Really," Ella asked. "I thought this whole thing was for a fundraiser."

Jack shrugged. "A fundraiser with extremely rich people. Napper always donates the lion's share, of course, and this year he's giving a little something extra for the reader of the poem."

Ella pressed her lips together. She and Vivi hadn't talked about college and paying for it, but Ella knew that Vivi hadn't spent the last sixteen years saving to send a kid to school. "How much is a little something extra?" Ella asked.

"$25,000," Jack said with a smile.

"You're kidding," Ella said, sitting back on the couch.

Jack laughed and said, "But scholarship aside, I need you to come. We'll protect each other from old people overdose."

Ella smiled and Jack winked.

CHAPTER 38

Napper wasn't used to being surprised. And with the discovery of the Ursa Minor, he had been.

He was glad that no one had taken the ring, and he hoped The Rogue would stay out of his way and leave it alone. It was more important to have the child's trust than the bauble on a gold band.

Still, he was more concerned about the Ursa Minor than he had let on. Which is why he had lied to the Senator. He did, in fact, know where the Ursa Major was. He had been watching it since August when the renowned folklorist had arrived in a small town in Indiana. Did the old teacher really think he could slip in under Napper's radar? Napper doubted it.

So if David Witten didn't believe he was unseen, what exactly did he believe? He was here for the Festival—there was no doubt. But to what end? And did he—he who could handle silver unscathed, strengthened even—was he the one who had been responsible for the deaths of the council members. Napper pursed his lips together. *Was* Witten the Rogue? It seemed like it should make sense. And yet it didn't. First of all, Witten should know better than that. He should know that a few killings could not stop a man in Napper's position. He should know, in fact, that a few killings would only heighten the risk of those Witten wished to protect.

And then, of course, there was the issue of teeth. Witten, he was fairly certain, would not want them.

ELLA SAT STARING AT MR. WITTEN'S SILVER BRACELET. NOW THAT she'd seen Jones' work, she could see his hand in it. The band was blocky, thick, not perfectly symmetrical, rustic. That wasn't the weird part.

The weird part was that the metal square that had been connected to it was ornate and delicate, the sides and surface smooth, with an engraving Ella never got a good look at. In a lot of ways the band and the metal square didn't seem to match—one chunky and bohemian, the other intricate and graceful—like two different personalities had gotten stuck together.

Witten wore it every day.

Today they were discussing a lesser-known British tale called "The Ring and the Fish." It was about a wealthy magician who divined that his son would marry a poor peasant girl. The magician promptly sought out the girl and tried to kill her. Because, apparently, that's what you do to a poor person who tries to marry your rich son. The murder plot didn't work and, eventually, the girl married the magician's son. The magician then threatened to push her off a cliff. When she begged mercy, he threw a ring to the river below and told her he didn't want to see her again until she could present the ring to him. Naturally, later when she was employed as a kitchen maid in an inn, the magician and his son came in. And she, hidden away in the kitchens, prepared them a fish which—tada—had the ring inside it. The magician concluded that you couldn't fight destiny and allowed the girl to claim her place as his son's wife.

Lucky her.

The feminists in the class had gone twitchy and were practically dislocating their shoulders in an effort to get their hands the highest so they could comment first.

Behind her, Ella heard Sam mutter, "Who comes up with this crap?"

Ella didn't feel twitchy or annoyed. She felt weird. There was something about the story that reminded her of something in the jewelry box, something her mother had written.

When once a man of perfect wealth
Perfect form and perfect health.
Feared a girl of lowly birth
Planned a plot, her life to curse.
Yet curses cut along both sides
When moonlight floods the black night skies.
A portion of herself, the cost
To break their twine, his fate, his loss.

At that, Ella raised her hand and said, "I think the feminist tones come into this story in the power the girl held throughout over the magician. He just couldn't get rid of her. Or her role in his life." Ella paused. "Granted a modern story might give us a stronger ending."

"Perhaps a retelling then," Mr. Witten said, smiling.

Ella nodded, but inside she groaned. She was dreading doing a story retelling.

She tried to make eye contact with Sam—to share an eye roll or a smile. But he wouldn't look up. He'd been like that a lot lately. Ella leaned forward in her chair, looked down at her mostly blank notebook, and sighed.

SAM HADN'T REALIZED HOW MESSED UP MOST FAIRY TALES WERE UNTIL they'd started talking about them in Folklore. No Disney princesses need apply.

One thing about today's story had gotten him thinking though. The ring—it had been hidden. But the fish was right there in plain sight. Which, of course, is the best way to hide a thing.

Now Sam sat in history class doodling on his notebook. They'd been talking about World War II for weeks. It was actually interesting enough stuff, except that it seemed Mr. Dillimon worked extra hard to make it uninteresting.

The kid next to Sam had been nodding off almost since class began, and now he had fully given it up and was leaning his head forward, drooling over his notes. Mr. Dillimon kept shooting him dirty looks, which Sam figured were pretty ineffective considering the kid's state of consciousness.

Sam managed to keep his eyes open, but his head was somewhere else. He thought of Ella, and how he was supposed to stay away from her. He thought of Zinnie and her strange number.

Over and over he sketched the number the old woman had given him. He wrote it in a circle, then backwards, inside out, upside down.

Sam knew he needed to think about the numbers in a different way, but he couldn't figure out how. He had looked for a pattern between the numbers; he'd added, subtracted, multiplied, square rooted. He'd taken to running past the Havensborough Unit in the evenings after it closed and trying each new number in the keyboard. If they'd had a security camera outside, they surely would have admitted him by now.

Sam felt almost sure that the number Zinnie had given him would lead him to another number that would let him in. But why hadn't she just given him the number if she knew it? And what was the number? Sam hated a problem he couldn't solve. He hated a pattern he couldn't find.

Mr. Dillimon droned on about World War II, and then there it was. The answer.

During the Second World War, the U.S. used a group of Navajo men who were also fluent in English to out-code the German and Japanese codebreakers. Navajo was so little known that these men— the Navajo code talkers—would nickname a plane, say, "Hummingbird," and then use the Navajo word, Da-he-tih-hi, to talk about it. In this way, the Americans stayed a step ahead of their enemies.

Zinnie wasn't speaking Navajo, but Sam felt certain she was giving him a word. And then that word…? Sam thought about it for a minute —that word would be typed into the keypad in the same way you'd type 1-800-PAPAJOHNS into a phone. The letters would match up with certain numbers on a keypad.

But first Sam had to figure out the word.

While his teacher went on about the conclusion of the war, Sam wrote out the number Zinnie had given him:

1891471121681

It would be tricky to crack it because the numbers could match up to letters of the alphabet as single digits or double digits—1 2 could be A B or it could be the 12th letter, L.

He wrote out the alphabet with the numbers underneath:

A	B	C	D	E	F	G	H	I	J	K	L	M
1	2	3	4	5	6	7	8	9	10	11	12	13
N	O	P	Q	R	S	T	U	V	W	X	Y	Z
14	15	16	17	18	19	20	21	22	23	24	25	26

Then he wrote the number code as if each number was its own letter:

A	H	I	A	D	G	A	A	B	A	F	H	A
1	8	9	1	4	7	1	1	2	1	6	8	1

That was a lot of 1's/A's. Some of them were surely combined, but there were combinations of numbers that wouldn't work like 47 or 81. That meant that the last letter had to be an A. He'd try the rest as combinations.

18—R
9—I
14—N
7—G
11—K
2—B
16—P
8—H
1—A

That gave him RINGKBPHA. Sam cocked his head to the side and looked at it.

RING.

RING something. Something in plain sight that he was just missing.

He looked at the numbers again. And then he saw it. Instead of 11, he could leave the first 1 as an A and combine the 12 that followed it. That would give him RINGALPHA. RingAlpha. The Ring of the Alpha. The mob his father had mentioned—that was Zinnie's code. But why? And why was she making him work so hard for this?

He'd figure that out later. For now, he needed a number. If RINGALPHA was the letter code and he typed that into a keyboard with numbers, he'd get:

746425742

There, the number was in his head. Unfortunately, no information about the last half of Mr. Dillimon's lecture was.

"Samuel," Mr. Dillimon said, tapping Sam's desk. "I see that you are anxiously engaged in your notes. Could you please explain to the class the cultural reasons for Japan's resistance to the idea of surrender, even when it became clear they would lose the war?"

Sam cleared his throat and felt the sweat prick up along his back. He was sick of losing face in every class that didn't involve numbers.

Suddenly, he looked up. "The Japanese did not want to lose face," Sam said, glancing at the previous day's notes. "Their image and honor had been culturally important to them throughout the war."

Mr. Dillimon glanced down at Sam's notebook just as Sam closed it.

"Yes, Samuel, that pretty much sums it up." Mr. Dillimon looked disappointed.

Sam didn't mind. Mr. Dillimon had given him something this history class had never given him before. It had opened a door. At least Sam hoped it had.

~

SAM SHOWED UP AT ELLA'S HOUSE AS THE SKY BROKE INTO ORANGE streaks and the temperature began to drop. No one was home. He'd wanted to show her—show her he wasn't crazy before he told her they were cousins. He knocked on the door three times before giving up and walking slowly down her street. He was wearing faded cargo pants and the old tennis shoes he always wore. Walking past driveways with hybrids and Lexuses he became somewhat more aware of himself as he walked faster and faster, slipping into a run the way some people sink into sleep.

When he got to the Havensborough Unit, his hands were shaking. 746425742

The click was quiet, but solid. Sam pushed open the door and held it for a moment before letting it fall closed behind him.

He stood in a waiting room—a stark, geometrical office that contained a desk with a flat screen computer. The door to his right would lead to the main hospital. The door to his left—he had no idea—doctor's offices probably with the patients' rooms on the floors above. The light was fading fast and Sam was starving. He shivered.

The bareness of the room was odd. There were no pictures of loved ones, no cat memes or cute calendars. There wasn't so much as a coffee mug.

Sam moved the chair away from the computer—he didn't want to sit in it. Instead he knelt in front of the desk. The computer asked for a password. Sam typed in the code again and just like that the screen whirred into action.

"Well, that was easy," he muttered to himself, frowning.

After having to navigate a code that went from number to word and back to number to get here, something didn't feel quite right about easy.

He began looking for Zinnie's name among the lists of patients with room numbers.

She wasn't there.

Sam realized that that didn't surprise him at all. And yet he felt sure Zinnie was in here, hidden beneath another code he didn't understand.

Sam clicked through patient after patient—there were pictures, home addresses, even next of kin. There were diagnoses—depression, schizophrenia, bipolar disorders I and II, narcolepsy, phobias, anxieties, and psychoses of various types. Two types of psychosis appeared more often than anything else: icanthropy and pTr4. Sam had never heard of either of them.

Perhaps even stranger was another diagnosis—listed only once, at the bottom of the page. It was not attached to a patient name, and not a common word.

Still, something felt familiar about it, some memory Sam couldn't grab.

Miscegenatosis.

Underneath the word Sam read the name of a single medication with the words 'patent pending' beside it.

Sam clicked an icon in the right corner hoping for more information about the diagnosis. Instead, he came to a screen reading, "Further identification required; please insert disc." Sam tapped his finger against the desk for a minute, but the sound was too loud for the room. Pinching his lips together, he back-clicked and tried another link. There he found spreadsheets for billing, telephone numbers, death certificates. He found everything.

Except Zinnie.

Outside the sun hung only a pale wisp over the horizon. Soon it would be completely dark. Sam shut down the computer and stood to leave. There was something wrong about tonight.

Obvious. But out of sight.

Like any good code.

CHAPTER 39

Ella sifted through her mother's papers, looking for a bit of inspiration for her own retelling. She'd always loved Beauty and the Beast as well as Sleeping Beauty. Rapunzel was cool, too.

But her mother just wrote wolves. Wolves, wolves, and wolves.

Once, in a land turned on its head, two sons were born to a Lord of the Silver—he who could handle the potent metal, drawing strength from it, instead of harm. The Silverlord had possessed a powerful stone, but it was not his to bear, and when the right time had come, he'd given it up to a human boy.

This stone now haunted the sons of the Silverlord—calling to them, though in different ways.

The oldest watched as his kind were driven from the land—forced back by the human queen's penchant for silver. From the woods the oldest son gathered his kind, rousing them to action, fighting so hard for equality that he began to forget the balance of the word—too eager to tip the scales in the favor of his people, to restore them to what had been. He remembered the myths of the stone, the stories that sang of the Promise Giver—the great Sarak who had touched the stone, sacrificing himself, and leaving his mark. Because of the small power Sarak had infused into the stone, the shifters might have power to turn back the worlds, igniting their fates and changing the tide. But they would need both the stone and the Bearer.

The younger brother sought the stone for different reasons. He recognized that, though it had brought some evil, the stone had also given much good. The humans and shifters could now be equal partners. And many were—working together to build and run cities, to farm, to industrialize, marrying and bearing children. The dogs and wolves had run of the land and its bounty. And the attachment of some of the canines to the humans had grown into bonds of friendship that often lasted through generations. Thus, the younger son did not seek the stone to keep or use it, only to uphold his father's legacy, to protect the stone and with it the stone Bearers.

Time went on. As the older hunted, the younger shielded. As the older sought out, the younger concealed. As the older rallied shifters, the younger tried to still them.

The sons grew into fathers and grandfathers. Their lineage spread. Among their progeny, few could handle the mighty silver as their father had been able to do, although occasionally one would arise among them able to touch the untouchable.

And so it is to this day. The sons of the first seek the stone—its power and ability to change the sun and with it the balance of power. While the sons of the second seek to protect the stone and the Bearers —to fulfill their duty as Silverlords, to save the humans and their own.

Ella smiled. Her mother had often ended her stories that way. "To this day…" as though beasts and princes still wandered among them. Ella sighed—holding the papers to her chest. She missed her mother. Missed her like she would the sun if it fell from the sky.

THE ROGUE WALKED IN TO THE POST OFFICE AND QUIETLY SLID A KEY into the post office box. The package had come today just as promised.

Another shiny bullet double-wrapped and placed in a tiny copper box. Tied up with a bit of red floss.

The Rogue smiled, glad the silver supplier was so punctual. The Rogue did not wish to have bits of silver sitting around for any longer than necessary. A bullet would be needed this month. And the next. Tomorrow night would be especially busy. After that, the Rogue hoped there would be no more worrying about what to do with the council.

The Rogue walked several blocks, slipped into an old coffee shop and found the corner booth.

Napper had been annoyingly prompt in recruiting new members for the council. There were several in town right now who could, if Napper wished, take their place among the Ring. Still, they both knew that the new members could not possibly learn everything it had taken decades for the old members to know. That, of course, was a practical matter—an advantage to the plan.

The revenge, on the other hand, that the silver bullets had given— that was purely sweet. The Rogue sipped the espresso, quietly licking the empty holes where four sharp canine teeth should have been.

CHAPTER 40

Ella walked home with her coat tight around her. Fall was slowly closing its doors, and the days were so short that by the time school let out dusty pinks were already rising from the horizon—gentle for another hour or so until the weight of the sun darkened and deepened into the reds and purples of dusk. The steam from her breath misted around her face and she burrowed deeper into her coat.

Vivi would be home in an hour. She'd taken to buying Ella pizza on Monday night, though Vivi usually just had a chicken breast herself.

Tonight Ella had a different idea.

She walked past the still-green lawn of the country club and up her aunt's trim little street. Her street, Ella reminded herself. Her street, her house, her aunt. She and Vivi still didn't connect well, but Ella was trying to do better.

She walked up to her bedroom and took off her shoes. Vivi often went to the country club in the evenings. Tonight, instead of bumming a ride from Sarah to go to the farm, Ella intended to ask Vivi if she was up for a game of tennis.

Ella's mother had loved tennis and taught Ella at a young age. Even when money was tight they'd throw on their Goodwill shorts and old tshirts and head to the free courts to play. Her mother had not often spoken of her estranged family, but sometimes on those cracking, weedy courts, her mother would tell stories about her older sister teaching her to play.

Ella didn't have to wear an old t-shirt and shorts now. When she'd told Vivi she liked tennis, her aunt had bought her a white tennis skirt and matching polo. She put it on and hurried down to catch Vivi as she came through the front door.

Her aunt looked up as Ella came down. "Hey," Vivi said, walking toward the kitchen. "You headed to the club?"

"Yeah," Ella said. "Well maybe." She tried to catch her aunt's eye. "I was hoping to catch a ride with you. I thought maybe we could play a few rounds of tennis together."

Her aunt smiled. "Oh, that'd be great, Ella, but I actually have some work to catch up on tonight." She pulled out a bag of lettuce.

Ella felt the openness of her smile fade.

Maybe Vivi noticed Ella's response because she put down her tomato and said, "You go today without me. Maybe next week we can go for a swim together."

Ella looked at her aunt for a minute. "You don't want to play tennis?" Ella asked.

"Well," Vivi said, still smiling with so many white teeth that Ella wished just one would turn brown right then and there. "The truth is, I'm just not that good."

Ella did her best to hide her reaction—the anger pushed from her stomach, like fire into her lungs and then burst into her skull. "Oh, um, okay. Maybe another day." She turned quickly. A look of concern crossed Vivi's face. Ella didn't care. She ran up the steps two at a time, then stripped off her clothes and threw on a flannel and jeans. Why would Vivi lie like that? Right to her face? Ella knew her aunt could play tennis. It was the one precious detail her mother had bothered to share about the aunt that would one day show up and become her guardian.

Ella took several deep breaths, trying to think it through. Maybe her aunt had gotten injured at some point. Or maybe she was out of shape. Or maybe—Ella felt her body slump on the bed and the explosion in her head turn to a black hole—maybe Vivi didn't want to. Maybe tennis reminded her of Ella's mother. Just as quickly as the rage had burned through her, Ella felt it snuff out—a trail of ashes through her guts.

Ella heard a soft tap at the door.

"Ella," Vivi's voice said. "Why don't you go to the club today? I'm sure I can spare a few minutes to give you a ride."

"No," Ella said loudly enough for Vivi to hear through the door that she wasn't quite ready to open. "It's okay. I'll text Sarah and figure something out."

"You sure?" Vivi said.

"Yup," Ella chirped, all the brightness she could muster in that one little word.

Ella listened to her aunt's nearly soundless footsteps pad down the hall before she texted Sarah. "Wanna take me to the farm tonight? I'll introduce you to the dogs."

"Sounds good, but I can only stay a few minutes. I have dance tonight at 5:00. I'll pick you up after and we'll do something."

"K," Ella tapped back.

"Maybe I'll bring Sam."

Ella smiled and texted an emoji with a fat pair of lips back to Sarah. Maybe she and Vivi would never be normal, but she had friends at least—slightly crazy friends, yes, but friends who could do normal things like crush on each other and try to pretend they weren't.

Sarah texted back—" my butt."

～

JONES WASN'T AROUND WHEN ELLA AND SARAH GOT TO THE FARM. A few weeks ago that would have made Ella uncomfortable, but she'd spent almost every weekday afternoon here for most of November, and she felt at home with the animals. She and Sarah sat in the front yard while the chickens pecked through the cornfields to the south. Ella put two fingers in her mouth and whistled three shrill blasts.

"You trying to call them or deafen them?" Sarah asked, pressing her ears.

Loco was the first one there. Ella was happy to see him—happier than she ever felt to go home to Vivi's house. The other dogs joined them, most bounding over, a few trickling in. Sheila walked right over to Sarah and sat on her haunches, looking up.

"Well, aren't you just the prettiest, sweetest thing," Sarah cooed.

Ella swore that Sheila smiled, pressing her head against Sarah's thigh, sniffing.

"I have got to bring Mom out here," Sarah said, scratching Sheila's neck. "She'd just die to see this lady."

Ella nodded, distracted. Where were the other dogs? At least three were missing and Ella noticed one, limping slowly toward the yard. She had named her Foxy because she was fast, smart, and small, but now it looked like her paw was tucked up against her leg.

Without taking her eyes off of the dog, Ella started walking toward her. Loco followed closely behind. When Foxy got to the edge of the yard, Ella could see that her paw was not hurt, but missing—completely gone, the stump wrapped tight in a bandage.

"Oh my gosh," Ella said, dropping to look at the small dog. "What happened?"

The dog looked into her eyes like she was about to reply just as a voice said, "We've had a couple wolf attacks lately. Last night, they got three. Foxy was the only one that came back."

Ella stood as Jones flopped a bag of chicken scratch near the chickens' pen. Ella scanned the faces of the dogs again—Curly, Leonard, and Blossom—they were gone.

"But I thought the wolves couldn't leave The Property," Ella stammered. "I thought that was the law."

The farmer shrugged, then made a clicking noise with his mouth. "Supposedly they can't. But there's been a shift in wolf migration patterns. Usually, they just follow the deer herds north or south, but recently several wolf packs from Canada and Montana have headed this way. Even an arctic wolf was purportedly photographed in Indiana recently."

"Crazy," Sarah said, coming up next to Ella with Sheila close.

"Hello, miss," Jones said politely, but with a slightly impatient edge as though annoyed that Ella was bringing even more people to his quiet little farm.

"This is my friend, Sarah," Ella said.

"Nice to meet you," Jones replied, though to Ella's ear it didn't sound quite like he thought it was so nice.

"We met a few years back," Sarah said. "My mom is Fiona Price. She's gotten a couple dogs from you."

"Ah, yes," he said softening. "She's a good woman, Dr. Price." He turned to Ella. "Haven't seen you for a few of days."

"I know I..." she began, but couldn't think up an excuse. She'd met with Jack one night, and there'd been the dress. Vivi had insisted on taking her shopping for shoes right after school the next day, though Ella still wasn't sure she wanted to take part in the Festival.

"Not got much left to do today," Jones said. You guys wanna feed chickens?"

That was better than bathing dogs. Ella turned to Sarah. "Don't you have a dance class?" she whispered.

"Whatever," Sarah said. "I'm skipping it. We get to feed chickens."

They filled up the water trough and feeders and then sprinkled corn among the hens as they scratched and pecked.

"It's like a storybook," Sarah said, her breath misting against the cool evening.

Ella stood with Loco while several of the dogs ran among the chickens. Sheila stayed by Sarah's side. And it *was* like a storybook. Jones brought out hot chocolates and they sat watching the full moon rise.

Slowly, a howling started up near the east reaches of the farm. Ella saw Jones' jaw tighten up and he said, "Let's take these guys in for the night."

To Ella's surprise, they led the dogs into a little barn near the house, and then locked them up like the poultry. Ella could tell the dogs hated it. Several started barking or whining when the door shut. "What about the chickens?" Ella asked.

"Chickens seem safer than the dogs at this point," Jones replied. "Doesn't make sense." He paused. "Those wolves are causing me all kinds of grief. I'm having more trouble training the dogs, especially when I have to lock them up. They're like restless teenage boys."

Ella chewed her thumb nail. The dogs did look like that—like Sam looked pent up in his tiny trailer—like a monster ready to break out.

Jones began to walk back to the house, and when he did, Ella turned to the one small window in the barn. Quietly, she cracked it open. It was just a small space—no animal could possibly get in or out, but at least they would have some fresh air and the unfiltered light from the full moon shining in.

As Ella turned from the barn, she heard one of the dogs bark, but it didn't sound like a bark. Instead, it sounded like a deep throaty voice, a voice that said, 'thank you.'

Ella shook her head. "You hear that," she asked Sarah. "That bark sounded like 'thank you.'"

"Sure, whatever," Sarah said. "Let's go. I hate to see them penned like that."

Ella walked behind her friend. The bark came again, though this time it sounded even less like a bark and more like the words "Thank you"—a sound that was so much like the "Look down" she'd heard in the corn maze that it made Ella shudder. And Loco—Loco had been in the corn maze with her. But of course it couldn't have been him she'd heard speaking.

And then Ella stopped. She remembered the mental illness she'd seen on her aunt's computer, the one Napper had developed a serum to detect. PTr4. For those who started hallucinating that animals could talk.

Her heart skipped a beat and she trotted to catch up with Sarah, her normal friend who was taking her someplace for a normal pizza on this very normal night.

S ARAH DROVE THEM TO THE COUNTRY CLUB FOR PIZZA. S HE COULDN'T quit talking about Sheila and had big plans to ask for the dog for Christmas.

Sam couldn't come. He had a killer headache. Or so he said. Lately, Ella felt like he had an excuse every time she wanted to hang out.

Ella sat in a dark corner of the booth, looking out over the indoor tennis courts and thinking about the look in Loco's eye as Jones had shut the door—hurt, intelligent, desperate, and a little wild.

Ella chewed on a hangnail.

In front of her, only one of the courts was being used. The ball seemed to bounce back and forth endlessly—lulling Ella into a comforting trance. Until a familiar figure walked onto one of the empty courts.

Ella gasped and Sarah stopped mid-sentence to see what she was looking at.

Vivi faced a man who held up a ball and racket, seemingly explaining the basics of how to hold them.

The man walked to the other side of the net and slowly, deliberately served the ball straight at Vivi's racket.

Her aunt swung. And missed.

Ella held her breath.

"What?" Sarah asked. "Are you grounded or something? Do we need to get you out of here before she sees you?"

Ella shook her head. "What's she doing?"

Sarah gave Ella a weird look. "Taking a tennis lesson. Obviously. That's Harold, the beginner instructor."

Ella shook her head again. "Vivi's supposed to be really good," she said.

"Who told you that?" Sarah said, laughing. "She doesn't seem to know a racquet from a broom."

"She doesn't seem to know *anything*," Ella said.

Sarah quieted, and looked at her friend, then said slowly, "And?"

"And my mom always said she was really good."

It just didn't make any sense. There was no reason for her mom to lie. And no way she could have overestimated her aunt's skill level this much. Besides, Ella's mom had been good. And she must have learned from someone.

"Maybe she's trying to date the instructor," Sarah said.

"Maybe," Ella responded. It was the only thing that made any sense, but Ella couldn't shake the feeling that it was a pretty thin straw to grasp at.

When Ella got home, it was after nine and Vivi wasn't there. She'd left a note reading, "Had to drive out to do some research. Probably won't be home until very late."

Ella set it down. Maybe Vivi *was* dating the instructor.

CHAPTER 41

Sam's head thudded like drums in a tribal war zone. His window was still broken out. His father had said nothing about it, but Sam had come home from school one day to find a large piece of plywood covering the opening. Classy.

It made Sam's room—which hadn't exactly been a suite at the Hilton—even more dismal. No sunshine came in. No moon either. Which made sleeping easy, but otherwise he stayed out.

Tonight nothing sounded better than the blackness of his room. He could see why his dad had his own bedroom window covered in dark curtains. When the headaches came, it helped.

Sam kicked off his shoes and crawled into bed with his clothes still on. He just wanted to close his eyes and try to sleep.

He didn't succeed.

Through the thin walls and even thinner plywood, he began to hear calls of night animals—owls first, followed by the barks of foxes, and then the slow, lonely howl of one of Napper's wolves. The call was soon joined by a chorus, followed by the sound of running. And then the scream of a rabbit.

Sam bolted up. His head was pounding, but he was furiously hungry.

He got out of bed. He *had* to eat. But then a dizziness hit, an ache in his shoulders, swelling in his hands. He could smell the blood of the rabbit—the trail it made as it was carried away in the mouth of another hunter.

Without thinking Sam slammed his fist against the plywood. It splintered and broke, but Sam didn't feel like he'd struck it hard. He hit it again—not thinking, just letting his body move like it wanted to move. The plywood broke out and he climbed through.

He could feel it now—the expansion of his body, the skin stretched taut yet thick—teeth, nails, strength. It seemed like he should be afraid —something was happening, something was wrong. But what he felt was nothing like fear, nothing like terror.

Raw, ravenous, driven.

He jumped, and when he did he flew high up, like a tiger into a tree. He jumped again—this time with intention and landed on a branch. The moon was full and clear, the night cold. It pumped into his blood like fuel, like adrenaline, like force.

From the tree where Sam stood, Napper's fence looked small and thin. He wouldn't have to crawl through some tiny licorice stick hole now. He wouldn't have to fear the wolves. He wouldn't have to fear anything.

He jumped down, ran to the fence—a few steps, then one leap over. Sam laughed out loud—deep, raspy. That's what he thought of Napper's chains and locks; that's what he thought of keeping a poor kid off this beautiful property.

Sam looked out over the acres and acres of The Property—woods, ponds, creeks, deer paths, huge outcroppings of stone. Sam had always loved running—the blood and oxygen pumping into his body until it burned. Now he *ran* and it felt like he had never run before.

He jumped tree trunks, splashed over cold creeks, climbed up large boulders like they were short steps to the sky. He stopped at a glossy pond lit by the moon, and stared down at himself. He was huge, muscled, with hair over most of his face and body. His hands were enormous—nails sharp and white, face square and broad, arms stretched out in lines of muscle so defined that they rippled like eddies of water with every movement. He clenched a fist, watching his forearm tighten into strings of strength. Only his eyes were familiar—the same brown discs they had always been. Something about that surprised Sam, calmed him. He remembered for a moment the human inside of him.

And then he heard it again—the howlings—feral and rich. There were clearly many more than nine wolves. He climbed up a tall tree and watched. The nine were there, but in the distance he saw grays and whites, blacks and reds—dozens, hundreds maybe. They all surrounded a small stone altar on top of a cliff near an overhang. Standing around the altar, the large group of wolves howled in unison until an elderly wolf stepped from them.

Except that he was no wolf at all. He walked on two legs, but was covered in black fur with silver shot through it—the fur on his muzzle lighter than that on his body. He used a dark, familiar-looking staff to walk forward, though Sam could see he didn't need it. And when he struck the staff against the ground, four more werewolves came forward—two females and two males—young, strong, some ugly, some strikingly beautiful. One of the females had a long jagged scar running up her thigh and looked at the staff resentfully, as though she would like it broken in half. The other female was light-furred and flawless.

The old black werewolf was clearly the alpha, the scarred female the beta, with the other two males obeying readily. The final female, the smallest and most beautiful, was pushed to the end of the line—the omega. Next to the alpha stood a dark, mottled wolf—ears pricked upward—a sentinel.

The council, which it seemed to be, convened with Dark Staff taking the lead.

Sam was still a good distance off. He looked to the next thick tree over and then, quietly, he leapt. The ten-foot jump was easy. He settled into the thick-needled evergreen and listened.

"Tonight," Dark Staff said, "we gaze toward the last moon of this earth."

The wolves howled toward the thick disc of light.

"When the solstice comes, so comes the new day. We will be led there, as we were brought here so many moons ago—by a child. Inferior. Ignorant. Human. And yet necessary to this cause through the stone she will bear."

As he spoke, the other four werewolves lit fires around the stone altar. The flames blazed red and gold, licking to the sky, tall as steeples.

Even from where Sam hid, he could feel the warmth creeping into the night. He wondered what would happen if he got caught here listening. He was, after all, one of them. But not. No, not.

Of all the things his father had told him recently, he had tried to make that the most clear. Sam had pressed his father—pressed him for more than the cryptic hints about weird mob bosses with wolvish names. His father had refused to say more. But Sam had wondered—maybe even suspected.

If he wasn't crazy, then what was he?

He was this.

He looked at his hands. But *this*, this was not the same as *them*. Sam put the pieces together. His mother was human; his father was not. That made Sam half. That was why his father had refused to tell him more. His father had been hoping that the human half would win, that Sam would not become this. But why? Why wish away the strength and power of a god? And why keep him from others who might be like him?

Sam looked around and there, two branches down, sat the little cat Gabby—like a stump-tailed Cheshire, watching.

The stumped tail.

Zinnie was not here. But there. In the institution.

For a minute Sam felt guilty. In the euphoria of all his strength and speed, he had not even considered checking on her.

Sam thought suddenly of the strange diagnosis he'd seen on the computer at the Havensborough Unit. Miscegenatosis. From the word Miscegenation. He'd looked it up on the internet after he'd broken into the Havensborough Unit—the intermarrying of two races. Sam had seen that word somewhere else. He pushed deep into his memory, and there it sat on his father's desk—some old medical papers—a diagnosis. But for whom? Now he knew. A diagnosis for him. Miscegenatosis. Half-breeds. They were half-breeds. He was. And Zinnie was.

Looking down to the cat, he said, "You're not her, are you?" He spoke softly through the tree branches. "You're not Zinnie transformed?"

"No boy," the cat said, and Sam nearly fell off his tree. "Though I do wish it were so. My lady is not here. She is presently in her containment."

Sam swallowed. "Will I be contained as well for imagining you speak?"

"If you are contained, it will not be for *imagining* anything," the cat said, a bit of offense in her voice. "A boy turned wolf who cannot conceive of a cat speaking. I mean, really?"

"Are you a human, then?" he asked, trying to be polite. "On the other days?" he said, nodding to the moon.

"Well, of course not. You've seen me on most days. I'm a cat through and through—though somewhat improved when My Lady is not in that awful confinement." Gabby looked sadly at her tail stump.

"But you can speak," Sam said.

"Cats can always speak to those who listen. Which is usually no one, especially teenage boys. So listen well because I will not speak often, if I do so again at all." Gabby made a strange sound in her throat like she was clearing it, and then she looked Sam dead in the eyes,

> *"Before the rise of men*
> *There were wolves.*
> *Before the fall of maidens*
> *There were witches*
> *Before the beauty, there was changing.*
> *Before the solstice there was aging."*

"You know poetry," Sam said, confused, but still trying to be polite.

"It's not poetry," the cat said, her small voice indignant. "It's prophecy. Now, of my lady's containment: you must get her out. They are treating it out of her—the werewolf, the witch. They're making her human so she will die."

"She won't die as she is right now?"

"Miscegenates—half-breeds—have always been special. She is especially so—daughter to a volatile match of werewolf king and human apothecary. She is one of the two who have seen this world from its start."

"And she is part wolf?" Sam asked.

"No," the cat said, looking at Sam like he was stupid. "She is part werewolf. Which has made her part magic—that is the gift her genes received. The Changers are both wolf and magician. Some better than others."

"And I?" Sam asked. "Can I do magic?"

"No," Gabby said, as if explaining something to someone even denser than the tree. "It is quite clear; is it not?"

Sam looked at her like it was definitely not.

He wasn't sure a cat could roll her eyes, but she gave him that impression. "You, my boy, are also half werewolf, but for whatever reasons, your genes have chosen the wolf—and a fine, strong strand indeed, but as half-breed you can only be half. You cannot be magician and changeling; and if you could, you would likely be neither well. You are no more magical than your human mother. Though you will call yourself lucky if you inherited even half of her strength."

"But my father is weak."

"Your father is afraid. Which is often much the same, though it is fear born out of love for you. Which is really quite different. Now be quiet and listen," the cat hissed. "Or we shall miss the important bits."

The werewolf of lowest ranking looked to Dark Staff.

"But, my lord, if it fails," she was saying. "If the girl proves less bendable than we'd hoped. Perhaps it is well to have a back-up plan in which we break her." The omega looked down submissively as she spoke.

The old werewolf looked at the female with some disdain. "You know the mighty Grey metal that holds so much power over most of our kind. The humans know that to shape it, it must be heated, purified, refined, molded, and then bent. To crack and break it will never form it into the tools and weapons they wish it to be. I have spent a lifetime bending humans. They are really quite pliable, my dear, and so much more useful as such. To break them is so untidy. And then they are gone before we can enjoy their full use. Think of the girl's mother, think how helpful it would have been to have her here."

"I was glad to see her broken," the omega murmured.

"Don't be ridiculous," the other female snapped. "She could have been useful. There are others much more important to break. Like she who, even as her bones stoop and her breath thins, can shift both winds and fate." The beta looked to the staff and then her scar. "She has done much wrong to our kind."

"My dears," Dark Staff said softly. "We break who we must when we must. But we shouldn't be reckless. To be so is to become as foolish as the Rogue, who endangers our cause with his carelessness." He scowled briefly over the treetops and Sam held his breath.

"The humans," he said, turning back to the omega. "They resist breaking, fight against it. But if we can raise the temperature gradually, soften them up and then gently, but surely, ply them to the shapes we need. Well, then they seem hardly intelligent enough to notice, much less resist. She will come. And she will come gladly. You yourself will see to that."

The omega nodded meekly.

"Now let us celebrate our coming Change."

Into five golden chalices, he poured a dark burgundy liquid. Each werewolf took a glass, raised it to the moon, and then—instead of drinking the liquid, threw it to the fires, which burst into explosions of red flame that shot into the sky.

The five of them linked their long-clawed fingers together around the stone altar, forming a dark star of black silhouettes—a chain of demons.

The smoke made Sam feel dizzy. It clouded the sky and his thoughts. He took a step back, pressed against a thin branch. It broke, tumbling down to where the cat had been. She was gone.

In the distance, Sam felt the wolves turn a collective face to him.

Which was odd. They couldn't have heard him—that one broken branch separated from all the sounds of the wood. Yet they were clumping together, forming a mass, ready to move. The mottled sentinel sniffed at the air—a deep breath inward, consuming.

Sam did not wait. He jumped from tree to tree—light like a bird, fast as a panther. Hawks rose up, startled in their perches. He sprang forward out of the wood, over the fence, and through the trailer park. Away from the ugliness—the ugliness of the wood with its black smoke and blood howls; and away from the ugliness of the south side —with its peeling paint and tornado-vacant lots.

Instead, he ran to the one thing of beauty he could be sure he wanted to see.

THE SENATOR DRAGGED TO THE LITTLE DESK IN HER HOTEL ROOM, exhausted. She'd been up all night. Not that she really wanted to go to bed on a night like this, with the moon so full it hurt to look at it. She always felt safe when she was with Napper, but now, adding some finishing touches to a bill he'd asked her to write, she was ready to crawl into bed. Dawn couldn't come soon enough.

As soon as the silver shootings had started, she'd hired two body-guards. They stood outside of her room. The guards did not make her feel safe exactly, but she assumed that she would at least hear a scuffle if they were attacked.

She assumed wrong.

The senator sensed the presence as soon as she stood up. "Who are you?" she asked, not turning or moving.

No one answered, yet on that night when the moon hung fat, her senses were heightened and she could hear every sound, including the calm, even breaths of the silver shooter. She could also smell. Fire— the shooter smelled like fire.

The senator moved more quickly than seemed possible, trying to lash out at the killer, but before she could turn, the round barrel of the old gun was against her temple, pressed cold into her skin.

"You will not even give me the chance for an honest fight?" the senator asked.

"A fair fight was not given to me. Only to them whom we claim to despise," the shooter said sweetly.

The voice. It was too impossible.

"But I'm afraid that even if I wanted to," the shooter continued, "I haven't got time for fairness right now, as I have other important business to attend to tonight. I'm sure you understand."

The senator turned suddenly, pulling away from the gun, hoping to lunge at the traitor, but her attacker moved too fast. One shot between the eyes.

By morning her teeth would be gone.

CHAPTER 42

The light of the full moon throbbed through the gauzy curtains of Ella's room. She tossed in bed, remembering the voice she thought she'd heard at the farm, how Loco had looked when the door had shut, Foxy's stump of a foot. It seemed strange for the wolves to attack the dogs, especially if they weren't after the chickens. In fact, it seemed strange that the wolves were there at all. Why was the movement of their packs changing? And what, on earth, was bringing them here?

As Ella drifted into her dreams she saw her aunt missing tennis ball after tennis ball until finally she lobbed one all the way out of the country club, through a field, and to a wolf, who brought it back playfully.

Ella's breath caught in her throat as she heard a thump. It woke her. Ella pushed down into her pillow, shifting around and trying to get comfortable. She realized that she was listening for the noise again. Had it been real or just part of her dreaming?

Finally, she got up and went downstairs to get a drink. She turned on the faucet and there it was again—a distinct thump. She turned the water off, silence. She turned it on again, thump.

Something was acting up with the water valve in the basement. Ella had seen her mother mess with noisy valves in some of their rentals. She wondered if she could just go downstairs and adjust it so that she didn't have to be startled out of bizarre dreams every time Vivi got up to go the bathroom.

Ella walked through the dark to the basement door. She'd only gone down there a handful of times, but she knew the water valve was in a corner near a small window. She held up her phone with its blue glow and felt her way down the wooden unfinished stairs. It got colder as she went down.

At the bottom, she clicked through her apps, trying to find the flashlight. When she did, it beamed on without much more light than the screen had had.

She scuffled toward the water valve, feeling for a light switch when she heard it again—THUMP. The noise was really loud in the basement.

She shined her light around, her heart beating harder. Had Vivi just turned the water on? Was Vivi even home yet? Was it something else acting up?

Ella hurried toward the water valve, eager to tighten it and make that noise stop. She twisted the valve and heard the noise again. But this time something became clear—the noise had not come from the pipe or the valve.

Someone's in the house, Ella thought, afraid to move. She crouched down, hardly breathing.

Nothing moved.

Quietly, she held her phone low to the floor, trying to hide its light. She began to dial. 9-1-.... Something kicked her phone—fast as light, quiet as darkness. The phone flew out of her hand.

She gasped and tried to scream, but the intruder clamped his hand over her mouth and started to drag her to the window, which she realized was open. Ella kicked and elbowed the intruder, but he was tall with strong, angular arms that were not big, but still felt like rocks through the dark camo shirt. She couldn't see his face, which was covered by black pantyhose tied up into a mask, but his hands were lean and long—almost womanly—each nail slender and sharp, though the backs of his hands were covered with hair that extended up part of his fingers.

Until Vivi's house, Ella had only lived in apartments in bad parts of big towns. She'd heard fights and seen scuffles. But in all those places, she'd never been mugged, touched, or followed.

Here in this sleepy little town, she'd been grabbed twice.

Still holding Ella's mouth closed, the man in camo banged Ella against the laundry table. She bit his finger. He released her mouth for only an instant before pressing against her nose and mouth harder than before. She could breathe, but it wasn't easy.

He picked up a rag from the laundry table and quickly wrapped it around her head and across her mouth—creating a gag that tasted like Downy fabric softener. Then he held her arms in front of her, tying them up with sticky, shiny tape.

Ella kicked back—banging her bare foot against his shin. She wasn't even sure he felt it, though he did toss her up onto the table and tie up her ankles just as quickly as he had her hands. Then the man jumped up to the laundry table—a good four feet—like he was hopping up a step.

The man in camo lifted her up and tossed her through the garden-level window like she was a doll. He followed, shimmying through the tiny window with ease.

Ella didn't know why in books people always fainted when these things happened. Every nerve in her body felt like it had been shot through with electricity.

Near the curb, she noticed a sleek, black car that she'd never seen in her neighborhood before. Using her bound legs, she tried to drag herself back through the window. Her attacker pulled her up as though she weighed no more than a toddler, then dropped her on the ground like a sack of garbage.

She squirmed to her knees, trying to think of where she could go and how she could get there.

On the road, the car sat with the lights off, but the ignition running —ready to drive away.

Ella's breaths came in short, intense bursts of panic and energy.

Camo Man reached down to lift her up. Ella clawed at the grass, dug dirt deep into her fingernails. The kidnapper jerked her to her feet. Ella let all her weight fall. She tried to be as heavy and useless as she could. Camo Man held up his hand like he was going to hit her, but just then, another stranger jumped from the shadows.

Ella tried to scream, and gagged on her Downy-flavored rag. She let her body go limp. Camo Man was distracted, and let Ella fall to the ground.

The other man stepped slowly toward her attacker. "You must be this Rogue I've heard so much about," he said.

"Must I?" Camo Man replied, his voice a subdued tenor. "It seems that you are more of a rogue than I am—fighting for the weak whom you call your friends."

"Lives that need protection," the man replied. His voice was deeper, though muffled by a thick gray mask.

"Lives that don't deserve protection," Camo Man said. "The Alpha and I don't see eye to eye on most things, but we can agree—at least—on that."

"Which makes it all the more unfortunate that you are both wrong," the gray-masked man replied.

Ella inched back toward the window—hoping she could drop back in, slam it shut somehow and crawl to her phone. She could still use her fingers to call the police. Her attacker noticed her moving away and grabbed her arm, jerking her up. It hurt, but she hung there, not putting even an ounce of weight into her feet. As she dangled like a rag doll, the other man—the one she thought might be an accomplice—punched her attacker in the face.

Camo Man dropped her. Ella gasped, but that made her gag and cough. She swung her arms up and banged her attacker in the knees. Camo Man knocked Ella down, sending little tingling shots of pain up to her shoulder.

The other man hit her attacker again, but this time Camo Man was ready. Camo Man grabbed the other man's hand and then slashed out at his throat with those long nails.

Although the other man was wearing a ski mask, a small part of his neck was exposed and Ella could see the long bloody lines Camo Man had made.

With her clumsy taped hands, Ella grabbed at the gag, trying to get the rag out of her mouth.

"Why do you fight it?" Camo Man asked with his high, muted voice. Ella looked up, thinking he was talking to her, but he was looking directly at Gray Mask and advancing slowly. "Our kind must have the girl."

"Because there is another way."

Her attacker laughed. "To you there is no way at all—you love the oppressive humans. Your sister—she has married one of them. Produced offspring."

"I am your kin."

"You are no kin of mine." Camo Man swung at the other man's face and then lunged.

Ella wiggled the gag mostly out of her mouth just as Camo Man came back to her and jerked her up again.

"You will not have her," Gray Mask said, his voice fierce and low, yet with a tone that struck Ella as familiar.

"If I do not, another will. And—frankly—I'd like to have her my way."

"Your way will destroy more than you know."

"My way will restore us all. And without the pretty civility the Alpha wishes to use. A civility that has too much potential to fire back in his face."

"He has the stone," the other man said.

"And now I have the girl," Camo Man replied. "So maybe we can make a deal. What do you have?" Camo Man asked, laughing. "You have nothing."

"I need nothing," Gray Mask said. Then with a quick movement he kicked Camo Man in the side, making him crumple to the ground, dropping Ella. She rolled and wormed like a caterpillar toward the window.

"Of course you don't need anything," Camo Man said, standing up more quickly than Ella could imagine was possible, considering the way he'd just been kicked. "You don't even have a dog in the fight."

The other man laughed. "I have all the dogs in the fight."

"The dogs are idiots. They have everything to gain—their voices, their stories, their freedom. Still they fight for your cause, loving the humans even more than you do." Camo Man punched Gray Mask hard in the mouth.

Ella scooted toward the window as the two men fought. Her attacker punched at the gut of the gray-masked man.

Gray Mask did not double over like she expected him to, but jabbed an elbow into the attacker's neck. "Are you," Gray Mask said, "going to fight me on two feet like a man?"

Ella swore her attacker smiled through his panty-hose mask. "No," he said, the word a tight sound in his throat. And then he lunged—using not his two legs, but all four limbs to propel him forward like an animal.

Gray Mask pushed against his body with his shoulders like a wrestler. Ella looked up past the maple tree in her aunt's yard. The moon was so full, so bright, not a sliver missing.

The attacker was gaining ground—biting and scratching, while the other man, the one Ella began to realize might be there to help her, or at least did not seem to be there to hurt her—stood upright punching and jabbing until the attacker dug his long nails into his shoulders.

Gray Mask howled—almost like a dog, and sank to his knees. When he did, he seemed to grow huge in the moonlight, his eyes dark, his neck and shoulders now shadowed with gray hair. The attacker laughed, and Gray Mask leapt onto him—four limbs like legs, a quick twisting movement, and then a crack. Camo Man howled—a wolf's howl in her aunt's backyard. Gray Mask bit at the other's pantyhose-covered face, then pulled Camo Man's upper body off the ground and banged it back down.

Camo Man lay there, not moving.

Ella swung her tied legs through the window just as Gray Mask ran for her and another, much closer man's voice spoke into her ear. Ella felt exhausted and achy, but she could swear it was the same voice she had heard in the corn maze.

"I'm sorry," the voice said, just as Gray Mask came up and shoved a wet rag into her face; and then everything went black.

SAM PERCHED ON SARAH'S WINDOWSILL LIKE A GARGOYLE—LARGE and bulky, but oddly graceful in his roost. Her room was on the second floor and her curtains had been left open. The glossy moon hit the pane of the window, reflecting.

Sam had been sitting for hours. His body didn't ache, but his hunger had grown. He watched Sarah on her bed. She slept on her side, curled into a soft ball—the hair she wore straight to school lay in clumps of messy, wavy tangle. Sam wanted to touch it, to feel the fine strands fall between his clawed fingers. Her body moved slowly up and down. He could almost feel his hand on her side—could almost taste that feeling in his mouth. She was small and vulnerable. And he could have that under his fingers because he was large and powerful.

Quietly, he slid his fingers under the edge of her closed window just as the first light of autumn dawn broke the horizon. He felt it like a kick to his gut. He laid a hand—a paw—on Sarah's window and paused. The sun crept up and he shook his head, now fuzzy and confused. Would Sarah want him to come in? Would she recognize him? Of course not. And she'd be terrified. Just like Ella had looked in the cornfield.

Sam pulled back.

For a moment, he had felt that Sarah was his to take. For a moment, the monster had overpowered him—the same demons he'd run from on the hill. They were him—inside of him. Trying to overtake the human that he was.

Without a sound, Sam dropped from the ledge. It stung his feet a bit. When he looked down, they were still wolfish, but Sam-sized.

"I have to get home," he mumbled, starting into a run.

He thought of his father, the bottle of Aleve by his bed. Sam had always considered his father weak—fearful, cowering, clumsy. And his father was those things. His father could have power, be power. Instead, he spent every full moon hunched over a toilet bowl, quivering.

And yet, thinking of Sarah, Sam hesitated.

The power he had felt just now—the power to take. It wasn't exactly power at all, but impulse, urge, and a strange type of submission to that urge. Which was the opposite of power. Yet, to give up what he had felt tonight—Sam could still smell the spruce on his hands—Sam wasn't sure that was strength either.

He ran into the dawn, beating at the confusion with the cold air that burned into his lungs. It was almost eight miles back to his house. By the time he dragged up to the trailer, all that remained from the night was a rasping in his voice. His dad sat on the porch, pale and waiting.

Sam walked past him and spoke. "So if I ever transform…" Sam asked, limping to the door.

"Do not go near the ones you love," his father replied softly.

Sam stopped.

"Go inside, son," his dad said.

Sam went inside.

ELLA WOKE THE NEXT MORNING IN HER BED WITH HER PHONE BESIDE her, the alarm going off. Everything was in place.

"So real," she mumbled, rolling over to turn off her alarm. She'd been sleeping on her side and now it tingled and stabbed all the way up to her shoulder as the nerves came back to life. Her head hurt and her mouth tasted awful. She licked her lips and the dreadful taste on her tongue seemed strange but familiar. She was sure she had the worst morning breath in history.

She sat up and looked at her phone. In its case, it was perfect. Even the box seemed fine—no new dents or scratches.

"So real," she said again, putting the phone down.

The dream had been a horrible combination of corn maze flashback meets basement horror story. At its end, someone had put her in her bed. She could no longer picture him clearly, though she was sure it was a man. She had asked him how he knew to come and help her.

"The dogs," he had said, "are in the fight."

"Loco?" she'd asked, her head fuzzy. "He told you?" She'd leaned her head back on the pillow. "He only tells me things in my dreams," she'd mumbled.

The man had responded, "Well, child, there will come a time when that changes."

Ella pressed her hand into her forehead. Maybe she had a fever. But everything seemed fine. She got up, took a Tylenol for her aching body, and then dressed quickly before going downstairs.

She walked through the kitchen, then paused at the top of the basement stairs, staring into the darkness below. It had all been so real; she didn't want to go down there. But she knew that that was why she needed to. Step by step, she walked over to the water valve. Everything was fine. Winter light poured through the basement windows, which were neither broken nor open. It had been a really horrible dream.

"Ella," she heard her aunt calling. She jumped.

"I'm up," Ella yelled, as she ran up the stairs by twos. She poured a bowl of cereal, hoping that would help wash down the taste on her tongue, and picked up her phone to text Sarah for a ride.

There, on the screen were two numbers: 9-1.

She put her spoon in her bowl and stared at them. She must have done it in her sleep. She had never had a dream that vivid before.

"Sounded like you slept badly last night," Vivi said, coming into the kitchen with a mud mask still on her face as she poured herself a big cup of coffee.

"Did it?" Ella asked, still staring at her phone, barely noticing her aunt. "I had some kind of crazy dream."

Vivi nodded, and got out a package of bacon.

"You're limping," Ella said.

"Yeah," Vivi replied. "I think I'm kind of sore from a workout I did."

The tennis lesson. It had made Vivi sore. Ella tried to catch her aunt's eye, but Vivi had turned to the coffee maker and was topping off her cup.

"Hurry up, Ella," she said. "The bus will be here in a minute."

Ella still hadn't texted Sarah, and she definitely didn't have time to walk, so the bus it would have to be. She brushed her teeth and ran out the door. The only other kid on the bus was a quiet boy who sat in front of her in biology class. They'd once dissected a frog together.

Ella stopped in the aisle. Her mouth—it had tasted like that smell—the chloroform the dead frogs had come in.

"Find a seat," the bus driver said, not sweetly.

Ella flopped down near the back, the nerves in her head like tiny fires pushing against her skull.

CHAPTER 43

Loco found it first—the large black lump that looked like a garbage bag discarded at the side of the road.

He circled twice before the half-dead creature growled, barely raising her head, pulling her lips back over her teeth in a way that made her look like the corpse she almost was.

Jones saw the dogs running—toward the woods that rested at the edge of his cornfield. They would often run for a squirrel or falling leaf, but they would never run with any kind of organized precision. They did now.

Jones jumped from the table and grabbed his gun.

The half-dead wolf lay between two trees. Loco stood in front of her pacing. Jones wasn't sure if that meant he was protecting her from the other dogs, or merely claiming her as his own prize. Either way, Jones ordered the dogs back where they formed a humming, whining, fidgeting clump of disgruntled obedience.

Jones stood a pace back from the wolf, raised the gun to his shoulder, and took aim.

It was what he should do. Mercy and justice both demanded it. The wolf was a threat to his animals as well as all the livestock of the other farmers in the area. For all he knew, it had been the one ripping his dogs to shreds all along. But even if wasn't the guilty wolf, the animal now lay in a drying pool of its own blood. It was clear that the kindest thing he could do was end the animal's life in the fastest way possible.

As he raised his eye to the scope, he could see that the wolf was likely a female—slight in frame, a softness in the face the males did not possess. The animal met his gaze, almost seemed to nod, and then looked away, staring through the trees as though eager to look at a thing of beauty on her way out. The animal had given her permission, almost requested that she be shot.

And yet Jones couldn't. In that small gesture—the tilt of the head, the stare through the trees, he'd seen every wounded, broken dog he'd ever taken in. He could not now leave her here to die and he could not, it seemed, help to hasten that death.

So he did another thing he should not have done. He sat, just a few feet away from the animal, gun lowered, and watched her. She placed her head on her paw, defeated, as though resigned now to die a natural, slow death, and with a stranger there to witness it.

From his pocket, Jones pulled a large strip of jerky, which he pushed toward the wolf with a nearby stick. He placed it directly in front of the animal's mouth. If she did not eat, he would kill her. But already he could see her sniffing, the tongue tapping against her teeth. And then in a quick movement, she opened her mouth, clamped down on the jerky, and swallowed.

The farmer pressed his lips together. She would be thirsty now. Jones had brought a water bottle with him, but he didn't dare move close enough to the wolf to pour it for her. Near him was a large, cradle-shaped piece of bark. He took it, filled it half way with water, and scooted the small vessel toward the wolf. He thought she might not even be able to lift her head to lap it up, but she raised up an inch and let her tongue drop to the water over and over until, exhausted, she rested again against her paw.

This time, however, when she put her head down, it was with her face toward the farmer. *More*, he could see her begging, *I need more.*

Quietly, he stood. Wolves, he knew, ate several pounds of meat a day. He doubted any kind of kibble would do either.

He walked back to his house slowly, the dogs running in eager, confused circles around him as he trekked to the chest freezer in the barn. From his freezer, he took two pounds of hamburger meat, which he thawed in the sink. Outside, the dogs were whining for him. The farmer shook his head. He could actually use a little help from Ella right now.

The girl had not come by since the full moon. Thanksgiving had just passed; Christmas was coming. The girl would surely be busy. And she was a teenager. Into one thing until another caught her eye. Maybe she had a boyfriend, or a new sport, or who knew what else—something more interesting than an old farm. But it was clear that the dogs missed her, especially Loco. The truth was that even Jones had gotten used to having her come around.

When the meat had thawed enough, he put it in a large dish. He walked the road again to the injured wolf, setting the food and some more water near her, then scooting it in her direction. She lifted her head fully this time to eat and drink—one paw pushing her up while the other lay useless and twisted beneath her. That, Jones began to see, was the source of the blood. Or at least one source.

The next day when he walked out with a pan of bacon fat and several scraps, the black hump was no longer there. He sighed a small breath of relief. She had run off—to die or live, but he had nothing more to do with it. He turned to walk back to his house, and there to the left he saw her, deeper into the corn rows and closer to his property. He pressed his eyebrows together, walked toward the animal and said, "If you're going to live, you're going to have to let me bind up that foot. And anything else that needs binding."

As if she understood, the wolf rolled to the side revealing the twisted leg and a large gash across her chest that would need stitching.

"Good glory," the farmer muttered. "What happened to you?"

He left the scraps and fat and returned with another bowl of ground pork and a wheelbarrow full of supplies—a pair of scissors, needle, and a small brown bottle. He was wearing thick leather gloves that extended nearly to his shoulders. He hoped they were thick enough.

He put the food in front of her, then carefully washed and sterilized the foot. She stopped eating for a minute, bared her teeth, and growled, but then went back to the bowl—too hungry to stop him.

The farmer guessed that the leg had gone numb days ago—damage to the nerves and sinews. She would not use it again, but he could keep infection from forming and spreading up her leg. The wound was different than the little dog Foxy's, more torn up, like ragged shreds of meat on bone.

The chest wound was another matter. It was deep and vulnerable—he could never bind such a wound in this position without her biting him. For that wound, he had brought a little something special.

He'd gotten the tranquilizer from the vet when the attacks had started. He'd wanted to be able to help his dogs if they needed it. Now, as the female wolf gulped down her food, he readied the needle and plunged it into her side.

In a few minutes she was sedate enough to stitch up. After he was done, he placed her in the wheelbarrow he'd brought his supplies in, and took her to his barn. He'd locked the dogs into the shed.

He set the wolf on an old towel on the ground, unlocked the shed, and told the dogs to stand in place. They lined up like a group of soldiers—a group of soldiers who whined and fidgeted a lot, but did not break rank.

"Okay," the farmer said to them. "I know this is a little different than our usual routine, but you can see she's in no position to hurt you and you aren't going to hurt her either."

He knew they couldn't understand his words, but he was pretty sure they still got his meaning.

Jones looked each of the animals in the eye and then said, "Loco, come."

Each dog came forward in turn, sat, and was allowed to sniff the wolf. He wasn't sure if it would help. He'd brought every kind of bad dog to this group, but he'd never brought something that smelled so wild that even he could sense it. Most of the dogs came forward, usually with their hackles raised and mouths open. Some refused to get close, circling instead. And Foxy stayed back, unmoving.

CHAPTER 44

Ella had planned to take the bus to the farm on Saturday morning—she hadn't been since Monday and she missed the dogs. But when she came downstairs Vivi was sitting at the table, waiting for her. Ella might have just ignored that except that as soon as Ella got down a box of cereal, Vivi cleared her throat. "Ella," she said pausing. "Have you thought about the Festival?"

Ella groaned inside. She had been trying not to think about it. She still didn't know what to do.

"A little," Ella said.

"And…" Vivi said, "have you decided what you want to do?" Vivi put down the pencil she'd been fiddling with. "I don't want to pressure you, but Mr. Napper told me yesterday that he needs to know by Monday. If you're not going to do it, they'll have to hold an audition for someone else."

A lot of things flashed through Ella's head—twenty-five thousand dollars, the perfect red dress, Napper's mansion, Jack's beautiful face.

But Ella could also see Sarah. She knew her friend would be disappointed not to have a shot at the part. Of course, having a shot wouldn't mean Sarah would get it. And Ella could tell from the way

Sarah talked about Napper that she wasn't a huge fan. Maybe Sarah wouldn't even try out.

Plus, it was obvious that Vivi thought Ella should do the part—that Vivi *wanted* her to do the part. And they'd had such a hard time connecting. The pros clearly out-stacked the cons. But what seemed right didn't quite feel right, and that wormed around in Ella's gut.

Ella opened her mouth, still not sure whether a yes or no would come out when Vivi tossed her hair over her shoulder and looked out the window. On the back of her aunt's neck was a small tattoo—a swirling black "C" that looked exactly like the "C" on Ella's ring. Her aunt—who seemed not to care for her sister at all had once cared enough to tattoo Christa's initial to her neck. That same woman now cared enough to take in her stranger of a niece and offer her every opportunity that existed in this town. How could she say no?

"Y-yes," Ella stammered. "Yes, I've decided to do it."

ELLA LET VIVI PERSUADE HER TO GO TO A STONE-WALLED, SLEEK-lined jewelry store at the most expensive corner downtown. Once inside, Vivi led Ella to a case of delicate gold chains that housed deep red garnets of various sizes and shapes.

"I want to buy you one," Vivi said, her voice insistent. "To celebrate."

Ella shook her head. "Oh no, you don't have to."

"Of course not," Vivi said, smiling, "but it will look beautiful with your gown, don't you think?"

Ella did, but she still resisted. "You've already given me so much. It's okay, really," Ella said.

"Ella," Vivi said, "it's something I want to do for the only niece, the only family, I have. Please. Choose one."

Ella could not resist that. She chose a slender chain with a smooth, bezzled gem. Vivi told the shopkeeper to get some earrings to match.

Ella had never left a store carrying a plain white bag that held two square boxes tied up with soft ribbon. She'd never walked down a cobbled street with that small weight in her hand, never felt it bump against her leg with the tap of something important. Now she did. People smiled when she passed. She smiled back.

When she got home, Ella set the boxes on her dresser—they didn't seem right in her mother's jewelry box—and carefully folded up the bag and tucked it in her journal.

The next day a blurb about Ella as the bearer at the Festival sat in the top of the Events section of the Sunday paper. Vivi left it on the table for Ella to see. Ella was pretty sure she hadn't looked at a newspaper in, well, ever. So she didn't expect anyone else to notice the news either. She was wrong.

Monday, when she showed up in school, Brandt stood at her locker, waiting.

"Heard you'll be doing the reading at the festival," he said, falling into step with her as she walked to homeroom.

"How'd you hear?" Ella asked. She had just barely texted Sarah. Sam didn't even know yet.

"Little bird told me," he said coyly, and then, "My family knows your aunt. And it was in the paper, right?"

It didn't take long for Ella to realize what living in a small town really meant. By lunch time, she was pretty sure the whole school had mentioned it to her. She'd been worried about people finding out, but besides a few senior girls in the Thespian club, most of the kids seemed honestly excited for her.

Ella hadn't realized how excluded she'd felt until suddenly she wasn't. People smiled at her as she passed them in the halls, a few kids asked her about it and congratulated her, and several boys stopped to stare as if noticing her for the very first time.

Ella fought the urge to slouch forward over her books and scamper through the halls. Instead, she pulled her shoulders back and returned smiles until her face hurt. She pushed her hair out of her eyes and answered questions about the dress and shoes she would wear.

That night Vivi was on the computer when she called Ella over. "I'm ordering some things from Anna's Boutique in Chicago. You want anything?"

Ella tentatively picked out a striped crewneck shirt.

"Anything else?" Vivi asked. "They're having a holiday sale."

Ella bent under the small pressure. She picked out two pairs of skinny jeans, a sweater, another shirt, and some chandelier earrings.

Two days later the box arrived. And just like that, the misfit orphan on the fringe who walked through ditches to school was a person of importance in her town.

That weekend she went with Vivi to get her hair cut. She let herself be talked into some wine-colored highlights. And later that week they went back for manicures.

All the beauticians commented on her beauty, her grace—from her nail beds to her soft heels.

"You must be so proud," they told Vivi.

And, strangest of all, Vivi did look proud. Or at least not tired. Ella was no longer a cumbersome accessory her aunt had to drag around. She was now a prize worthy of display. Ella tried to let that annoy her, but as the contact list on her phone filled up and any guy at the country club was happy to invite her for tennis, she found she didn't care that much if she was an accessory for her aunt or not. It was good to be included, wanted, respected. Her mother would surely have approved.

Ella found herself reading her mother's poems and fables less and less. She didn't have time to miss her walks to school or her weird runs with Sam. She didn't have time to obsess over the silver shootings, or even read very much about the latest one. She just had time now for school and her very busy life.

Which felt great. Or at least, not empty.

And that was good enough.

CHAPTER 45

Sarah was trying not to begrudge Ella of the part she'd gotten for the Festival. It was wrong to be jealous of your orphaned friend who'd grown up in the inner city of a big town and never known anything but poverty. It was wrong to envy her when she got a break. Even if it was a really cool break.

Sarah had been hoping for some type of audition, but apparently Ella just knew the right people. Which was what you needed in Napper. Sarah knew that. And it wasn't Ella's fault her aunt worked with the mighty Charles Napper.

Maybe it wouldn't have bothered Sarah so much if Ella still felt like Ella—old jeans, brown hair, phone she almost never touched, homework she always did.

Sarah sighed—there she went again. She'd liked Ella better as an oddball. It was like Sarah had been using Ella as some sort of toy—the friend who needed Sarah more than Sarah needed her.

Now the tables had turned. And Sarah was lonely. She'd come to really value Ella as a friend. And now Ella had lots of other options. She'd been busy every day that week—playing tennis, going out with guys who seemed to have come out of the woodwork, hanging out with new friends.

She and Ella had started saying, "Hey, we should get together soon." But then they didn't. It worried Sarah. When you started talking like middle-aged women who don't have time for lunch, it was kind of over.

Just yesterday, Ella had suggested they go get their nails done that weekend. Whatever. Sarah hated getting her nails done at those stinky salons. She'd made up some lame excuse and found herself wishing they could go to that stinky farm instead. That sounded way more interesting.

Being with Ella had been fun because Ella had just been Ella. Most of the kids Sarah had grown up with weren't at ease in their skin. And now they'd gotten under her best friend's skin and were morphing her into someone else.

Sarah hated that.

At least she still had Sam. Nice, crazy Sam. Sam who apparently was not as into her as she was into him. Sam, who would never kiss her or even ask her out.

She sighed. Lately, he'd been acting weird too—well, weirder—only on the other extreme. He'd mostly stopped talking to her or anyone else, and walked around looking haunted half the time. She'd seen him running by the institution the other day and he'd stopped at the Havensborough Unit and stared up—like he was looking for a camera or trying to communicate with the stars or something. He had looked, Sarah had to admit, like he belonged a little more inside the psychiatric institution than out. And yet he was the most true person she knew, the only one in the school who would walk around just being himself.

It was because of Sam that Sarah had let the black fade out of her hair and stopped with the dark lips and eyes. She'd realized that just because you were trying to be different than everyone else didn't mean you were trying to be yourself. She'd spent the months since meeting Sam trying to figure out who she was. Which, apparently, was a jealous jerk who begrudged one friend's success while judging her other friend for his obvious eccentricities.

She texted Ella—"You still up for that mani-pedi? I'm going purple; how 'bout you?"

Sam still hadn't come up with a way to tell Ella she was his cousin without sounding like a whack job. The truth was that the harder he tried to look *not* crazy, the crazier everything became.

Sam looked down at his utterly normal hands—long, slim fingers that were a good match for his tall skinny body. When he had changed he hadn't been afraid. He was afraid now—terrified of it happening again and just as terrified that it would never happen again. When he'd dragged himself home that night, he'd insisted his father talk to him, tell him as much as he could. Which wasn't as much as Sam would have liked.

"I've never had a half-breed son before," his dad had said, a wry sadness in his voice.

"You've always had a half-breed son," Sam shot back. "You just haven't wanted one."

"I've always been happy with what I had," his father said, looking him in the eye.

"Well, good for you," Sam said, slicing a hand through the air. "Just tell me if this will happen again. If you can tell me *anything* useful at all."

"I don't know if or how often it will happen again," his father had said. "But I know this. To stop it from happening, don't eat meat, don't look at the moon, and a bit of Aleve won't hurt either."

Of course his father would assume he never wanted to transform again. Sam had let out a snort.

His father had ignored it. "But whether it happens or not, don't go near the ones you love."

"Why?" Sam had asked.

His father had actually laughed. "Because," he'd said with a bit of his own snort, "you could hurt them. And even if you don't, you could lead others to them who will. Get used to it, son, this world doesn't have a ton of room for people like us."

Sam had stomped off to his room, angry—angry that what his father said was actually true. But determined as well. He would tell Ella.

Sam had never been one to run with his instincts before, but in his transformation a piece of that had changed. It was true that he didn't want to hurt anyone if he transformed again, but it didn't seem any better to stand back and let others get hurt because you refused to stand up and be who you actually were.

Ella was his best friend. And his cousin. Something crazy was going on and Sam and Ella were in the middle of it. The only difference was that Sam knew this, and Ella didn't.

No. That wasn't the only difference.

The other difference was that Sam wanted to figure it out, was ready to run toward it, while it seemed that Ella was more than happy to step back, look away. She'd come to school last week with some dark highlights in her hair, new clothes, new nails, tan skin—her own transformation into her own kind of half-breed.

Today Sarah had told Sam that she was going to help Ella practice her part for the festival. Sam figured he could corner Ella in the theater when she was done and talk to her then.

SAM GOT TO THE STAGE JUST AFTER SARAH. HE WAITED IN THE darkness of the wing as Sarah bustled around finding a stool and a microphone, then plugging things in. He had told her he was coming, but he was pretty sure she didn't know he was here, and he hated to interrupt her. Besides he kind of enjoyed watching her in her element. After a few minutes, Ella came through the audience doors of the theater, texting as she walked up the aisle toward the stage.

Ella didn't look up until she got to the stage where Sarah was standing. They both smiled at each other, and maybe it was the dim lighting, but Sam felt like Sarah looked a little strained. She motioned for Ella to come up onto the stage, and then Sarah stood Ella in front of the curtain with just a few lights on, as though ready for a big opening act. Gently, Sarah adjusted Ella's posture, pressed her shoulder's down, told her to stand with one foot slightly in front of the other.

Ella still looked really nervous. Her shoulders had already tensed back up, and her legs with their bent knees looked like she was gearing up for a sprint off the stage.

"Ella," Sarah said, laughing. "Relax; it's just me."

"I know," Ella mumbled so Sam could just barely hear her. "I'm just not good at this stuff."

"Well, of course you are. Why else would they have picked you?" Sarah looked sideways as she said it. Ella did too.

Sam guessed that they both knew. A connection was worth a thousand auditions. And Ella apparently had a good one.

"Okay," Sarah was saying. "You'll probably have a mic for the event, so we're going to practice with one. Testing," she said, tapping into it. It echoed back at her and she positioned the stand in front of Ella.

Sam couldn't help but stare. Sarah's small hands flitted over the equipment with ease, her hair falling forward. She had always been eye-catching, but as Ella's hair had become less natural, Sarah's was fading back into a reddish brown. Parts of it caught the lights on the stage, amber strands flitting like fairies down her back. It made Sarah's eyes seem greener and her pale skin pinker. And the plain black shirt and black pants she usually wore—those had always done her a lot of favors. Sam wished he was watching a long, long play, so he could sit and stare at her for hours.

It was almost like she knew, because for a minute she blinked in his direction. But the wings were too dark, and Sam had always been good at going unnoticed.

Sarah's eyes went back to Ella. She patted Ella's shoulders down again and told her to take a deep breath.

Ella spoke into the microphone. But instead of her part, she asked, "So are you going to be there with your parents?"

"No," Sarah said. "My parents won't be there."

"Why not?" Ella asked. "Are you guys going out of town for the break?"

"No," Sarah said. "My parents weren't invited. They're never invited to Napper's fundraisers."

Ella tipped her head to one side. "Seriously?" she asked. "I thought your parents were pretty well off."

The comment obviously annoyed Sarah, although Ella didn't seem to notice.

"Yeah, they do okay," Sarah said. "Better than okay. But this party's about more than money. It's like Hollywood. It's all about status. And my parents lack that a little. My dad's politics don't always line up with Napper's."

"Really?" Ella said, like she'd only been half listening. "That's too bad."

"Is it?" Sarah asked.

"I mean that they won't—that you won't—be there."

"Yeah, I guess," Sarah said. "The food is supposed to be amazing."

"And there's dancing," Ella said.

Sarah shrugged. "With old people."

Ella smiled. "And Jack."

"Yup. Old people. And their rich relatives."

Ella looked hurt. "What do you mean?"

"Jack is Napper's great nephew; didn't you know?" Sarah said. And then quickly added, "Anyway—I was just kidding about the old people. It's going to be a blast."

Sarah tapped on the mic one more time.

"Now let's do this thing so you can go in there and impress everyone."

Ella took a deep breath.

White moon rising. Red sun blush.
Melt the old world to a hush.
To bring anew a refreshed land,
I place this stone with purity of hand.
The sun will rise, bright new star.

New definitions of who we are.

Ella whispered and mumbled her way through and when she was done, Sam bit his lip. The poem wasn't great to begin with, but Ella was *awful*. She'd sped through most of it, stopping only to take a desperate breath at awkward points in the middle of phrases, her voice shaky and weak. Sam had heard her read in class and she'd always done well, but here—with lights and the microphone, caught into something that was supposed to be a performance, she sounded like a zombie.

"Okay," Sarah said, obviously a little surprised as well. "Just slow it down a little. At first just imagine you're reading in class—no big deal. Pause at the end of each line, breathe, and then move on. Slowly. Try it again."

"Okay," Ella said. "I'm also supposed to place some ceremonial stone at the end of it."

Sarah shook her head. "Napper's a weird one," she said. "Place it where?"

"I don't know," Ella said. "I figured they'd show me."

"Okay, well, read the poem and then place your imaginary stone on the ground or something. Just be sure to bend down with your knees together and to the side—don't bend at the hips and stick your butt out at everyone, though old Napper would probably love that."

Both girls giggled and the ice finally broke.

Ella read the poem and placed her "stone." Her reading was better. At least as good as it was when she read a passage in folklore.

"Okay," Sarah said. "Now kind of try to flow with the words a bit. Don't overdo it or anything. But when you talk about the moon, picture the moon. You'll be surprised how well the images and your feelings about them will connect to your language without any overacting."

Ella said the first few lines and they were pretty good. Really good. Sam found himself feeling proud of his friends—both teacher and student. Also, he figured at this rate, he'd have a chance to steal a few minutes with Ella, but she had begun pulling her phone out to check it.

"Thanks, Sarah," she said the minute they got through the whole poem. "This has helped me a lot, but I've got to run."

Sarah looked at her watch. "Where are you headed? I was kind of hoping we could go for pizza or something. Sam was supposed to be here soon too."

Ella's eyes lit up. For a second Sam was flattered. Until Ella said, "Actually Vivi is taking me to look at some cars. She said maybe for Christmas."

"Cool," Sarah said. "That *is* more motivating than pizza." She turned off the mic and wound up the cord. "What kind are you looking at?"

"I don't know," Ella gushed. "Honestly, I don't know anything about cars, but Jack does. He told Vivi he'd help her look."

"So Jack's coming?" Sarah said, her hands slowing on the cord. Sam held his breath; it was obvious Sarah didn't like Ella's counselor.

"Yeah," Ella said, grabbing her bag and shoving her phone into her pocket. "And maybe Brandt. They know a ton about cars."

"Mmm-hmmm," Sarah said.

Ella hopped off the side of the stage and jogged up the aisle and to the audience doors. For a minute, Sam saw his old friend—ponytail bouncing, bag slung over her back. But just before the exit, she paused, adjusted her hair, and walked carefully out the doors.

Sam watched Sarah as she stared at the door that shut behind Ella. He felt like he should say something so he didn't startle her, but she seemed so lost in thought that he was pretty sure anything would startle her.

Sam stepped forward, still in the shadows, but closer to Sarah. She put away the microphone, picked up her bag, and went to the lights to flip them off. Her fingers brushed the switches down, leaving only the aisle and exit light shining, and still he held her in his gaze. He liked the way the dim lights traced her profile—the deep set eyes, angular nose, full lips. She turned and began to walk in his direction. Then, for a minute, she stood there in what would have been his long shadow if the lights behind him had been on. She turned and went back for something she'd forgotten.

Sam shook himself out of it. There was a light switch near him and he flipped it on. "Hey," he said, as though he'd just come in.

"Hey," she said, not quite looking up. When Sam caught her eye, he could see that her eyes were full of tears.

"Hey," he said again, moving closer. "You okay?"

"Yeah," she said, pulling a tissue from her pocket. "It's just—" Her voice shook a bit and she paused. "It's just a lot of things. I can't…I can't even explain it. I'm—" She dabbed at her eyes. "I'm a little jealous I guess."

Sam could see the relief break like sunshine through a mist as she said it.

She laughed. "Yeah, I'm definitely jealous. Ella's reading was actually really terrible to start with—almost like she was trying to be intentionally bad. And the poem is just terrible. Some rich donor must have written it and asked for it to be read. And…I don't think Ella even really wants to do it."

Sam nodded. He didn't think it seemed like Ella wanted to do it either.

"But she's a quick learner." Sarah dabbed at her eyes and put on her coat. "So there's my jealousy on the one hand," she said. "And… and on the other hand. I kind of miss her. She's been so busy. With Brandt and Jack and Lila and Nicole and who knows who else?"

Sam laughed and they began walking toward the back door.

"I mean, why can't she see it?" Sarah said. "That she's too young for Jack and that Brandt's kind of a jerk."

Sam shrugged. Girls, he'd noticed, often seemed to have this problem, but he didn't point that out to Sarah.

"It just would have been fun if you and me and Ella could have hung out or something. You know?" She looked at him with her big, shiny eyes.

He wanted to touch her face, to comfort her. He could feel how her skin would be under his fingers. It made him sweat.

Sam cleared his throat. "Well, maybe we could do something fun— you and me. We could maybe go get ice cream or something."

"I like ice cream," Sarah said smiling. "Even when it's freezing outside."

"We could get hot chocolate instead," he said quickly. "That new coffee shop has—"

"No," she said interrupting. "I think ice cream sounds good."

They walked through the empty halls, their arms occasionally brushing. Sam felt the warmth of her fingers. He hadn't held her hand since the corn maze.

Sarah glanced at him and he pushed open the door to the parking lot. Sarah walked through.

Sam took a deep breath and fingered the hundred dollar bill he'd folded into his pocket three very long weeks ago. It'd been washed several times since then and still it stayed folded and tucked away— evidence that Sam wasn't nuts. That he wasn't poor and that he could grab a thing he wanted and keep it close. He hoped it was true.

CHAPTER 46

Sam took Sarah to a small little ice cream shop called Percil's. He'd never been there, but back in August when school had started, he'd heard kids at school talking about it like it was Disneyland. At the beginning of December, the place was still packed.

He opened his wallet and plunked a twenty down on the counter before either of them had even ordered. He wanted it to be clear that he would pay, that this was his treat for her, and that he wouldn't have to scrounge around for pennies either.

Sarah got the almond cherry swirl, but Sam just went for a basic chocolate. He was still, in that way, his father's son. He didn't want to waste money on some fancy flavor he didn't like.

"Chocolate, huh?" she said.

Sam shrugged.

"You know you could have tasted some other flavors before you ordered. If you wanted to."

"I know what I want," he said. But he was found out. For a minute, he'd felt like he was taking some girl out on a first date, like it was a totally new start with a totally new Sam. But first real date or not, this girl already knew him; and she could tell he might have wanted to try another flavor if he'd known which one to try. There was something scary in being known, especially for a kid who'd moved every few months of his life.

But before Sam had time to think about it, Sarah said, "Here, taste this." She held her spoon up to him and he hesitated.

"Taste it," she growled at him, scooting closer and pushing the spoon toward him with a laugh.

He did. The almond was really good and the cherry might have been a nice fit with it, except that it tasted too fake and cough syrupy for Sam. "It's alright," he said.

"Yeah, that maraschino flavor isn't working for me either. I got it," she said with a bit of confession in her tone, "because they said it was the most popular flavor. Come on, let's try some other flavors and get what we really want."

There must have been forty flavors lined up in the tubs in front of them: Chipotle Honey Swig, Rum Raisin Rumble, Pistachio Cream… the list kept going. After trying at least ten flavors they each ordered another scoop of their favorite one. Double Almond Crunch for Sam and a surprisingly simple Vanilla Beany for Sarah.

When they left they were both shivering and laughing. Sarah kicked up the heat in her car. "Where should we go now?" she asked.

Sam had no idea.

"What about Zinnie?" Sarah asked. "Do you think she's home?"

Sam cleared his throat. He'd been steering clear of mentioning Zinnie or anything else Sarah might think was weird. Cautiously, he said, "I don't know, maybe. She'll try to feed us more if she is and I'm stuffed. Besides we'll have to crawl along the cold ground to get to her property, and—"

"Let's go," Sarah said, swinging out of the parking lot.

ZINNIE WAS NOT HOME. THE HOUSE WAS COLD, DARK, AND ABANDONED. Sarah began shivering in earnest. Sam knew he could take her to his trailer and they could watch a movie or something, but he had a better idea. "I wonder if she'd mind if we lit a fire," Sam said.

Sarah shrugged. "Probably not. But there's no wood or matches and I don't even know how to start a fire."

Sam did. He'd spent several months living in an abandoned RV with no power. He could build a fire. And cook on one too. But he didn't tell Sarah that. "Stay here," he said.

He was back in a few minutes with twigs and a few logs that were stacked by the house. After he and his dad had left the old RV, he'd kept a match in his wallet as a good luck charm, hoping they'd never go back. The match was still there.

It was just a few minutes before a cheerful flame licked up the back of the fireplace.

"Nice," Sarah said. "So you can navigate corn mazes, get bumped into honors physics, and build a fire. What other surprises have you got?"

That he'd been technically homeless more than once in his life, that until today he'd never once taken a girl out, that he could find a nickel in a packed parking lot.

That he'd broken into the mental hospital to make sure he himself was sane, that his father had hidden thousands of dollars in a hollow door to hide the fact that his family had been involved with some kind of werewolf mafia, that his mother had died because she'd kept her cancer a secret.

And then there was the charming little fact that he could shift shape under the full moon.

Nope. He couldn't tell her anything more that he wanted her to know. "Zinnie," he said, changing the subject. "You've never actually met her."

"Not yet," Sarah said.

"But you don't think I'm a nut job?"

"You're absolutely a nut job," she said, sitting cross-legged in front of the fire. "But I let you bring me to abandoned buildings, so I guess it doesn't concern me too much."

"Your hair looks nice," he said, sitting beside her, and then, "I went to the hospital again and used Zinnie's code a different way. She's real, in case you were wondering."

"So you got in?" Sarah said.

"Yeah," Sam said. "I did."

"Code cracker," she said. "Add that to the list."

"It's redundant," he said. "The corn maze, physics—they're all codes."

She turned to him. "I kind of wish you'd just made the Zinnie thing up to lure me here. But you brought Ella and spooked yourselves. But you're not"—she stopped—"you're not interested in Ella, right. Like, at all? I mean, you wanted to see her today, and I kind of just happened to be there."

"I did want to see her," Sam said. "But I'm definitely not interested in her in that way. I actually think—this will sound a little crazy—I think we're related. Cousins actually. So, yeah, no romantic interest."

"Are you freakin' kidding me?" Sarah said, turning sharply. "You think you're cousins? How?"

Sam swallowed. He hadn't really meant to bring it up. And how did he know? Because he'd found an old picture of his grandmother that his father had tried to hide. Because he had a dead aunt who had a daughter? Because his father had lied to him about it all? "Ancestry.-com," he said.

"Seriously," she said. "You're into that too?"

"Well, my dad was showing me my mother's, um, family line."

"Your mom, huh? They divorced?"

"Um, no, she died when I was little. Cancer. They didn't catch it early. And then she went fast."

"I'm sorry," Sarah said, looking straight ahead—the fire reflecting off her hair like sunset.

"Me too," Sam said. "But…but I found Ella's picture. Well, sort of," he said, thinking of the picture of his young grandmother who looked just like Ella. "I mean, on Ancestry." Sam paused. "Look. Could we not talk about this?"

"Yeah," she said. "Sure."

"And…and don't tell her, okay. I want to."

"I bet," she said, then more softly. "Cousins. Cool."

"What about you?" he said. "I don't know much about you."

She laughed. "Only child. Two dogs. Dentist mother. Accountant father. Seriously, Sam, as hard as I try not to be, I'm hopelessly boring."

"Sounds wonderful," he said, and then without thinking, picked up a piece of her hair and twisted it around his fingers.

"Sam," she said, but before he could reply, she'd put a hand to his neck and pulled him to her. Their lips met in a hard press. It was easy. Kissing her was easy.

She pulled back, but kept her face close to his. "You're a scaredy cat, Sam."

He wanted to say, *No, I'm not*. And then, *I know*. But he found that he couldn't say anything.

She moved her face an inch closer so that their mouths were almost touching again, and then she squinted slightly into Sam's eyes, her face tipped up to him.

He pushed a section of hair away from her face, and touched her neck.

She smiled, the light from the flames golden on her skin, her eyes closing like flower petals at night.

He leaned down, touching his lips to hers, softly, in pieces—taking one part of her mouth at a time—gently, top to bottom. Then he pressed his lips full against hers.

He wrapped his arms around her back and pulled her as close as possible. He could have stayed there forever, but after a minute Sarah pulled back slightly, looking into the dark of his eyes. She touched his cheek, his hair, pressed at his sideburns with her thumbs. "I was hoping you had it in you," she said, smiling.

He kissed her again—her mouth so soft, sweet.

"Yeah," he said, pulling back. "I definitely had it in me. It's just… codes are so much easier to figure out. I'm sorry I made you kiss me first."

"You didn't make me," she said, kissing him quick again, then laughing. "It did take you super forever though."

"I'll make up for lost time," he said, leaning down—kissing her forehead, then cheek.

And then there was a quick flash of light and a cracking sound.

Sam opened his eyes. "Was that thunder?" he asked.

"I don't think so," she said. "It was different."

What it was was a gun—right outside the window. It cracked again. "Whoever you are, you better come out," a low, harsh voice shouted.

"Come on," Sam whispered. "Hurry."

They crawled out the back and through the licorice post. They ran all the way to Sarah's car near Sam's house. When they got there, Sarah burst out laughing. "And that, sir, is why you don't go onto some rich guy's property to make out. He'll call the cops on you. Although I still think I'd choose that over my mother peering at us out the window, which is what would have happened if we'd been at my house."

Sam blushed at the thought—hot from his neck to his hair. He found it all so disconcerting. It was good to know Dr. Price wasn't standing at a window with a pair of binoculars. But getting chased from Zinnie's house by some guy with a gun—it was bizarre.

It was not, however, disconcerting enough to stop Sam from leaning down one more time and kissing Sarah.

It was late. He knew it. He opened her car door for her and then he watched her drive off, all the way until he couldn't see her taillights anymore.

His dad had gotten one thing right—the hunger was the worst part. But kind of the best part too.

WHEN ZINNIE OPENED HER EYES THE ALPHA WAS THERE, AS SHE'D known he would be. He enjoyed watching her suffer. He enjoyed watching her suffer while taking especial care to erase any physical pain she might have had. It was an odd, but perfect cruelty. When physical suffering was eliminated, it opened you up to experience other types of pain. Degradation, submission, shame, indignity—those were Napper's specialties.

Quietly, he adjusted her IV, then checked her vitals before placing a bowl of warm soup next to the bed.

"There now, we're almost done. Soon this ugly business will all be over."

"It will just be beginning," Zinnie said.

"Well, your part in it will be ended. Then you can rest." Napper smiled. "And you won't even have to be burned at the stake. Or any such gruesomeness. Look at you—a simple needle in your arm like a regular old woman."

"I will never be regular."

"We shall see." He adjusted the drip for the IV. She knew that it contained several pain medications as well as something strange— something of Napper's own creation. A new drug made just for her, and one that would sap the immortality from her, make her merely human. As a mere human, she did not have much longer to live.

She bit her lip, inviting pain.

Gently, he pushed the soup toward her. "You know one of my men made it onto your little property last night. We've never been able to do that before. A boy and girl were in the house. I sent a wolf to keep his eye on the girl." He paused, smiling at Zinnie's face. "I should also tell you the chimney was cracked—a deep line straight through. It won't be long now before it crumbles."

CHAPTER 47

Sam woke with a jerk remembering that he'd left a fire burning in an old house. He ran to Zinnie's. When he got to the grounds, he wasn't sure what he expected to see—charred walls, ashen trees, nothing maybe.

What he saw was the same old empty house, dusty and abandoned, but when he looked up, the chimney had completely collapsed. Sam banged through the front door. Dust from the collapse was thick, but otherwise the house was as it had been the night before, except for one thing. When Sam looked into the small kitchen, the stove was blackened and broken—a deep, dark gash up its side.

He had been there. He had left a fire. A fire burning in an old house with an old chimney.

He stood for a minute worrying, and then he heard the wolves in the distance—a long howling that raised the hair on his neck.

They were coming his way.

Zinnie had told him to use the back door—that that would protect him. And Sam had always felt perfectly safe with that promise, even when the house was empty. Somehow, though, he didn't anymore.

He ran for the licorice post, scurrying through as the wolves came around the corner, running in a pack after a small, frightened animal.

"Gabby," Sam called. The tiny cat bolted from the wolves through the narrow slits of the fence. Sam and the cat ran for Sam's house as the wolves growled through the cast iron bars.

∼

SAM'S DAD DIDN'T EVEN BOTHER TO TURN AROUND WHEN SAM brought the cat in and opened a can of tuna.

"Her tail's gone again," Sam's father said, looking out the window and listening to the wolves.

"You know the cat?" Sam said, surprised, but not.

"She dislikes me," his father said.

Sam shook his head. "And if you know the cat..."

"Yes," his father cut in. "The old woman." He didn't look at Sam. "I know of her."

"Well, since you know so much, maybe you know that part of Zinnie's house is gone too?"

His dad turned sharply. "What?" he said.

"The house—the chimney's collapsed." Sam was startled by his father's sudden reaction; it brought back his guilt. "I..." he said. "I'm worried I burned it down."

"How could you have done that?" his father asked, voice rising.

"I was there last night," Sam said. "With Sarah. I started a fire. To keep us warm. And then some guy chased us out. But I forgot about the fire. Do you think I burned it down?"

"No," his father said. He was gathering objects—cans of food, a few dishes—setting these things on the table as though grouping them.

"What are you doing?"

"Whether you burned it down or not, if the house is crumbling, we have to leave." His dad took out a duffel bag, threw in the cans, two plates, a handful of silverware.

"No," Sam said. "No."

"She," his dad said, "she was a barrier of protection. If the house is going, we have to go."

"What?" Sam asked.

"The house," his father replied. "The house and the old woman are connected—each strengthening the other, each weakening when the other is weak."

"Then Zinnie is in danger?"

"If the house is crumbling, yes." His father paused. "And if she is at risk, then so are we."

"We have to get her out," Sam said. "We have to help her."

"She's stronger than we are, son. If they can hurt her, they'll kill us." He paused. "We're going."

"No," Sam repeated, unaware that his voice had begun to rise. "No. You can go, but I won't. I'll move in with Ella or Sarah's parents. I'll report you to CPS or the mental institution. I'll do whatever I have to do to stay."

His father whirled toward him as though he was going to start yelling, but instead he whispered, "Then fix the house." He turned away. "And fix it quickly."

"What?" Sam said.

"It won't need much, but the walls must stay standing, and the chimney. And the stove."

"The stove is cracked," Sam said.

"That will have to be fixed too," his father replied.

"That's not possible," Sam said.

"Isn't it?" his father asked. "Then we go."

Sam looked at him. "Help me," he said. "Help me build it back."

"I can't," his father said.

"Won't."

"Can't." His father paused. "Well, not in the building of it. They'd smell me—the wolves." He looked down. "But I can get you some supplies. And then you can use that physics class for something besides a gold star on your college application."

It seemed impossible, to fix a house as old as that one—reinforce the walls, rebuild the chimney. Sam chewed on his cheek, trying to think. He'd always dreamed of building a playhouse. He'd even written the plans when he was younger, then carried them from new home to new home. He still had them.

But something bothered him that his dad had said. "Why won't the wolves smell me?" he asked.

"Because you're a half breed, and you're young. If they do smell you, it won't be as strong. Just," his father said, pausing. "Just don't eat any meat. And keep your distance from them."

Sam wondered if he'd kept enough distance when they'd been chasing Gabby.

"You don't eat meat," Sam said. "Why would they smell you?"

"Because I am from a very long, very pure line of shifters. If I get into their territory without Zinnie as a protection, they'll smell me no matter what I've eaten."

Sam nodded. He went to his room, got the plans for his playhouse, and laid them out for his father. "We can reinforce the walls with a few planks in triangle shapes, like this," he said. "And I'll have to learn how to brick the chimney. The good news is that it's not high up. But the stove…"

"The stove will be tricky to repair," his father said, picking up a pencil and starting to sketch. "But I think you can do it with a little welding equipment from your school." He paused to consider the drawing, and then, as though startled, he looked up. "You and Sarah were both in the house?"

"Yes," Sam said, looking at his father.

"Have you heard from her today?"

Sam shrugged. "No."

"You should give her a call," his dad said, looking down at the sketch, trying—Sam could see—to be casual, but not succeeding.

The phone rang over fifty times. Her voice mail never picked up. Sam looked at his dad who'd been watching as he'd dialed over and over again. His father's eyebrows dipped down. "I'm sorry, son."

Sam threw the phone, and ran.

THERE HAD BEEN A WOLF AT THE DOOR—THAT'S WHAT HER DAUGHTER had told her.

A wolf.

At the door.

A wolf whose fur was gray and red and black—mixed, textured. Stone-cut eyes. Sarah had screamed and her father had run down the steps two at a time. But there was no wolf.

A lie. A drama. Like all the other dramas that filled up her daughter's life.

But this time Fiona Price had refused to let it go. They'd taken her in for a consultation with one of the psychiatrists. And then everything had gone wrong.

"She'll have to be admitted," the tech had said.

Fiona and her husband had bulked and refused. But they couldn't refuse. A new law had been signed—making it possible to hold children struggling with certain types of hallucinations, even without parental consent.

Fiona had started to cry—the same as her daughter, but the tech had been calm. "Don't worry," he'd said. "It's for her own good. Children with these hallucinations became a danger—certainly to others, but mostly to themselves. Often," the tech had continued, "those with such hallucinations throw themselves off cliffs or in front of cars or shoot themselves in the heart just to escape the monsters they think they see."

The tech had pulled up several cases to show her.

Fiona had looked away in tears. "How long?" she'd asked.

The tech had smiled kindly, so kindly. "Not long, Dr. Price. It just depends on how well she responds to the meds and how quickly we can help her concede that these creatures of her imagining are not real at all."

She had agreed to let her daughter stay for observation. What else could she have done?

And yet there was something—something that needled at Fiona Price. A tiny word the technician had used. *Concede.* They were going to help her concede that the creatures weren't real. He should have used a term like "realize," "recognize," "understand"—something that implied a healing rather than a…a covering up.

Quietly, Fiona Price typed in the password of her daughter's phone and began to scroll down.

SAM WAS NOT HOME. HIS FATHER OFFERED THE WOMAN WHO announced herself as Fiona Price toast, and together the two sat eating the odd meal in silence.

When Sam burst through the door, it was like a clap of thunder. The boy even looked like a storm—hair sticking up at odd points, torn t-shirt, sweaty from running.

"Where is she?" he asked without even pausing to say hello.

"They're keeping her for observation."

"They are not," he said.

The small, red-headed woman in front of him closed her lips tightly. "She said your name." She paused. "As they took her away."

CHAPTER 48

"Hey, Ella girl," Lila's voice rang down the hallway, "Looks like you don't have to ditch your tagalong after all. Sam went and got himself suspended."

"What?" Ella asked, trying not to sound as shocked as she felt. "What'd he do?"

"Punched Luther Bradberry in the mouth," Lila said as Nicole and a girl named Kate came up beside them.

"Sam?"

"The one and super only," Nicole said, inspecting her new manicure.

"Why?" Ella asked, inspecting her own finger nails and trying not to sound like she cared.

"Because," Nicole said, "he couldn't bear to hear that his beloved Sarah Price got doped up and freaked out on her parents."

"But Sarah's not on drugs," Ella said.

"Whatever," Lila said.

"That's what she gets for not sharing," Kate added, ignoring Ella.

"Who cares," Nicole said. "The good news is that Sam isn't here to stare at you all weird all the time. Maybe he's on drugs, too."

"Sam?" Ella said again.

"The one and super only," Nicole said, laughing at her joke. "That kid is whacked. He's probably the one selling them."

Ella stepped uncomfortably back and forth, not sure what to say. Brandt came up to the group and flipped Ella's ponytail. "You guys talking about Sammy."

"Who else?" Nicole said. "Ella says he's selling drugs." She laughed at herself again.

"I did not," Ella said, laughing uncomfortably. Brandt looked at her, and Ella added, "Although he does act a little doped sometimes."

Ella felt the guilt flow in as soon as the words left her mouth. She pushed it down her throat.

"More like dopey," Lila said.

Ella laughed again. She looked around. Sam wasn't there. No one else was. There was no chance he had overheard and even if someone else had, who was going to tell Sam? No one. So why did she care that she was joshing on him with some kids?

Brandt smiled and said, "I might have texted you sooner if you hadn't always been with him." He put a hand on her shoulder, letting his finger graze the back of her neck when he did.

"Seriously," Lila said. "It was high time to dump him."

"He wasn't my boyfriend," Ella said, surprised at the weak tittering laugh she produced.

"Didn't have to be; some friends need dumping just as bad," Nicole said.

Everyone laughed again. Ella smiled, but couldn't make another laugh come out. Ella had been a lot of crappy things in her life, but she'd never been mean.

Further down the hall, Mr. Witten began to walk toward them. Her friends scattered and Ella gathered up her books for the night. As her teacher passed her, he paused and said, "See you tomorrow, Ella. Enjoy your reading of Snow White. Remember, the essay is about the multiplicity of the queen. I think it'll make for a good discussion, don't you?"

Ella was sure that it would make for a very good discussion—one in which she didn't plan to participate.

THE BLACK WOLF HAD LAIN NEAR THE BARN FOR TWO WEEKS—LONG enough that the chickens had forgotten the threat and now pecked happily around the black animal as though she was nothing more than an old broken tractor.

Foxy was not quite as bold or stupid as the chickens, but she was a good deal kinder. She made her way to the barn and lay down near the black wolf, staring into the dark eyes.

Loco followed a ways behind the small dog, watching. He was worried at first that Foxy had gone to confront the wolf, to face her fears. But as she stopped in front of the wolf, he realized that Foxy pitied the animal, pitied her with an understanding deeper than the rest of the dogs possessed. Losing a leg was not an endgame for a canine, but it cost you speed, dignity, and beauty.

The black wolf had not yet spoken to any of the dogs. Now she raised her head to stare at Foxy. Loco stood around the corner of the barn and listened.

"It's rude to stare," the black wolf began.

"It's ruder to sulk," Foxy replied.

Loco was ready for the black wolf to lunge or snap at Foxy, and was surprised to hear a low teetering sound at the bottom of the wolf's throat, a sound Loco realized was a laugh.

"I know it's bad," Foxy said. "But it's not the end of the world."

"I wish it was," the wolf said.

"Well, then, I suppose the end of the world *is* why you're all here," Foxy replied in her careful, quick way.

Again, the wolf laughed. "What do they call you, blunt one?"

"For many years I was one of the un-named. Now they call me after the small red foxes that sometimes hunt these parts."

"Fitting," the wolf replied.

"And yours?" Foxy asked.

"Ezazh," the black wolf answered.

Loco stepped closer. The black wolf sniffed the air, sensing him, and laid her head again against her paw, silent.

"Hmm," Foxy said, also sniffing the air. "You hungry? I'll find you a scrap or two. Perhaps some garlic. Doesn't do much for the breath, but it helps with recovery."

The black wolf turned away as Foxy left and Loco stepped forward, sitting on his haunches, unwilling to lie down as Foxy had in order to be level with the wolf.

"I see that you begin to recover," he began.

The black wolf did not even look him in the eyes. "Do not think that you saved me, sheep dog, just because you were the first to notice I was there."

"I do not claim that I did," he said, annoyed. "And I am not a sheep dog."

"Pardon me," she said. "Mutt."

"I believe the term you're looking for is 'mixed breed,'" Loco said.

"Very well then, mixed breed, do not now come to me as though you are one of my own."

Loco felt his temper flare. He certainly hadn't come to her as one of her own. "Your own left you to die."

"There is dignity in that," she replied, her voice like shutters snapping. "Not that the dogs would know anything about that."

"Neither, it seems, do you, having been just as ready to take food from the hand of a human."

"Death is a door that swings only one way," she said, her voice quieting. "I was not ready."

"Nor did you need to be ready. Accepting help from another is not weakness."

"Accepting help from a human is treason to the Alpha."

"Who did not himself extend help."

"Help I would not have needed were it not for the savage traps of the humans."

Loco looked into her face, the eye teeth draped down over the perfectly black skin of her muzzle. Without the maimed foot and muti-lated chest, she would have easily risen in rank among her kind.

"But my injuries are no business of yours."

"Fine," Loco replied. "Keep your injuries and your business."

The wolf's eyes were as black as her fur, blending into that face of perfect darkness. Ezazh closed her eyes, a long blink that did not wish to remember, but would not forget. "It was a claw—metallic. Not created to capture those of my kind. But used as such nevertheless."

A bear trap, Loco realized. One of the neighboring farmers must have put it out. There were no bears in these parts. The trap had been intended for the wolves.

"And why do you come, running through these lands that are not your homes, risking the ire and the fear of the humans, the danger of their tools?"

"We come when the Alpha calls."

"And he has called?"

"Of course."

"Of course," Loco said with a sigh. "The Alpha. Ready to destroy us and those we love."

"The wolves are not against you, foolish dog."

"Are they not?" Loco asked,

"Of course not. They are simply for themselves. They don't care one way or another for the dogs."

"How comforting."

"Comfort was not my intent, only understanding. The wolves wish you no ill. They wish only to protect and empower themselves, their packs, and their young. To do this, they follow the call of the Alpha."

"*They*," Loco asked.

"We," Ezazh corrected.

"Except that they have now abandoned you, as is their way."

"What else should they do? I cannot hunt. I will slow them, endanger them. Of course I can no longer roam among them—lower even than the omega."

"A lone wolf," Loco said.

"Yes," she replied. "For now."

"And you will not now join us—even as our Keeper tends to your wounds?"

"Your Keeper is not my Alpha—nor, I think, is he yours."

"The dogs do not bow under the weight of an Alpha in the same way the wolves do."

At that Ezazh laughed, but not with the friendliness she had shared with Foxy. "You may not bow to an alpha, but you bow in ways much less dignified than that. You bow to those who call you pet, to those who auction off your young for others to call pet."

Loco bristled, but did not reply.

"You have come to love them—your captors—like maidens stolen from themselves when too young."

"Only because most of the humans have come to love us. Which is more than can be said for your Alpha."

"Love is not necessary, only fidelity. I know what to expect from the Alpha."

"You question our lack of alpha, or pack. We have both, though in different form than the wolves."

"In human form," she spat.

"Yes," he said.

They fell silent as the farmer came into view, moving toward them with a change of bandages for Ezazh.

Just like Foxy, the farmer sat level with the wolf, preparing an ointment, then donning his thick shoulder-length gloves.

Ezazh growled and snapped, but the farmer held firm, dabbing the wound, then re-wrapping it.

Ezazh's words sat heavy in his stomach. The Alpha was not good, but it was true—he was consistent. Humans were not. Ella had not come back since the full moon. She was busy, distracted. Young. Loco paused. And perhaps she was also worried. Worried that she thought she could hear a dog talk.

In a town where any mention of a gift like that would get you thrown into an institution, that made sense.

Still, Loco was hurt. Ella was the *She*—the one with the power to stop the changing of the suns, or to complete it. But power did not equal courage.

For the first time, Loco wondered if Ella would have enough strength to do what was best for her kind. For both of their kinds, and the mutual bonds they had spent generations developing. All of that would be lost if the suns changed and the worlds ticked back to that ancient time.

Loco walked in the cornfields beyond the spot where the Keeper had found Ezazh. Loco knew the farmer wasn't sure if what he had done was right. Loco wasn't sure either. It was hard, he was learning, to be sure when what you'd done was right and what you'd done was wrong.

The last night he'd seen Ella she had heard him speak, heard him like only she could when the moon hung full and the world ticked back to a time before this time. A time when their voices could connect with those of her race, a time from a world of monsters and children and powerful songs. She was the last of her kind. That was why the Alpha needed her so badly.

Loco hadn't sung for ages; it was too dangerous. But that night when she'd left the window cracked, he had sung to the moon—his fears, his hopes, his history. The others had joined in, a tapestry of voices that wove together in a way the howling of the Gevudan never would.

Most couldn't hear it. Even on the night of the changing. But there were those who could. The Grey One had come to him after midnight and opened the window.

"Take me to her," he'd said. "Or The Rogue will get her first."

Loco had led the Grey One to Ella, spoken to her in the shadows just before the Grey One had covered her mouth with a rag of chlorophyll in an effort to protect her, in an effort to help her forget. Loco had run all the miles back to the farm.

The Gevudan and their masters had not followed. No. Another of their council had been shot. Shot toothless. The council had been too concerned with that to send anyone after a stray dog. The council was used to being the hunters, not the hunted. They were used to walking away from those who wished them harm.

Loco continued to pace. As dusk settled, Foxy joined him in his walk, staying close, limping faster than many dogs could run. If it weren't for those like her, it might be tempting to turn back the sun and return to the time when their kind ran free through the woods, singing and scavenging. But looking at Foxy, it was easy to see that the Alpha and his council did not have the dogs' best interests at heart, no matter what pretty promises they tried to make.

"Was it a mistake?" Loco said to Foxy. "To let one such as Ezazh remain among us?"

"If it is, it is a mistake that has already been made," Foxy replied. "You cannot now undo it with your thoughts or worries."

"I worry about more than that," Loco said.

"And those worries are likely just as ineffective," Foxy replied, stretching her rear legs.

"Do you think," Loco said slowly, "that our associations with the humans make us a lesser animal, repressed or used?"

"At times," she said, "yes. But they also make us more civilized, interconnected," she replied.

"But civilized is not necessarily free."

"Nor is wildness," Foxy replied. "Look at Ezazh. She is deformed and has been cast out. It is the way with their packs. They consider themselves so superior with their order and supposed emancipation. But it comes at a cost."

"As does our interaction and co-habitation with the humans."

"Correct," she said in her small, precise voice. "There is a cost— there is always a cost no matter your choice." She looked down at her maimed leg. "But with the cost, there is also, always, a benefit. I have not been cast out and left to die. I have been granted an asylum with the Keeper; and with you. Ezazh has too. And though she will likely not stay, I believe she will always remember. Our kind and theirs share one great commonality—we are loyal—fiercely so. She will not join us, but she will not betray us either. Watch."

With that, Foxy lay near Loco, scooting her good front paw under his belly. For many minutes, Loco did not relax into her touch, sitting up straight and still, looking at the moon until gradually his breathing slowed and he laid his head near her face—feeling her warmth, breathing to the rhythm of her steady soft sleep.

CHAPTER 49

It was just as well that Sam was suspended. Each morning he visited Sarah, hoping she would wake up from the medicated mist that held her captive. And each afternoon he worked on building Zinnie's house. It took him a lot longer than he thought it would. He had to feed several 2x4's through the cast iron posts of Napper's fence, then a load of bricks, a bag of concrete mix, and more tools than he ever could have imagined his dad owning.

It took an entire day just to get the corner 2x4's to stand up straight. He secured them with several other diagonal planks, expecting to be torn apart by a pack of wolves at any second, but none came. Gabby lay near him as he worked—in the spot Sam was pretty sure had been a chair by the hearth.

On the second day, he begged his father to help.

"I can't," his father repeated. "If I come, they'll find you."

The third day, it poured cold, vicious rain. Which made Sam less worried about wolves. He finished reinforcing the walls.

That afternoon, when the rain had stopped, he bricked a tall, wide chimney that he was sure was not in any way up to any code ever in the universe, but he figured that once Zinnie was back, she could fix it.

When he was done, Sam turned to the stove and picked up the

"

welder his shop teacher had let him borrow. How his dad had talked Mr. Waters into that, Sam had no idea. *Hey, let's lend the violent, suspended kid a fire-shooting gun.* Some adults, Sam was learning, were either crazy morons or people who actually cared. Probably a little of both.

Sam spent the next several hours trying to mend the wounded stove. He wasn't sure it did any good, but when he was done, he bricked around and in front of it, creating a simple, flat hearth.

Finally, he pulled out one of his mother's old doilies that he'd found in the suitcase with his grandmother's picture, and placed that at the center of the hearth. It was snowing outside in the darkness—sleety wet flakes that pounded on the tin roof and leaked into the corners in a way Zinnie surely wouldn't have approved. But it was the best he could do in a few days. And—Sam thought with a bit of pride—it was better than any play house. Well, a little.

It'd been a couple weeks since Ella had dipped into her mother's jewelry box, but today she wrote on small bits of paper, scribbling all the names of all the friends she had, and then at the end, she wrote on a last piece of paper, *CONFUSED*. She dropped it into the cacophony of paper slips before lifting the bottom section and sliding out the stack of her mother's papers.

She didn't thumb through them as had been her habit. She just plopped them open and began to read.

Once in the land of the high white sun, the years flew by—rising and falling in a steady rhythm that did not, could not, relent. All of the Originators had long passed, their mortal shells crumbling to dust after the manner of every creature under the high white sun. None were granted the near perpetual life the Changers had once known, and none were denied the glory and birth of children. Except two. These continued while everyone else passed on.

The Remainers spent their days in woods where ancient trees and babbling creeks would die and change before they did. Seas dried up, rivers moved course, mountains withered to hills. The Remainers still aged, but so slowly as to be nearly imperceptible to those who lived and died among them.

The Tea-drinker provided refuge in her woods. Any who wished to build and not destroy were welcome. While the Unthroned hid, ashamed of his fate, tortured by a life that would not end. He avoided all until eventually, mercifully, his legacy dimmed, mostly forgotten.

Both watched as their new world slipped by into centuries—evil and good traipsing before them in an ever reliable succession of years.

WHEN SAM CAME BACK TO SCHOOL ON FRIDAY THE EMPTINESS OF NOT seeing Sarah was everywhere he looked. Of course, everyone else thought she'd been hallucinating or making something up, but Sam knew that there had been a wolf at her door—Sam himself had shown it the way.

Do not go near the ones you love.

"Sam," Mr. Witten was saying. "Sam."

Sam looked up.

"May I speak to you in the hall please?"

Sam expected a lecture. He'd missed at least one paper during his suspension.

"I'm sorry," Mr. Witten said, "about your girlfriend."

Sam wanted to say that Sarah wasn't his girlfriend, that he was fine, that whatever. Instead he said, "There's a hole. I can't close it."

"A hole," Mr. Witten said, "is an opening that can lead someone through to somewhere else."

Witten took off his bracelet, held it out to Sam. "I knew your mother when we were younger," he said slowly. "And lately I've been worried about you. This is a little piece of our combined past. Maybe it will open up some doors for you."

That was not what Sam had expected to hear. Sam felt like he should have been shocked, maybe even angry at this new piece of information, but nothing surprised him now.

He found that he was not interested in memories. Or secrets. They all hurt, every one, in their different ways. And at this point he hurt too much for a new scratch to register very much.

He looked at the bracelet. The copper piece on the silver band was a square the size of an SD card, only slightly thicker, with ornate circles engraved around a delicately scripted "N." Whatever that stood for. Sam didn't care.

He nodded roughly at his teacher and took the bracelet, his hand brushing against the copper piece, which had the grain and thickness of a small, square key.

The semester was almost over. Today Mr. Witten would be reading selections from several of the stories they'd discussed this semester. He started with Hansel and Gretel—pacing the room, opening the tale, his rich voice filling it up until you forgot about his small, portly body.

The class stared at Witten with more attention than they'd given him all year—realizing, it seemed, what it meant that their teacher was a world-renowned folklorist—a man who could spin a tale like golden threads until you forgot.

"Once," Sam's teacher began. "There lived a boy and a girl at the edge of a wood—a wood deep with secrets, dark with wolves."

CHAPTER 50

Ella had not been at the farm for almost three weeks. It felt like an eternity. Thanksgiving had come and gone—a fancy, French restaurant being Vivi's only form of celebration. Ella was grateful. The less tradition, the less reason to think about her mother. The same went for Vivi's Christmas preparations, which mostly focused around the Festival of the Red Candle.

Ella had gone shopping with Vivi several times, and had a ballroom dance lesson twice a week. Plus, people kept inviting her to get together to see a movie or play tennis or to shop some more. Ella was getting to bed later and sleeping in as long as she could. One Saturday, she had actually slept in until nearly noon.

When she thought about it, it felt weird to be just like a normal kid with a cell phone and this season's boots. She'd never been a normal kid—not as the poor kid of a single mom, not as the orphaned kid of a dead mom. But slowly, steadily, her life had started to tilt toward normal. Some days she felt guilty enjoying it—the fluffy comforter on her bed, the cash that sat like an invitation in her new purse, the phone, the country club, the everyday indulgences that were part of life with Vivi.

At first she'd struggled to sleep in the perfect silence of Vivi's house, but now she wasn't sure if she'd ever be able to go back to the lullaby of rat feet in the ceiling overhead. At first she'd struggled to accept Vivi's money, but now she was coming to expect it. At first she'd pushed against the easiness of her new life. Now, apparently, she could sleep until noon and not look back. Well, almost.

Lately Ella had been thinking some things through, ready to make some changes to her new life. It was time to leave certain things behind, and make other things permanent.

That afternoon, Ella took the bus like she had on her first trip out to the farm. It seemed like years since she'd ridden a bus to the farm. She could have gotten a ride from Lila or Nicole, but she didn't want them to know what she did in her free time.

She wished she could have gotten a ride from Sarah—Sarah who'd liked her in spite of her weirdness, maybe even because of her weirdness. Sarah who'd liked her, Ella realized, because they were both trying to figure out who they were.

But Sarah wasn't here. Ella didn't care if Lila and Nicole said Sarah was on drugs, or Kate and Brandt said Sarah had gone off the deep end with the goth thing. Ella was pretty sure that neither was true. Sarah had definitely been the most sane of the three friends, despite her efforts not to be. So why was she the one gone, *institutionalized*? Ella tasted the ugly word, then pushed the thought away, staring out the window and thinking about what she would say when she got to the farm.

She had decided that today she would talk to Jones about adopting Loco. Even with her new friends and new clothes and new status as *non*-loser, she had missed the dogs. She figured if she could bring one home, that ache would subside. She hoped so anyway.

She hadn't talked to Vivi yet about adopting a dog, but she was pretty sure it'd be fine. Loco was perfectly trained, and what was a dog compared to an iPhone or—come Christmas—an Audi. It seemed like if Vivi would agree to those other things, she would certainly agree to taking in a pet.

When Ella got to the stop, she wrapped her coat tight around her. December had come quietly, and now the temperatures were dropping into the twenties at night. When she stepped off the bus, it was nearly dark.

Ella thought she saw a black form in the woods—like one of the dogs, except that it was running on only three legs. Ella squinted into the corn fields to the side of the road. It couldn't be Foxy. It was too big. A rustle of old corn husks, and the shadowy animal was gone.

Ella ran her fastest to the farm. When she got there, she was surprised to see Jones outside in the gathering darkness with a bunch of lights set up—the dogs sitting eagerly around, as though waiting for a party.

Inside the circle of light, Jones had placed a table with several tubes and jars and a propane torch on the side.

"Hello, Ella," he said, putting on a pair of gloves. "Wasn't expecting to see you tonight."

Ella was staring at the table and couldn't think of a response. She hadn't really expected to be here.

Jones dumped out a bag of foreign, silver coins.

Ella found her voice. "What are you doing?"

The farmer smiled. "I'm making silver. Well, sort of. I bought these old Australian coins off of Ebay. They were cheap, but they're fifty percent silver. I can refine them and reduce them down to almost pure silver. Then I can use them for whatever else I want to make."

Jones fired up the torch. "Here, I'll show you how it's done."

He placed the coins in an old jar. "First, you add a mix of nitric acid and water." The liquid changed color, becoming a bluish-green, while an ugly yellow gas formed at the top of the glass and began to drift off.

Ella felt like she was watching a witch at work, but she couldn't move or take her eyes off of it.

Jones stepped back for just a moment. "You have to be outside because the nitric acid releases dangerous fumes. The dogs can smell it —they always back off."

And they did. Ella did too. As Ella watched, the coins seemed to melt away, leaving nothing but blue liquid behind. That didn't seem to bother Jones. He added more water and then poured the liquid through a coffee filter into another jar.

"It's…it's gone," Ella said. "The coins are gone."

Jones just smiled and put a coiled copper wire into the blue liquid. "Watch," he said.

Ella found that she couldn't not watch. Gradually, the copper wire began to attract what appeared to be dust-like specks of gray. As it did, the copper wire itself grew smaller and smaller. Soon the wire was almost gone and a strange clump of gray matter was left in its place.

The farmer looked at her, waiting for her to ask the question.

She just shook her head.

"The copper atoms traded place with the dissolved silver—so the silver solidified from the liquid as the copper went into the liquid. An interesting exchange."

Jones poured the blue liquid and gray dust through another coffee filter, catching all the gray particles. When the particles were dry, Jones got out the blow torch.

Ella took a step back, though all the dogs seemed to lean in. Jones put some of the gray particles on—of all things—half a potato, which he set on a large brick slab. "The metal won't bind to the potato like it would a brick," he said. Then he turned the blow torch toward the particles. As the potato blackened, the gray particles began to come together. Jones added more gray particles until they'd all been heated and there, on the blackened potato, sat a tiny, shiny button of silver.

Jones stood back to admire it. "That there," he said, "is nearly pure silver—99.9%. Pretty huh?" He stepped closer and touched it quickly to see if it had cooled. When it had, he held it up in the light.

It was pretty—one of the prettiest little stones Ella had ever seen. But she stepped back anyway because when the farmer held the small piece of silver up to the light, it looked exactly like a small bullet for a small gun. She tried to shake off a shudder, but didn't succeed.

Jones looked at her. "You cold?" he asked. "Come on inside for a cup of hot chocolate."

"No," Ella said. "No, thank you. I actually can't stay long. I just came because I needed to tell you that I won't be able to come out to the farm much anymore. Maybe not at all. It's just been really busy with the end of the school semester and Christmas coming."

"And the Festival," Jones added.

"Yes," Ella said, not sure why she was surprised that he knew about it. "And the Festival." She took a quick breath. "But Mr. Jones," she said. "I also wanted to talk to you about adopting Loco."

Jones paused for what seemed like a very long moment. "Of course," he finally said. "Now, I have to tell you I don't actually do the adoptions. Miss Mandy at the Humane Society will have to take care of that side of the business. I'll give her a call and maybe we can shoot for this Tuesday. How does that sound?"

Ella didn't know. She hadn't even discussed it with Vivi. "Okay," Ella said. "That will probably work."

Jones stared thoughtfully toward one of the lanterns and as he did, Ella noticed that he wiggled something in his mouth. She watched as he moved it up and down, almost as though it was a mouthpiece of some sort. Jones turned quickly and saw her staring at him.

"I was just thinking," he said, and as he said it he seemed to click a few of his teeth back into place, "that I'm going to miss that old dog. He'll be in good hands though." Jones winked.

Ella barely registered it. She was staring at his mouth.

"Sorry," Jones said. "Bad habit. Cow kicked two of my teeth out when I was a kid. That's why I only raise corn and chickens."

Ella nodded, but could not find it in herself to smile. She'd just seen Jones fashion old coins into tiny silver nuggets that looked like bullets. And he was missing teeth.

It seemed impossible—surely she hadn't spent the last few months doing volunteer work for a serial killer. He took care of dogs. He ran a corn maze. Ella paused. A corn maze with a famous silver bullet.

"I, um, I've got to hurry to catch the bus."

"Do you want me to walk you there?" he asked. "You look a little ill."

"No," she said. "It's okay. The cold air feels good." Ella turned up the gravel drive, walking quickly, then trotting, before breaking into a full run. She didn't slow until the bus rumbled down the country road, pulling to a creaky stop in front of her.

ELLA LET THE BUS GO PAST HER STOP—WELL PAST. THE THOUGHT OF going home to Vivi's perfect house seemed hard.

When she got off the bus, she realized she'd gone down into the southern quarter of town. It was now nearly eight o'clock, and she was standing in front of a building of old, run-down apartments with a "For Rent—Cheap" sign in front of them. This is where her mother would have lived if she'd ever lived in Napper. The only gates in her community would have been on the apartment windows—and that was if she was lucky. *One bedroom, one bath, mice optional.*

Ella walked all around the building, smelling booze and Mexican food and old, empty room smells that seemed to drip from the walls.

The buses had stopped running. It was probably a good three miles from here to her house, and Ella felt suddenly very, very tired. Sam's trailer park, she knew, was just a few blocks away.

By the time she got to his house, it was really cold. Sam looked thin and pale when he opened the door.

"Ella," he said, letting her in quickly. He had just come back to school and she'd been avoiding him. "What's up?"

Ella took a deep breath. "I went to the farm," she said, "but I missed my stop. I must have fallen asleep. Do you think your dad could give me a ride to Vivi's house?"

Sam's dad had come up behind him, and Ella was pretty sure that his dad looked like the very last thing he'd like to do in this world is give her a ride home, but he dug his keys out of his pocket anyway.

"Yeah, sure," Sam said, getting his coat. The three of them walked out to the old van.

It wasn't a long ride, but it was surprisingly quiet.

Ella noticed that Sam was staring at her in a strange way—kind of like he had when they first met, only even stranger, like he wanted to tell her something.

She sighed. Sam was definitely a weird one. She hoped no one would see her get out of the van. She wasn't sure how she'd explain that to her friends. She turned away toward the window and Sam looked down at Ella's hand, staring at her ring.

"So," Sam's dad finally said, breaking the silence. "You live with your aunt. This is your dad's sister?"

"No," Ella said. "I think my dad was an only child, but I know almost nothing about him. This is my mom's older sister."

Mr. Calhoun nodded, but when Ella looked over at his profile, it looked like all his facial muscles had been snapped tight.

She got out and thanked him. He nodded. Sam said good-bye and that they should hang out sometime. Ella tipped her head, not quite committing.

~

WHEN THEY GOT BACK HOME ROBERT CALHOUN SAT IN THE DARKNESS of his room for a very long time. He knew just who Ella's mother's sister was. And it was not the woman living in that house. Robert wasn't entirely sure who was pretending to be his dead wife, but he had a pretty good idea.

Robert could hear Sam tap lightly on the door. "Dad, you still awake?"

Robert did not answer. Let his son think he was asleep. Let him think that everything was okay and that they would stay in this haunted little town. In the morning, they would leave and never come back.

CHAPTER 51

Sam could tell when his father was ready to run. But he also knew that his dad would do almost anything to avoid getting the police or a social worker involved. And so Sam had run first.

He didn't want to hide. He didn't want to worry his dad. But just because his dad was ready to bolt didn't mean Sam was. He'd spent the day slouching along the south side, a black hoodie over his head.

Dusk settled before the Napper Psychiatric Institution had even closed. Sam waited patiently, feeding bits of hamburger bun to the ducks in the pond at the center of the grounds until all the normal workers had gone home. The lights had come on along the pathways, and the building was locked up tight.

Then he went and stood outside the side door in the nearly perfect darkness of the overcast sky. Sam had noticed something about cloudy nights. They left him feeling tired, a little weak, hungry, but listless.

Tonight that didn't matter too much because the lack of moonlight would cover a skinny white kid in darkness.

He'd only typed in three numbers of the code when a groundskeeper appeared from around the corner. Sam gasped.

The groundskeeper didn't. He just looked at Sam and smiled. "I'll tell you what, every time I think the old woman has lost it, she goes and proves me wrong again."

"Excuse me?" Sam said, his voice a whisper.

The janitor moved closer. "Of course, we should be quiet. You're right. The old woman," he continued. "She said you would probably be here tonight. And that you would remember her number. Usually she gives it to me, but she was not even conscious till a couple days ago when she bolted up in bed, good as new. But she can't remember her number. I told her she didn't need it, and that I would help her out anyway. As a friend. But she told me you'd be here tonight to give it to me."

"Her number?" Sam asked.

"Yes," the janitor replied, stepping back as though worried he'd made a mistake.

"The number she uses to get out of the hospital?"

"Yes," the janitor whispered, looking relieved. "Just type it into my phone."

"Which number?" Sam asked.

The janitor shrugged. "Far as I know, she's only got one. Uses it to pay me to get her out every time." The janitor pushed a cell phone toward Sam. "Here, I already typed in the zeros at the beginning."

Sam stared at the phone for a very long minute.

"Account numbers never work without the right number of zeros."

Account number. "So she just pays you to let her go?" Sam asked.

"Pretty much," the guy said. "Boss acts like he thinks it's magic."

Sam blinked. Apparently being a witch was cool and all, but nothing worked as well as a good old fashioned bribe.

The janitor went on. "If she was herself, she would have just given me the number." He looked down at his keys like he felt a little sad, then looked up and said, "Somebody's got to take care of the old crow. She might be a little quirky but she makes the best cake this side of the Mississippi, and probably the other side too. Plus she's always been good to me."

"You're extorting money from her," Sam said.

"Well, son," the janitor said, pulling his phone back a bit. "I don't see it as no bribe. I told her she didn't need to give me nothing to get her out, but she insisted on paying me for my troubles. Truth is, I wouldn't a let her go at all, money or no, except that every time she comes in here, she ends up looking worse than when she got here. Some hospital." He shook his head.

Sam looked at the phone and hesitated. Was he really going to give this number that was also a secret code to some random guy? Then he heard Zinnie's words in his head. *My number*, she had said, *If I ever need you to check me out of the hospital.*

Sam had to admit that he'd used that number in a lot of ways for a lot of things, but he'd never actually used it to get Zinnie out.

He looked at the janitor. It didn't really seem like he should trust some old guy who took money in exchange for releasing Zinnie. But then, it *did* seem like you could trust a nice, rich philanthropist like Napper. And Sam was pretty sure you couldn't.

Sam chomped on his cheek, his mind fluttering over the original thirteen numbers Zinnie had given him. Zinnie's number. The one she had used to tell him so many things—the number that was a clue about The Ring of the Alpha, a code for the office of the Havensborough Unit, and now a credit card number to get Zinnie out of her confinement.

Zinnie was the furthest thing from a woman with Alzheimer's in the world.

Sam looked at the janitor and decided that he was just the person Zinnie would trust with her money. Sam took the phone and typed in the number. "Take good care of her Mr., um…"

"Marcus," the man replied.

"And I'd appreciate it if you wouldn't mention seeing me here tonight," Sam added.

"Right," the janitor said. "I'll just go help the old woman out now. What are you here for anyway?" he asked.

Sam stared at the janitor, trying to think up a lie. He couldn't. "A girl," he said. "I came to see a girl."

"Well then," the janitor said, winking. "You got my word."

∾

SAM WAITED UNTIL THE MAN WAS OUT OF SIGHT AND THEN STOOD FOR A few more minutes before typing in the code and stepping quietly through the door. He walked soundlessly to Sarah's room. Visiting hours had ended, but that didn't matter to Sam. He knew where each fire exit was as well as the stair well, and an old fire escape that dripped down the south wall.

The night nurses, however, he didn't know. He figured that was best. There were only two on the floor after visiting hours. One had her nose in the computer and one had her back to Sam and was talking almost non-stop.

Sam slipped around two corners. Sarah's door had always been open when Sam had come. Which didn't matter. Because her eyes had been closed. Every time. Once she'd groaned and said his name, moving her hand as though she was feeling around for something in a dark room.

Sam's heart had raced and he'd touched her hand, taking it in his, but then she'd gone limp—back into a restless, but persistent sleep that the institution called healing. This meant that during their visits, he'd done all the talking—apologized for getting her stuck here, touched her rust-colored hair, told her he loved it—everything he'd ever wanted to say, he'd said.

Sam got to the door, pressing slightly on the handle.

It was locked.

It didn't have a traditional key hole for a traditional key, or even the type where you slide a card through. Instead, there was a small port where a person might press a small square.

Sam took out the bracelet Witten had given him. It was a hunch—a hopeless, crazy hunch, but Sam held the bracelet and awkwardly pressed the square into position. The light above the handle flashed red. Sam took it out and took a deep breath. Each sound he made seemed impossibly loud—the click of the metal, the scratching as he slid it out.

He turned the square a quarter turn and pushed it in again. Another red light, and then a sound. From the room. Sarah had gasped.

Sam pulled the square from the port. He heard Sarah moving, the crinkly plastic sound of the hospital bed, the press of a button.

"Someone's out there," she whispered. "There's scratching."

Down the hall, Sam heard the call go through at the nurse's station. He braced to run. "Sarah," he hissed, his voice low.

"It knows my name," she shouted to the intercom.

Sam felt his muscles tighten, ready to sprint, until down the hall, he heard a laugh. "There she goes again. Wonder what it is this time? Big foot?"

The computer nurse didn't laugh. She let out a heavy breath. "I guess we'd better check on her. But first I have to finish this paperwork. Check the computer for her dosage," she barked at the other nurse.

Quickly, Sam turned the square again, but he was shaking now. The nurses would be coming, and inside the room, Sarah seemed to be crying softly.

"They're trying to get in," she said over and over. "I can hear the wolves scratching."

Sam wanted to cry too. Could he do something, anything, that wouldn't hurt her?

He turned the square again to the last possible side. The key still didn't let him in, but this time it made a noise—three angry beeps in quick succession. He jerked out the key just as he heard one of the nurses jump up. "Oh crap. Someone is down there, tampering with the key coder."

She ran down the hall—the plodding footfall of a heavy woman. Sam was glad for that. He could easily outpace her.

"Jenni," the nurse said, panting. "Hit the button to lock all the doors. And call security!"

Sam banged through one of the fire doors, setting off an alarm.

"Jenni," the other nurse screamed.

"I'm calling security," Jenni shouted back.

"Hit the button."

"Where is it?"

"Under the desk."

Sam heard her chair go down—knocked over in her haste. But that was all he heard because after that he was standing on the south side fire escape—hand over hand down the old rungs until he jumped the last eight feet.

It hurt, and for a moment Sam cursed the clouded night. He'd landed unevenly, jolting one ankle much harder than the other, but he didn't have time to feel sorry for himself.

Around the corner came the long beam of a bright flashlight, and attached to the beam was the strongest-looking security guard Sam had ever seen. The guard ran, shining the flashlight in every direction.

Sam pulled his black hoodie over his head and sprinted away—his ankle stabbing every time his foot hit the ground. He turned in to a stand of trees, zigzagging out at a different point.

When he did, the guard was there. He caught Sam's profile in a beam of light. "Hey, kid!"

The security guard ran after Sam, beginning to catch up, but Sam knew the paths better. He ran along the quiet, grassy sections, darting. In the distance, he heard sirens—screeching down Main Street in his direction.

Sam stopped.

He was nearly cornered, and almost ready to give up and make up some embarrassing excuse about why he was trying to break into a girl's room in the middle of the night when he heard a voice straight above him. "Climb, son."

Sam looked up, and nearly at the top of the tree sat his father petting the little cat Gabby. Sam stepped up a low limb, climbing as quickly as he could, favoring his right ankle.

When he reached the top, he saw the security guard run onto the path—the flashlight shining every direction but up. The guard kept running until Sam could tell he'd reached the street because the screaming of the sirens stopped and Sam heard voices, shouting back and forth.

The voices fanned out across the area.

"They'll find us," Sam whispered.

"Shhh," his father said. "And no. The guard is a human."

"So," Sam said.

"Humans never think to look up."

"And the cops?"

"I don't know what they are, but look." His father scooted into a hollow area of the thick evergreen. Sam looked straight at him and still almost couldn't tell he was there.

His father gestured for him to come over. "You're just lucky," he said, "that Gabby saved you a spot."

Sam slept squished against his father, a purring cat on his lap. In a way, it reminded him of when he was young and they'd driven across the country. Sam had sometimes fallen asleep slouched against his father's shoulder. He hadn't done that in years and was surprised when the sleep slipped over him just like it had then.

In the almost morning, when the pre-dawn gray pressed itself across the sky, his father finally moved. "Come on, son," he said. "They're gone."

Stiff and cold, they climbed down from the tree and walked—two dark shadows turned to men as the pale December sun creaked over the horizon.

⁓

LATE IN THE AFTERNOON, ROBERT CALHOUN WOKE UP. SPENDING THE night in a tree was exhausting. Spending the night in a tree with a boy who had a thick band of silver in his pocket was worse.

Robert walked to The Property, counting his way along the cast iron fence posts until he got to the one he knew was there. Licorice or not, there was no way he would make it through it. Through the bare winter trees he could see the small hut. It looked frail, but a thin wisp of smoke snaked out of the chimney—the chimney his son had built.

"Zinnegael," he called through the fence.

She did not answer, but the small tabby appeared at the gate, her smooth long tail curled around her like a scarf.

"Gabriella," he said formally.

"You'll have to use the front door," the cat said. "I do hope you haven't had any meat."

He hadn't. He hadn't had meat for the last sixteen years, and he'd barely eaten anything these last two weeks.

Slowly, he walked back to the fence, the padlocks hanging open except for a small one on the bottom. Without her staff, the witch's magic was now too weak to open them all. Robert jiggled the lock, then stomped it with his foot, breaking it. He slid through the gate and up the path into Zinnie's house, then sat down, breathing heavily.

The house was warm, but just barely. Zinnie wore a thin shawl over her narrow shoulders and walked now with a significant stoop. The house itself seemed smaller, the furniture ragged and old. Only Sam's handiwork looked newer—and even that seemed to have acquired some wear.

"Hello, Robby," Zinnie said. "I was just thanking your son for all he's done."

Sam was sitting at a small table, cinnamon roll in hand. When he saw his father, he stopped chewing, the bun hanging loosely from his fingers.

"You got in?" Sam said.

His father didn't reply. He only waved a hand at Zinnie who was trying to put a cinnamon roll on his plate and said, "Just tea for me, thank you."

"Sam's done a lovely job with the chimney and stove, don't you think?" Zinnie said, pouring the tea. "I know you don't normally take sugar and cream, but I'm adding a spot anyway." She tossed in two cubes of sugar. "You look too thin."

"He's done well," Robert replied, taking the sweetened tea without argument. "But it won't last long, will it, Zinnegael?"

The old woman pursed her lips. "No dear, it won't."

"I'm sorry," Sam broke in, as though trying to process all that was happening. "But how did you get in?"

"I broke a lock," Robert replied.

Zinnie frowned, aware it seemed, of what that meant. "Oh, but I do miss my staff," she murmured under her breath.

"You know how he likes his tea," Sam said. "I didn't even know he liked tea."

"I don't," his father said. After a short pause, he continued, "There are some of our kind who know Zinnegael very well. She is a guardian of the forest and its kind, a controller of storm and wind. She is a protector of those who wish to hide from the Alpha. Though it has cost her much." Robert nodded with a touch of gratitude to the stooped woman. "Right now she is the only reason they can't smell me."

Sam shook his head. "And what do you mean, the chimney won't last? I know it's not perfect, but it should last for a little while at least. I did the best I could."

"And it is very good," Zinnie said, refilling his cup, though he'd barely drunk any tea. "But there are powers outside of your control, and the medicine has become very strong."

"Medicine," Sam asked.

Zinnie ignored him. "When my age catches up with me, it will catch up with this house as well. And then we will crumble."

Sam set his sticky bun on the table.

"But your work on the house has been like a little vitamin for me," she added fondly. "A boost that will extend my time longer than the Alpha expects." She laughed. "So before this house and I return to dust, I have several batches of cookies and a few good tricks up my sleeve. Now," she said, "take your father home."

CHAPTER 52

It had been many, many years since Witten had worked at the compound—hired to keep their records. At the time, they'd not known who he was. At the time, he himself had just been figuring it out.

Had they known that he was one of them but not the same, had they known the lineage of his family—they would have ripped his throat out before he set foot on their property, much less plunked his nose into their important documents.

The human boy had been hired to work on the cars. It was unusual to have a human worker on the compound, but all could agree that the humans were superior in their use of tools and the welding and crafting of metals. They assumed he would look at The Ranch as an exclusive sort of retreat and nothing else.

What they had failed to assume was that he would notice the two sisters, brought to the psychiatric ranch retreat in order to cure their acute case of pTr4 hallucinations.

Napper—in all his genius—had often overlooked the obvious, ignoring something he considered human folly. Something like young love. Until that human folly took off in one of his best cars with the human sisters he'd been cultivating at The Ranch for a very long time.

The car had exploded at the bottom of the cliff. Cliché of course, but when a plan is cooked up by two twenty-something young males—one of them totally love sick and one of them desperate to escape, explosions just make sense. And it had worked. For many years the four of them were thought dead.

After the explosion, they had separated—Patrick and Christa going to the nearest town to elope; Vivian hitchhiking her way across the state and eventually meeting Robert; and him, Witten—limping away. He was sure he'd get caught by the Alpha until he was found instead by a hunter and his dogs—the hurt ankle healed, a square, copper piece of metal extracted from the wound.

IN RETROSPECT ELLA REALIZED THAT SHE SHOULD HAVE MADE VIVI brownies or at least a good cup of coffee.

As it was, she brought up the adoption of Loco just after dinner on Monday night. Vivi did not blow up exactly. Her words were as cool and clear as ever. But her jaw clenched shut with a strange little click and her eyes rounded into angry, dark discs. "You have been going to this farm without my permission?"

Ella was slightly taken back. As far as she knew she hadn't really needed permission for anything. Vivi didn't much seem to care where she went, or with whom.

"I…I'm sorry," Ella said. "I didn't realize I needed permission."

"The farm is several miles out, in the middle of nowhere. The dogs run loose. What if one had bitten you? Or something else had happened?"

Something else had happened at that farm, much worse than a dog bite, but now didn't seem like the best time to mention the corn maze attack.

"It's safe," Ella said, feeling the lie in her voice as she said it. She hadn't been safe the first time she'd gone to the farm. And she hadn't felt safe the last time she'd been there either. In fact, part of the reason she wanted to adopt Loco was to get him off of the farm and closer to her.

"Frankly, Ella, that farm has a reputation. And it's not one of safety."

"What do you mean?" Ella asked.

"They run that corn maze. Several times people have been lost in it."

"Oh," Ella said as neutrally as possible. She didn't want Vivi to know that she already knew that.

"When the lost were recovered, some were okay, but one had a serious concussion and at least three had to be admitted to the psychiatric institution for several days due to some strange side effects that they were suffering."

That was new.

"Some kind of emotional trauma?" Ella asked.

"I suppose," Vivi said. "They were talking jibberish by the time they were found—moaning about the things they'd heard—dogs and talking and some such nonsense."

"And the man who runs it," Vivi continued. "Look, he's probably perfectly nice, but he's known for not hiring any hands. He likes to work alone. A single, older man being with you alone is not a safe environment for a young girl. Do you understand what I'm saying?" Vivi looked at her in a way that made Ella extra sure she didn't want Vivi to have to explain.

"Yes, ma'am," Ella said softly.

Vivi turned to leave, and Ella blurted, "But Vivi, I've already been to the farm and I'm fine. I won't go back," she added quickly, seeing Vivi's look. "But could we at least go out and adopt the dog? We wouldn't even have to go to the farm. We would meet at the Humane Society to sign the papers."

"The Humane Society," Vivi almost barked, and then more quietly she said. "Ella, look, I'm sorry, but I'm incredibly allergic to dogs. I can't go to the Humane Society. And a dog is simply out of the question."

Ella was not used to pressing her aunt. She had never needed to. "I could keep him out back, tied up or something."

A small muscle twitched in Vivi's cheek. It had been a terrible suggestion.

"Or maybe even kenneled somehow and I could visit him on weekends," she added quickly. "Like people do with horses."

"That hardly seems worth the expense or energy, Ella. I'm sorry. I know you must have had your heart set on this dog, but it's not something we can do right now." Her aunt paused. "Or ever."

Ella felt the tears like a busted pipe. She turned from her aunt, but not quickly enough.

"Ella," Vivi said. "What was it you called the dog? Maybe I could call the Humane Society and talk to them. Maybe something could be arranged. At least be sure he goes somewhere really nice."

Ella felt the tears burning down her cheeks. She kept her face turned from Vivi. "His name is Loco," she said. "Or at least that's what I called him."

~

ELLA SAT ON HER BED, STARING AT THE BLUE WALLS THAT WOULD HAVE been white if Vivi had had her way.

Why had she named him Loco? Why had she come to this town and named the dog Loco? Because she had felt like they were two lonely drifters—a little off kilter, a little different. But different wasn't crazy. Crazy was crazy. Loco. Lunar.

Ella sifted through the slips of paper in her mother's jewelry box— the bits of poetry and song and observation. There it was. A little rhyme her mother had taught her when she was young to help her pronounce her L's.

> *Lovely Luna Lunatic*
> *Longed a lolly to take a lick*
> *Instead she found a licorice stick.*
> *Lonely Luna Lunatic.*

Ella held the paper for a long time in her hand, repeating the rhyme over and over just as she had as a child, the L's tapping behind her top teeth.

THE FOLLOWING DAY WHEN THEY COULD HAVE BEEN SIGNING THE papers for Loco, Vivi called the Humane Society to tell them they wouldn't be there to pick up the dog. She nodded and hmmm'd into her phone.

"Ella," she said when she was done. "Are you sure that dog was supposed to be there today?"

"Yes," Ella said, "I'm sure."

"Because the woman on the phone said that Mr. Jones hadn't brought any animals down to the shelter, and that she didn't have any dog by that name. I asked her to try to get a hold of Mr. Jones, but she said she's been trying to reach him all weekend and he hasn't returned her calls. I'm so sorry."

What she was sorry for, Ella wasn't sure. Vivi hadn't wanted a dog, couldn't keep a dog. Ella realized as she looked into Vivi's face that she didn't believe her—not one word. "Okay," Ella said. "Well, I guess we did what we could. And it's for the best if Jones keeps the dog anyway."

Ella went upstairs to her room, shut the door, and then did something she'd never thought to do in her life. She climbed out her window, onto a tree, and into the cold December.

WHEN SHE GOT TO THE FARM, NO DOGS RAN OUT TO GREET HER, NO lights came on in the house. Everything was empty. As empty as Sam's old woman's house.

Well, almost.

Among the impeccably clean couches and tables now cleared of silver or any other trinkets lay a small black box with Ella's name on it.

Inside was a necklace with a little note. *Ella, I've got to leave town for a spell, but if you happen to stop by, the dogs and I made this for you. If you're ever missing us, try it out.*

The chain she held in her hand was strangely familiar. In fact, it looked just like the chain her mother's stone had hung on. Which was impossible. Silver chains, after all, were not one of a kind.

That didn't change the fact that Ella could tell from Jones' masculine touch that the latch on the back had been redone—as though the necklace had been broken and then repaired by him.

On the chain hung a tiny silver cylinder. It was incredibly small, but hollow with one small hole near its top.

"You're kidding me," she whispered, fingering the charm. It was obviously a miniature dog whistle, and Ella had no idea how Jones with his clunky hands and lack of finesse had fashioned such a perfect miniature.

She supposed she should probably give it to the police, although when she thought about how to make such a phone call—"Hi, I snuck out of my aunt's house and broke into an empty house and took this necklace. I think it might belong to the Silver Shooter"—she just couldn't make it work.

Besides, she found that she had no desire to give the necklace up. The chain reminded her of her mother, and the whistle reminded her of her dog. And if Jones really was on the lam, this wouldn't help anybody out anyway. Ella slipped it carefully into her pocket.

CHAPTER 53

Sam didn't really want to talk to his father about the bracelet. He didn't want to bring it up at all, but it was a link he couldn't figure out in a chain he needed to understand.

Sam looked at his father across the table and held out the thick, silver bracelet. "I thought it was a key," he said. "Mr…Someone said it would open doors."

"Doesn't look like a key," his father said, standing up and trying not to give it a glance.

Sam held it out for his father to take.

Robert Calhoun, however, didn't touch it. In fact, he stared at the thick band of silver and took a step away. "I need you to have a look at my SD card," he said.

Sam narrowed his eyes. "Why? So you can reveal the mysteries of the universe to me through our seven-year-old computer?"

His dad ignored him, handing him the SD card, which was actually two pieces—an outer adapter that fit into the slot in their computer and the micro SD card that slid into the outer piece and carried the information.

Sam took it and gave it a quick glance. "Dad, you've been eating near it. You've gotten crumbs or something into one of the grooves."

Sam picked at it with a toothpick from the table and then slid the small piece back into the outer electronic casing.

And then it hit him.

The two together created a device. Without the inner piece the outer wouldn't work. And the outer was what connected the inner to everything else. They needed each other—these two pieces.

Sam held up the bracelet at his dad's eye level, gripping it tightly. "What else," he said. "What else do you know? Please tell me."

His father sighed. "I've never seen the square before, but I know what it's supposed to look like. And it does."

"What does?"

"The letter," Robert said. "The letter 'N.'"

It would seem that in the weeks since finding out his dad was a millionaire werewolf who lived like a pauper in a trailer there wouldn't be a lot that could surprise Sam, but somehow that one small comment did.

"The '*N*?'" Sam asked.

"Yes," his father said, pointing to the engraving on the square of the bracelet. "It matches the 'C.'" He looked at Sam. "The 'C's' that were branded onto everything he owned, including them."

"Who?" Sam asked.

"The sisters," his father said. "Your mother and your aunt. They each had a 'C' tattooed to the back of their necks. They all did—all those who worked for Napper. It was a sign of allegiance. This 'N' is of the same script. As I knew it would be. The square you have is the outer part—the part called the Ursa Major. The problem is finding the other part—the Ursa Minor as your mother called it."

"And what if I told you that Ella has a square-topped ring with a small 'C' engraved on it that matches this 'N?'"

"I would say she's nearly Napper's property," his father said, looking away.

Sam sighed and closed his eyes.

"What I might also tell you," his father said, "is that the woman your cousin lives with is not her aunt."

"What?" Sam asked, eyes flashing open.

"The woman Ella lives with is not her aunt."

"How do you know?" Sam asked.

"Because Ella said it was her mother's sister, and her mother only had one sister, and that woman isn't it."

"You mean that woman is claiming to be my mother?"

"It would appear that way."

How had Sam not put it together before? He'd been so focused on the whole cousin thing; he hadn't even thought about what "aunt" was housing his cousin. "Who is she?" Sam asked. "And please don't tell me you don't know."

"I don't know," his father said, not even bothering to smile. "But I have a guess. At The Ranch, your mother and her sister were watched over by a young woman—well, not a human woman; she was a shifter. She was the one who let another member of the staff have the keys to the vehicles, which she wasn't supposed to do. But she was charmed by this guy—the accountant, and she gave him the keys, the keys that let him escape from The Ranch with the two sisters and the mechanic. A mistake for which she was surely punished. So it would seem logical that she might—after all these years—be the one to try to get the sisters back. Or what is left of them. Which is Ella."

"Will they kill her?" Sam asked. "Ella."

"Oh no," his father said. "They will do anything to keep her alive." He paused. "Until the solstice."

"The Festival," Sam said.

"Of course."

"And who was the mechanic?"

"Ella's father."

Sam shook his head, trying to put it all together. "And why is all of this so important? Why the Festival?"

His father sighed. "There are myths of a world in which my kind reigned supreme—ran free and unafraid of the humans, a world with a great red sun and an ever-hanging moon. A world where our strength and magic didn't dull with the wax and wane of the moon, when we didn't have to hide, avoid meat, or vomit into commodes if we wanted to avoid changing. And, according to the myths, there is a time when that world ended—the result of a boy even younger than you placing a magically empowered stone and changing the suns."

Sam raised his eyebrow.

"I told you they were myths," his father said, "so don't look at me like that."

Sam held up his hands in mock surrender and his father continued. "Before the boy changed the sun there were two shifters—friends, but also competitors. One, a werewolf prince, aided the boy in the empowerment of the stone. The other, called Sarak, fought his friend—touching the stone, though he knew doing so would overpower and kill him. Through that touch, Sarak added a spark of his desires for his people. Through that touch, Sarak made it possible for the stone to change the sun again if the need arose—if the humans were ever driven to hunt and despise my kind. Which, of course, they have done for a very long time."

His father paused and rubbed his head. "Many of my kind have sought the stone, many have plotted and even killed to get it. At the winter solstice when the moon is full—an alignment of season and sky that happens only every hundred years or so—the stone can be used. Thus, the Festival."

"So, at the full moon during the winter solstice, the stone can open some sort of other dimension?" Sam asked.

His father seemed to chew on his answer for several long moments. "No," he finally said. "It is this world. But shifted. Transformed into something different—a place where the humans are fettered and the werewolves are not."

"Then why can't they place their own dumb stone."

"They cannot touch it," his father replied. "Not without harm. Well, one can, and they will need this shifter to empower it and bring it to the place of changing."

"And Ella?" Sam asked. "Why is she needed?"

His father did not look at him. "Per the stories, both a werewolf *and* a human are needed. The shifter must be an anomaly—one who gains strength, not weakness, from the metals that can kill the rest of us."

"Like silver?" Sam asked.

"Yes," his father replied. "And other substances too ancient for this world to remember. This shifter will bring the stone to the place of empowerment. But he cannot place it without becoming too strong for anyone—even the Alpha—to contain. And so a human is also needed —a descendant of the boy who placed the stone so long ago. This human will also be an anomaly—last in a long, dwindling bloodline of humans, humans who can hear dogs speak at the full moon. If they can find that person, if they can use that person to place the stone, they can change the suns, and return this world to the old form."

"And after they use her?"

"I don't know," Robert Calhoun said, looking away.

"You don't care," Sam said.

"I care a great deal," Robert said, beginning to pace. "I see you when I look at the girl; I see Vivian's smile. I see people I care about through that child, and I cannot help but care about her as well, but at this point the girl is outside my reach. Many of my kind will do *anything* to get her, *anything* to keep her."

"Many of *our* kind," Sam said, folding his arms over his chest, still annoyed at his father's unwillingness to include him. "And we should stop them."

"Many of *my* kind," his father said. "You, son, are not completely of my kind. It is a difference you must accept because it is a difference that means a great deal to the Changers. Your kind—the half-breeds— will never wish for a changing of the suns because in the old world, half-breeds were quickly exterminated if they had the misfortune to exist at all." He took a breath. "So it is *my* kind who seek the stone, *my* kind who wish to shift the world. You don't understand what they will do to accomplish the changing of the suns."

Sam had no reply.

His father sat down. "But futile or not, it's true that there are those of us who do resist. Quietly, perhaps, but we resist. *Your* kind, son, are why many of us have learned to control our shifting, contain our appetites, go unseen, unscented. We control our shifting because we love those whom many of my kind believe we should hate. We control our shifting because through that love come beautiful children with genes wrapped around in unusual ways—part human, part shifter. These young, our children, are always at risk from both worlds—human and werewolf. Especially during the delicate years when they have not yet learned to control themselves."

Robert gave Sam a pointed look, which Sam ignored.

"So, do you ever wish for the old sun, the old world to come back," Sam asked, sitting across from his father, "to release you from the bondage of your control?"

"There are certain things I wish for, but going back is not one of them. Under the old sun, the humans were disdained, repressed. Under the old sun your mother and I never could have met and married. Under the old sun there could never have been a you." He paused. "Going back is not worth any amount of power to me. Though there is no denying that this world could be improved upon too."

"But what if there was a way to fix the old world?" Sam asked.

"I believe that the creatures who most wish to go back are not those with a good deal of change in mind. Looking back is rarely the type of thing that propels a group of people forward."

"But," Sam said, "you often hold back."

"Holding back is not going back," his father said. "You would do well to learn the difference."

"Holding back may not be the same, but if you're not careful the end result will be the same," Sam retorted. "If they get Ella, which you say they practically have—if they use her, then the suns will turn back. And if what you say is true, then not only will she be doomed, but I will as well."

Sam set the bracelet on the table between them, turning it, trying to see how it could best be used.

His father set his face, then held out his hand for the bracelet. Sam hesitated. His father waited, hand outstretched, palm open. "If you don't want me to hold back, then give me the bracelet."

Sam looked into his father's eyes—the same deep brown as his own, and set the bracelet in his father's hand. His father stood, twisting the metal of the bracelet, crushing it in his hands.

Sam gasped, jumping forward, grabbing his father's wrist. "You're destroying it!" he screamed.

"No," his father said, hands shaking, fingers white, blue veins bulging. "I'm releasing it." He dropped the mangled silver bracelet, letting it fall to the floor.

Sam ran for the silver bracelet.

"Leave it," his father said, opening his fist to reveal the unharmed copper square.

Sam walked to his father, who leaned against the thin walls of the trailer. He could not even raise his weakened arm to hand the square to Sam.

"Attaching it to a thick silver band was smart," his father said. "It makes accessing it so much harder."

Sam took the ornate piece of copper. "Now tell me how this is going to help. After all, it's not a magical stone."

"That," his father said, nodding at the copper square, "is a different type of power source. And one Napper tried to protect just as much as the stone."

"So what does it contain?" Sam asked.

His father almost smiled. "Information," he said. "And not a little."

Sam turned it around in his hand, trying to put the puzzle together in his mind. "But it's only the outer half."

"Yes," his father replied, standing up a little straighter. "Napper created it in two pieces so they could be taken apart and the information safeguarded." He pressed his forehead, still looking pale. "Those who fled The Ranch stole it too, but during the crash, one of the pieces went missing. By the time it was found, everyone from the group had travelled to different places."

His father reached out and touched the square. "They tried, but could never find a safe way to meet up and put the pieces together."

Sam fingered the perfectly smooth edges, finding an almost imperceptible ridge where a smaller piece could be inserted.

"So I still need the other piece," Sam said.

"Yes, son," Robert replied, kicking the mangled silver bracelet toward the wall. "And the other piece needs you."

~

Sam didn't know what else to do, but go at it directly. He jogged to Ella's house when he knew Vivi would still be at work.

"Sam," Ella said, opening the door for him.

"Hey," he replied, almost certain that when Ella let him in, she had looked both ways down her street to be sure no one had seen.

"I'm sorry," Ella began, "I can't go running today. I've got a ton of stuff—"

Sam interrupted her. "I don't want to go running," he said quickly, feeling like Vivi would pop in any minute. "Look, this is going to sound really weird, but I need your ring."

Ella narrowed her eyes, just a bit. "What ring?" she asked slowly.

"Your mother's ring—the one you wear. I won't need it forever, but it fits into this thing—this part of a bracelet that Mr….that someone gave me, and I need part of your ring to…"

"What?" Ella said, a little loudly. "You need *part* of my ring?"

"Well, yes," Sam said, stumbling over his words. How could he explain that he needed a piece to fit into another piece so that the parts would be complete, but he still wasn't sure what to do with it after that? It didn't help that when he looked down at Ella, she seemed mad. "I need it to fit into…"

"Sam," Ella snapped. "Stop it."

"But Ella," he said.

"Look, Sam, I just need you to, just to listen," Ella said, sounding less mad and a little more desperate.

"No," he said. "I need you to listen. I know it sounds weird…"

"No," Ella shouted. "It sounds crazy."

Sam stepped back like she'd hit him.

She bit her lip, softening. "Look, Sam, I've never said you were crazy. I've been your friend, even when others weren't. I've even tried to believe you when you said bizarre, whacked out things. But to come and ask for my mother's jewelry, to hint that you'll be taking it apart for who knows what—it's just a little too much."

Sam's face fell and Ella paused.

"Look," she said. "I know you miss Sarah. I miss her too, but you've got to pull yourself together. Something went wrong with her. It happens. Hopefully she'll get the help she needs."

"You stop it," Sam said, his own voice rising. He just couldn't listen anymore—the mind-numbing way Ella talked like there were simple answers to all life's questions when he knew she knew there weren't. It was like her heart had fallen out when she put on her brand-name clothes.

"Sam," Ella said. "Please. Just listen."

He put his hands over his ears, turned his face away—like a child.

Ella's eyes welled up with tears. Gently, she put her hands up and took Sam's hands off his ears. "Look, Sam, I know you don't want to hear this—any of this. But maybe you should try to get some help too. They have doctors, medicines."

Sam pulled his hands away from Ella.

"I'm sorry," Ella said. "I'm only saying this because I care about you. I'm your friend."

Sam wanted to turn away again, but he looked straight into Ella's face. "No," he said, taking a deep breath. "You're not my friend. You're my cousin."

And then he ran—the long, lanky legs hitting the pavement in strides much faster than Ella could have matched.

ELLA SHOOK HER HEAD, WATCHING HIM. SHE THOUGHT ABOUT TRYING to catch up to him, but she'd never be able to. And even if she did, what could she do? Ella sat down right on her porch and held her head in her hands.

"Oh man," she said, looking down the road where he'd run. "Sam needs help."

Slowly she stood, stretching out her legs. On top of everything else, he'd somehow convinced himself that they were cousins.

Feeling like she had an ugly hangover, Ella walked up the steps to her room. She sat down on her bed, surrounded by the blue walls of her room. She was glad she'd painted them. When they'd been just white, it had felt like an asylum.

Ella bit her lip. She hadn't gone to visit Sarah—hadn't even checked on the visiting hours. Ella sighed and held up her phone, googling the psychiatric institution. She had till six o'clock today. It was nearly five now. And she had no car, no bike.

Ella put on her running leggings, then laced up her shoes. Vivi had bought her a Dri-fit jacket—light but warm. She zipped it up tight, grabbed her earbuds and her phone, and stepped out the door.

CHAPTER 54

Sarah was sleeping when Ella stepped into her room—white bed, white room, creepy. It smelled that white smell too—sterile alcohol clean. Ella would take the burrito armpit smell of her old apartments any day.

Sarah was just supposed to be in here for observation, so Ella had expected it to be a little more like a dorm room—relaxed with maybe some color and bad art. Instead it looked like a hospital room: moveable bed, moveable table, bare walls, linoleum floor. The only life was from the flowers and cards that sat on a table next to her hospital bed. Sarah's mother had put up a few photographs of their family.

Ella picked one up. Sarah's mother looked a lot like Sarah—broad smile, green eyes, red hair. Her father was darker and taller, balding a bit, but handsome. Ella set the picture down, wondering how long she should hang out if Sarah was just sleeping when suddenly Sarah opened her eyes and rolled over.

"Oh, hey," Sarah said, struggling to sit up. She hoisted herself onto one elbow and looked at Ella through foggy eyes rimmed at the edges with red. "I feel like I've been sleeping for days."

Ella thought that that was pretty much how she looked too. Sarah wasn't wearing a hospital gown, but it was some sort of jump suit that Ella could tell was issued to her.

"So is the nightmare over yet?" Sarah asked, cracking a crooked smile, and slurring the last part of her sentence.

"Umm," Ella said, not sure if she should wise crack back at her friend, or make some overly cheerful statement about how it wasn't so bad.

"Nope. Nightmare's still going," Sarah said, dropping back onto her pillow, as though staying up on her arm had been too exhausting.

"So," Ella asked, "how is everything?"

"Well," Sarah said, slurring again. "I'm officially crazy. I hear howling and see things that aren't there. The nurses keep medicating me so I won't wake up screaming when I sleep."

That explained the slurring and sleepiness, Ella thought. But it didn't explain how her non-crazy friend had suddenly gone crazy. It didn't explain that at all.

"What do you see?" Ella asked, unable to resist.

"Wolves actually," Sarah said. "I'll roll over at night and see one —*think* I see one—looking at me through the window over there. Even if I go to sleep with the blinds closed, they'll get opened and there will be the wolf face." She shuddered. "Just staring. They're not pretty wolves either, not the National Geographic kind with blue eyes and white fur. Instead, they're brown and mottled gray, deep set eyes like empty stones, wolves like the ones Napper got. What are they called?"

"Gevudan," Ella said, without pausing.

"Yeah, that," Sarah said. "Hairy and scruffy and mean. That's what I see."

"But you've never seen them before this?" Ella hesitated. "Before here?"

"No," Sarah said, pausing as though she was trying to think it through and struggling. "Never before. Not till I saw one at my door —*thought* I saw one at my door."

Ella felt her eyebrows come together like they did when she wanted to cry. Sarah had never been perfect—she'd always been offbeat, sarcastic, a little moody. But she'd never been dull or slow.

Seeing all the sharp vividness sapped from her friend was all wrong. Sarah had hallucinated a wolf at her door. Just like Sam had hallucinated an old woman in that house. Just like—Ella paused—just like she had thought she'd heard a dog talking to her.

Ella sat by Sarah's bed. Sarah had dozed off again, her mouth open like an old woman.

Visiting hours were almost over. Ella stood to slip out of the room, then bent down to touch Sarah on her forehead in good-bye. It seemed strange that three stone sober kids would come to this town, meet, and start imagining things. Really, when she thought about it, that seemed like the craziest thing of all.

Ella jogged back, her feet pounding out the rhythm her head couldn't let go.

Lovely Luna Lunatic,
Longed a lolly to take a lick,
Instead she found a licorice stick.
Lonely Luna Lunatic.

Luna. Lolly. Lunatic. Lonely. Licorice licorice licorice. Luna.

When Ella got home, she tore into the jewelry box, searching for the piece of paper. On its back was the other rhyme, a tongue twister her mother had made up. Children's games. Children's words. Stories, riddles. Ella stopped on the last thought. Riddles.

When once a witch went walking
Woods and animals talking
When once a witch went walking
Woods and wolf stalking
When once a witch went walking
Went a walking witch which way
Which walking witch went wandering
Which walking witch went wondering
Which way the walking witch must wander

> *When the witch must ever wonder*
> *Which way walked the witch?*

Ella held the paper in her hand for a long time. Sam had called the old woman Zinnie. In her mother's stories, there was a witch who lived in a hut in the woods—a protector, a keeper of secrets and stories. With the witch, those who were good found safety. Werewolf or human. To her the evil could not go.

Ella swayed slightly. Her mother had owned a stone—round and glistening. And it was gone. Her mother had written of a witch. And she was gone.

Were they stories?

Ella spun her mother's ring around her finger, turning the small square into her palm and pressing it against her skin.

WHEN SARAH OPENED HER EYES AGAIN, ELLA WAS GONE. HOW LONG had she been sleeping? It felt like a thousand years. Down the hall, she heard the tidy clip of a man's dress shoes, then the click of the lock on her door.

"Good evening, dear," he said, shutting the door behind him.

"Mr. Napper," Sarah said.

He was dressed in a suit and tie, and Sarah felt like he'd been here before, though she couldn't remember if that was true or just strange dreaming. Napper sat down beside her and patted her hand.

"They tell me it's been a tricky recovery for you," he said. "So I wanted to stop by."

He leaned forward to look into her eyes—his own gray eyes so much like the wolves that she pulled back.

"I'm afraid you've gotten caught at the center of a spinning circle," he said. "It's difficult to step away without falling."

Sarah shook her head, unsure of what he was talking about. She felt so tired.

"So many connections," Napper said with his steady stare. "Things that I need—your friend, the old house, maybe even that boy. It just seemed safest to keep you here."

The smell. Sarah sniffed the air. She could smell a wolf—the same smell as when she'd opened the door, as when the wolf had been there.

But there were no wolves, then or now. Just one old man staring down into her eyes. And why was he here again? Or maybe it was just a dream—a psychedelic dream where she was at the center of a Tilt-a-Whirl that swooped and orbited without stopping.

She closed her eyes, her head spinning, dizzy, as her thoughts sank to the center, her feet slipping; and she fell.

CHAPTER 55

Ella stood by the licorice post in the dark, wondering if Sam was crazy. Or she was. Maybe both.

She'd never gone in without Sam. Slowly, she pushed the licorice to the side and crawled in. She ran to the cottage, afraid of the wolves, and banged through the back door just like Sarah had two months ago.

But there wasn't a dusty shack. There was warm light, the smell of chocolate, and a very old woman sitting in a chair.

"So you've figured it out, Christazdoter."

"Excuse me?" Ella squeaked.

"You've figured it out."

The woman was incredibly old—thin paper glued to bone.

"No," Ella said, still out of breath. "I haven't figured anything out at all."

"But of course you have," the old woman said. "Look at you standing here with me—that's something."

Ella shook her head. "You do seem to be real," she said, not quite sure that she believed it.

"And," the woman said, pouring a cup of tea and setting a chipped saucer underneath it.

"And if you're real, then Sam is not crazy," Ella said. "Or not *as* crazy anyway."

The woman chuckled and took a bite of a brown cookie with slivered nuts on top.

"Not at all crazy, I'm afraid," she said with her mouth slightly full. "Terrible dull stuff, sanity."

"I'm not sure I would know," Ella murmured.

"Have a cookie, dear."

"No thank you," Ella said.

Zinnie set two cookies on Ella's plate anyway.

"Did you know my mother?" Ella asked.

"I knew of her," Zinnie said. "And she of me. Eventually we might have crossed paths if things had not ended the way they did."

Ella nodded, not sure what else to say, and then blurted, "You made Sam think he was crazy. You made me think Sam was crazy."

"I did not make anyone think anything."

"But you left."

"I was taken. My strength is no longer quite what it was in your mother's stories."

"But you always find your way home."

"Yes, as long as there is a home to come to, I will find my way to it."

"How?" Ella asked.

The woman was crumbling her cookie into her tea. Watching the crumbs fall reminded Ella of Hansel and Gretel—their trail of stones and crumbs.

"Because I know where home is," the woman replied simply.

The comment made Ella's insides hurt.

"Is Sam home?" Ella asked.

"I expect," the old woman replied. "Sam's home is not far you know."

"Yes," Ella said. "I know."

"Do you then?" the witch asked. Pausing, she added, "And your home?"

Ella did not answer. She was not sure there was a trail of crumb long or wide enough to ever lead her back home. She turned from the witch and looked out the window.

Zinnie dabbed the edges of her wrinkled mouth with a linen napkin. "If you want to find the things you've lost, you need to help others find the things they seek. That's just common courtesy," she said.

"You want me to give Sam the ring."

"Sam does not need the ring," Zinnie said. "Only the small piece on top of it."

"Which is attached to the ring," Ella said, still not sure either of them was sane.

Zinnie raised a bushy, gray eyebrow.

Ella shook her head. Since she apparently wasn't being courteous enough, she might as well ask her question. "Do you have all your teeth?"

Zinnie smiled as broad as the Cheshire cat. "Yes," she chuckled. "Every one."

Ella took a cookie after all.

WHEN ELLA GOT TO SAM'S HOUSE SHE HELD OUT A SMALL, parchment-wrapped cookie and Sam took it.

"You saw her," he said.

"Or we're both crazy," Ella said. "But I think she's real. Of course I also think she's a witch, so maybe we're just both crazy."

Sam tasted the cookie—a moist chocolate almond bar with powdered sugar on top. "Lovely Luna Lunatic," Sam murmured.

Ella squinted at Sam for a minute and then added, "Longed a lolly to take a lick." She cocked her head. "How do you know that rhyme?"

"My mother used to say it to me at bedtime."

"Mine too," Ella added. And then, after a pause, "Sam, I'm sorry."

"It's okay," he said. "It's not like I said a single thing that didn't sound crazy."

"You've got that right," Ella mumbled, and then smiled.

~

SAM HAD SAID THAT THE TWO SQUARES WOULD FORM SOME TYPE OF A master key. With it he hoped to break Sarah out of the institution.

Everything Sam said sounded like something out of a looney bird's mouth, but Ella had to admit that it did look like the two square pieces would slide together—one fitting inside of the other.

Which didn't mean that she wanted to watch Sam hammer away at her mother's ring. He'd lined up several delicate tools, but it didn't look like any of them was going to be much help.

"Ella, I'm going to have to break it," he said nervously, examining the ring from every side.

"I don't think you're really breaking it," she said, trying to sound brave about it. "You're just setting it free."

"I'm not sure you believe that," Sam said, giving the ring a gentle twist, "but thanks for letting me do this." Sam twisted a bit harder. The ring wouldn't budge. He looked at Ella. She nodded and he twisted harder.

Ella closed her eyes, expecting to hear a pop or a crack. Instead, when she opened her eyes, Sam was turning the small square round and round, as though unscrewing it from the band of the ring. After several turns the tiny square dropped off, leaving the ring with a raised, ridged bezel that contained a small, clear diamond. Sam laughed, a giddy sort of sound.

Ella was too stunned. She stared at the ring for several minutes while Sam took one of his father's tools and carefully chipped off the remaining bits of metal from the square until it was perfectly smooth.

Ella slipped the ring back onto her finger. She could never wear it in front of Vivi now, but she would wear it here, today. In his hand, Sam held the large copper square as well as the small golden one that had been attached to the ring.

"CN," Ella said, looking at the letters. "I always thought the 'C' was my mother's initial," she said.

"I know," Sam said. "I'm sure everyone did."

Together they looked at the two swooping letters—the letters that had connected and complicated pieces of their pasts, the letters that would connect and further complicate their combined futures. CN. Charles Napper.

CHAPTER 56

Jones had gone against his better judgment in leaving Ella that note.

Why he'd let Witten drag him into this whole business, he couldn't say. It was just like the first time, only worse.

All those years ago, Witten had limped into his camp, claiming a car wreck and needing Jones's steady hand to extract a piece of metal from a deep, angry wound in his ankle. Jones had used a pair of tweezers and a small tool made of silver that he'd been planning to recycle. With them he picked the embedded square of metal from Witten's leg. Using the silver pick, he'd pushed the skin back over the wound, planning to thread a needle and stitch it up. But by the time he'd worked the flap of skin so it was next to the other skin, the wound had started to heal.

Witten had taken the silver pick from his hand and continued to run it gently along the line of the wound until all that remained of the cut was a faint pink line.

Jones was shocked. He'd never seen a home remedy like that before—maybe all those mystics with their crystals and coppers were on to something. Witten didn't seem surprised at all.

When Jones had asked him how he'd gotten a square of metal stuck in his leg, Witten had said he didn't want to talk about it.

Jones got that. There were plenty of things he hadn't wanted to talk about either—like the fact that he'd left his father's farm to seek his own way, hunting and fishing with his dogs and his camper. He'd seen a lot of the world, but he'd started to feel lonely and listless—like he lacked purpose in the deep, beautiful world around him.

For several days Witten had stayed on at the little camp. He seemed to enjoy the dogs on the same deep level that Jones appreciated them. They'd hiked and fished in peaceful silence, and then at night they'd fried up their catch, talking and telling stories. Witten told better stories than any of the other travelers Jones had known. Yet underneath it all, he could tell that Witten was anxious about something, restless, unsettled.

Jones was still surprised to wake up one morning to find that Witten had taken off in the middle of the night.

The next day two investigators had shown up seeking a missing person. Jones could have set them on his trail, given them a description of what he'd been wearing, sought some kind of revenge, but he found he didn't have the heart.

Witten was practically a kid—a troubled kid maybe, but a very young man finding his way. Jones had been like that when he'd left his father's farm ten years earlier. He understood how it felt.

Jones had given the investigators vague, evasive answers to their questions. The next day, he'd come back from hunting to find his camper burned to the ground, the dog he'd left to keep watch shot through beside it.

And just like that, his world had turned. The tragedy propelled Jones to return to his ailing father's farm. It had also given him a vision about how to proceed. Jones had a gift with dogs, and it turned out he wasn't a terrible farmer either—respecting things like land, animal, and soil in a way his peers did not, making extra money through his dogs and his metalwork. Within his profession he could even have been considered successful.

And then that vagrant storyteller had shown up in his town and everything had fallen apart again. Jones wasn't sure he could rebuild his life the way he'd done twenty-five years earlier.

The FBI had come this time—with a search warrant. They'd confiscated almost every drop of silver Jones had owned, though he kept a few special pieces in a few special places. When the investigators left, their lips were pressed tight together. Jones considered that as good as a promise to return.

It was true that Jones had run because he was afraid. After all, he wasn't quite sure he was innocent. He did ship silver "bullets" to anyone who ordered them. They were one of the most popular party and novelty items sold from his online silver shop. And they should have been nearly useless as actual bullets. Silver was a soft metal, difficult to use in weaponry in general.

Or so he'd thought until those horrible shootings had begun.

He should have stopped selling the bullets then, but requests had suddenly skyrocketed, swinging into a morbid trend. And farmers weren't known for being rich.

Still, Jones should have quit making them, cut his losses. As it was, the FBI had found an entire box full of the things, as well as payment records, including his most recent shipment—sent that morning—one silver and one titanium bullet. Which didn't look great for Jones.

But being afraid was only half the reason Jones had run.

The real reason, the deeper reason, was because in his gut he felt that something bigger was forming—something not entirely normal, something someone wanted and needed him for. Well, maybe not him, but his dogs.

And Jones wouldn't let his dogs be used, not like some chip in a game Jones didn't know how to play. To him, the dogs weren't just resources or weapons or pieces on a chessboard. To Jones, they were souls; they were friends. If they did help anyone, it would be because they chose to do so. And they might. Loco had already left—following after the child, he was sure. Because of this Jones had decided to give the girl a tool, a tool to call the dogs if she ever needed them.

He could do no more.

CHAPTER 57

A master key could work in a lot of places, but Sam suspected that a master key would get the most results in a master computer. Sam was sure one was hidden in plain sight like everything else. Which didn't mean he could see it.

Sam had spent the last few days manically trying the key all over town. He'd tried the key in the library computer, the school computer, the computer in the sparse office at the Havensborough Unit. He'd found encrypted information in all of them.

At Havensborough, he'd found information about Zinnie's diagnosis and medications. He'd even found, at last, Zinnie's room number, which wasn't a room number at all, but an entire wing. He'd also found a log with dates of each of her escapes or "releases" as the record called them.

At the library computer he'd found listings of books, articles, and myths about wolves. Several had sections highlighted with notes. He'd also been able to open dozens of articles from URL's that no longer existed—articles about wolf migration and its steady and recent shift toward the Midwest. He also read blood-chilling stories of Gevudan wolves attacking families and animals in France—eating their flesh till the bones were dry.

At school, he uncovered some of the simplest and most disturbing information of all.

Lists of students and faculty—their names color-coded. Purple for the shifters, blue for the humans, black for the half-breeds, and white. Sam found himself under the white category, and it was then that he figured it out. Whites were the unknowns—possibly human, but possibly not.

He didn't have time to go through most of the names, but among all the names there were two aberrations—Ella, of course, who was marked deep red. They needed her for the Festival.

And David Witten—who was silver.

It was strange to stop thinking of Vivi as her aunt—strange, but not.

The truth was that it had actually been a whole lot harder to learn to think of Vivi as her mother's sister than it was to accept the fact that she was really a psychopath imposter. In fact, of all the crazy things Sam had ever said, this one had somehow been the easiest to believe— Vivi was neither blood nor water.

All the wondering why her aunt acted the way she did, all the worrying about why they couldn't connect—it all lifted off, leaving Ella with a sense of relief, of freedom. It was good to have the cards on the table, even if Ella was playing a losing hand.

This new freedom made it easy for Ella to use Sam's master key to sneak into Vivi's personal computer as well as the laptop Vivi used for work. There was no betrayal anymore, just a sense of self-preservation.

Once hooked up to Vivi's computers, Ella found more information on Charles Napper than she or Sam could ever get through. She read information on Napper's long career, his work with mental illness— particularly hallucinations, his philanthropic endeavors which always included efforts to find and "cure" those with such hallucinations.

She found information on his work in the field of chemistry—how he'd taken a strain of very old DNA procured from an ancient ear, and used that to find matches for the pTr4 genome—the one Napper believed would lead him to another with similar DNA. This is how he had developed the test tubes that had been used in hospitals around the U.S. This is how he had first found the sisters after they'd gone in for blood work and a psychiatric workup in rural Ohio. It was all intensely interesting and fanatical and mad-sciencey.

But none of the computers—not the ones Sam had tapped into around town, not Vivi's own computers—contained the *everything* that Sam was looking for. What they would do with the *everything* when they found it, Ella wasn't sure.

THEY WERE SITTING TOGETHER AT ELLA'S HOUSE, LOGGED INTO VIVI'S computer researching Napper and the Central Indiana Hospital when Ella's phone buzzed. She picked it up and clicked on the smiley icon that was Brandt's face.

"Ugh," Sam said. "I don't like that guy."

Ella ignored him.

"You know I saw him pound a kid half to death once. I should have looked him up on the school computer."

Ella shrugged, more curious than she let on. "You said yourself that being a Changer didn't mean you changed necessarily. Like your dad."

"Means you can," Sam said. "And that guy does. Just because he doesn't grow fur doesn't mean he can't flip from smiling guy to angry lunatic in two minutes flat."

Ella had to agree with that. It was another reason to favor Jack with his calm, easygoing demeanor. But Jack wasn't the one willing to text her; Brandt was.

Suddenly, Sam grabbed Ella's phone from her.

"Hey," she said.

"In plain sight," Sam mumbled. "So plain you'd see it every day and never even think of it, right?"

"Right," Ella said sarcastically. "Because they'd want to give a teenager a super computer to carry around."

"Why not? Sam said. "It could keep track of you. And they'd want that."

"Yeah," said Ella. "Until I accidently drop it off the bleachers at some football game."

But Sam wasn't listening. He was unscrewing the case to get a better look. At its side was a slot for a memory card—a little bigger than you would expect on someone's phone.

"Doesn't mean anything," Ella said, though she'd begun to think that it probably did. "Besides," Ella said. "How would they even be able to access the information?"

"Oh, I don't know," Sam said. "Supposing they don't have some awesome spyware installed, I guess maybe they could put an evil, fake relative in the same house as you. I'm sure Vivi could look at your phone almost any time she wanted."

The thought of Vivi slinking into her room at night to download information from her phone was possibly the creepiest thought yet. "I hope it just uses spyware," Ella said.

Sam held the slender, silver case and slipped the key into the side.

The first thing that popped up were Ella's vitals, heart rate, pulse, and oxygen levels.

Ella grabbed the phone back. "Oh crap," she said, scrolling down. It knew her age to the day, her height, weight, hormone levels, nutrient intake, everything.

And then there it was—too much.

Volumes from decades or maybe centuries of information. There were names, dates, histories, fairy tales. There were maps, records from jewelry stores and silver mines. Books worth of information on chemistry, physics, alchemy, witches, werewolves, trials, killings. Everything.

There was just no way to start it all or end it all. Until they came to their mother's names.

Ella started to cry. Sam put an awkward arm around her. And together they scrolled down into the pieces of their family's past that would become their future.

THEY FOUND OFFICIAL RECORDS, MEDICAL RECORDS, PICTURES, AND journal entries from the sisters—photocopied and recorded. Slowly, Sam and Ella pieced the information together.

Their mothers had been taken to a rehabilitative ranch when they were teenagers—at ages seventeen and fifteen. They'd been having hallucinations—imagining they could hear dogs speak at every full moon.

Mysteriously, their parents had died in a car accident shortly after the girls were taken into The Ranch. And oddly, a will was found giving the philanthropist who funded The Ranch custody over the girls.

For several years, the sisters grew up on The Ranch, taking medications and receiving every privilege that two young girls could enjoy. They had a cook, governess, driver, tutors, doctors, horses, and nice clothes.

Everything except family.

And so they clung to each other as only teenage girls can. Until a mechanic—a young man named Patrick—came to the ranch to fix some classic cars. Unlike the other workers, he did more than his job. He told jokes, smuggled in magazines and candy, taught the girls tricks for rigging engines. He cared for them in a way no one else had. And then one day he smuggled in a small silver bracelet for the youngest sister. Three years had passed. It was Christa's eighteenth birthday.

Her governess exploded when she saw the bracelet—removed it from Christa's wrist with tongs like it was a poisonous snake. She sent it in a copper box with the driver to be removed from The Ranch.

When questioned about where she had received such a thing, Christa had lied. Firmly. Believably. She'd found it, she said, behind a fat rock on one of the hiking paths, half buried in the dirt. She'd thought it beautiful and brought it back to wear. The mechanic had helped her polish and repair it. And she'd worn it—good as new. What was wrong with that?

The governess, they were told, had an allergy to silver, quite severe.

Maybe it would have ended there if the next week Patrick had come back to The Ranch. But he didn't. Their governess, Raquel, told them he'd quit. One lie too many—one thing Christa knew with her heart wasn't true. After that, life changed. Something was wrong at The Ranch.

The girls dug through files, read long history books, studied geology, uncovered secrets. The girls were different, it turned out. But not crazy. They were needed by a group—a cult of sorts—to help place a stone, a stone that was made of a substance that none of this cult could touch.

The cult believed that this stone would change the sun so that a new world would be reborn—a world in which this cult, a group now known as The Ring of the Alpha, would rule as kings.

The changing would not happen until the first winter solstice that coincided with a full moon. Which would be in another twenty years. The girls were trapped. Except that they hadn't been Patrick's only friends on The Ranch. And they weren't the only ones with reason to leave.

The bookkeeper came to them. He was a member of the cult, but he had been a friend to Patrick. He was also an outlier—an outlier who had begun to feel himself in danger. Vivian and Christa weren't sure he could be trusted, but their options were limited.

The bookkeeper was an insider, and—perhaps most importantly—their governess had a crush on him. Raquel made him sweets, laughed too loud in his presence, and stared at him when he wasn't looking. For better or worse, the bookkeeper David was needed. He contacted Patrick; they cooked up a plan.

Before they left, Christa took something from The Ranch headquarters—a stone that had been entombed in a thick, padded safe.

Vivian had helped crack the code for the safe. If the cult was going to steal girls in order to force them to use a stone, then the girls would steal the stone in order to save other girls.

The bookkeeper stole something too—an unusual chip with two pieces that fitted together. Then he took the girls and picked up Patrick. Together they fled and together they "died."

Ella had been scrolling, clicking from journal entries to newspaper articles, to ledger books. Now she stopped, let the phone rest in her lap.

Sam looked at her. Then picked up her phone.

"What are you looking for?" Ella asked.

"Death records," Sam answered. "Real ones. After the crash, they all separated—your parents eloping, my mom laying low nearby, which is where she met my dad. And I know they hoped to reunite." Sam clicked a link, his eyes scrolling through the records. "But—" Sam stopped. He clicked a footnote and there it was. Patrick Peterson had died in a mine cave in in West Virginia. Vivian Calhoun at a cancer unit in Arizona. Christa Peterson in a car accident in Indianapolis. Only one of the four had survived. He had never married or had children. He had given up accounting and taken up literature.

Sam and Ella looked at each other. The silver name on the school roster.

Mr. Witten.

"He's one of them," Sam said. "But different."

"So are you," Ella said.

"No," Sam said. "I'm not one of them. Witten is a full breed, but different somehow."

"Silver," Ella said slowly. "He can touch it. The rest of them can't. Or if they do, it weakens them. That's why werewolves can be killed with a silver bullet. But Witten—he's worn that bracelet all year. And he used to be friends with Jones, who is a silver smith."

"Witten can touch silver…" Sam said, racking his brain to remember what his dad had told him. "And you…"

Ella had stopped scrolling through her phone. She didn't need a master key anymore. Or a master computer. She had her mother's stories and they told her the rest. She began to speak.

"Once, at the beginning of worlds and end of days, a mighty race ruled under a violet sky. Wolves, shifters, dogs, and men. All lived under the same scarlet sun. But all did not have access to its power.

"Incredible strength, incredible magic, and sometimes incredible intrigue propelled the Changers into the monarchy where they ruled

with wolves at their side, humans at their heel, and dogs at their hands.

"From this world arose a poor human boy and a magic-less Changeling prince. Together, and aided by the dogs, these enemies-turned-friends found a stone of ancient source, of ageless power—a stone that few others could touch. Yet, hiding under the werewolf prince's magic-less fingers was a gift.

"He could touch a metal none of his race could withstand.

"As lord of the silver, the prince became responsible for empowering the stone—turning its use against his own corrupt people. After that, the boy could place the stone and change the sun. But there was one—a friend to the prince who, torn between fellowship to the prince and loyalty to his race, fought with the prince. He could not overtake the empowered stone. But to it, he added his essence, his hopes, and much of his strength. To it, he gave a glimmer of power—enabling the stone to return the world to the one it had been should the need ever arise.

"But to return the world to what it was, the Changers would need the stone.

"And one to carry it.

Ella stopped in her telling of the story. *One to carry it.* One from a long line of gifted humans, a line Napper had spent his life seeking. Her mother. Her aunt. And now her. The carrier, the *bearer*, and the only one left.

"We do belong in the asylum," Sam said when she was done telling her mother's story.

Ella was chewing her cuticle. There were, she understood now, two surefire ways to stop the Changers' plan. The stone could be destroyed. Or she could.

One of those things, it was clear, was much easier to get rid of than the other. The stone, after all, had been around for eons, and longer. That didn't exactly give Ella a ton of hope. After the stone was placed, the Changers would surely dispose of her. And before the stone was placed, if some human found out and wanted to stop the Changers, he might not think it too great a crime to get rid of her either—in the name of humanity and all.

That didn't leave Ella with a whole lot of friends. She counted them. Sam—one. Loco—two. Sarah, who was in the mental institution—three. That was more friends than she'd had most of her life. The problem was that her tally of potential enemies had risen from zero to almost everyone. The Changers needed her, but only to use her for a short period of time. And the humans might not want her to die, but they also might find in necessary if that meant saving everyone else.

Sam seemed to be putting together what she was thinking. "No one's going to hurt you, Ella."

Ella shook her head. "They will if they know. They'll have to. To save me will be to destroy everyone else—at least all the humans and half-breeds. That's me and you and a lot of other people."

"Then let's come up with a different plan for saving the human race, and make sure no one finds out about you," Sam said.

He took Ella's phone from her unresisting hand. "Should we head to the tallest bleachers?"

"I'm sure the information's backed up somewhere," Ella said, staring at nothing. "And the bleachers aren't high enough."

"Maybe," Sam said. "Probably. But lucky for us, we live in a city by a river."

Together, in jeans and winter coats, they ran through the south side of town until they came to a creek, which widened before emptying out into the river.

Sam removed the master key from Ella's phone and put it carefully in his pocket. Then he took the super computer that was Ella's phone and drew his arm back to throw it. Ella sucked in her breath and Sam stopped.

"You do it, Ella," he said, turning to her.

She looked dazed for a moment and then something focused in her eyes. She took the phone and scrolled through the numbers. Brandt and Lila, Kate and Nicole. She was pretty sure that all of them would give her up for humanity, or, when she was honest with herself, a whole lot of less important causes as well—like maybe what brand her jeans were and how well she wore them. And who needed a phone full of contacts who weren't really her friends?

She yanked her arm back, and threw the phone so hard it hit a tree near the water on the other bank and cracked before sliding down the edge and into the creek.

Ella sat on the cold ground and cried. Sam looked uncomfortable, but he patted her back occasionally. Maybe he thought she was crying because of the phone. Really she was wondering how—how she could have had a phone, a life, full of people who had not really been her friends, who would throw her—quite literally if they had to—to the wolves.

Her mother wouldn't have filled her life with fake people. Her mother hadn't. Ella dried her face and stood up. The Festival was in two days. There was a lot to do.

No one believed he was a king, he thought, pushing the half-full grocery cart around the fence that surrounded The Property. But he had been all those years ago—king of all, king of everything.

In a time before this time there was one who had taken it away from him, left him to bow and grovel in his weak, magic-less skin. It would have been a cruel fate for any of his kind. But the curse had run deep, deeper than he or she could have imagined. He had grown old, bald, ugly, but his body had refused to die. All these years it had pressed on him—years of achy bones and weakened teeth, years to see what his own prejudices and punishments had done to others. He had resisted learning it—the lesson his curse was trying to force on him. Until Charles Napper had taken up in the forest and built himself that mansion—a perfect reflection of the king-that-once-was—calm, disdainful, cruel.

And so, the king-that-once-was had gone, after all these years, to see the tea-maker, the balance-bringer, the girl-who-was-now-old. And she had told him: one act of restitution, one good deed to those half-breeds whom he had despised. That was all it would cost him. When that act was complete, the curse would be broken. His aged body would fall from him, and he would be released.

He bent to pick up a crumpled, red can, listening to the distant voices of the wolves. Their numbers continued to increase even as their food sources diminished. The Alpha was pulling them to him. But not all would stay. The blackened Ezazh had already been abandoned. Eventually she had found her way to him—scented his authority when the humans could not, when the Changers would not. The wolves would still trust him if the need for a leader arose. One good deed.

"I will call them," he muttered to his shopping cart. "If the Alpha falls, I will call the wolves to me."

CHAPTER 58

It was the last day of the semester. Ella walked slowly to Mr. Witten's room, set her retelling on his desk, and waited.

Her teacher looked up, smiling. "Anxious to know your score, are you?" he asked.

"Not exactly," Ella said. "This is really just a draft."

Mr. Witten raised an eyebrow. "Ella, it's due today."

"I know," Ella said. "I guess I was hoping you'd let me email it to you or something. The truth is, I'm just wondering if there's anything more about the original wolf lore that I should know—anything that might help me make the re-telling more impactful."

"Yes," he said, skimming through the paper, the lines on his face deepening as he read. "I see."

For several minutes they both sat in the silence of the empty classroom. Finally, Mr. Witten cleared his throat and said, "Of course there are always many ways that a story retelling could go."

"Yes," she said. "Exactly. Those who once worked together could now work in opposition to one another. That could also be part of an effective retelling, don't you think?"

Witten looked into Ella's eyes. "Yes, I suppose it could be very effective and a nice twist. Though I must admit that I personally dislike retellings that make old friends into enemies."

Witten paused and looked at Ella. "There are always other twists you could use as well. One thing you might think about is that the mythical werewolves in the stories would have had children. In your retelling, it would be interesting to imagine that now the descendants from those werewolf lords could have multiplied and intermixed with other races, as family lines often do. And so, just like some of the children in the myths of Greece and Rome, many of these creatures would now be halflings—partial werewolves if you will—with blood that has been combined with regular humans. These half-bred descendants of the full blood werewolves might be disliked, even endangered by the full bloods. Yet, there might also be a few full bloods who would wish to protect them if they could."

"Yes," Ella said. "That would be a nice addition. I'll work on it and get it to you tonight."

"Very good," her teacher said, shuffling his papers and looking down at his desk. "Good luck at the Festival, Ella. I'll probably see you there."

Ella smiled. "I'm pretty nervous."

"I bet."

So Witten was on their side, or at least not on the side of the Changers. Witten considered himself one who wished to help and protect the half-breeds—at least if Ella was interpreting their conversation correctly. That was good, or at least nice to know.

The rest of everything was a mess. Ella and Sam had different plans. The idea was that these plans would eventually work their way into the same plan as the night of the Festival progressed. But Ella thought that seemed overly optimistic. Especially considering both plans had approximately 10,000 holes, she and Sam were just teenagers, Napper was an evil genius, and it would be the full moon, which meant there would be a wood full of wolves and werewolves.

Ella paused for a second as something else clicked into her brain. The full moon.

The news never caught stories of werewolves or half-breeds. But every month, for the last five months, the news had been filled with stories of a silver bullet on a moon-filled night.

Ella looked up to the darkening sky, the moon scattering light through the trees. Suddenly it seemed quite possible that, in addition to wolves and werewolves, the Silver Shooter might also make an appearance at the Festival of the Red Candle.

And Ella really had no idea whose side he was on.

THE ROGUE TOOK ALL THEIR TEETH, SO AS NOT TO AROUSE SUSPICION. To take only the incisors might have alerted the Alpha. Although probably not.

It was a common punishment—to remove the sharpest teeth—the most powerful, the most beautiful. And the Alpha had not known to whom the punishment would be given. She had been an inconsequential female working as a governess at The Ranch.

An inconsequential female with her first real crush. On the wrong man. Naturally. She laughed at the cliché. Her superiors had told her that she was never to release anyone from the compound. And yet she had. Witten had touched her hand, holding his fingers there—lingering as he'd asked for the keys, taken them. He had just wanted to go on a little joy ride, he'd said. There had been no rush, no urgency, and it had seemed so harmless. He, after all, was one of their kind.

And then he was gone with the mechanic and the sisters. They'd escaped through backroads and staged the crash and the explosion—so beautifully done that even the Alpha had believed them to be gone—burned up at cliff's bottom where only twisted metal and smoking remains had been found.

The chosen ones were gone. It had been her fault.

"Whoever was responsible," the Alpha had said, "remove the teeth."

The Italian had reported the infraction. The rancher had executed her punishment. They had been the first to go. After that, she'd gone after the Alpha's favorites—those who weren't necessary to secure the girl's presence at the Festival, but whom he preferred, whom he listened to when he never listened to her at all.

The Rogue smiled as the bridge of her fake eye teeth soaked for the night. Because he hadn't been there, because she'd grown into a woman—a woman who'd chosen a different name and a different face —because she could hide her infirmity, she'd moved up through his ranks. Strong, smart, beautiful. The humans, she thought darkly, never questioned beauty. Among them, an attractive, wealthy woman could do no wrong. This had served her well among their kind. And her own. She could slip into any position in human society. They always trusted a pretty face.

She slid the bridge back into her mouth and smiled—perfect teeth between perfect lips in a perfect face. She wanted to be sure the Alpha believed the Rogue was after the girl and had failed to get her. In reality, she had failed at nothing. Her efforts to take the girl were merely distractions from the messier work of weakening the council by reducing its numbers. Although the girl would have been a good card to play.

The Rogue set both gift boxes on the table. One she left closed and triple wrapped as usual. The other she opened to look at her newest bauble. This bullet was special—not silver as she'd needed for the others, but titanium—shiny as moonbeams, ready to be stained garnet as the blood sun. She had commissioned it for one final bit of business she needed to complete before the work of the Festival was done. It would be, she thought smiling, a special surprise.

CHAPTER 59

The rehearsal breakfast was held in a large indoor patio to the north side of Napper's mansion. It was decorated in spring pastels though outside a light sleet was falling. The food was spring-like too—strawberry rhubarb crumbles, fresh eggs balanced on tiny bowls, and bright melons cut into flower shapes of different sizes. Wealth and power, Ella could see, had no regard for the seasons.

After breakfast, they walked from the patio to what appeared to be a large atrium. Instead of normal walls, windows stretched from the floor to a ceiling that was also made entirely of glass. Standing in the domed room, they could see everything outside and in. The room was being prepared for dancing. The stone floor had been polished and large groups of people milled around carrying flowers, dishes, and gauzy red tablecloths.

But what was most remarkable about the glass-encased room was that at the back of it two marble staircases climbed up a full story, emptying out at the top of a large hill—not a balcony that looked like a hill, but an actual hillside that formed the back wall of the atrium. Napper had built this room up and around the top of the hill, encasing it in a building of glass and marble. As such, the hill looked startlingly out of place and all the more beautiful.

Vivi saw Ella staring and explained, "He's a bit of an eccentric. He wanted to build his house around the natural beauties of the land."

And so he had. Wildflowers, grasses, and herbs sprouted up on the face of the hill. There were butterflies and bees that occasionally flitted through the main room before finding their way back to the natural landscape at its back, unaware that through the glass window panes that comprised the ceilings and walls, winter hovered, waiting for its entrance.

At the center of the hilltop sat an old stone structure that looked like it'd be more at home with Greek ruins than in southern Indiana. It was pock-marked and ugly with a cement pedestal that held a round basin at its top—almost like an ancient bird bath. Napper obviously liked it. It seemed his mansion and this room had been built onto the hillside with the express purpose of preserving the relic.

"Come," Vivi said, leading Ella to one of the marble staircases. The staircases were wide and open with works of art, statues, portraits, and artifacts encased in glass cabinets at different points as you walked up the stairs.

Ella stopped to admire several of the paintings that she knew she'd seen in her mother's old art history book, as well as several ancient weapons that Vivi told her had been discovered on the grounds when the first Nappers had settled the town. The craftsmanship was amazing —double-edged swords, spears, daggers, and scythes—all with etchings of unusual birds, insects, and calligraphy-type letters. Ella wished she could open a case and hold one—just for a minute. She placed her fingers gently on the glass.

"They don't make things the way they used to now, do they, my dear?"

Ella jumped. Napper had come up behind her just as quietly as Vivi usually did. He held a carved wooden walking stick in his left hand and was wearing a suit that was clearly tailored, but looked old-fashioned —like Napper had just walked out of a 1935 boutique. He was much taller than Ella had realized, without any stoop to his features. His hair was gray and his face bore several dignified wrinkles, but his hands were smooth, white, and impeccably groomed.

"Ella," Vivi was saying. "This is Mister Napper."

"Pleased to meet you at last," Napper said, holding out a delicate hand.

Ella took it and he pressed gently.

"Quite a privilege to meet the young lady who will complete our little ceremony tomorrow night."

Ella nodded stupidly, and together Napper and Vivi walked with her back to the bottom level.

They stood directly in the center of the room and Ella realized there was a third staircase—built, or formed, into the rocky edge of the hillside that protruded into Mr. Napper's house. Napper and Vivi paused, and Ella realized that this was where the ceremony would begin.

Vivi and Napper were hushed, staring at her with a silence that seemed to need breaking.

"So, are we waiting for anyone else?" Ella asked, a little too loudly.

Vivi pinched her lips together, but Napper smiled. "Mostly this rehearsal is so you feel comfortable tomorrow night. Others will have small roles to play, but yours, my dear, will be the biggest."

Ella nodded. "And this is where I'll go?" she asked, nodding at the staircase carved into the hillside.

"Yes," Vivi said. "The ceremony will begin exactly at midnight. You'll wait for the twelve strokes of the clock, and then you'll begin your ascent."

Napper nodded encouragingly at Ella. "Give it a try."

Ella placed a tentative foot on the bottom step. It seemed solid enough. "Don't worry, my dear," Napper said. "Each step will be illuminated by a small, red candle. But do be careful. We wouldn't want you to lose your footing and hurt yourself."

Ella put a foot on the bottom stair, then turned back. "And the stone," Ella asked. "Where will I get it?"

"It will be presented to you at the bottom of the staircase," Napper said. "Simply take it in both hands"—he cupped his hands as if to demonstrate—"before ascending the stairs."

Ella thought it odd that the person who was to give her the stone was not also at the rehearsal breakfast.

Slowly, Ella climbed the staircase. The steps were uneven—some short, some tall, some narrow, some wide, but they were all sturdy and Ella made it to the top with Vivi and Napper following behind. The stone staircase opened out beautifully onto the balcony-hilltop. In front of her was the odd stone structure that resembled a concrete birdbath. Except that as she got closer, she realized that it was an old sun dial, lined and etched with worn symbols representing sun and moon.

"Wow," she said.

"Indeed," Napper replied. "Now when you get to the top, I, your aunt, and several others will be standing behind this tablet, candles at our feet. You'll come here and turn to face the crowd—no need for a microphone; the acoustics are remarkable. When you're facing the crowd, we'll be behind you." He demonstrated by standing behind her, slightly to her left. "We'll pick up our candles and you'll begin reciting the poem."

Ella took her place and began reciting the poem.

Napper cut her off after only a few words. "Very good, my dear. At its conclusion, you'll place the stone here in this indentation." He pointed to a small indent that looked like a tiny moon belonged in it.

"Then," Napper continued, "there will be, I'm sure, some applause, and the party will resume."

"And when I'm done, where will I go?" Ella asked, looking Napper directly in the eyes.

He smiled. "When you're done, I or your dear aunt will lead you to your place among your peers."

Ella glanced at Vivi, though she didn't dare look her in the eyes, didn't dare ask where exactly she and her "peers" would then be led.

Witten opened the door of his small apartment to see his niece standing in front of him with a box of chocolates in her hands.

"Emmaline," Witten said, more than a little surprised. "I thought you weren't coming for Christmas. Where is your mother?"

"She could not come," the little girl said. "But an old gentleman accompanied me here."

Napper stepped from the shadows of the hallway and tipped his hat at the stunned teacher. "It was the least I could do this holiday season," he said. "We wouldn't want families to be apart."

"Where is my sister?" Witten asked.

"Oh, she is quite well in Paris," Napper said. "Though she does hope you'll keep the child safe during her stay here."

Witten felt like all the blood had fallen to his feet. He held the door frame for support.

"Not to worry," the philanthropist said cheerfully. "All we need you to do is your part."

And with that, he left the girl and her uncle.

"Isn't it wonderful, *oncle*?" the little girl cooed. "Come, have a *chocolat*."

But Witten was not the least bit hungry. He shut the door, bolting the heavy lock, though it was—he knew—a useless gesture.

CHAPTER 60

On the morning of the Festival, they drove to Vivi's salon. At least there were some advantages to being the fatted calf. For the next four hours, Ella was pampered as she'd never been before. They put fresh highlights in her hair—red streaks like rubies. They did her nails and exfoliated her feet, smoothed her skin and massaged her scalp, then layered on a dizzying succession of concealers and foundations, eye shadows and liners. Her hair was then washed, dried, and pulled through what seemed to Ella a confusing combination of curling irons and straightening tools until Ella felt that her face and hair were just as smooth and clear as polished stone. And just as blank.

Ella was grateful for that. Every time she looked at Vivi she was worried she'd give herself away. But throughout the day, Vivi barely acknowledged her.

A limo would arrive just before eight. Vivi tapped on Ella's door close to seven thirty. "Are you about ready?"

Ella stepped from her bathroom with the perfect red dress and stood in front of the full-length fairy tale mirror. Vivi had bought her delicate, satin gold slippers to go with it and a small golden clutch. For one small moment, Ella looked at herself and wished that she could forget about evil schemes and shapeshifting geniuses, that she could just swirl around in a beautiful dress, and dance.

When Ella stepped from the room, Vivi smiled—her teeth lined up in two spotless, alabaster rows. Ella knew that this was not her aunt, that this woman was an imposter who was *not* on her side.

Still, to look at Vivi was almost to trust her. She wore a silk evening gown, purple so dark it was almost black. When Vivi moved it was like the deepest waters of a midnight pond. The hem fell to the floor in a direct line that seemed purposeful and concrete while the shoulder straps were gauzy and feminine, highlighting Vivi's collarbone and flawless skin. Her heels clicked like those of an important woman and her hair was a combination of tight and loose curl pinned up with garnet barrettes so that it fell or stayed put just as if Vivi had photoshopped it there.

"It's almost time," Vivi said, handing Ella a tube of crimson red lipstick. "The limo should be here any minute."

Ella lined her lips with care, then filled them in—her mouth like roses, like beetles, like blood. She felt like a geisha, a child bride—ready to be led to her new destiny, powerless to change it.

Ella hoped things were less chic and more productive on Sam's end.

～

SAM REALIZED SOMETHING ON HIS SECOND TRIP TO THE NAPPER Psychiatric Institution in the middle of the night. Things were easy when you had a master key.

Of course, he'd always known this. Things were easy for people with lots of money or really good looks, connections, status. Those were all types of master keys and they did all kinds of things. Master keys got you into places you shouldn't be, and out of trouble if someone found you there.

And so it was for him. Into the institution, into Sarah's room just like that. No one heard him walking through the halls, no one noticed the small click of the key. In the office downstairs he'd taken a moment to disable the entire security system. That was where a master key got you.

But there was one thing a master key could not do. It could not wake Sarah up. She lay there, hooked up to her tubes and monitors and medicines, sleeping like she could go on for a hundred years. It would have been nice if a kiss could awaken her. But tonight he needed something stronger.

Sam had avoided looking at the moon all night. He had worn sunglasses to the institution and walked through halls and rooms with no windows. But even without looking, he had felt the moon. It, he knew, had risen slowly, brilliantly from the southeast and now sat cock-eyed on the horizon—a white snowdrop ready to welcome winter into its gaze. Even the knowledge of this made him hungry.

He took a package of beef jerky from his coat pocket and opened it. He hadn't had meat for weeks, and he didn't eat it yet.

For a moment, he sat beside Sarah, watching her chest rise and fall, her hands soft at her sides, her hair sprawling across the pillow in waves of burnt red, rebelling against the forced slumber, the white sheets. He touched her hair, then sat for a minute holding her hand. On her wrist was a hospital bracelet, one with a small chip inside that would set off an alarm if she left the room.

Gently, he leaned down and pressed his mouth softly to her forehead. It was, after all, worth a try.

She didn't move. But Sam wanted to remember anyway. After tonight, it was likely she would refuse to see him again, if there was a him left to see.

He released her hand and placed it on the bed. Then he stood up and dug into the bag of jerky, finishing every last bit in only a few minutes. He threw the bag away and opened the thick shades that covered her window. The moon was so white the edges blurred into silver against the winter sky. Sam took off his sunglasses and met the moon with his gaze.

His heart pumped, his head pounded. He wanted to shut his eyes to close it out, or jump right into it. Instead, he sat and stared. From across the city he heard noises—music, dancing, laughter. The Festival had begun. From across the city he smelled food—roast pheasant and pig, chickens in creamy wine sauces, veal cut into delicate slices. They were not avoiding meat.

Without turning back to Sarah, Sam opened his mouth, feeling each sharp new tooth with his tongue. And then he hit the window hard with his now large, thick shoulder. The double pane shattered into a thousand pieces which fell like angry sleet to the grass below. Sarah stirred. From the nurses station Sam heard noises—papers dropped, the scrape of chairs, and then footsteps. So slow and soft, their human feet.

In a solid movement, he scooped Sarah into his arms, ripping the tubes and needles from her sweet, smooth skin, and then he climbed to the window, and jumped.

By the time the nurses banged into the ruined room, he was across the grounds and over the fence.

Sarah was awake now, if you could call it that. Her eyes were glazed and glassy, forehead slick with sweat. "Stop it," she said, shaking her head at nothing. "Stop it."

Weakly, she pressed away from Sam, pushing against his chest. "Leave me alone, you nightmare," she said, slurring her words.

"Sarah," he said, slowing in his run near the south side of The Property. "Can you hear me?"

"Stop it," she said again. "I hear you every night. I don't want to anymore."

The words stung, even though Sam knew they weren't really for him. They were for the monsters in her drug-induced dreams, the monsters intended to keep her in the institution, not get her out, the monsters that looked a lot like him.

"Sarah," he said again. "I'm taking you somewhere safe. Safe from the night and the moon and the creatures it provokes."

Sarah kicked him in the gut, pounded his shoulder with her fists. "Stop it," she said, crying now. Each blow was like tiny butterfly punches to Sam's thick skin, but it still hurt.

"Sarah," he said, setting her down by the fence posts of The Property and holding her shoulders so she wouldn't slump on her weakened legs. "I'm taking you to meet Zinnie. You'd like that, wouldn't you? I'm taking you there."

Sarah looked at his face for the first time that night, squinting through the confusion that still threatened to overtake her. "Zinnie," she said, without slurring.

"Yes," Sam said, slightly relieved. "Zinnie. My friend."

"Zinnie," she said again, shaking her head, and then adding, "Sam?"

He wanted to lean in and hug her. Instead he turned from her and her question. He faced the posts in front of them, ready to bend them open so they could step through.

"If you're Sam, then crawl," she said. "Crawl through the licorice post."

In the distance, Sam heard police sirens start up—heading off into different sections of town—searching.

"I never said I was Sam," he replied, bending a post and creating an opening.

She had dropped to her knees and was searching for the candy post. Two sirens pummeled toward the south side of town.

"Please Sarah; we have to hurry."

"Then find it," she said. "And crawl through."

"I can't. I'm too big."

"Then help me," she said.

"I am," he roared, reaching toward her as though to grab her and drag her through the opening he'd made.

She scuttled back from him, scooting away like a drunken crab. Sam stopped, opened his mouth to curse, and then shut it again silently. He turned, running along the fence to the licorice post. He pushed it aside and held it for Sarah. "Come on," he said.

She crawled through almost on her belly. Behind them they heard a sound. Sam turned. His neighbor stood in the lawn, staring. He was wearing only boxer shorts and holding a joint. "It's medicinal," the man said, his mouth hanging half open.

"Good," Sam said, nodding politely before turning to the fence and bending an opening big enough for a werewolf to fit through.

He took Sarah's hand and half pulled, half helped her up the path and then stopped. There was smoke everywhere. Sam paused. Not smoke, but dust. Sam waved it away, coughing. Sarah held her sleeve over her mouth. Out of the fog came a figure, pale and sallow-skinned, her mostly bald head dotted with sparse patches of long white hair that dangled from it like drift weed.

Sarah screamed.

The woman smiled sadly. Her lips were cracked and gray, teeth yellow, though still square and strong as ever.

"Zinnie," Sam whispered.

"I'm sorry, dear," Zinnie said, reaching up a papery hand to touch his cheek. "The house is crumbling. I'm afraid we won't make it through the night."

"You can't stay," Sam said. A chunk of Zinnie's house fell to the earth—from brick to dust in no more than seconds.

Zinnie laughed—a tinge of her youth hanging onto the sound. "No dear," she said. "What I can't do is go." She handed Sam a small vial of a tonic he had requested. Then she held up a basket of cakes with a thermos of tea. "This tea should clear her mind," the old witch said. "Now take her somewhere safe."

Sam took the basket, then bent down to kiss Zinnie's balding head. When he turned back to Sarah, she was crying. All the sirens were heading this way now—four cars down four different roads. The south side wasn't that big. They would be here soon.

"Leave," Zinnie said, as pieces of her age-old house wafted through the air like mist.

Sam knew of only one other place in the world where he had always been safe, one constant point where Sam felt the evil could not go.

He pulled Sarah back through the fence, then lifted her as he ran, past his neighbors' trailers, around his front porch, and to his father's old van.

His dad was waiting there in the darkness, sunglasses on, leaning against the van, keys in hand.

Sam opened the door and tossed the basket in. He could hear a police car as it sped its way toward the trailer park, turning in. "Go," Sam said, lifting Sarah into the backseat and gently buckling her in. She wiggled and pushed against Sam.

"They've gone up the east road," Sam said.

"I know," his father replied, starting the van, which Sam now realized was surprisingly quiet for an old van.

"Keep her safe," Sam said.

"Get in son," his father said.

"No."

Sarah kicked Sam hard in the shin. He gently put her leg back into the car and shut the door.

Robert Calhoun kept his sunglasses on and drove slowly, silently, through the west exit and into the night.

Jones had arrived at the door to the enormous kitchen with thirty of his slaughtered chickens that afternoon. He couldn't exactly care for the chickens now that he had left the farm, so it made sense to donate them to the party.

Except that it didn't make sense at all because this was the last place where Mitchell Jones wanted to be.

Still, Jones had lingered near the kitchen after they had taken the plucked and gutted chickens into the house. He'd waited for the old cook to come back and then offered to help her. She'd taken his offer gladly—the birds would need to be prepared and she was behind.

Together they had spent the last several hours chatting. Jones told her stories from his travelling days—stories of Bigfoot that he'd heard at almost every campsite in the hills of Montana. The cook had laughed as they'd seasoned and basted, roasted and braised until each bird was cooked, until the sun had sunk into its evening sleep.

The orchestra was playing now—an opening sonata in the ballroom while the tuxedoed wait staff stood at attention, ready to carry out plates and goblets, appetizers and drinks.

The old cook wiped her forehead and helped herself to a glass of amber champagne while Jones took a seat by the window and watched. Guests were arriving in fancy cars and limousines. And then there she was—stepping out of a black snake of a limo with a tall, attractive woman following close behind.

The dogs, he knew, would come. Jones wasn't quite sure what was going on. But he was sure of this: Napper was a man with not one face, but two. And you couldn't trust a man like that.

So he would trust his dogs. And his dogs cared about Ella.

Whatever Ella was to do, the dogs would help her. He wasn't sure how to help the girl, but he knew what he could do to help his dogs. He wouldn't leave them to battle their way through whatever dangers lurked on this hill when he could easily let them in through the kitchen door.

He stood near the door as the cook nodded off. Through the darkness of the trees, he watched, waiting for the moment when one of his dogs would rise up over the hill, waiting for the moment when he would take out his own silver whistle, and blow.

WHEN WITTEN ARRIVED AT THE ENTRANCE TO NAPPER'S MANSION, HIS car was taken by the valet and Witten took the hand of his tiny niece, wrapping her fingers protectively in his own. He paused at the entrance, not eager to go in, and after a few minutes he could smell the old beggar come up behind him. He could also smell the quiet creature that hid in the shadows—the black wolf that might have become the alpha female if her front leg hadn't been maimed in a human trap. It was a cruel world for the wolves—Witten had to admit that.

"Tonight," the old man said.

Witten turned halfway, not meeting the old man's gaze. The young girl looked at the homeless man with wide eyes.

"Tonight what, *oncle*?" the small girl said.

"Tonight we find out how your dear red cap turns out," Witten said, a sad smile turning up his lips.

"Will you be reading?" she asked with excitement.

"No, but another will. A student of mine just a few years older than you."

Emmaline clapped her hands.

The beggar stared at the girl, stepping closer. "Your sister's child?" he asked.

Witten nodded.

"She looks just like my deceased wife," he said, squatting to get a better look at the girl who hid from him behind Witten's legs and waist.

Witten looked to the mansion, about to step forward.

"By the laws of the old world, she would be killed as a half-breed," the old man said.

"Don't frighten the child with your crazy talk," Witten replied sharply.

"I can help," the old man said.

"Then do," Witten said without looking back.

CHAPTER 61

The Festival of the Red Candle was *not* a casual event. What struck Ella most when they arrived was that the windowed walls of the atrium had been draped with long, thick curtains that fell from ceiling to floor while the ceiling windows remained uncovered. The stars shown down on the party-goers like hundreds of tiny white Christmas lights, but the moon had not yet risen high enough to be seen through the glass.

Ella felt, in fact, that she was in an entirely different place than she had been the morning before. The room was lit with candles and small twinkling lights. Long tables were draped with shimmering red clothes that reached to the ground and then spread out like petals onto the floor. Live plants had been brought in—vases and pots with peonies and roses as well as several native trees on which living birds perched —cardinals and chickadees, goldfinches and sparrows.

In the center of the floor, couples danced in clothes that would have fit well on any Hollywood red carpet. But what the pictures in maga-zines could never capture was the soft flow of the fabrics as women brushed past, the glitter and shine of the gemstones on necks and ears, the sweet muted smell of perfumes and money. It was bedazzling.

Jack came up behind Ella and tapped her shoulder. "Want to

dance?" he said, holding out an arm. "I should have let Brandt have the first shot at you, but he's over at the bar trying to convince them he's twenty-one."

Ella smiled and took Jack's arm. He was wearing a deeply black tux that made his blue eyes stand out like an ocean. Ella thought she might drown.

Jack took her hand, moving her across the floor like she was a doll, a puppet, an appendage to his own graceful movements.

When the song ended, Ella felt not like she had stopped, but like she had landed. Jack held her close to him still—one hand pressed lightly against her back, the other cupping her small hand in his long, soft fingers, gently stroking the scar on her wrist—all that was left from the attack in the corn maze. His face was only inches from hers—fair-skinned and clean shaven. He smelled like soap and cologne and new tuxedo fabric. Jack pulled her hand against his chest and held it there for a moment before moving a stray lock of Ella's hair from the side of her face.

"You look so beautiful tonight," he said, leaning his face down so that his lips were so close to hers she could feel their warmth. His fingers grazed her cheek, then gently touched the side of her neck.

Just then Brandt came up and tapped his brother's shoulder. "Do I get the next dance?" he said.

Jack stepped back, laughing, and Ella tried to smile, though she could feel the blush spread across her collarbone and up her face.

"You look great, Ella," Brandt said, his breath just a little boozy.

"Thanks," Ella said as Brandt took her hand in his.

"How crazy is this?" Brandt said, gesturing around them. Several tuxedoed servers were bringing out a large pig on a platter as well as several roast birds that looked like chickens. Tiny plates of pate and chicken hearts, a leg of lamb.

"I know, right," Ella said, following Brandt's movements through the dance. Ella had to admit that he was so tall and big that it made her feel small and feminine in a way that might have made her swoony, except that right now all she could do was look past Brandt's shoulder to see where Jack had gone.

In one year and three months, she would be eighteen—a legal adult, just a few years younger than Jack. She stumbled over Brandt's foot just a bit.

"Sorry," she mumbled.

"No problem," Brandt said, pulling her a little closer. Her left hand was on his shoulder and he turned her right wrist over to look at it. "What happened here?" he asked.

"Just an accident a few months ago," Ella mumbled.

"Ouch," Brandt said. "At least it didn't get your face. Could have been way worse." He smiled.

Ella nodded, stumbling and blushing. She knew it was meant to be a compliment, but something about the conversation was bothering her.

They finished the dance and Brandt took a step back. "You wanna drink?" he asked. "I can get you something from the bar."

"Um, no, that's okay," Ella said. Brandt shrugged and walked away.

Ella held her wrist where both Jack and Brandt had just touched her scar. Two months ago after the corn maze, Ella had told Jack about the attack. He had immediately looked at her wrist. So sympathetic. So kind.

But she hadn't told him which wrist, and she'd been wearing long sleeves. She remembered because Jack had had to move her sleeve up to see the cut.

How had he known which wrist had been cut? It could have been a fluke, a lucky guess, a coincidence—a reaction where he pulled her arm forward and it just happened to be the right one.

Or not.

Ella looked up at the windowed ceiling—at the cold first night of official winter. In the arctic when the dark winter pressed across the land, some travelers, so struck by the bright moon over the snow would follow it—often walking into snowstorms or falling into icy waters just to catch the moon—the moon that neither noticed, nor cared when they fell.

In her purse, Ella carried two silver cufflinks. Jones had given them to her after that first week of helping out on the farm. She'd brought them tonight as a gift for Jack. He'd seemed so perfect; he'd smelled so good. She didn't want him to be anything more than she thought he was.

But she had to know. She had to find Jack. And give him his present.

~

THEY WERE ALMOST AN HOUR OUT OF TOWN WHEN SARAH'S HEAD WAS clear enough to really think.

"Turn around," she said, tapping the seat in front of her. "We have to go back."

Robert Calhoun ignored her.

"Seriously," she said, her voice rising. "You can't take a person against her will like this."

"I've texted your mother. She'll be at the meeting place," Calhoun said calmly.

"Well, text her again and say we won't. We're going back. She can turn around, same as you." Sarah didn't really want to be rude, only to be heard. And she was feeling kind of cranky after being drugged for two weeks.

Sam's father sighed, but he didn't slow down or turn around. "Listen," he said. "My son has lived in a lot of places and known a lot of people. But until we came here, he hasn't had someone to care about. I can't risk letting him lose that." Calhoun's throat caught on the last two words—just a small pinch, but Sarah heard it.

"But caring," she said. "It doesn't only go one way. It has to go two."

Calhoun nodded, barely. "So you do not care?"

Sarah took a deep breath. It was all so awkward and embarrassing. "No, I care enough to go back. Caring doesn't run off and leave someone."

"Sometimes it does," he said quietly. "Sometimes it dies a quick death in a hospital bed before you've even have time to say a real good-bye."

"Not on purpose," Sarah replied just as softly. "People who care don't leave on purpose; people who care don't run *away*."

Calhoun pulled to a stoplight, silent as silk. And then, without waiting for the light to turn green, he spun the car into the other lane and started to drive back to Napper, tossing Sarah his phone. "Text your mother."

"No," Sarah said. "Not yet. I think it'd be better if she waited for a while before coming."

"She might call the cops if we don't show up."

"After the last two weeks," Sarah said. "I doubt it." She turned to look out the window at the empty winter hills which blew past them in a brown blur. They were driving home. And fast.

TEN MINUTES OUTSIDE OF TOWN, CALHOUN TOOK OFF HIS SUNGLASSES and pulled into a dimly lit taco drive through. He pulled a $100 bill out of his wallet and asked the kid at the window, "How many grilled steak tacos will this get me—just the meat?"

Thirty piles of taco meat later, they stood outside The Property, listening to the music which crept from the mansion on cold breezes. Robert Calhoun was breathing deeply, his breath catching in raspy licks up and down his throat. It had been a long time.

SAM'S DAD WAS HUGE. SARAH HAD THOUGHT WHEN SHE FIRST SAW Sam in his changed condition that he was the largest creature she'd ever seen. But now that his father had shifted, it was clear that Sam was only a boy, and not a full-bred werewolf.

Sam hadn't smelled so bad for one thing. Sarah took a perverse kind of pride in that; and Sam's facial features had not been so feral or pronounced. His father's ears were several inches long and hairy, the eyes deep brown, but not as wide as Sam's had been. Mr. Calhoun's hands were yellowed with chalky nails that were long and smelly. Against her will, Sarah shuddered.

Mr. Calhoun smiled. "You see then, why I haven't shifted for so many years. Stinky business, this whole thing."

Sarah smiled weakly. This terrifying creature, this man-wolf in front of her was one of the good guys.

Maybe it had been a bad idea to come back. But having bad ideas had never stopped Sarah before.

CHAPTER 62

Ella wandered to the refreshment table. Most of it was meat and foreign cheeses, and Ella didn't feel hungry. Even so she chose a small mascarpone pastry and set it on a crystal plate, breaking it into pieces as she drifted into a dark corner. There she set the plate down and took the tiny whistle from her clutch, fingering the silver chain like a rosary. Quietly, she put the whistle to her mouth and blew.

Nothing.

Not so much as a tiny, tinny sound came out of it, much less a high, shrill blast that would call the dogs to her. The darkness of the hall, the soundless emptiness of the whistle—they made her feel lonelier than ever.

It was then that she saw Mr. Witten seated at a nearby table with a young girl instead of a date. He was wearing the ugliest brown suit that Ella had ever seen with an olive and chartreuse colored tie. The outfit would have been pretty awful anywhere, but here in a sea of black and gray tuxedos, he looked like a moth in a swarm of exotic butterflies. Ella stared at Witten for several minutes before she caught his eye. He nodded at her and stood, bringing the child over to meet her. The girl was the youngest at the party—eight or nine years old with dark, delicate features.

"Hello, Ella," Mr. Witten said. "I'd like you to meet my niece, Emmaline. Emmaline, this is Ella. I teach her at the school."

"How do you do," the girl replied with a tidy French accent.

"Hello," Ella replied, charmed in spite of the circumstances. "Are you here for the holidays?"

"Yes," Witten said evenly. "It was quite the surprise when she showed up. Napper was kind enough to escort her here from Paris."

And then Ella knew—the girl was not a guest, but a prisoner; and because of that Witten was captive too. The girl was a ransom note and, watching them together, Ella knew Witten would pay the ransom, whatever it was.

EZAZH STOOD WITH THE ANCIENT ONE BY THE ALTAR IN THE WOOD. Both faced toward the atrium-encased hill. In the woods all around that hill, the wolves were gathering. None of them had accepted Ezazh back into their packs. She had her infirmity; she had the lingering scent of human and medicine in her wounds.

And so she had found the old one. Together they had scavenged for food and eaten—sitting around a campfire at night as the ancient one cooked the food that she tore from the bones of her prey. Ezazh was not the hunter she had once been, but her wounds had healed well and she could still catch pheasants and small rodents.

Occasionally, the cat Gabby dragged a rabbit to their circle and the three would eat together. Tonight the cat was with her mistress— keeping vigil over the crumbling house, staying by the side of the dissolving woman. If the old woman had access to her staff, the witch's powers might surge one last time before she returned to the dust.

Ezazh looked to the altar. At the top of the stones and sticks lay a long piece of archaic wood—the staff the Alpha had taken from the witch. Tonight, Napper had traded the old staff for a gentleman's cane. Ezazh stepped toward the altar where the staff lay, waiting to be burned after midnight. Ezazh took the staff in her mouth and then, following the scent of the small cat through the forest, the deformed wolf thundered through the cold woods to the old woman's crumpling house.

~

Jack was easy to find—dancing a sultry foxtrot with a tall blond who was wearing an incredibly short dress and the spikiest heels Ella had ever seen.

A wave of jealousy nipped at Ella's stomach—ridiculous and irrational. Supposing Jack was actually *not* a werewolf, he was still an adult. And she wasn't.

Jack smiled at her and Ella smiled weakly in return, waiting for the lingering blonde to move away, which after a brief, but significant look from Jack, she did. That didn't help Ella's stomach at all, but it did give her the courage to pull out the cufflinks.

"So," she started, "this might sound silly, but a few months ago, I bought these. And—" She paused. "—and I want to give them to you." She held out her palm with the small silver squares resting on it.

Jack took a step back. The smile never left his face, his posture never changed, but there was significant space between them now. Ella was sad about that. She held out the small links and smiled as big as she could.

"I just," she said, "I wanted to thank you for all you've done for me. Here, let me put them on for you."

Jack seemed to be breathing a little heavily. Ella wanted him to just take the cuff links. She wanted it so badly. Over Jack's shoulder, she caught a flit of movement.

"Here," she said.

Jack took a long, deep breath, and then smiled again. "No," he said, gently, pressing her fingers closed around the silver, careful not to touch it himself. "I can't. I have a terrible allergy."

"To silver?" Ella asked, her voice pitched a tone too high. "Oh no. This is sterling silver. Your allergy is probably to nickel, which is sometimes combined with silver, but these cuffs are made of fine, pure silver."

"No," Jack said again, holding her hand firmly closed and looking her in the eyes, as the tiniest edge of the moon crept into view through the glass ceiling above them. "I could never," he began—and on the last word, Ella thought she saw a strange glint in his mouth, the teeth so white, so long—"I could never take such a thing from a child."

On the word 'child,' something in his face flickered and changed.

Ella might have excused it away—the darkened features, the stone gray eyes, the lengthening ears—were it not for the scent, a scent that lingered in the air even after his face had returned to normal. It was a scent she knew—putrid, troubled—the smell from the corn maze two months ago.

Ella looked down, masking her shock as hurt. "Oh. Okay then."

Jack seemed to sigh in relief, his features softening and lightening, just as the lights dimmed, the curtains began to be drawn open, and the music stopped.

The room was now in perfect blackness, except for the stars and moon casting splashes of wraith-like shadow throughout the crowd. Then, slowly, one by one tiny, red candles began to flicker—lit along the edges of the room, then up the three staircases, ending in a circle of light around the balcony-hilltop.

Jack, Ella noticed, had stepped away from her, and she stood alone in the center of the ballroom. She began to walk forward, like a bride without a groom, a *sati* heading toward her burning pyre.

Around her, a room full of champagne glasses clinked, toasting the ceremony that was about to begin. As she walked, the chimes began. Twelve solid tones which matched her footfall. When the last tone struck, she heard the partygoers behind her as they sighed and sank into their seats or onto the floor. That was good. It meant that Sam had gotten Zinnie's tonic into the champagne. Only those participating in the ceremony had not taken part in the toast; the rest had fallen into a deep slumber. But this was no hundred year's sleep. They had one hour, no more.

At the base of the hillside, Ella paused. It was here she was to receive the stone. The moon stood nearly at its highest point—a cool blue disc in the night sky. Through the darkness, slow heavy footsteps came toward her—a tread unwilling, yet persistent.

When Ella looked up into her English teacher's face, he tried to smile. "Do not place it," he whispered almost soundlessly.

Ella stared forward as though she hadn't heard.

"You have a gift in this," he said softly. "You are unattached. There is no one for them to dangle over you—no mother or father, sister or brother."

Ella looked him in the eyes—the moon lighting his features which had slowly, insistently, begun to change. She thought about Sam whom she had seen flitting through the crowd; she thought about Sarah drugged in a bed in Napper's hospital.

"You're wrong," she said, taking the stone as Witten's pale face fell into gray whiskers that climbed his cheeks and forehead like ashen flames.

ELLA FELT THE STEPS THROUGH HER SOFT, GOLDEN SLIPPERS. SHE HAD thought the trip up the staircase would be hard, but felt as though the moon above them was drawing her to it. Behind the stone tablet stood five tall figures, their candles on the floor, their faces in darkness. Ella took her place behind the tablet and heard each of them lift their candles. Even with the dim candles it was impossible to see the sleeping crowd—only dark figures positioned throughout the shadows. Behind her she heard one of the shifters lick its lips. And then it was silent. In a voice that began small and built into a gradual crescendo, Ella recited the words that had been running through her head for the last month.

> *White moon rising. Red sun blush.*
> *Melt the old world to a hush.*
> *To bring anew a refreshed land,*
> *I place this stone with purity of hand.*

The sun will rise, bright new star.
New definitions of who we are.

Ella held the stone above its final resting place. A group of birds rustled through the trees—several finches taking flight at once as though startled. And then Ella dropped the stone. Straight to the floor.

Ella had not really thought it would break, but she was still disappointed when it didn't so much as chip. What surprised her most was that there hadn't been a rush from the Changers behind her. No one scrambled forward to keep the stone from cracking or rolling over the hillside edge.

Instead, the stone gave a sad little flop toward Ella's golden slippers and stopped. "So I'm the only one who can touch this thing," Ella began, bending down to pick up the stone again. "Me and Mr. Witten?"

Ella did not turn to the group behind her. She did not yet want to see the terror their shifted forms had become. She bit her lip, picked up the stone and said, "What if I told you I know what it's for."

"Be quiet you foolish girl and place the stone," Vivi said, her voice deeper, but familiar. It was a man's voice almost, a jagged tenor.

"Why?" Ella asked, finally turning. "So you can kill me all the faster?" Ella saw the shifters lined up, standing on two legs, wearing thick cloaks of gold and red. She knew that the shifters would be huge and terrifying, but she had hoped that they would be merely vile, ugly.

And some of them were.

Jack was shockingly grotesque. She recognized his horrible scent more than his face, which was deathly black with yellow teeth and nails. Brandt was brown and huge and obviously drunk. Another, whom Ella believed was the veterinarian who had released the wolves to Napper's property, was the tallest of the group. He had ruddy fur and eyes that matched his fur exactly—his hands meaty, sallow things that looked jaundiced and cruel.

Yet Vivi was still delicate and wiry, the fur of her face soft, almost inviting. When Ella's eyes rested on Vivi's fingers, she realized something she should have figured out before. Those were the hands that had held her tied with a Downy-scented gag in her mouth. Ella had been so certain that a creature of that strength would be a man that she hadn't thought to consider anything else.

Now she did.

At the center of the line-up stood Napper. He was simply beautiful. Clearly the oldest of the shifters, his black fur was salted with dignified whites, his eyes a soft, clear gray—like they'd been crafted from the gems of the hill. His fingers were slender, long, and strong with white pearly nails that extended out into perfect points. He had no odor at all and his voice was seemingly unaltered from the shifting.

"My dear child," Napper said, his voice gentle and calm. "It is not our wish to go around murdering people. And you, of all people, would not be killed. Placing that stone would grant you a position of honor among our kind. You would earn your seat among the gods."

"Exactly," Ella said. "I'm not quite sure I wish to join up with the gods just yet."

Jack piped up, his voice a crash of raspy, dark tones. "What he means is that you would be more respected; you would be revered." Jack's voice softened a bit and he stepped toward her. Ella could see his form sink and smooth as he shifted back into the slender man who had been her counselor. "By all of our kind and yours as well. You would pave the way for our kind and your kind to be together. Please, Ella. I know it's hard to understand. But place the stone."

As he said this, his voice sank into sweetness. She could tell that it took a great effort with the moon high above him. But she could still smell the werewolf on him, and with that, she could feel herself being dragged through the corn. "For you?" she asked gently.

"For us," he replied, his tones honey.

"Then no," Ella shouted, and with all her strength, she threw the stone. It arched over the sleeping crowd and struck the far window, a hairline fracture creeping up the glass like a thin, singular strand of a spider's web.

Jack reached his arm back, transforming as he did so, and slapped her, his nails drawing three red marks across her cheek.

"Enough," Napper shouted. "Do not lay another hand on her."

Jack slunk back as Napper walked to the edge of the balcony and called down, "David, find the stone. And quickly."

Napper looked out on the crowd, realizing for the first time that the mob he'd gathered was completely unconscious. He made a small clicking sound and turned to Ella, his mouth a firm, straight line. "I see that you have somehow managed to drug my crowd. I'm forced to respect that since drugging people is one of my specialties as well. Unfortunately," he paused, "it will do you no good." He smiled. "Now, my dear, if you will not consider your future, consider your present. There are people in this town you care about, are there not?"

Ella set her face and didn't answer.

"Of course there are. The girl I have in my asylum, the boy who brought you to the old house—they are friends of yours. And there are more people in this building and town that you might not know, but wouldn't want harmed."

Again, Ella didn't answer.

"There are parents in Napper, children, dogs, and cats. There are innocents."

At last Ella nodded.

Napper smiled and patted her head as though she were a very small child. "Within these woods, hundreds of wolves have gathered—drawn to their ancient forefathers, the Gevudan. And to me."

He got down on one knee in front of her and looked directly into her eyes. "If you place that stone, all will be well with those you care for and with those others who now slumber in innocent ignorance— here and in the towns beyond us. But if you do not—" He stood, looking toward the large windows of the atrium. "—I will release the wolves. They are hungry and strong and have not found enough to eat in the paltry woods of this preserve. They will tear through this building and then through the town, felling and consuming those who come into their path. And many others who do not." Napper did not smile or frown, his face as smooth as his voice. "The hunger of the wolves, my dear, is deep."

He turned away from the windows and looked at Ella again. "Listen."

Napper paused, allowing Ella to hear the hundreds of mournful howls. They rose up outside the glass walls, from the top of the hill to the base of the atrium. The wolves had surrounded them.

Napper stepped back into his place among the council as Witten climbed the stairs, holding the stone that started to glow when he reached the top.

Witten faced Ella, across the ancient sundial—the light of the stone coming through his fingers, until gradually it seemed to seep into his skin; Witten began to glow.

Behind her, Ella heard gasps from the council. Napper cursed. "You were not to ascend the stairs, David."

Ella, frightened, held out her hand to take the stone. But Witten did not give it. Looking down, he moved his hand as though to place the stone himself.

"David," Napper said sharply, but Witten stood transfixed, unhearing.

As his hand came down with the stone, Napper jumped forward and Ella heard Vivi's husky werewolf voice scream, "No." Then the quick cock of a gun and the discharge of a bullet. The bullet struck Witten in the right shoulder, its force pushing him backwards so that he toppled down the hillside, crumpling at its base.

"*Oncle*," a small voice screamed out, but Ella barely heard it. She was looking instead at Vivi, who was holding a small, ornate gun, and smiling. Where her four eye teeth should have been were empty black holes.

The council of Changers broke formation as Vivi loaded a small silver orb into her gun.

"Ella, Napper," she said, walking from her place at the end of the line to face them. "I did want it to be more of a surprise, but someone had to stop him and he had *that* a long time coming. Now, how about we speed things up a bit."

She held the gun toward Napper. "Do you know who I am?"

"You are many things," Napper replied. "The Rogue of our race, the Silver Shooter to theirs. But mostly," he said calmly, "you are a traitor."

"That," she replied, "is a very ugly word for a girl who had her most lovely teeth torn from her at a young age simply because she made one small mistake—to trust the one who now lies dead on your floor." She smiled again. "When I took the teeth of the others, I simply took back what was taken from me all those years ago. With interest."

She held the gun pointed to Napper's chest. "Now the games are over. Diplomacy has gotten us nowhere. The girl will place the stone or she will be killed." Vivi looked cruelly to Ella. "And I won't kill you with a bullet either. If you do not place the stone, I will tear you to pieces—first your teeth, then eyes and ears, skin and hair, limbs and innards. They will be delicious—so young and tender."

"I don't have the stone," Ella said. "It fell with Witten."

Napper scowled at Vivi who replied bluntly, "The Silverlord was going to place that stone himself—taking the power of this world and ours into his hands."

Napper pinched his lips shut before turning to Ella. "Go fetch the stone, child."

Ella descended the stairs where the small French girl was sobbing over her uncle's half-conscious body. Ella stopped in front of the body. Looking at him with his face in the shadow, she realized for the first time that he was the gray-masked creature who had saved her the night she'd been kidnapped from the basement.

The child looked defiantly at Ella and shouted, *"Vous ne pouvez pas l'avoir.* You can't have it." In her small hands was the stone, a faint glow still lingering at its edges.

"You can hold it?" Ella asked.

"Obviously," she retorted.

"Good," Ella said. "I don't want it—not to keep, but I have to try *something.* Your uncle is dying."

"I don't trust you," the girl said.

"I know," Ella began. "It's hard to know who to trust." She sat back on her heels to think. As she did, Witten moved a white hand to the girl's lap, and motioned weakly for Ella to take the stone.

The girl looked up at Ella with wide, brown eyes, but still she clung to the stone. Ella bit her lip and was about to say something when Jack bounded down from the balcony-hilltop, running for the young girl. Emmaline screamed. Ella jumped up and stood in front of the child.

"Jack, stop," she yelled.

Jack smacked into Ella's shoulder, throwing her to the side. Ella fell hard on her ribs as the girl shouted angrily in French and threw the rock. Ella struggled to push her bruised body up off the floor as something huge came crashing down beside her.

Jack lay just a few feet away from her, a tiny red spot on his forehead where the rock had struck him, barely drawing blood.

Ella did not immediately reach down to take the stone. Emmaline stood near it, looking at the enormous werewolf she had knocked to the ground. The small French girl bent over and picked up the stone. She held it in both hands, bringing them high over her head before swinging both arms down at the werewolf's head, hitting him squarely between the eyes. And then she sat down and started to cry.

Ella knew how she felt. She crawled over and wrapped her arms around the girl. "Here," she said, handing Emmaline the silver cufflinks. "Place them on your uncle's wounds—front and back. I think it will help."

Emmaline wiped her face with her sleeve and handed the stone to Ella. "Take it," she said. "I don't want it."

"I know," Ella said, taking the small stone that had been her mother's—light enough to wear on her neck, though right now it felt almost too heavy to hold.

AGAIN ELLA FELT HER WAY UP THE HILLSIDE STAIRCASE. THE RED candles that lined them had burned into puddled nubs. Outside the walls on all sides, Ella could see the yellow and brown eyes and dark forms of the wolves, staring at her.

When Ella got to the top, Vivi stood facing Napper, Brandt, and the veterinarian.

"Quickly," Vivi said. She had her gun trained on Napper, and Ella noticed the smallest tremble in her hand. Vivi had one silver bullet in the gun and she would have had to keep it close to her the entire night. It was weakening her.

"Do I need to say the poem again?" Ella asked, launching into the recitation.

"No," Vivi said, cutting her off. "Just place the stone." Vivi looked up to the moon, which still seemed to hover above them, though soon it would begin its descent.

Ella took a deep breath, gripping the stone so hard it hurt. And then from the right staircase, something flew past her and struck Vivi so hard she fell. The gun slipped from her fingers, sliding to the front of the hilltop near the center stairs. In the moonlight, a figure in a white jumpsuit stepped up from the center staircase onto the balcony, and picked up the gun.

"Ella, you have no idea how much I hate heights," Sarah said, stepping toward her and looking down the steep hillside.

"What are you doing here?" Ella asked, looking to the right for the person who had thrown the stone. Sarah was not the one she had expected to see.

"I don't know," Sarah said. "I guess this is what jealous friends do when they want the part." She almost smiled.

Ella didn't smile back. She felt like crying. Sarah might have been holding a gun, but there was still just no way for them to win. The gun held one bullet and as soon as it was used, the rest of the Changers would be safe to force Ella to place the stone. And then they were done.

Below them, Ella heard the wolves begin to bang against the glass windows—thumps and crashes as their heavy shoulders hit the glass.

Vivi stood, her forehead swollen and bloody. "Put that gun down," Vivi hissed at Sarah.

Sarah wrapped her fingers tight around the handle. "You know we used guns like these in our spring play," she said. "An Agatha Christie mystery. I was in my most morbid phase back then so I totally researched everything." She waved the gun around, and each of the Changers stepped back. "These things aren't easy to use," she said, smiling at Vivi. "But I wanted my performance to be realistic." She cocked the gun and pointed it at the woman who had called herself Ella's aunt.

The wolves continued to pound against the windows, the sound louder and louder as the glass shuddered and shook. And then from both side staircases, Ella heard footsteps—not two-legged, but four—the stamp of paws, the clack of nails.

The wolves, they were coming.

SARAH PRICE COULD PUT ON A VERY GOOD SHOW. BUT SARAH PRICE had held a real gun only once before in her life. Hearing the rush of paws shook her and her hand began to sweat. Stage guns and real guns were different in one important way. On stage you didn't kill anything. Here, you did.

Except that Sarah couldn't.

Sarah's hand trembled and the gun shook. The werewolf who was the Silver Shooter saw it, and laughed—the four gaping holes in her mouth more sinister than fangs.

Sarah tried to level the gun but she felt frozen, out of breath, her fingers stiff. The Silver Shooter leapt toward her, claws outstretched. Sarah closed her eyes as a sharp pain jolted her, but not in her chest or neck as she'd expected. Rather, something sharp clamped down on her wrist, causing her hand to jerk and pull the trigger. The Silver Shooter collapsed just feet away, eyes open in shock, blood pooling beneath her chest.

The dog, Sheila, sat beside Sarah, panting. Sarah dropped the gun, spots of blood sprouting up along her arm where the dog had bitten her to jolt her into firing the weapon. Sarah stood by the dog, putting her good hand on the soft fur of the animal's back while tears ran down her face.

And then the shocked quiet of the balcony broke into a thunder of confusion.

CHAPTER 63

The dogs had come, not the wolves. Ella didn't know how they would have gotten in when the wolves continued to pace and bang on the cracking windows. But she knew they had come at the whistle's call.

Loco, Foxy, and Sheila stood at the edge of the balcony, ready to fight. Sarah stood at the center, trembling and bleeding. Ella scanned the right edge of the balcony, looking for the one person who was still missing. He was almost impossible to see, but perched on a large pear tree sat a werewolf—a werewolf with Sam's eyes.

Unfortunately, Ella was not the only one who saw him. Napper nodded to the veterinarian, whom he called Tomas. The tall shifter turned with a precision that made Ella's throat thicken.

"Sam, watch out," Sarah screamed, just as Brandt ran at her, grabbing her by the waist and throwing her over his shoulder. Sheila and Foxy tore after Sarah, biting at Brandt's calves and knees, and skidding down the marble stairs.

Sam jumped from the tree and ran down the other stairs, breaking the glass of a display case and grabbing a sword on his way.

ONCE ON THE BALLROOM FLOOR, SAM SWUNG THE SWORD BACK AND forth, like a fencer on crack. It was clear that he was a runner, not a fighter. He had no aim, no idea how to place a blow with a sword. And most importantly, he had no silver.

The best Sam could do was parry and jab—little scratches to the other werewolf's skin that were about as damaging as paper cuts. Laughing, Tomas stepped forward, grabbed the sword by its blade and pulled it from Sam's hand. Then, with one quick movement, he punched Sam hard in the stomach.

Sam crumpled just as another Changer stepped from the shadows. He was the largest, ugliest shifter Sam had ever seen. His fur was mottled with browns, reds, and patches of gray. His ears were long, and one had a piece torn off with a bald, scarred patch of skin near it. Its fingernails were yellow and smelled like the bottom corner of a dumpster.

Calmly, the werewolf came up behind Tomas. Sam stood up, bracing to run from the two of them when the enormous werewolf struck Tomas with one large fist to the back of the head. Tomas fell to the ground. He lifted himself on his arms, trying to stand back up, but he never got the chance. The mottled werewolf struck him again—two more quick punches to the head, and that was it—Tomas collapsed into a heap of fur and blood on the floor.

Sam backed away, reaching down to pick up the useless sword when a familiar voice actually laughed. "You can thank me for your fur and fang, but your mother's genes definitely prettified you," Robert Calhoun said.

Sam almost dropped his sword. He stared at the hideous werewolf with his father's voice. His father was close enough now that he could see his eyes in the dark hall. They were, Sam was surprised to notice, just like his father, brown and warm. And right now they were not the least bit afraid.

Suddenly, Sam remembered Sarah. She had been dragged to the opposite end of the ballroom. "Sarah," Sam whispered.

"I'll help you," his father said.

"No," Sam said. "There's a little girl, and Mr. Witten got shot. They need help too. You should go to them."

They were stopped by a loud crack—high-pitched, almost shrieking as a deep line raced up one of the glass windows toward the ceiling—thin, long tinsels of glass falling like needles to the floor. Outside the building the wolves paused to let out a unified howl before resuming their rhythmic pounding—louder and louder, harder and harder, faster and faster until, at once, the chasm of glass opened and quivered, the east wall cascading down like a thousand waterfalls.

The wolves poured forward, a river that had broken through—hundreds of feet running into the ballroom. Then suddenly a strange swirl of air blew across the east wall and around the wolves, circling the atrium before becoming a barrier of wind and snow, a thick pane of storm. The wolves pushed against it, unable to break through the heavy, windy wall.

"Zinnie," Sam whispered. "She's still alive."

His father frowned. "But she won't be for long. A magical snow storm is not as easy to conjure as restorative tea."

Sam turned, running as quickly as he could to where Brandt was dragging Sarah and kicking at the dogs, his ankles a mess of bloody bites. The three-legged dog was down, one of her remaining legs broken. She lay on the floor, still growling.

But the other dog was fierce, jumping high and hard at Brandt's arms and sides, tearing into his skin. Every time she did, he struck at her face, neck, and back with fists or elbows, cracking the dog's bones and teeth.

Sarah, for her part was kicking, punching, and wiggling in an effort to get loose. But Sam knew that to the enormous Changer, she was no more than a stuffed toy. And that softness in the arms of such brute, cruel strength made something in Sam break open.

He lunged at the werewolf.

Brandt turned around and caught Sam in the face—a simple slash with his free hand. It tore across Sam's forehead and through his eyebrow—blood dripping down the side of his cheek.

Brandt laughed. "Suits you, half-breed. I'll get you a hair bow to go with it. Crimson. Like the sun will be when we're done." He nodded to the hill.

Sam knew he needed to help Ella too, but right now he had to get Sarah away from Brandt.

Brandt smiled again. "Just like a half-brained half-breed to choose the wrong priority. But no matter what you do, I'll still have your girl. Bet I can do all kinds of fun things with her after you're gone."

Sarah bit into his shoulder, and it must have been a good bite because Brandt flinched, then cursed, grabbing for her throat.

Sam flew at Brandt's arm, this time with his teeth instead of his fists. He ripped into Brandt's skin, tearing it, so that it hung off his forearm, exposing the bone.

Brandt dropped Sarah and ran at Sam.

Sam had never seen so much blood. It was getting to him more than the actual fight—dripping into huge puddles on the floor. It made him feel dizzy.

Brandt slammed his hand into Sam's face, sending him to the ground, flat on his back. Sam gasped and stood up. Blood was everywhere. Sam couldn't tell what was his and what was Brandt's. Sam closed his eyes. Then he could only smell it, and he found that, as a werewolf, that wasn't half bad.

He ran with his head down toward Brandt—an angry goose. It probably wasn't the coolest move ever, but it knocked the wind out of his opponent. Brandt took a few steps back, still dripping blood wherever he went. Sam bit his lip, willing the wooziness away and trying to pull himself together. Brandt was feeling the effects of the lost blood too—his face pale, his breath fast. Still he seemed to sense Sam's weakness and ran at him with his bloody arm outstretched—little flicks of blood flying everywhere.

Sam took a deep breath and rammed into Brandt with his shoulder —hitting him solidly under the outstretched arm. But Brandt was heavier than Sam. He used his weight to fall forward, dragging Sam to the ground with him. They both smacked into the stone floor. And then Brandt raised himself up and began to pummel his good fist into Sam's back and face. Sam had seen this move before—seen the way Brandt could punch a kid into submission.

Brandt hit Sam's eye, then cheek. Sam felt dizzy from the blood and punches. Golden daggers stabbed into his vision. He couldn't beat Brandt with weight or force. He needed to think, but how could he when his face was being broken into bits?

Sam rolled over, holding his hands over his head. *Force equals mass times acceleration….* Everything was foggy. From what seemed like millions of miles away, Sam heard screaming. And then almost in his ear, Brandt let out a terrible yowl.

Sarah had stabbed Brandt's foot with the sword. Brandt stood up and turned on her, running with a limp, but still easily fast enough to catch Sarah. He lifted her up like he was going to throw her body into the hillside in front of him. And then she swung her legs, which were just below his waist, and kicked him. Right in the balls. Some things just work better than physics.

Brandt dropped her and staggered back a step.

Sam grabbed the sword, putting his weight behind it and running his fastest with the blunt end forward. He hit Brandt in the skull with as much speed and acceleration as he could muster. When he did, Brandt crumpled. This time he didn't get up.

Sarah stood shaking, and walked around the unconscious body, then over to Sam.

"That's two points for you," Sam said. "I was about to pass out. So far, you've taken out Vivi and Brandt." Sam smiled, but Sarah broke into tears, hysterical gasps that seemed they would break her in half.

She pressed her body into Sam's huge chest, burying her face in his fur. And then he realized it—he was still a furry beast, and she was willing to touch him.

Gently, he pushed the hair back from her face and wrapped his arms around her, holding her until the crying slowed, and then—when he looked down at his friend, he saw that his own arms had shrunk back to human size along with everything else.

"You know, it's experiences like this that formed the basis for Beauty and the Beast," Witten said from several feet away. His niece was seated in his lap, her head against Witten's shoulder. Mr. Witten was sitting up, pale and in his human form. He looked like he'd suffered from a fainting spell, not been shot in the chest and then fallen down a cliff.

Near them Jack was laid out flat, his eye and face swollen and bleeding.

Sam stared, "Is he…"

"He's alive," Witten said, playing with a curl on the little girl's head.

"Don't know how much good he'll be if he's bleeding inside his skull as much as he's bleeding outside," Sam's dad said, looking to the hilltop.

"Did you do that?" Sam asked, stunned at the thought that his father could strike another creature like that.

"This little lady had already weakened him for me," Sam's dad said. "But he was starting to come to, so I made sure he was done for the night." He tried to smile, but he was looking to the balcony, his forehead a crush of worry.

Sarah was staring at the hilltop as well. "Ella," she whispered. "He's still got her."

Sam started to run toward the stone steps, but his father—the only one left in a wolvish form—grabbed his shoulder. "Stop son," he said. "She's the only one who can do this."

"How can she?" Sam said.

"If she can't, there's nothing on this earth you can do to help her."

The old anger poured into Sam, and he felt himself shifting back into beast. "You don't care. You're just afraid."

"I am afraid. But I do care. Only, son, you've got to realize it's not always weakness to leave another to find her strength."

With that, he smiled at Sarah.

Sam looked up to the hill, then over to Sarah and his father. And then a mighty crack shook the ballroom—the sound of thunder at its last, its greatest, the sound of one final jolt before the storm withers and blows away. Witten hovered over his niece, Sam over Sarah, and his dad over both of them. And then at once, the snow storm keeping the wolves contained wavered and stopped—melting snow left in a circle around the atrium.

"Zinnie!" Sam screamed. Nothing screamed back except the normal winter wind that swept through the ballroom, chasing the birds and butterflies to the hill.

Hundreds of wolves filled the hall, surrounding the room like they themselves were a new wall. They wandered among the sleeping party-goers, sometimes sniffing, sometimes stopping as though to stand as a sentinels.

A small pack of fierce, black wolves ran toward Sam, Sarah, Robert, Witten, and Emmaline. They formed a tight circle around the group, pacing and drooling, their eyes wild and bloodshot, their ribs a stark outline through their underfed bodies.

"They're starving," Sarah said, as one looked at her directly in the eyes and growled.

"*Oncle?*" Emmaline asked in a trembling voice.

"They will wait," he answered tensely. "Until the Alpha gives the sign for attack."

CHAPTER 64

Loco was the only friend now left at Ella's side. From his mouth, he dropped a small round bullet. It looked like a simple copper bullet from a regular gun.

"It's not silver," Loco said, his voice still startling to Ella, though she knew that he would speak. "Jones gave this to me when he let us into the mansion," Loco said, worry soaking into his brown eyes.

Ella picked up the bullet and held it near the gun. There were too many questions; she couldn't ask them all.

Napper had been waiting for the wolves to break the wall and surround her friends. Now he smiled, every line and feature of his face kind and grandfatherly, except for his eyes which burned with a sharp, deliberate hatred. "Here, dear," he said, grabbing the gun and bullet before Ella could move, and loading the gun. Then he smiled again and set the gun on the stone tablet. "Now that that's loaded and completely useless against me, let's get on with this, shall we?"

Loco growled low, but didn't move.

Ella looked down at him. "It's okay, Loco. It's okay."

Napper laughed. "No," he said, striking Loco on the head with his fist, "it's not."

The dog collapsed instantly.

Ella sucked in her breath, feeling the room spin around her, sure it would collapse just like Loco had.

Below them, released from their snowy wall, the wolves howled triumphantly.

"I won't place it," Ella whispered, tears covering her cheeks. Napper had told her that if she placed the stone, the innocents would be spared. It wasn't true. If she placed the stone, hundreds of people would die. People and dogs and half-breeds—Ella had a best friend in each of those categories. If they weren't already dead, then they would be when she placed the stone. The wolves would kill them, the Changers would kill them, or Napper himself would kill them.

"I won't place it," she repeated, louder this time. "You lose." She stood with her back to the stone tablet, and looked Napper squarely in the face.

Again, he smiled, no grandfather left in any of his features—all of them stone, brass, and sharp-tipped diamond.

He moved so quickly, she almost didn't see him. In less than a second, he had grabbed her right arm, twisting it behind her back so that her hand with the stone dangled behind her, over the tablet. He held her there—arm wrenched in an awkward and painful position, his face and body in front of her, so close they were almost hugging. "In this game there's only one way to win and one way to lose," Napper hissed, no silk left in his voice, no sweetness left in his scent. He was the most repulsive of them all. "Now place the stone."

"No," she whispered.

Napper dug his claws into Ella's wrist so that her blood began seeping into his fur. She leaned back, pulling her face and chest away from him. He laughed and dug harder into her wrist.

"Place it," he said.

Ella felt the tears roll down her cheeks. She couldn't run and she couldn't hold the stone much longer. She was only a human girl with human wrists and when enough pressure was applied to the tendons and nerves, she would drop the stone. When she did, it would fall onto the tablet and she would have placed the stone.

But, Ella realized, there was one other way to stop the ritual from happening.

On the tablet sat Vivi's gun with its plain copper bullet. Quickly, before she could think, Ella reached behind her and picked it up with her left hand—the hand Napper had considered too useless and weak to restrain.

Napper laughed. "It will bounce off of me like a rubber ball," he growled.

"I know," Ella said, meeting Napper's eyes as she fired. The small piece of metal—no bigger than her fingernail, no wider than a bean—tore through her skin too fast to feel. It slashed through muscle, blasting through her clavicle, then into her body—bone shattering like thousands of fires in her chest, and then the fires were gone—ash, blackness.

Ella crumpled, falling, as the bullet exited through her scapula and hit the stone, which splintered into thousands of shards. They sprayed in all directions striking Napper, the walls, the glass ceiling.

Napper fell to the ground as glass poured down like rain on his dead body. For an instant, the wolves bounded forward, and then stopped.

Nothing moved, the air barely shifting until, from deep in the distance, an ancient voice cried out—royal, commanding—calling the wolves.

The wolves paused, sniffing; then turned, breaking away, following the command, pulling back to the wild.

People woke up as if a spell was broken just as Fiona Price and her husband arrived with their lawyer and the FBI.

Her daughter, however, she found racing to the top of a hill, screaming, then crying over another girl's still body.

They would call it a mass shooting, mob related. Several were dead from bullets or shards to the heart.

The Silver Shooter—a woman identified as Raquel Wilhelmson and a member of a mob the FBI identified as The Ring of the Alpha—was also dead—seemingly from accidental gunfire. Most of her accomplices were dead or seriously injured and had been taken into custody.

Nothing found in any of Charles Napper's remaining documents could connect him to the mob. That didn't change the fact that he was dead.

Charles Napper had left no will and no heirs. Consequently, his property would be donated to the city and operated by a new city planner, a gentleman by the name of Robert Calhoun who had—per his resume—spent the last several years moving to various cities throughout the country and studying a diversity of city plans, layouts, and landscaping. The Property would be in good hands.

In the southern corner of The Property, a small historical structure would be rebuilt—a tiny hut with a large hearth—one of the original houses in the city of Napper. Around it would be several community gardens containing flowers, herbs, and vegetables, which could be accessed and used by all the residents of Napper, including those from the south end.

Already the padlocks on the southern gate had been removed. In the years to come, this entrance would be hung with a large sign that read, "Zinnie's Landing: All Welcome."

~

SARAH HAD SWORN SHE WOULD NEVER GO BACK TO ANY HOSPITAL EVER again, but on Christmas morning she walked the snowy path up to the Napper Trauma Unit, and let herself in. Ella had been unconscious for two days, but now she was awake. Fortunately for everyone, shooting with your left hand and trying to hit your heart wasn't the easiest thing to do. Ella had managed to muff her own suicide. Sarah thought it was the best Christmas present ever.

With the adoption of Sheila being a close second.

Ella's story had been all over the news—the girl who had stopped a huge mob operation right here in little old Napper.

Sam and Robert were already at the hospital filling Ella in on the details she had missed while being nearly dead.

"What I just don't get," Sam was saying, "is why the stone shattered. I mean nothing else could break it. It's been around for millennia. Why that bullet?"

His father shrugged. "Ella was the last in a very long line of Bearers. Perhaps when her body shattered, so did the stone."

"Maybe," Sarah said, putting a huge pink poinsettia on Ella's table. "It seems to me that great sacrifices always bring about great gifts. Unusual gifts. Miraculous gifts."

Sarah sat by the bed and looked at her friend. Ella's shoulder was bound up with a bandage that looked too simple to cover a wound that had punctured a lung, broken several ribs, and shattered part of her scapula and clavicle. Her right wrist had several puncture wounds that ran deep and had damaged both muscle and nerve. She'd be affected by the wounds—changed—for the rest of her life.

Loco was sleeping next to her. He and Foxy had been patched up by Jones, and then deemed therapy animals—allowed to stay with Ella until she went home. Home. A place with her real uncle and real cousin.

"So," Sarah said, looking at Ella. "What do you want for Christmas?"

Ella looked weak, pale with some of the color just coming back into her lips. "I'd say being alive is a pretty good start," she said.

"Whatever," Sarah said. "Don't get all mushy-gushy on us. Seriously, what do you want?'

"How about some better food?" Sam said, looking at the paste-colored soup at her bedside.

"A new house to come home to," Robert added.

"With walls every color but white," Sarah said.

"That sounds pretty good," Ella replied, smiling. "But what I really want right now is for someone to tell me a story—one with a good beginning. And a happy ending."

Sam raised an eyebrow and looked at Sarah. He cleared his throat. "Once," he began, "there lived a boy and a girl and a really hot other girl…"

"Oh, be quiet," Sarah said and pushed him aside. "Once," she said, her voice hushed, "there lived three young children trapped between walls that pressed in on them, growing tighter every day."

"Did they get out?" Ella asked, taking Sarah's hand.

"Shhh," Sarah said. "You'll have to wait and see."

"Yes," Sam whispered to Ella, quietly enough that Sarah wouldn't hear.

He took Ella's other hand and together the three friends sat as the story wound around, holding them—as stories do—tightly.

ACKNOWLEDGMENTS

Books take a long time to write. Whole streams of people are involved and all they get is this lousy t-shirt. Wait, they don't even get that. But we'd still really like to thank them. First, a huge shout out to our beta readers this go round: Becca, Emilee, Rebecca, Emily, and Tori. Thank you for treading through a half-baked manuscript and giving us advice. A special thank you goes to Mirandine for checking the French in the manuscript. We'd also like to thank Vanessa and Anna-Lisa for their input on tricky bits. And of course we need to give a really big high five to our tween and teen readers: Mark, Elizabeth, Peter, and Alyson.

Thanks to all the family and friends who let us (especially Jean, because she is an OCD pest) send 700 minutely different versions of the same two paragraphs and ask for opinions. And a big thank you to those who blog, share, and re-tweet. We love you, too.

We also appreciate all the libraries, schools, book stores, students, and fans who've had us for events and loved on our books. May we have many more years together.

There were many local places and a few local people who inspired scenery and characters for this book. The real life Ella (Jake's daughter) says, "Thanks to Mr. Whitten, one of the best teachers ever. He taught the 4th grade Rat Pack how fun each day could be. He inspired us to be the best we can be."

Thank you to our original publisher, Ink Smith, and our editor and jack-of-all-book-trades, Corinne.

The biggest, warmest hugs (kisses, special dinners and/or nights out, etc. and etc.) go to Kip and Cara for being the best spouses in the world. You're the ones who find us slumped over our work, dare to pat our backs and tell us it's time to go to bed and that things will look better in the morning. They usually do. Especially when you've got kids so great that you can model whole characters around their awesomeness.

—Jean and Jake

ABOUT THE AUTHORS

Jean Knight Pace is the co-author of *Grey Stone* as well as the author of *Hugging Death: Essays on Motherhood and Saying Goodbye*. She has had essays and short stories published in *Puerto del Sol*, *The Lakeview Review*, and other literary magazines. She lives in Indiana with her husband, four children, eight ducks, four chickens, and a cat. You can find more about her at jeanknightpace.com.

Jacob Kennedy is an ER doctor who dreams werewolves and tournaments in his free time. He is also the co-author of *Grey Stone*. Find him on Facebook @jacobkennedybooks.